ALISON LEONARD was born in Yorkshire and lives there again now. As well as writing fiction, she has written plays for BBC Radio and for stage and community production. Her poetry has been published widely in anthologies and she has broadcast on local and national radio on spiritual themes. She is married, and has two daughters and two grandchildren.

Also by Alison Leonard

(Fiction)
An Inch of Candle (YA)
Tinker's Career (YA)
Kiss the Kremlin Goodbye (YA)
Heavenly Lilies
Flesh & Bronze
Thirteen Months to Christmas (short stories)

(Non-fiction)
Telling Our Stories
Living in Godless Times

THE
UNEXPECTED
MARRIAGE
OF
MARY BENNET

Alison Leonard

Published by Goosander Press
Copyright © Alison Leonard 2023

Cover design by Nell Wood

Typeset in ITC Galliard Std and AntiquarianScribeW01
(AntiquarianScribeW01 font created by Brian Wilson.)

British Library Cataloguing in Publication Data
A catalogue record for this book is available from the British
Library.

ISBN: 9798392635825

i.m. Diana Sidaway,
who asked the right questions

PART I

1

The Summons

LOOKING BACK, it felt like an awakening.

It was simply a glance. Mary saw it: an oddly conspiratorial glance from Annie to Lizzy over the dinner table. The steam was rising from the bowl of beef broth as Annie lowered it to Mama's place on the tablecloth. But, as Annie lifted her hands from the bowl, her eyes met Lizzy's across the table, and in that instant, Mary realised that Lizzy, sitting beside her, had locked her gaze with Annie's.

Mary recalled the scene clearly as she woke the following morning. Mama's plea to Papa had pierced both the line of the glance and the wafting aroma of beefiness: "But *I* need Luke, for Meryton! For my buff silk *thread*! Why should *you* always have him?" Papa's gaze drifted up towards the ceiling, and Mama, losing the thread of her own thinking, had looked vaguely around the table in case anyone else might know her mind better than she herself did.

The fact that Mary had noticed the glance was in itself odd; that she had been alert to it, her sight not blurred in the perception of it. Was that because she had nudged her chair nearer to her sister's, in recognition of Lizzy's imminent departure from Longbourn? And that Mary would miss her when she was gone? Or perhaps the opposite: that she might be relieved to see her go?

Time and again, over the course of her life, Mary had sensed that something important was afoot but that she had failed to pick up the crucial clue. So, when this particular moment struck her – a perception that, for once, she had not missed, but recorded clearly in her mind's eye – it struck with a vital force.

Having noted it, though, she still could not grasp its significance. What private message could have passed between Lizzy, who was Family, and Annie, who was Servantry? What circumstances might have given rise to such an understanding? An understanding from which she, and maybe her other sisters (had they been present) were excluded?

Annie was special, of course. Like Mrs Hill. And Luke, too. They were different from the kitchen maids, the maids-of-all-work and personal servants Lizzy had brought with her from Pemberley, the laundry women who came in from the village when needed, the extra stable-boys who exercised the horses if Luke was busy.

Those three, they were different. But they were still servants.

And Lizzy, of all the five sisters, was the most aware of every gradation of status. She had to be, in her position as Mrs Darcy.

So why this glance?

Come on, said Mary to herself. There was no point wondering and dawdling. She must be up and about and down to breakfast.

Steadily she clothed herself, item by item, in the layers she had laid out neatly the night before: the simple chemise and comfortable old stays, stockings up to her thighs with their reliable garters; then some splendid new bloomers (the result of her mother's persuasion), a plain linen petticoat, and last, her one walking costume in modest laurel green. Spring was here, and soon she could relinquish her linen petticoat. But not her stays.

What a fuss women made about *stays*, she thought for the hundredth time as she pulled the lace at the back and fixed it firm. She herself would prefer not to bother with a corset of any sort. Especially the kind that revealed one's bosom. Her bosom was thankfully small. Once, when she had broached to her mother the possibility of going without stays, it almost induced a fainting attack. "Even *Hill* wears *stays!*"

The memory of her mother's reproach brought a flush to Mary's throat, even now. She had withdrawn the suggestion immediately, but then made up for it by continuing to refuse help from either Annie or Mrs Hill, and insisting on lacing up her own stays.

∞

A few weeks later, soon after Mayday in the year of the new king's reign, when the hawthorn on the hedges around Longbourn was a mist of white froth and there had been no more trouble from the Radicals rioting in the North, the small Bennet family scattered themselves around the large breakfast table and a letter arrived from Lizzy at Pemberley.

The letter seemed rather long, considering how recent was her last visit. Mary nibbled on one of the crusts she had carefully sliced off her toast, and waited.

Mama tore the wax seal, opened the pages, and gave a little shriek of pleasure. Mary, knowing her mother's moods, could feel this pleasure muted by a certain clouding of her mother's eyes, caused no doubt by the cordial Balm of Gilead she had taken first thing. Also by tears, due to the absence of her sisters: not only Lizzy, but also Jane (always, now, referred to as "poor dear Jane") and Lydia to their own homes, and Kitty to the spreading of her presence around the three elder sisters for as long as could be tolerated by each.

"'Now, dear Mama, read this and see if it does not provide a remedy for your poor nerves.' See how insolent she is become," chortled Mrs Bennet, "since she has made me thrice a grandmother, and one with a nursery governess already? Mary dear, those crusts are for the discard bucket in the kitchen. Oh! My eye has slipped down the page and caught your name! And something about… Oh! Mary!"

Mary pushed the last crust obediently to the side of her plate and reached for a fresh slice. If only Mama could be so overcome with the news from Pemberley that she must release the letter into the hands of Papa, and Calm. But no, Papa's eyes were lowered towards the table, magnetised by the news in the *Times*.

"Listen well, Mary, do. 'Lady Agatha Manton, who, as you know, is our neighbour and dear friend, has in her gift the living of St Michael and All Angels in the pretty little village of Humbole. Lady Manton has let it be known – '" (here Mrs Bennet's voice faltered into a girlish giggle) "'that her present clerical... cum...cum...incumb...ent...' Oh, Mary dear! In her 'pin...opinion, must, must...' I can barely read... 'be furnished with a wife'."

A painful flush rose from Mary's chest to her forehead, then downwards till it reached her fingers. Only the entrance of Annie with a fresh plate of cherry jam gave some relief. For Annie had a way of nodding to Mary – not conspiratorially, but amiably – indicating that her plight was but one of many plights in this slow-moving world, empty of sisters: different from Annie's own, yet to a small extent shared.

৩৩

Annie, earwigging at the door, didn't wait for a pause in Mrs Bennet's reading of Miss Lizzy's letter before entering to slide the plate of jam between her mistress's elbow and the butter dish; she even gave Mrs Bennet's shoulder a nudge to point out that this was her favourite jam and she should be grateful for it. Clearly Her Ladyship, neighbour of Miss Lizzy's at Pemberley, Derbyshire, was so much mistress of her estate that, should she consider this clerical incumbent to be requiring of a spouse, she could rustle one up through the good offices of her friend Mrs Darcy. By way of contrast, Annie's own spouse, Luke, had been secured through risk to life itself. And now illness stalked the family: apart from her own children's tendency to croup, her beloved mother-in-law Mrs Hill was suffering bouts of pain and bleeding, which affected the whole household, both above and below stairs.

"'…So if it could be arranged for Mary to make the journey to Derbyshire with due (though not undue) haste, that would suit Lady Manton's purposes splendidly'."

Annie allowed her out-breath to be so audible that Mr Bennet raised his head briefly from his newspaper: enough of a moment to raise her own eyebrows and say, to no one in particular, "And who will accompany Miss Mary to Derbyshire? That may be a question?" And she strode to the door before any of the breakfasters could attempt an answer.

Miss Mary would make an excellent clerical wife. But she was a puzzle, right enough. Underneath her tremble, behind her magnifying glass, she had grit. She clearly wanted to escape from her mother, and from Longbourn. But she refused to attend balls, and clung to her books and her sermons and her piano. Here was a chance to take a risk. Would she rise to it, or not?

⁘

Mary knew that her mother would follow her father out of the breakfast room and thence to his library, there to discuss the precise degree of haste with which they might despatch her to Pemberley. How many minutes would it take for Papa to shake off Mama's insistence that he should play his part in such petty details? Five, at most. She could pause amidst the crumbs of Bath buns and hope for a snatched word with Annie. Yet Annie might be detained with Mrs Hill, if there had been another of her bleeds in the night. Mary stared at her plate and counted the left-over crusts. It was difficult: as with the rest of her life, the details blurred into one another. Her mother did not allow her to bring the magnifying glass to breakfast. "You must try to live without such things, Mary, if you are to get anywhere in life!"

On the other hand, Mrs Bennet's attempt to persuade Mr Bennet into correct fatherly behaviour might last only seconds. In better times, each of them could have consulted Mrs Hill separately. But these were not better times.

Must she go to Derbyshire as she was bid? And with whom as chaperone?

The prospect of Pemberley was in itself a mountain to climb. Mary had not so far visited this august mansion. But, if she did visit Pemberley, another momentous visit lay ahead. A far, perhaps impossible, summit. She was to be introduced to a gentleman, to become acquainted with him, and to please him enough to be taken on as his life companion. This was the sort of behaviour that could be expected of any of her sisters, but not Mary. Mary's fate was written in the stones of Longbourn. The good Lord, for whatever reason, had decreed this fate, and without seeing any alternative she had accepted it. 'Let the woman be silent, and submit', said St Paul.

But St Paul also said, 'Wives, submit to your husbands'. Was she now being directed by St Paul, via Lady Manton and Pemberley, towards the holy state of matrimony? How could she know where God, or St Paul, might be leading her?

And what did she herself want? Was she allowed to want anything? Even supposing she secured this apparently eager clergyman, could she feel happy at the prospect of wedded bliss? She recalled a phrase from the poet Southey: 'A vague, a dizzy, a tumultuous joy'. If all mountains could be climbed, and she became betrothed, could she expect to feel 'dizzy joy' at the prospect of union with...what was his name?

Annie slid in through the door.

"Oh Annie! What will become of me?"

"Miss Mary, now. Now then."

"Will you accompany me, Annie dear?"

"Oh, no, Miss Mary. I couldn't leave my little ones, even for you."

Mary knew that Annie's two children, John-James and Edie, were recovering from a nasty bout of croup. But she could not stop herself bursting out, "I cannot go alone! If only I could have been selfish and demanded a lady's maid when Mama pressed me to do so! Yet I *am* selfish, am I not, Annie dear? I should have asked after dear Hill. Did she have a good night's sleep?"

"Slept a treat last night, thank you for your kindness, and is all the better for it. Luke popped over to her after doing the horses and she hardly woke to greet him. She is trying to dress just now, and may be down for an hour in the kitchen."

"She will not give up. Who knows, with God's grace she may make a full recovery."

Annie barely concealed a *harrumph*. "God's grace is for those who can afford it, begging your pardon, Miss Mary."

"It is free, Annie – free!"

"You and God together, you'd make a splendid wife for this clerical man, Miss Mary. Think! So close to Miss Lizzy!"

"But Lizzy might only... Lizzy would..."

Mary, about to say *Lizzy would only be as hard a task-mistress as Mama*, stopped herself just in time. In fact, she stopped the words more from surprise at the thought than from any notion of self-discipline in front of a servant. Was Lizzy a hard task-mistress?

Yes, she was. Now that she had fulfilled her dream, Lizzy had become impatient with those who failed to fulfil theirs.

But Lizzy must be forgiven. Not only because our Lord commanded us to forgive, but because Lizzy, more than any of them, felt the loss of poor dear Jane.

৩৩

Annie hardly heard Miss Mary's hesitant closing words. She was weary of hearing about Lizzy, Lizzy, Lizzy. Life was easy enough for Mrs Darcy, with all those thousands a year, three wild children and a queue of nurserymaids to whisk them away when she'd had enough of them; whereas she and Luke had to care for their children through every childhood illness, and all the while keep the Bennet household running smoothly from top to bottom.

Ah, well! At least old Boneypart was long gone, and for Luke there was no more need to fear capture as a deserter. No more terror of the bounty-hunters, the flogging of precious flesh, imprisonment, then back to the battlefield. The end of war was the biggest gift that Miss Mary's God could ever offer. Yes, there were food protests, but they were far away. And that other insurrection, up in Manchester, the one they called 'Peterloo'; that was The North. Far away, like Yorkshire with its rioting weavers.

If she could have torn herself away from her children (the two who'd survived; the two who weren't laid in the corner of the churchyard without headstones to commemorate them) she could have embarked on this visit to Pemberley as Miss Mary's lady's maid. But, for Edie and John-James's sake, she couldn't. Wouldn't.

To be fair to her, Miss Lizzy had once berated her father for his use and misuse of Mrs Flora Hill. On that single occasion, as she listened through the door while Mrs Bennet slept the sleep of the drugged, Annie had heard Lizzy's fury and seen 'dear Flora' rising in her imagination; not as her mother-in-law Mrs Hill, nor as Luke's mother, but as a girl: striking rather than pretty in presence, with her strong jaw and wide brow softened by mole-brown curls, her bosom full and her hips wide. Those hips: ideal for child-bearing. Utterly unlike the woman Mr Bennet had chosen to marry, whose narrow frame took her to the brink of death during each of those five births. Five. Each one a girl. Whereas Luke... Luke was a by-blow. Misbegotten.

Wrong side of the blanket. Baseborn. Bantling. Whoreson. Born of the bar sinister. Illegitimate, illicit, unacknowledged in law.

Who else, beyond Miss Lizzy, knew the truth of Luke's fathering? Miss Jane, certainly, for (until recent years) there had been no secrets between Miss Lizzy and Miss Jane. Miss Lyddy and Miss Kitty? Indeed not: they didn't know what a secret *was*, never mind how to keep one. Mrs Bennet? Of course she didn't know – but, at the same time, surely, she *did* know. Why else would her slumbers need to be induced, in its myriad forms, by laudanum?

Did Miss Mary know? Miss Mary, bless her, knew nothing. About anything.

☙

Mary, alone at last at the piano in its small upstairs room, picked out the easiest Bach Prelude with heavy fingers. Right hand: dum-diddle-diddle-dum dum dum. Left hand: progress up, then back to doh, then fah... This had been her first success, the one she could always return to. Old Mr Prendergast, whose enthusiastic spit had landed so often on the keys that his veined and knuckly hand must wipe it away with a grubby handkerchief; he had taught her Bach (progressing from Preludes to Fugues), and Handel. His own arrangement of the dear *Water Music*! And a little of his beloved Mozart. Though 'not enough to ruin it', he said.

Working from memory, she moved from the easy Prelude into the much more difficult Fugue, her fingers first stumbling, then finding their way with more confidence, breaking loose from both her blurry eyesight and her brain. The music flowed through her while her thoughts wandered elsewhere. Broadwood... London... Darcy... Pemberley... Humbole. Would there be a piano at the Vicarage in Humbole?

That wasn't right. It wasn't a Vicarage. It was superior to that – a *Rectory*.

What if there were no piano? Might she, incredibly, request one?

Never. She must please, not expect to be pleased.

But she must also live. She could not live without a piano.

What if there were a piano, but in a public room, where she could be heard practising? What if? What if?

What if the Rector took one look at Mary and decided that, Lady Manton or no Lady Manton, he could not survive a moment in her company? What if she were only the first in a long list of possible Mrs Rectors (what was the man's name again? Something to do with sewing), who could easily be disposed of if the second, third, or fifteenth candidate showed more promising looks or temperament? What if she were the last woman on earth whom any man would wish to marry? Who, if the rocks underneath Hertfordshire and Derbyshire were to open and swallow up all other women in existence, would remain alone, at home, to look after Mama until she died, or until she herself collapsed from sheer frustration?

Or what if, with the wedding arranged, Mama refused at the last moment to let her go? Three of her daughters had married well, and Darcy might hire lawyers to see off the dreaded Entail. There was no need for Mary to quit the family home. Mama could not manage without her.

Calm down. Return to Bach. Reach for the magnifying glass on the top of the piano, peer through it at the notes once more, and let the fingers return replenished to the keys.

By the end of the piece, she had resolved to go to Pemberley.

If Mrs Hill, bless her, could recover sufficiently to act as her lady's maid, Mary would prepare herself for the, until now, unthinkable. She would ask Papa to reply in the affirmative to Lady Manton. She would beg Annie to pack enough towelling in case her monthly visitor came inconveniently early, and alert Mrs Hill to that possible predicament. She would face Pemberley, and the formalities and introductions, with as little trembling as she could. She would open her mouth, if only once or twice, to speak to the Reverend Sewing-Something. These were the small steps which might enable her to make a bid for freedom from Mama, and Longbourn, forever.

Her fingers went back to the Prelude. Dum-diddle-diddle-dum dum dum. Yes-Mary's-going-to-go-there, hum, *yes* Mary's-going-to-go-there, hum. She would. She would.

2

The Clergyman

THE LEATHER WAS silky smooth, the padding easy on her bony bottom, the damask curtains pleated and neat, the wheels covered in some substance that minimised the bumps in the road. Still, Mary wished that she were travelling in the homely Longbourn chaise, with Luke in charge. That way the two of them could have helped Mrs Hill towards cheerfulness, and Mary might have distracted her mind from what lay ahead.

But no, Lizzy had insisted on sending one of Pemberley's liveried carriages. For privacy, she said; for the luxury of an under-coachman and extra footman as well as the regular pair of men up top, and so that highwaymen would know by the coat of arms that this family's jewels were stored in underground vaults, not carried around like currency in exchange for one's life or one's modesty. The Bennet chaise would never survive the journey from Hertfordshire to Derbyshire and back again in one piece. And what would they do for horses? Leave Rosie at the first post-house and collect her, days later, on the way back? How would the farm manage without her? No, no. Mary must become accustomed to accepting Pemberley's generosity.

Mary's grasp of geography was woefully small. She knew that Hertfordshire was not far from London, and civilised. But Derbyshire – the entire North – must be throbbing with villains. The Darcys would be protected by their vast parks, while the lower orders would be exposed to cut-purses, rogues, jostlers and vagabonds of every sort.

How much of England were they covering? Jane and Lizzy knew about geography. Since they were scarce grown, the two elder girls had taken off with the Gardiner side of the family in a dizzying variety of coaches and carriages to pretty places like Derbyshire and the Lake District, leaving Kitty and Lyddy to make mischief at home, and Mary all alone. Mary had been, well, nowhere, in her whole life. Aunt Gardiner looked at her rather as she might look at a piece of furniture or the pattern on wallpaper: ever there, never noticed, and certainly never invited to *go* anywhere.

This journey, so suddenly demanded, so hastily prepared for, exposed the thinness of Mary's knowledge. Her education had been fitful and ragged. Papa always congratulated himself on providing the best tutors, selected by interview, by himself, alone. Yet not one of these wrinkled old men, sweaty, often tattily dressed and frequently dismissed, had introduced his daughters to a map of England, Scotland, Wales, and Ireland. "Get them a governess!" her mother would demand. But her father would find endless reasons, none of which Mary could recall, to scoff at the idea.

Except… *Too tempting*.

Had Papa actually said those words? Or did Mama use them, some time during the same old argument? An argument that, on one particular day, took a different turn? 'Tempting'? In what way? Tempting to whom?

Hill would have made an excellent governess. She knew more than anyone about who did what, and when, and who would be expected to do what, and why. Though even Hill could not say how far it was from Hertfordshire to Derbyshire, only that they would spend three nights at coaching inns on the way.

Hill sat opposite Mary now, quiet, her mouth slightly open and her eyes closed. But Mary sensed by her restlessness that she was not asleep. She had assured Mary, while they were packing, that there would be plenty of towelling for 'untoward occasions'. Annie, running up and down stairs with items for the trunk while keeping an anxious Mama at bay, whispered to Mary that she'd packed the 'necessaries'; adding that Mrs Hill wore towelling pads herself most of the time now, and she'd have words with her counterpart at Pemberley for dealing with the resulting laundry during their stay.

How did Annie know that such conversations could happen at, of all places, Pemberley? Servants knew these things. And Mary had to trust Annie to know what she was doing.

She twitched the curtains of the coach and peered outside. Everything – verges, trees, fields – was a blur. She fumbled for her magnifying glass and held it to her eyes. But that, with the movement of the carriage, only worsened the blur.

She was surprised not to feel sick. But she felt quite well. In fact, so long as she stopped herself thinking about Mr...Sewing-Word? Needleman!...she felt remarkably well. Even somewhat elated. She had always wondered what Life was like out there, in the world that Jane and Lizzy inhabited. Now she was to find out.

Nevertheless, she did wish that Luke had been in charge of this carriage rather than the unknown and fierce-looking Pemberley coachman and his purse-lipped underlings. Each time they stopped for a change of horses the pursed lips pushed themselves through the window, barked an unintelligible question, waited for a non-existent reply, and vanished. Every second horse-change she and Hill hauled themselves up from the upholstery of the carriage, tottered into the unknown, refreshed themselves in each modest billet, washed in a grubby bowl, and returned to their coach. Each time, the underling appeared just too late to help them back inside. They might be in Mrs Darcy's liveried coach, but they were not Class. Servants knew these distinctions. She was sure that Luke would have helped them inside.

Since the arrival of Lady Manton's letter a few weeks ago, Mary had seen more than usual of Luke and the Longbourn stables that were his domain. For she had taken it into her head to start to ride.

She had walked across to the stables to ask Luke. Luke, pausing in his grooming of Papa's horse Bradwell, had seemed hardly to hear her.

"Start to…?"

"I did ride, long ago. With Kitty and Lydia. On ponies. Before you were here."

His hand, holding the brush, fell to his side. "Well. Now you're a lady, you'd need to go *aside*. Side-saddle."

Mary was taken aback. She remembered the firm feel of the saddle between her knees, the snuffling nose of the friendly pony, the heady, wildish smells of dung and of hay. It had been such fun. Side-saddle would be the opposite of fun. Side-saddle had to be elegant, poised; one would need a man to help one to mount and dismount; and if one fell off, one found oneself tangled in the straps and dragged along the ground, and injured. Maybe even killed.

She had assumed she could climb onto Blossom or Rosie, settle her small bottom comfortably in the middle, and just *ride*. As she used to, but with everything bigger. But no, it had to be difficult. It showed her up, as so often, to have blundered.

"Could I not go astride? Catherine the Great of R-r-russia, *she* rode astride."

Where had that bit of history popped up from? Would Luke have heard of Russia? He must have. Luke had fought in the War. He knew about Boney and the Iberian Peninsula; he had *fought. Suffered.* But…Catherine the Great?

Luke was hidden from view by Bradwell's shining

flank. She heard his steady breathing as he worked away at creating that shine on the other side.

He was silent.

"Jane," she began again, thinking it best to retreat from the Empress of Russia. "Jane and Lizzy, they used to ride, when Blossom and Rosie weren't needed on the farm? No one thought..." *No one thought to ask* me *if* I *wanted to ride*, were the words that rose in her throat. But she stopped them. She must not be plaintive. "I thought that riding might be a pleasant change from my books and my music. I'd like to get a little colour in my cheeks." Surely Luke would realise why? He was a man, though a servant. He must have courted Annie. He might understand that colour in one's cheeks was an essential prerequisite of a wife?

Luke reappeared, flushed from his work, and spoke. "But Miss Jane and Miss Elizabeth, they rode aside. And them smaller astride saddles were sold back to the tannery when they were married off. There's only them saddles we have now." He waved his brush towards the far stable door, where Mary saw rows of huge hooks where the tack hung. Most of them were empty. "And Blossom..."

He disappeared again, and Mary remembered that dear old Blossom had been put out to grass last year after a fall. They had replaced her, but the replacement, a lively nag with dangerous-looking teeth, was safely out in the back field and used only for farm work.

Mary, having come so far, pictured the nag's teeth, and ran her tongue over her own. They were crooked; she was unworthy; but still she was determined to ride.

"And Rosie? You look after her so beautifully, and

she is only needed sometimes. She might be quiet enough for a small rider such as myself? Even if I rode on a larger saddle, astride?"

She remembered feeling a smile on her lips as the words came out of her mouth. *Myself. Astride.* What effrontery!

Now, looking across at Mrs Hill and seeing that a smooth stretch of road had allowed her to fall into a proper sleep, she recalled her effrontery and realised that it was a strange emotion to feel in relation to a servant.

It was a week later, when Luke had agreed she could ride Rosie when he had time to tack her up, and Annie had sewn padding into Mary's bloomers so that she would not become sore as she rode, that Mary, suddenly, from the delicious feeling of saddled height above him, asked Luke what seemed to be a simple question.

"Where did you *go*?"

Luke turned away with a sharp intake of breath, as though the horse had kicked him.

She persevered in this latest effrontery and asked: "When you went? All those years? Then came back?"

"What?"

Mary retreated into a stuttering apology. "I know it is not my business to ask. Forget I mentioned it. Do hand me the – "

But before she could say *reins*, Luke had whipped back round, lifted his head to look up at her, and said in a rush, "It's being a deserter, Miss Mary. A criminal. It was for hiding, this coming to Longbourn, for safety. But then they were chasing once more. So it was off again. No matter where. Everywhere, and nowhere. Till after the victory. Waterloo. Then it was possible. To come back."

Recalling his rush of speech, and the pain behind it, Mary found that his words might have referred not to himself but to some entirely other person.

Then a realisation shuffled alongside: that Hill, dear Hill whose boots now knocked against hers even in the spaciousness of Lizzy's carriage, must be the reason why Luke had returned to Longbourn. It was because he had begun here. It was where he belonged. Luke belonged in her home as much as Mary belonged there. Servants could be taken on and dismissed. But Luke had come and gone, and come and gone, for causes she could not fathom; disappeared for the war and then returned once more. Luke, for those unfathomable reasons, could never be dismissed now. Any more than Mrs Hill could be dismissed.

How could that be?

Because Luke belonged to Mrs Hill.

Mary looked at that fact, and let it go.

As for riding, she only took one turn around the yard, clutching mightily to the reins, before shouting that she must stop, and slithering down onto the cobbles. After that there was no point attempting to ride again.

☙

On her first early morning at Pemberley, at some dawn hour, Mary felt her nightgown lifted by her own movement, in sleep, up beyond her thighs. Dreamily but somehow purposefully she drew it up farther still, almost up to the pits of her arms. The whole of her body needed to feel the sheets. They were like an extra but more wholesome skin. Linen, surely; sheets were always linen; but these were of some heaven-sent lightness that gave them a surface of pure silk. What superior lye were they washed in? What gentleness of flat-iron had pressed them, inch by inch, and with such care that there was not a single crease to irritate? Her body, in contrast, felt rough: her finger-nails roughly snipped with inadequate scissors, her toe-nails likewise; the ungainly bumps of knuckles and knees. She must surely be spoiling the perfection of these silky, costly sheets.

The wrinkles of her nightgown irritated her. She wriggled out of it and lay in the manner of nature, embraced by luxury from every side.

Beyond her, in the great space of the room into which, late yesterday, she had been ushered, all was still. Not a crack between the floorboards let the sounds of kitchen and scullery through; the floor had a half-inch layer of Axminster almost edge to edge. She heard twittering from birds in the garden, and the clang of some tool as gardeners or coachmen prepared Pemberley and its scores of inhabitants for this new day.

Memories of her arrival came rushing now. The succession of Darcy family portraits on the first curving staircase. The chiming of grandfather clocks on each floor as the buxom maid led on, and on, and on.

There had been a screech!

Oh – a peacock. Her mother had once installed a

peacock in their garden, hoping that its exotic presence would seal Longbourn's status as the chief mansion in the neighbourhood. But Doctor Morgan had shot it, declaring it to be the precipitator of his wife's lunacy.

Another screech. And now two together. Pemberley had plenty of space for peacocks.

Up under the roof – how many floors up? Two, three, four? – Hill would be heaving herself out of sleep and maybe out of bed, kneeling to pull the chamber-pot out from under and relieving herself... *Oh, let her be well, please God, let her be well enough!* Well enough not to upset the events planned for the next few days, anyway.

But how selfish was this thought! Dear Hill, upon whom they all depended. Hill, who had survived the winter despite her bleeds; whom Doctor Morgan declared to be a living miracle. Who seemed to be related to Luke, but one was not allowed to ask how. Or even to think the question, because of where that might lead. Hill seemed not to have been able to care for Luke in his infancy: why not?

It was all too confusing. She was here, at Pemberley, at last.

There was movement outside in the corridor. It was not the clatter of clogs, or ill-fitting cast-off shoes like Annie and the others wore at Longbourn. These servants must wear footwear that allowed them to slide or glide, because all Mary could hear were coughs and hissed instructions. Yesterday, when Lizzy was giving orders to her lady's maid (Thwaite, she was called), Mary had heard shuffling behind her. That must have been the shuffling of many maids, picking up the orders and then disappearing, on these almost silent feet, to relay them on to countless others for action and effect.

Amid the awe engendered by her arrival, she had remembered to tell the ushering maid that she would need no assistance with dressing in the morning, thank you very much. She had needed say it twice in order to be understood. "Yes, even my stays," she had insisted to the baffled and blinking face. No doubt the servants' quarters were echoing even now to shocked laughter at the thought.

∞

Longbourn,
June 3, Year 1 of the 4th George

Dear Miss Mary,

I trust you are well in body and mind this morning, and Mrs Hill also. The journey will have been taxing, but I believe we despatched you well-enough equipped for whatever may arise. (That's enough about health and well-being. We will hear soon enough if disaster has struck.) Brigands and robbers were there none, God willing. You would have a biblical text to offer them, I have no doubt.

As I remember the agenda for your first day, the scene will be full of children: happy voices, generously including their dear aunt in their play.

You will be amused to witness Henrietta on her home territory waging full-scale battles up and down the sculpture galleries and wide staircases of Pemberley. I hope she does not leave too many toy swords and baby helmets in her wake for you to trip over. Please, for your own sake, do keep your magnifying-glass close to hand.

George, being just eighteen months younger than his sister (poor Miss Lizzy, she had scarcely recovered from the first experience of childbirth before the next was upon her), will be his usual angelic self. Until his mother leaves the room, that is. Then he will set upon his older sister and younger brother with eager ferocity. George knows what every tin-pot Napoleon or Wellington knows: that surprise is the most effective weapon.

Then there is darling William, trailing around after the older ones, trying to keep up, but, when they bat him out of their way, going off on his own, enchanting every adult into laying down their work and playing with him instead. William is supposed to be fully trained, but Miss Lizzy was so desperate to have him returned from his nurse in the village that she cut short the essential period of training. Is he, I wonder, still leaving small contributions, liquid or solid, behind the furniture?

Miss Mary, I sometimes wish that Mrs Darcy would not confide so readily in me when she is staying here at Longbourn. Especially about Miss Jane.

Neither sister took well to childbirth. Did Mrs Bingley's first and most fearsome experience sour both herself and Mrs Darcy for each subsequent child's entry into the world? I did not pass their stories on to you, Miss Mary, for fear it would sour *you, too, should you anticipate the joy of motherhood yourself.*

And now you may be on your way to that joy, Miss Mary. I wonder, will Lady Manton be present in person to urge forward her project to marry off this Rector? From what I hear of Lady Manton, she may be busy with some quite different project by now.

I wonder how closely Miss Lizzy will watch over this match-making. I heard your mama reading out the last few sentences of her letter in which she regretted that Mr Darcy will miss your valued company on this occasion, as he must be in London on business. Increasingly, it seems, Mr Darcy is in London on business, generally in the company of dear Mr Bingley. So, during those times, she does not have his regular support in the discipline of their three lively children. She made it clear to me, if not to your mama, that this does not sit easily with her.

You may ask: how dare I make judgements on Mrs Darcy's family life, even on Mr Darcy's attentiveness or lack of it? My answer is, I dare very easily because, having found words for my observations, I have neither the time nor the paper and ink with which to write. I have composed it in my head while winding the mincer with the off-cut meats for our Thursday lunch, which are now ready to make into a fricassee.

Dear Miss Mary, I pray that all goes well with your encounter. You will miss my fricassee, but I recalled that it is not your favourite, so is best

offered in your absence. May your visit unfold as
you would wish. I will be thinking of you.
                    Your affectionate maid, Annie.

∽

Mrs Hill stood to the side of the main door to the gallery, in the gloom. Every so often she made herself take a couple of forward steps so that she could glance in at the glittering movements and the noise – the moving waves of conversation, the guffaws and titterings and coughs, the piano keys tinkling and breaking off and then tinkling again – and check that somewhere, in this pattern of colour and candle and carpet and fine Pemberley plush, Miss Mary was still standing.

Where…?

Yes, there, as if protected by a thick bottle of glass.

Someone must surely approach and speak to her?

Here was one: a gentleman, elderly, fat and no doubt farting, leaning towards Miss Mary with a kind gesture and a gruff word. Would she emerge from her bottle-glass cage, and respond?

She moved, but only within her bottle. The gentleman tweaked his beard and shuffled away towards more promising pastures.

Mrs Hill ached. Her legs ached, her back ached, her head ached, and most of all, something at the centre of her lower body ached. Three days on the road, three nights in unfamiliar beds, three sets of twenty-four hours managing her nightwear and her towels and her dread. Somewhere called North Hampton

Shire there had been a slight bleed – no more. Thank the Lord: Miss Mary's Lord, for she had heard her say her prayers faithfully, and at length, each bedtime. After the prayers came the mattresses which, even in the fancier establishments, were as lumpy as in any old post-house. Unless it was the lumps in her own body that kept her from sleeping? Or Miss Mary's comfortable breathing, interrupted every so often by a quickening of wakefulness, perhaps from dreams of this cleric who might, or might not, rescue her from permanent companionship to her poor mother?

At any rate, thought Mrs Hill, her bleeding was not so very bad. During the winter it seemed almost cured, but then it returned with the spring, and the pain with it. If she could get through this visit without pouring blood all over Pemberley's fine rugs or soft bed-linen, she would have triumphed.

Other servants, presumably servants of other evening visitors, hovered nearby. None of them spoke to her, and most of them stood some distance from the great doors, murmuring to one another. They would be familiar with their lady's or their gentleman's ways; they would sense which corner their gentleperson might gravitate towards, which drinks tray, bon-bon dish or member of the opposite sex they would be particularly attracted to. So they rarely needed to check on what was actually happening in the glittering room, while Mrs Hill, a stranger, must blink every few seconds to keep herself alert. She must be aware at all times of where her frail young charge was standing or sitting, and who, if anyone, was trying to make conversation with her. She hoped that she would finally recognise the cleric – Reverend Mr Needleman, Reverend Mr Needy Man – when he stepped into the small circle within which Miss Mary's inadequate eyes could be expected to see.

Why had Mr and Mrs Bennet denied Miss Mary permission to wear spectacles when it first became apparent to family and servants alike that she was alarmingly short-sighted? "Oh, no!" Mrs Bennet's tone had been beyond contradiction. "Spectacles would ruin the poor girl's chances!" Her cumbersome magnifying glass must be for reading only, and (reluctantly) for making sense of those dots on the pages of sheet music. Miss Mary insisted on taking it with her wherever she went.

Mrs Hill had herself said *No* to Miss Mary, rather sharply: *No*, she must not dangle that magnifying glass from her waist this evening. *Nor* must she peer at people as if they were exhibits in a museum. She must stand, and glide, and seem approachable. At Mrs Hill's use of the word 'approachable' Miss Mary had faltered, then raised herself to her small height, sniffed slightly, and made a nervous nod.

Knowing Miss Mary, it might turn out that Mr Needy Man would sidle in her direction but remain at a deferential distance, or try to find something polite to say but get no response from her at all. Whether from short-sightedness or from nerves, Miss Mary might miss her chance of happiness, or whatever else you might call it, without knowing that it had come within a few feet of her.

No, wait.

Here he was.

And here was the solution to it all: to the reason for Lady Manton's letter, to Miss Mary's invitation to Pemberley, to their lumpy journey, to everything.

Here he was, the Needy Man who needed Miss Mary. This was the reason why Lady Manton knew he needed someone like her. Mrs Hill saw it immediately.

∽

Mary wished she could die, or play the piano, or find someone who would talk to her about sermons. She remembered a phrase from *The Collected Sermons of the Very Reverend Dr Pratt Green*: 'Blessed indeed are the meek, for they offer quiet spaces to the soul.' But no, she must stand here, must continue to stand here, until some end came to the torture. There was a piano in the room somewhere; she had heard it. Might she sit down and play? No, she could not. For she recalled that dreadful occasion, years ago, when Papa had humiliated her as she sat at the piano at Netherfield with the words: *You have delighted us long enough, child*.

So she must smile, and think of sermons, of spaces, and souls.

Where was Hill? She must have Hill. "I won't be far, Miss Mary," she had promised. "I'll find a useful spot just out of sight." But *out of sight* was useless! She needed Hill here, now!

A voice. Close to her. "Miss Mary Bennet, I believe?"

A man, to her right, had entered her space. It was a man, though his voice was light and his jacket was of a somewhat paler colour than those around him.

She must speak. She coughed, and said, "Yes, I am Miss Mary Bennet." She heard the words and felt them emerge solidly, as if she was real, and really speaking.

"We were introduced earlier, but in the flurry of others you may have missed me."

The flurry of others. She liked that, but could not find any reply.

Apparently no reply was necessary. The man said, "My name is Robert Needleman. I understand that this is your first visit to Pemberley?"

I understand. Maybe he did understand. And she understood immediately that this was the Rector of Humbole. What a pleasant-sounding man.

She must respond. "It is. My sister Elizabeth…"

She dried up. If only she had been able to say *Lizzy* – but she knew she mustn't. *Lizzy* was no more. So was *Elizabeth.* Mrs Darcy was *ten thousand a year.*

He said it for her, this maybe-understanding man. "The delightful Mrs Darcy?"

"Invited me to stay." It was only half a sentence, but it was enough. She could manage half-sentences. Half anything.

"And she invited *me* to meet *you.*" The man bent towards her. "The Reverend Mr Robert Needleman, at your service."

He was nodding now, and smiling. She could do the same.

3

The Rectory

AT ONE POINT in the preparations for her visit to
Humbole Rectory, Mary did actually say to
Lizzy, "Lizzy, please do not fuss so." She had
wanted to follow this sentence with another: "I know
you are trying to save me from nervousness, but in
truth you are making me a great deal more nervous".
She had even practised the words in her head. In the
event, this latter sentence did not emerge. She felt
quite brave in letting loose the first. She had spent
most of the night in its composition.

Lizzy was all "Your bonnet sits too far forward.
How can you be comfortable, Mary, with all this
hair bunched up behind? The bonnet is supposed to
sit *thus*. But it will not, it positively refuses." Then:
"Just a little rouge. No? Mine is a delicate shade: most
natural, I assure you. Not even a little? Well, that is

your decision, but you may regret it." And then: "This delicate lace at the neckline. We chose well; it is pretty. Yet is it too high? The fashion is proceeding ever lower towards the... But you may be right. Perhaps this level of lace is more suitable. For you."

When it came to the time of their departure, Mary's concern was more about Hill than about herself. Hill had not appeared first thing, and when she did appear, she admitted that she had not breakfasted.

"I am perfectly well," she insisted. "I am better to travel without a full stomach. I know it is not far, but even so... Thank you, Miss Mary, I will just have a cup of tea. A half. Thank you."

Mary sat her down at the long table in the family's breakfast room. Two servants hovered around, confused as to whether this maid should be treated as Upstairs or Downstairs, or be persuaded to move back to her rightful place in one of the many kitchens. Mary waved a hand at them, as she would have done at Annie, and they backed away. Lizzy bustled in and said, "The carriage is out and ready!" She held something in one hand and laid the other on Mrs Hill's shoulder. "Ready for the day, Hill? Had a good night? Now, Mary, I have this new hairbrush for you. We can solve that wayward bonnet, I am sure. But, oh dear, if we are talking about hair, look at this!" She opened her hand to reveal a tatter of golden locks. "Henrietta's! George took them out! A whole fist-full! Before breakfast! Please, not a word of it to Darcy."

Mrs Hill and Mary exclaimed in different levels of horror at the sight, and Mary hoped that George's attack on poor Henrietta would distract Lizzy from

43

pressing the hairbrush upon her. But it was not to be. There would be ten more minutes of wrestling with her errant locks before the bonnet was finally pressed into place and they could go out into the spring air, be handed into the carriage, wave Mrs Darcy goodbye, and get under way.

"Never mind, Miss Mary," said Mrs Hill as the horses increased their pace through Pemberley's vast park. "She cares for you, she wishes your best happiness. It must be good to have a sister of that sort."

"Most likely you are right." Mary felt disloyal at that doubtful *most likely*, but could not prevent it coming out and sitting in the air between them.

They left the park gates behind, and the two were silent for the rest of the brief journey. Mary felt for the security of her magnifying glass, but knew she must not lift it to her eyes. She tried gazing out of the carriage window. This bleary countryside, this fuzzy road, that almost definable tree (was it oak? or beech?) might, if things went to plan, become her world. It was unimaginable. She could only try to keep breathing.

There was a turning, and a drive, a slowing and a stop. A pause for the liveried footman to dismount and open the carriage door.

She was aware of the footman standing and waiting for her to move. But how could she? Mrs Hill should go first. That was it. Mary leant forward, summoned breath, and whispered, "Hill? Could you…?"

"I cannot. Just for a moment. You go, Miss Mary."

There was no alternative. She must move.

She took her skirts in her hands and, as she rose, realised that during the last mile her fingers in their nervousness had scrunched together the newly-bought lace around her neck. She was a mess. This visit was pointless. She had failed already.

Here was the footman's hand – the step – her feet meeting the gravel – the hand withdrawn. She forced herself to look up. The Rectory's grey steps were a watery triangle before her, narrow at the apex, flowing down to a curve at the base. Just a few more footsteps now. How could she cross the divide? Were those steps made of real stone, or were they the rushing water that filled her eyes?

From the top of the waterfall a slim figure emerged. After a pause to take in the scene, the figure tripped lightly down the watery triangle and across the gravel. Mr Needleman swirled beside her, and she felt a touch on her arm.

"Miss Bennet! You are so very welcome."

She was swept upwards. Sensing only the guiding pressure of his arm and a blur of subterranean kitchen windows on either side, she was transported inside the Rectory.

Would the servants be lined up to meet her? No, this was only a preliminary visit. How many servants were there? Ought she to have discerned such facts already?

The guiding hand took her into a generous entrance hall: tiled, and well-lit from a large window halfway up the stairs.

A single figure stood before her, dark and square.

His mother? Lady Manton?

Neither. A dark unpatterned dress. No pinafore. Not young, not old. Solid.

Housekeeper.

As certainly as she was on show to the Reverend Mr Needleman, she was on show to his servants too.

⚬

Here she is, the minx.

They all try it, money-grubbing beggar-women that they are. They should take their Fate as I did, on the chin. Work for their living. As maid-of-all-work, up through to lady's maid, and finally to cook-housekeeper.

Of course they, the English, Victors of Waterloo as they are pleased to style themselves, have no perspective. England, England, England! They think nowhere else exists. We who come from across the water, who know the English from afar, most likely from the edge of a sword: we know that money must be earned, not merely married into. A gold band on their fingers, these minxes, and they assume they are gentlewomen for life. I come from County Down, from Ulster, and know otherwise.

My father taught me thus. He and Mr Prunty. They were scholars; they taught me that only by the labour of hand and mind shall I receive food in my belly and a roof above my head. And I a girl, a woman, too! Only thus do we deserve it: by labour. That was how my father and Mr Prunty reached the university of Cambridge; that was how I reached the good Rectory of Humbole, and the status I now hold in the eyes of RN. In the eyes of his congregation, too; of the whole parish. Not by mealy-mouthed simpering and pretty-bowed dressing-up.

We have seen them before. Here is another. We bade the others farewell; farewell will be the conclusion of this encounter also, despite the schemings of Lady Manton and her like.

And if, hearing my voice with its lilt of Strangford Lough and the mountains of Mourne, she dares enquire whether I am 'of the Roman persuasion', I shall leave her standing in the hall amid the echoes of her impertinent question, and leave RN to tell her the story of my father the Reverend Mr Beattie and his friend the Reverend Mr Prunty and how they finally joined the company of scholars in St John's College, Cambridge. I will leave *him* to explain how deep is his attachment to the Reverend Simon Hepplecraft; how necessary is that bond for the great work of coherent, evangelical, literary sermons. All of which she would wonder at, if she were to stay long enough to sit in our Episcopalian church of a Sunday and listen to the God-given words that the union of minds of RN and SH draws forth. Assisted by my good self.

But we will dispose of her before that. We will withstand this one, as we have withstood all previous. We will stand together, and she will retreat.

☙

It was a cold hand and a rough-skinned one that took Mary's.

The shape in front of her was full and broad; the flesh beneath the plain garb must be solid and strong. The woman's height was not much more than Mary's, but the woman's grasp made her stifle an intake of breath.

Mr Needleman spoke. "Miss Bennet, may I present the Rectory's esteemed housekeeper, Mrs Beattie. Mrs Beattie, Miss Bennet. Miss Mary is the younger sister of Mrs Darcy of Pemberley."

"As you informed me, Mr Needleman. Good morning, Miss Bennet."

What a strange voice was the housekeeper's! But this very strangeness helped Mary to step out of her anxiety and focus on things outside of herself. "I am delighted to meet you, Mrs Beastie."

Mr Needleman, still close at her elbow, shook with laughter. "No, the name is Beattie! Mrs *Beattie*."

Mary felt herself blush from her neck up to her forehead. How could she have been so rude?

The housekeeper remained impassive as she accepted Mary's bonnet. It took Mary agonising moments of discomfort to untie the ribbons and hand it over. "That will be tea in the drawing room, Mr Needleman?"

"Thank you, Mrs B. Then I will take Miss Mary on a tour of our house."

"But," said the housekeeper, "if you were to take the lady around the tour first, it would give Gladys and Patty time to boil the water and arrange the tray."

What was this? A housekeeper who gave orders to her master? Was that customary among the clergy? And Mr Needleman had referred to *our* house! What was meant by that?

Before Mr Needleman could respond, the housekeeper spoke again. "And where, may I ask, is Miss Bennet's lady's maid?"

Mary, shocked at her forgetfulness, burst out, "Hill! She remains outside in the carriage! She has not been well, Mrs Er…" Her voice drifted in dismay.

Mr Needleman turned to Mary. "How remiss of me. I should have asked immediately for one of the maids to go out and give assistance. Mrs B, could you attend to that? Then Miss Bennet and I can begin our tour. We will take in the kitchen first. That will alert Gladys and Patty as to the timing of tea."

The housekeeper stepped decisively forward. "Thank you, Mr N, but it is I who will give the orders to Gladys, and Patty who will attend to Miss Bennet's servant in the carriage." A swirl of dark skirt, and Mrs Beattie disappeared into a corner of the hall from where the back stairs emerged.

Mary found herself turning to Mr Needleman for, if not explanation, some relief. Words rose in her mind: *I hope I have not upset Mrs Beattie?* But all she could manage was, "I am sorry if I misunderstood?"

Mr Needleman, unexpectedly, laughed. "Not a bit, my dear. Mrs Beattie is from 'over the water', as she will no doubt tell you in due course. Which is why she expresses herself so forcefully."

"The water?"

"From Ireland."

"Oh! Does that mean she is one of the…?" Catholics? Romans? Papists? Which was the permissible term?

"No no no, she is not of the Roman persuasion. Never fear, she is Church of Ireland, and a good enough Protestant to pray with the rest of us. Which reminds me. If we have the time, I would like to show you the beauties of our dear St Michael and all Angels.

As you would expect, the church is but a stone's throw from the Rectory. It sits among its ancient yews in the most delightful manner.

"Now." He gave an encouraging nod. "Are you comfortable in leaving your maid's welfare to my good staff? Shall we take a peep into the drawing room first, then on to what I pretentiously call the Music Room, and my study? Then up these rather elegant stairs" – indeed, when Mary turned she saw them curving most graciously – "where we have converted one of the upstairs rooms into an extra sitting room?"

'Comfortable'? 'Shall we'? The speed at which this man was including her in the embrace of his household was dizzying. And who was included in that 'we'? She could only follow, and learn.

∽

Mrs Hill, alone in the Pemberley carriage, wondered whether curiosity had some curative properties. For she was so concerned to discover how Miss Mary would cope with this most challenging of visits that she began to feel stronger. Her towelling was in place, and so far as she could tell, not moistened in any untoward manner. By the time the portly red-faced maid came to fetch her and, when they were in the hallway, asked her whether she should stay put or follow her mistress into whichever room she'd got herself into, she could answer firmly, "I will go after Miss Mary, if that's amenable to you." And, after some opening and closing of doors, the maid's heavy footsteps took her into the drawing room.

Here stood the intriguing Mr Needleman. Miss Mary stood quite close to him. She glanced across the room with a smile as Mrs Hill was ushered in, then returned to gazing at the tall, slim, warmly gesticulating man beside her.

"The fireplace, as you will see, is Adam in style. Robert Adam, of course, not Luke or John. When my friend the Reverend Mr Hepplecraft visits to discuss our sermons, we sit here for a while, in the gloaming. But my study is also, of course, used for that purpose." He coughed, and turned. "I trust you are recovered from your journey, Mrs Er?"

"I am, sir. You are most kind."

"Er, Mrs Hill, without whom…" Miss Mary started to introduce her, a mere servant, to a gentleman, then realised her mistake.

Mrs Hill said quickly, "Do continue, sir, Miss Mary. Take no notice of me."

"You are welcome to join us if you wish, Mrs Hill. Gladys will no doubt bring the tea before too long." He added, almost conspiratorially, "Though, knowing Gladys, there may be some delay."

As the Rector pointed out the high ceilings with their carved roses, various mahogany cabinets and many jade doorknobs, Mrs Hill began to list a number of aspects of the house that her mistress might miss, or any hints of what this place, this future, might offer. For instance, the lack of snuff boxes. (Miss Mary hated her father's snuff habit – the paraphernalia of it and the disgusting smell.) The fact that there was no library for a man to hide in, but that every room had a small upright case containing books. The cleanliness of every surface. (The housekeeper, or cook-housekeeper or whatever, must be a meticulous supervisor of her staff.) The aroma of baked meats that she had detected on entering the house. That was good: no house should be without the welcoming smell of good food. But only such as would lie just below the awareness of the family and their visitors.

This, in Mrs Hill's opinion, was a house in which a family (should that be what Miss Mary was seeking) could be at ease.

But. There was a But. She was as sure of this as of everything else she took note of in the Rectory. It was a 'but' with implications that would not be apparent to Miss Mary. Again and again during their tour, the name of the "Reverend Mr Hepplecraft" occurred. Mr Hepplecraft's books lay on a table in the study, hard by the Rector's own desk. Reverend Mr Hepplecraft's spare overcoat hung in the lobby, and his hiking boots below them. "The weather is so pleasant for walking in this district. Such a relief after the smoke and clatter of the city. That is, Derby, where he himself resides." The words "my friend Mr Hepplecraft… alternate Wednesdays to discuss sermons" came several times. So, when the man was actually present in the Rectory (which was, it seemed, most regularly) what might that imply, wondered Mrs Hill, for the permanent presence of Miss Mary Bennet?

༄

Mary was admiring the piano in the Music Room when Mrs Hill begged to be relieved of further touring, and

Mr Needleman graciously offered to conduct her back to the drawing room. Finding herself unexpectedly alone, Mary seated herself on the piano stool and placed her hands lightly, silently, on the ivory keys.

"Aha!" came Mr Needleman's voice behind her. "Mrs Darcy mentioned that you were of a musical disposition!"

Mary turned guiltily. "But only of modest skills, I fear."

"Whatever your skills, my dear, they will surely exceed mine on the piano. I am a devotee of the church organ. I play, for my own amusement, our fine pipe organ at St Michael's. To use your own word: modestly. I bought this piano in the hope that it would assist my progress on the organ, but I find that, surprisingly, there is little similarity between the two instruments." Mary was about to stand and give way to him on the stool, but he demurred. "Stay, stay. Who is your favourite composer? Purcell? Bach? Mr Handel, perhaps? Or the extravagant newcomer, Herr Beethoven?"

"I have a little piece of Bach by heart."

"By heart? No need for the score? Splendid. Do play."

Mary, after a deep breath, managed the easy Prelude without an error.

"And the Fugue?"

"Oh no…" began Mary. But then her fingers found the opening bars and she continued, with only a few missed notes, till about halfway through. "That is the best that I can achieve, I fear." Turning on the stool, she found that she was smiling, and Mr Needleman was smiling in return.

"Now," he said, taking her hand, "we must return to the drawing room, for amidst your rendition of Bach I heard a bell tinkle to indicate the arrival of tea. I hope that Gladys has had the forethought to serve your maid while she was waiting."

As they emerged from the Music Room, however, Mr Needleman stopped in a pool of light from the high window. "But we must return to the study! The sun will be shining full on the garden, and I forgot to show you the view. Simon and I often join my manservant in the garden and help him to nurture the flowers."

Mary felt panic rising in her throat. How could she respond to a "view"? She would be able to see none of the garden's detail. She needed her magnifying glass! It could not be impolite, surely, to use it? But Mama had warned her: no man will want to marry a woman who constantly reaches for a magnifying glass. But surely, no man would want to marry a woman who could not see what he was trying to show her?

Half-running after Mr Needleman from the hall and into the study, she fumbled for her faithful glass. Enormous, heavy, but oh, so helpful.

Mr Needleman led her on to the big sash windows, and, as he predicted, the sun blazed directly over the lawn towards them. Dazzled, Mary put her magnifying glass up to her eyes.

"Come, see." Mr Needleman was encouraging her forward. "The slope of the landscape is kind to us, giving us that beautiful sweep of lawn from the house to the drive. The borders are splendid, are they not, at this time of year, with their flowering shrubs and blossoming cherries. My manservant is quite *au fait* with the latest in garden design. But I fear we have moles. A veritable plague of the beasts!"

Mary scarcely heard him. She murmured, "Please, if I may?" For, passing Mr Needleman's desk, which she had only briefly taken in on first viewing, she had noticed not only the heaps of books and papers (oh, for a companion who read books, who relished sermons!) but, in a pile, a collection of spectacles. As she turned back from the window, there they were, higgledy-piggledy, with none of them taking precedence in a way that could announce: *These are my spectacles, suitable for my eyes, for my work. The others are just extras.* Behind her, Mr Needleman was still talking about the need to catch moles.

Hoping that he would not be offended by her curiosity, she walked over, picked up the top pair of spectacles and put them up to her nose.

Mr Needleman strode back to her side. "You have caught me out, Miss Bennet. Oh, dear, spectacles! My friend picks them up in Derby in the hope that one pair or another will improve my short sight. But none of them do! I noticed your magnifier. I have several. Cumbersome, are they not?" Mary opened her mouth to reply, but he continued: "And molehills? Could you advise me on moles?"

Moles? Advise? Mary could not. Not if there were spectacles to investigate. "If I could just..."

"Any of them. Feel free."

Mary rapidly tried one pair of spectacles, then another, and then another. The third seemed, on first trial, to give her remarkable clarity. She tried the second pair again, just in case.

Mr Needleman turned towards the door and said, "Though we must not allow our tea to chill, or Mrs Beattie will be angry with us. And an angry Mrs Beattie is a fearsome sight indeed."

The second pair were no good. Mary returned to the third.

Here it was, the quality she had been dreaming of since a small child: clarity! Clarity of vision; she could see! She could see – properly, as other people saw!

Mr Needleman returned to her side. "Miss Bennet?"

Mary said, "Please? Might I wear these? To see the garden?"

"Do, do! It would be splendid if they helped you. But while you take in the view, I must go to the drawing room and explain our delay."

Mary breathed out as he left the room. She moved towards the window and the view and almost tripped over her shoes, so astonished was she by the sight of their midnight-blue ribbons and sharply pointed ends. Then the carpet: she could see its pattern repeating as far as the place where Mr Needleman had been standing at the window. If she walked across and stood where he had stood, she could see – oh, it was astounding – the whole expanse of the garden. Its lawn flowed like a green rug, speckled with petals from the cherry trees above. She could see every single one of them. And there were little piles of soil at the far end of the lawn. Those were what he was referring to! Moles! Mole hills! These were her first molehills, properly seen! By the time Mr Needleman returned, she was transfixed by the sunlight shining on the dark brown soily-ness of them.

"Your maid is well ensconced, and Gladys has been told by Mrs Beattie to bring some extra hot water. So we are excused." He seemed relieved. "But – do you like the garden? Miss Bennet, are you quite well?"

Mary was staring at him through wet eyes. "Indeed I am well, Mr Needleman." Her voice was quavering, but clear. "I see your garden as perfectly beautiful." She also saw Mr Needleman. Instead of being blurred, he was a series of swift, clear lines.

"Better than I do, no doubt! I would hate to think that it made you sad."

"Oh, no. It is these!" She took the spectacles off, passed them to him, and fumbled for her handkerchief to mop away her tears. She even unceremoniously sniffed. "With those, I can see. At some future time, please may I borrow them again, when you have time to tell me more about the flowering shrubs and trees?"

"My dear," he replied, "you may borrow them whenever you please. In fact, do take them with you into the drawing room, if that would suit. You may have them for your own."

"For my own? Myself?"

"Why not? They are of no use to me." She saw the bones of his cheeks, the fullness of his lips. "It would give me great happiness if they were of use to you."

She felt the spectacles on her nose, and adjusted the side attachments around the ears. The feel was odd, but not unpleasant. She could imagine herself wandering into her father's library and picking out a book, or going into Meryton to browse in shop windows as her younger sisters used to do. "Thank you. Thank you.

Thank you."

"You are welcome, my dear." Mr Needleman's voice was all warmth.

Then he shrugged his shoulders. "And we are expected in the drawing room." Blurred once again, he almost flew through the door.

Mary hurried after him. "Hill will be so happy for me!" Then she wondered if the strange Mrs Beattie would be hovering at the drawing room door, and if so, how she should behave in the presence of this fearsome housekeeper.

◌

Seated in the Rectory drawing room, Mrs Hill almost drifted into sleep. She was weary again: weary of pain, weary of Miss Mary's needs, weary of being away from Longbourn, where she had at least a measure of control. Sleep, however impolite in this complicated clergyman's domain, seemed so very attractive.

She dreamt, and in her dream she was being cared for at Pemberley. It was as if she herself were a Darcy, and could call upon every Pemberley service to make her comfortable. She was led to an upstairs room more gracious than any other she had ever met – a Family room, surely, not a servant's room – and invited by some gesture from her companion towards a well-appointed bed upon which the blankets were turned back in welcome. Slowly, confidently, she lay down. The pillow was patted around her head until she nodded: *yes, that will do*. Her companion turned their attention to her other needs. Her towelling, now quite damp, was removed, her private spaces gently sponged and a new piece of towelling (softer than the previous) edged into place. The hands that ministered to her were small, swift, and bony; the breaths from the effort came out like little puffs of wind. The face was hardly visible. In her dream, Mrs Hill was invisibly provided with all the care she had dreamed of all her life.

And then she woke up. Miss Mary was leaning over her, close, flustered, concerned.

Only it was a different Miss Mary. At first, Mrs Hill could not think what the difference was. Then Miss Mary blinked, and, blinking herself, Mrs Hill saw that there were two round shapes fixed horizontally between Miss Mary's eyes and her own, with a sort of bridge between them, over the spike of her nose.

Spectacles! Was she still dreaming?

Miss Mary stood back and brandished her hand in the air. "See, Hill? Look! No magnifier! No more need for that!"

"Magnifier?"

"Magnifying glass! Mr Needleman has wrought a miracle! As the cripple in the gospel leapt to his feet, so I leap to my sight! I can see!"

"Miss Mary, I cannot leap…"

Miss Mary coughed, then spoke more gently. "Dear Hill, we are to drink tea. Stir yourself, do. Gladys is on her way with extra hot water. And cake!"

"Just one moment…"

"Take your time. Mr Needleman is telling the Pemberley coachman that we will be here longer than expected. He is so handsome! Handsome in face, as well as in manners! Do not fret yourself, Hill dear. We have all the time in the world."

᠔

Mary saw that Mrs Hill remained pale, and refused a second piece of cake, but only seemed truly uncomfortable when indicating to Mary that it might be time for them to leave. Mary was in the midst of a discussion with Mr Needleman about Methodist theology as shown in the hymns of Charles Wesley, and was not in a hurry to go anywhere.

Mr Needleman was expounding the true meaning of atonement. "It comes, does it not, in the fourth stanza? When we reach the words, 'My chains fell off'?"

But then he glanced towards the door, and Mary turned her gaze likewise. In the doorway stood Mrs Beattie.

Mary flushed. "Hill! I believe we are out-staying our welcome!"

Mr Needleman leapt to his feet. "Not a bit, not a bit!"

Mrs Beattie, rigid in the doorway, coughed. Mary stumbled to her feet and helped Hill to hers. As they walked over to the door, Mary felt two hostile eyes taking in the significance of her new spectacles. Then Mrs Beattie backed off as Mr Needleman led Mary past an attractive antique bench and over the fine pattern of the hall tiles.

As Mary paused at the top of the steps to watch the Pemberley coach draw up, its two fine horses adjusting themselves to their correct position, she heard Hill breathing heavily behind her. Mr Needleman must have heard it too, because he murmured, "Allow me?" and she realised that he intended to see Hill to the carriage door. Another panic: should Mary go after them, on her own, or should she wait? With Mrs Beattie standing in the shadows behind her, watching her floundering?

Her feet made the decision for her. They stayed firmly at the top of the steps and waited for Mr Needleman to come back up.

As he approached her up the steps, she felt the weight of her magnifying glass swinging from the ribbon at her waist, and, with a return of nerves, picked at the ribbon.

But Mr Needleman smiled at her and said, "You will not need to carry that now?" His way of making a statement seem like a question softened the words, and reassured her. She undid the ribbons with no trembling at all, and gave the heavy object to him, hand to hand. He held it briefly up to his eyes, then said, "It is a better strength than any that I own. I could use it for trawling through *Cattermole's Selected Sermons*. That has so tiny a print. Might I keep it in my top drawer? Then, should you need it again, you will know where it is."

Later, back at Pemberley, Mary realised the significance of this statement. He had spoken as if the two of them had a future together. Those words were, in fact, tantamount to a marriage proposal.

4

Correction

WEIGHTLESS, SHE FELT, without her magnifying glass, as the carriage took them back to Pemberley. Relieved of that burden at last, and by so simple a solution as a pair of spectacles on her nose! A solution delivered by – no less – a man she might marry! Mama would not believe it. Mama might actually faint at the sight.

But faint Mama must, for there would now be no separation between Mary and her new-found vision. She could see out of the window! Trees! Not just trees, but (surely she would learn) beech trees, oak trees, ash trees, even field maple and weeping willow trees. Within this carriage she could see the texture of the leather lining of the door: it was rather like her skin. But of course, *skin* was what leather *was*! Ah! She would learn things: she would learn what others knew from their childhoods; she would catch up. She would marry Mr Needleman and be his consort, no longer confused and panicking, but learning more and more each day.

They drove though a group of tumbledown houses, and Mary saw a small, bedraggled horse pulling a small, broken-rimmed cart on which half a dozen small children dozed or fought. She wondered, suddenly, how many bedraggled horses and carts and children she had missed seeing in her life so far. Such children as these in the bedraggled cart might be the ones she could care for in the parish of Humbole! She could not, at the moment, contemplate producing offspring of her own. The poor had too many children; might she care for their surplus children in the Rectory?

But she could not, surely, deal with an infant's requirements in the 'necessary' sense? Or feed those children from her own (so small) bosom?

She would hire a wet-nurse! Yet would that not defeat the purpose of the endeavour? Which was to suffer the little children to come unto her (*Mark, 10:14*), for of such is the Kingdom of God?

And women from Good Families, such as theirs, generally put their infants out to a wet-nurse in the village for feeding, and even for training. Lizzy certainly had done so, in order to protect her figure and her sensitivities; to enable her, in fact, to keep functioning as Mrs Darcy. Jane must have done so too, given that she had been desperately ill after each of her confinements. So the idea of caring for the village children was nonsense.

It was far too early to consider such things. At the moment she should simply rejoice in having met, and reached a certain understanding with, Mr Needleman.

"It is a miracle, Hill!" She spoke to her companion seated opposite, while still gazing at the detail of the clouds in the sky: puffy, wispy, bubbly, bright white, grey-white…

"I am glad it makes you happy, Miss Mary." Hill's voice was not bright, nor puffy, nor bubbly. She did not appreciate Mary's miracle. But then, she was unwell. Mary could see the sag of her cheeks, the creases and bulges where her rough face-powder had worked itself into sweaty little streaks during their exhausting visit.

"Dear Hill, what a long morning it must have been for you. I will ask Lizzy to get her maid – Thwaite, I think, is her name – to provide a soothing balm. Yet, we must be happy, must we not? We have so much to be grateful for, do we not?"

Hill looked neither happy nor grateful. "If I have learned one thing in my life, Miss Mary, it is that not everything is exactly as it seems."

"Oh, come. There *are* miracles! Our Lord showed us! 'The blind shall have sight, the rough places be made plain'! Do you not believe?" Mary expected to see her companion's face soften and lift. But it did not. It grew tighter. She could see the muscles of Hill's jaw: they were clenched. "Are you in dreadful pain, my dear?"

"I am in some discomfort, thank you. But I am anxious on your behalf. The Reverend is a pleasant man, and means well, but…"

"He is so kind! So fond of music, so considerate to my needs! And, I must tell you – though I would not breathe a word to Lizzy, so please not to mention it at all, even to the maids, in case they might divulge – I must tell you, and you will be reassured, I know – he opened the doors of some of the upstairs rooms, and there are so many of them! Five bedchambers, at least! Not counting the attic for the servants! Was he not leading me to hope that one might have one's own accommodation? The word he used, dear Hill – the actual word he used – was *privacy*. He said, if I recall it correctly, 'I do recognise the value of privacy where sleeping accommodation is concerned'. Something like that. He was waving his hand around. You saw how he often did that, to explain something? He waved at all those doors and said important things about *privacy*." Breathless now, she sat back against the soft leather, certain that she had convinced Hill of the genuineness of this, and indeed every, aspect of Mr Needleman and his abode.

There was silence. Mary did not need to lean forward to see that Hill's eyes were now closed.

She waited. She adjusted the spectacles on her nose, and their arms over her ears. Her nose ached a little with the weight of them, but she would get used to that.

Hill opened her eyes and paused a few moments with a half-open mouth before speaking quite firmly. "Miss Mary, do you know I had a son?"

Mary frowned. "A son?"

"I have a son. I was not supposed to have had a son." Hill's tone was now more than firm. It was irritable. "You might know this? Someone would have told you? He was sent away from me, but there was still the matter of me having had him. In secret." She coughed. "But that's by the by. What I am trying to put over to you, Miss Mary, is that people, women, have secrets. Men, too." Her voice was beginning to fade. "And secrets lead to... Well, to covering them up. Finding something to do that covering. Like Mr Needley needing a wife. People don't just marry because... Oh, because Miss Lizzy or Lady What's-Her-Name says so. They do it because... You have to ask yourself *why*."

That last *why* came over to Mary with a thud. All the time Hill had been making this speech – the longest speech Mary had ever heard her deliver – Mary had wanted to interrupt her with *But... But...* When it came to that final *why*, the *Buts* in her mouth stopped.

Thud. Why? Why?

Mary did not think about what she was going to say next. She just heard the words as they came out of her mouth. "A son? You had a son? You *have* a son? Did he, did you, have a *Mr* Hill at all? A father to your..." Her sentence trailed off. She paused for some answer, but Hill did not give one. "What has this to do with Mr Needleman? I do not understand?" She was relapsing into Mr Needleman's own habit of making everything into a question. But then, everything was a question.

Mrs Hill suddenly spoke again. "I can't be telling you who and why and so forth. Yes, there was a father, and no, we couldn't be married. Don't ask me more, Miss Mary. I cannot take it."

"But…"

"I know, I know! About His Reverence! Well? Think what secrets he may have! What concealments! We all, or most of us, need some sort of concealment. Well, maybe not you, Miss Mary."

Mary heard the word *concealment* as if it were part of a melody, the melody of a song. The accompaniment of the song was the rhythm of the horses' hooves on the avenue and the wind in the trees. Ah, that was it! The old nursery rhyme: *The farmer wants a wife…*

With a sudden burst of energy, Hill sat up. "Don't tell anyone I said anything about concealments, Miss Mary! Don't ever, or I'll be after you with the carving knife! But you do need to think on. You do so need, even if you don't *want* to. And be grateful I warned you!"

Mary, shaking, took off her miraculous spectacles, as if seeing everything blurred again would help her to focus on what Hill was talking about. The song played on, with the rhythm of the wind and the hooves behind it.

Seeing Hill's closed eyes, Mary closed her own. Then opened them again and retrieved her magic spectacles. The carriage paused for the men to descend and open Pemberley's first set of gates.

The Reverend…needs a wife. Why?

She asked: "Did you see your son many times?"

Hill left a pause of some length, and Mary thought she might not respond. Then she did. "Once. Twice. When he were six. When he were ten."

"Are you saying that Mr Needleman may have secrets of that sort? To keep from me?"

Hill eventually murmured, "I can say no more, Miss Mary. If you please."

⚬

Mrs Hill, jogging at a leisurely pace through Pemberley's park, wished herself at home, at Longbourn. She longed not to be concerned any more about Miss Mary and her future.

About her own future she was very clear. Annie, too, was in no doubt. As for Luke: oh, he would fight it to the last, but he also, in some depths of himself, knew what lay in store. She longed to speak of her own concealings with those who understood it, who were part of it. She longed for this even more than she longed for the end to the bleeding, and the pain. Oh, the pain. She named it discomfort, but it was pain. She would be desolate to leave Luke and Annie and their blessed little ones, for they were the very life of her. But oh, to be in the place where pain is past.

How sweet that would be, how dream-like, to hear Luke's boots on the cobbles below, and the children running around him with their hoop, and feeling Annie's hand in hers while they talked, and talked, and talked. In this dream there was no labour, no rush. Just being together, and letting their words flow. Annie, gently, would ask how Pemberley was. And she, with her old strength and vigour, would reply: "Oh, Pemberley is as Pemberley will be! A world in itself, cotton-wool'd gainst all other worlds! Yet even the chandeliers and the tapestries cannot guard agin Mother Nature. Mr Darcy's Nature is his mansion, his park and his deer. But it is also his adoring of Miss Lizzy. Miss Lizzy's Nature is to bring forth the results of that adoration, and the subsequent delights and the squabblings that arise withal. And the Fear. Miss Lizzy smiles, and smiles, but under all is *Fear*. Fear of more confinements, more heirs to the Darcy line. And more pain and tearing, and the fevers, perhaps even the death that may ensue. The Honourable Gwentholen Manton, Lady Manton's nephew's wife, died in child-bed but last week."

But what of Miss Mary, Annie would say, for whom this tremendous journey had been made?

"Oh, Miss Mary was in Heaven. A whole boudoir of Heaven has floated down to Earth to enrapture her. Here is Kindness, in the shape of a man! A man who prates of *privacy*! What could be more enrapturing for a young woman who, most of all, wishes for *privacy* for herself?"

Such talk was but a dream. The pain was now so bad that she could not imagine what she might say or do, either at Pemberley nor, should they arrive safely home, at Longbourn.

Yet she *did* know what she wished most of all, this minute, to do. It was to take the pointed end of one of her fine mending needles and poke it into Miss Mary's bubble with a swift *prick*.

There were many possible – and hurtful – ways of delivering this prick. She chose the least hurtful she could muster.

She said, above the pain, "Do you wish for children, Miss Mary?"

"If the Good Lord should grant," Mary said,

"children may come. In the meantime I will find needy babies in the parish, and care for them, as our Lord exhorted us to do."

There was no suitable reply to that, and Mrs Hill gave up trying. She allowed herself to be swallowed up in the pain, and it overwhelmed her.

Her only comfort for the next few days was the hope that she might keep the same Pemberley maidservant as she had been offered so far. She could not recall what this person looked like, or even her name, but the girl must have few other duties to perform, for she could be at Mrs Hill's beck and call without ever having to rush away. There was something so gentle about this person's tending that it was almost like being in heaven. She would not mind going to this heaven, even if it required her to die and be buried in order to get there.

∽

There were so many more questions queuing up for Mary to ask, but she must resist the urge to pester Hill with them now. Pemberley's park spread out to right and left. They were approaching the final pair of gates before reaching the house.

She was taken with a sudden impulse. A parasol was perched between the seat and the door, put there by Lizzy to guard against the blazing June sunshine. Mary took it, lifted it, and tapped it tentatively on the carriage ceiling. Her wrist longed to bang it, one-two-three, peremptorily, as a man would do. But she was a mere woman, and must tap, not bang.

Still, the men up top heard her, as they were no doubt trained to do, and the horses were reined in at her command.

Hill opened her eyes in surprise. "What...?"

Mary spoke to the under-coachman whose face had appeared in the window. "Is there a longer way round the grounds to the house? I wish to see more of the park before we arrive."

"Indeed there is, Miss. By the gazebo, with a view of the deer."

"Drive that way, if you please. And pause when the deer are in view."

The man disappeared. The carriage heaved as the man climbed back up, and with some shouted commands, they turned around and took a different avenue.

"Deer!" said Mary. "But there is no need to excite yourself, Hill. I can view their splendidness alone." She needed time to absorb what Hill had been trying to tell her. She must have time to think.

Her space, at the Rectory of Humbole. What was it to be? It would be modest. Mr Needleman would be busy with sermons and Mr Hepplecraft. Hill had not been specific about what men *do*, but, as a lady, one accepted men's ways without question. She was happy that the two Reverends should indulge in theology.

There was, too, the work of running the 'living'. This, as Mr Collins had enunciated long ago, involved pleasing one's patron in every way.

When one considered the space given to Mr Hepplecraft and Lady Manton, her space in her husband's life would indeed be small.

Surely her space in the Rectory would be larger than her allotted space had been at Longbourn? Larger than her space as the lonely singleton between two inseparable pairs of sisters; larger still than the space left over from being Mama's daughter-companion?

She had tried to find space again in the stable, with the horses, with riding. She had failed that first time, but she could try again. She might ask Mr Needleman to summon his stable boy and request that she be seated – astride! She could take the reins and trot out along the lanes, rising in the saddle and falling back, rising, falling, in a rhythm of natural harmony.

Might this be too demanding? She must not demand. And she did not know the lanes around Humbole and Pemberley. What if she were to fall off?

No, she would not ride. She would stride. Around the parish. Become the Rector's wife, meeting and greeting, being benevolent.

There was a sudden *Herrrupppp!* from the coachman as the horses were reined in and the carriage came to a stop.

There was a shouted "Yon! Deer!" from the under-coachman. Mary realised that, to these servants, she might be a sister of Mrs Darcy, but she was not an august enough personage to warrant either of them getting down a second time from their great height up top.

Where were the deer? Ah!

With her new-found clarity she saw them. They were grazing. Some had antlers; they must be stags. Others, smaller, clustered in groups. Several of these were round in the belly: they must be ready to give birth. What was the word for their babies? She had some fragments of deer-related vocabulary (stags, antlers) but there was so much more to learn.

As she struggled to find deer words in her mind, Mary experienced a sudden rush of entirely other words.

Alien words. They related to Jane, and to childbirth.

Traumatic. Extended. Recommend... No, *prescribe*. Urgently. Laudanum (whenever). Seclusion. Recruitment (governesses, as the children grew, and extra maids). Cancelled (visits to Pemberley). Bingley, alone. Jane... *misses* (as in, *cannot bear to be with, cannot bear to be without*) children. Sisters. Everything.

Unfortunate, regrettable, inevitable. Mrs Darcy, sick visitation? Not advised. Children? Nurses, governesses, cope. Medical instructions, incontrovertible. Seclusion, complete.

Jane, alone. Without Lizzy, without her children, without any of that life with Bingley for which she had yearned. Poor, poor Jane.

One of the stags, slightly separate from the group, raised his head and shook his antlers. Would he roar, as she had heard that stags did? No, that was just in the autumn. Did human males roar as they gathered their females in the autumn? Oh, how ignorant she was.

She, Mary, must not become like Jane. She would say goodbye to her tiny space at Longbourn, and accept the invitation to share Mr Needleman's space in the Rectory, in Humbole, however 'convenient', however modest, however strange.

'Thwaite'. If only she could have kept her own name, Esther. It seemed like a theft, to have your name taken away. Especially as Milly could stay Milly. Low down as she was, lower than anyone, she mattered not a whit; so, strangely, she could keep the name their parents had given her. But she, Esther, the one who rose and rose through servant ranks: her name must go. 'Thwaite' was the name of Mrs Darcy's lady's maid. If Esther were to take up the post, Thwaite she must become.

"A chance in a million," said her father, while she was still Esther and the remnants of the family were still together. "The both of you, at Pemberley!" Other girls must work their way up through pretentious, middling little houses before landing such a plum. As it was, with their all-important Introductions, the two sisters could stay together. Where else but at Pemberley could such a blessedness occur? The Lord's hand was in it, her father had said, the furrows of his great brow knitting and un-knitting as he explained how mysterious were the ways of the Lord. *He plants His footsteps in the sea, And rides upon the storm.* It was the hymn her mother had sung as she lay dying. *He treasures up His bright designs And works His Sov'reign Will.*

So, in acknowledgement of the Sov'reign Will, she, Esther, worked her way up through the servant hierarchy under this one vast roof, with Milly at her side. At the start she'd no notion of reaching the unimaginable height of Lady's Maid. But, with Milly's eyes and her own swift learning, she did. It was only then that she must change her name. Some of the maids-of-all-work still called her Esther by mistake.

Of course, when they were alone, she and Milly didn't need to use names at all. They were the *Doovus*. The two of us. Always together, never apart. Listening out for Milly's witness, translating it into service to Mrs Darcy, she – they – made Thwaite indispensable.

She wasn't complaining. Just feeling. Just feeling what Esther would feel.

And now she was watching this day unfolding with its new dimension.

On the surface it was very straightforward. Mrs Darcy was one of a troupe of sisters, most of them catered for by a variety of marriages. Now one of the un-catered-for sisters had landed here, hoping to seek out a destiny of her own. It was all down to Lady Manton. Most machinations were down to Lady Manton, who wanted to mother everyone into happiness, and if that wasn't possible, she'd mother them through their misery. A marriage needs arranging: up pops Lady Manton. Not, of course, the marriage of a servant. Oh, no. Thwaites and their like did not seek husbands. If a likely mate appeared on the horizon, he was chivvied away like some bothersome bluebottle. But marriages for sisters of Mrs Darcy: yes.

Now that Lady Manton could trust Mrs Darcy to do the necessary, Lady Manton could absent herself from proceedings and all would be well.

Thwaite puzzled at this. She didn't puzzle at what was demanded of her; that was clear as glass. The visiting sister, even, wasn't too difficult. The puzzle was what this whole business did to Mrs Darcy. She was fired up like a hound on hunting day. Especially puzzling was how Mrs Darcy behaved around the so-called lady's maid from Hertfordshire, a Mrs Hill. The poor woman was terribly ill; anyone could see that. Then why had she come? Where was Miss Mary Bennet's proper lady's maid? Did she not have one? Why not? Was Longbourn (which Esther had briefly visited last autumn) so very short of servantry that lady's maids must be borrowed for the occasion?

Yes, those folks at Longbourn must indeed be short: short of money, of maids, of everything. And why? Because Mrs Darcy's own status was quite remarkably below that of Mr Darcy. He had stooped. Everyone was aware of it, always. In the name of love, he had stooped.

As for today, everything was a-bustle, and Mrs Darcy gave instructions that Milly be despatched to the east wing to care once more for Mrs Hill. Milly would do as Milly always did. Milly was one of the Lord's *bright designs*. No one other than Esther – Thwaite – would ever know the full truth of that.

༄

Mary saw her clearly: Mrs Darcy, Elizabeth, Lizzy, awaiting their return. First, as the carriage crossed the gravel and the horses snorted to a halt, she appeared as Mrs Darcy: a small but elegant figure embraced by Palladian pillars. Then in a trice she became the high-spirited Lizzy of old, skipping down the steps and across the gravel to meet her younger sister. And now, very close at the carriage window, she became Mrs Elizabeth Darcy, impatient for news as the under-coachman leaned to open the door.

"Oh Mary," cried Lizzy. Then – "Mary!"

Mary, as her foot reached the gravel, flinched. "Is something amiss, Lizzy? Hill has managed in a most stalwart manner…"

"It is not that!" Lizzy took a step back and cocked her head at Mary, as if she could not quite think what was wrong. Then: "A messenger came! A message! From Humbole! Were you delayed?"

"What? It was the stag, we stopped to admire…" Mary, lurching forward, almost fell into Lizzy's arms. "Already? A message? To say what?"

"What are those? On your face?" Lizzy took Mary's arm and led her up the steps and through the doors, then up and through and along, deep into the rich panelled immensity of Pemberley. "He invites you again! Not tomorrow, of course. Such enthusiasm would be indecent. But Thursday! The day *after* tomorrow."

As if, thought Mary irritably, she did not know that one day of the week followed another. Then Mr Needleman's words returned to her: …*comes to stay, which he does on alternate Wednesdays to discuss our sermons*. Mr Hepplemast. Craft! Mr *Hepplecraft*. It had a rhythm to it, in the same way as *Needleman* did. *Duh*-duh-duh. Two names in harmony with each other.

"But Lizzy, dear *Hill*! She has been… We must…"

"Never mind. The servants will help her. Come. Tell me about it. What are those spectacles on your nose? Where could you have acquired such things? Mama is sure to disapprove. What happened, Mary? At what point might we alert Lady Manton? Darcy is due back presently; he will wish to convey the news to her himself. But say, how did you achieve such a result?"

They were through at least five pairs of doors and across assorted marbled and carpeted surfaces before Mary could release herself from Lizzy's hold and say, "My spectacles were a gift from Mr Needleman."

She paused for a moment of satisfaction, and saw Lizzy's astonishment on hearing this: her beautiful eyes widening, the dimple in her cheek disappearing and then returning to its place in her softly powdered face.

Mary continued. "We cannot expect any more of dear Hill. She is, I dare not say, but she must be in dire need of... Please, Lizzy, can she be looked after?"

"Dear oh dear! I will send for Thwaite. Then you and I will seat ourselves in the lower withdrawing room for the details. The message-boy is waiting in the south kitchen. We must decide on the exact – the *appropriate* – wording of our response."

Lizzy rang the appropriate bell, her lady's maid appeared, they murmured together, and Thwaite vanished as swiftly as she had come. Lizzy re-linked her authoritative arm with Mary's, and drew her on.

5

Confirmation

MR NEEDLEMAN insisted on sending his phaeton. His message said that he could not, for propriety's sake, come himself, as he and Miss Mary Bennet were not yet betrothed. (Mary read those exact words. 'Not *yet* betrothed'.) But he trusted that Mrs Mill would be well enough to act as chaperone, as before.

'Mrs Mill' might have been well enough; Mrs Hill, though, was not. Thwaite gave the news to Mrs Darcy. Mrs Darcy, relaying the news to Miss Mary, followed it with: "Thwaite herself will accompany you in Mr Needleman's proffered phaeton." And swiftly to the weather. It looked set to remain sunny and bright, though the month of June could be subject to sudden downpours, so, as Mr Needleman's phaeton would be open to the elements, Lizzy would furnish them with umbrellas in addition to parasols.

Just one coachman drove the pretty tasselled phaeton: a silent man, a leisurely man, clicking the horse into action and setting them on their leisurely way. The countryside spread out on either side. Mary, through her spectacles, saw that it went on forever: the park gave way to farmland, which in its turn gave way to moor and rock, to bog and hill, and probably, in the end, to waterfall and mountain, and even beyond that, to shining ice-caps and scorching deserts. In the other direction it reached the sea. How much of all this was owned by the Darcy family? Mary had no idea.

"It must be good," Thwaite was remarking, "to be able to see properly for the first time. Very special."

How did this girl know how she felt? It was unnerving. Pleasantly unnerving.

"Indeed it is. Do you know Humbole? Have you visited the Rectory before?"

"Not the Rectory, but the village, yes. Mrs Darcy often takes a turn around the village. We went once into the church, and the Rector was there. He pointed out its historical features."

"The organ – did he show you the organ? Mr Needleman plays that remarkable instrument, you know."

"I do not recall the organ. The Rector was with another person, and we did not care to distract him. Though he was most polite."

Another person. Mr Hepplecraft? Or a member of the congregation, maybe one of the villagers. Congregants, with whom she would in due course make acquaintance. In whose eyes she would be the Rector's New Wife. With whom she might discuss the weather. Or salvation.

She caught her breath at the prospect. Could it be so?

Thwaite soothed her nervousness. "I will remain at your side, Miss Bennet. Mrs Darcy instructed me to act the chaperone in every particular."

Mary's tension vanished. This, she thought, is what it means to have a lady's maid. To have all one's needs noticed, and met.

๛

In the middle of the following night, cossetted by Pemberley's soft sheets, Mary woke in the darkness with a realisation. There were two types of blur. The first was the blurring of vision, which she had suffered before the advent of her wonderful spectacles. The second was the blurring of experience as it fell into memory. This was happening, now, to yesterday's experience with Mr Needleman.

What, actually, had taken place?

The behaviour of her spectacles had been impeccable. She had noted, for instance, the speck of flour on Mrs Beattie's middle finger as the hand approached to be shaken; then, later, the intricacy of the cream lace around Mr Hepplecraft's cuffs as he bowed extravagantly before her.

But what happened before and after the speck of flour, and before and after the cream lace, was not available to her. Her memory went into spasm, much as her muscles might spasm if the coach in which she was travelling were to hurtle off, out of control. This image, of hurtling and losing control, had woken her from a dream.

Complete wakefulness came slowly, but with a certain calm: *she had behaved well*. How could she have behaved quite so well? Because, by her side, there was always Thwaite. Thwaite's hand, with a murmured *This way*; Thwaite's eyes, turning in whatever direction they should next go; Thwaite's questions to the gentlemen – and even to the fearsome Mrs Beattie – as to what the procedure should be. After Reverend Mr Hepplecraft had taken his leave, and the two of them, Mary and the Reverend Mr Needleman, were about to be left alone together in the drawing room, Thwaite had said firmly: "I will be on hand in twenty minutes, Miss Mary, in case you have any requirements." Thwaite's eyes had then lifted to the clock on the Adam fireplace (*Robert* Adam, Mary remembered, like *Robert* Needleman), as if to confirm her attention throughout those twenty momentous minutes, distant though that attention might be.

After a little while Mary discovered that, just as the blur of her vision could be amended by spectacles, so the blur of her memory could be amended by lying in this soft cocoon and inviting the details of her second Rectory visit to appear. She could see clearly, now, Mr Needleman's frowning brow as he greeted her at the door; the small streak of grey at each of his temples as he turned his handsome head. She could appreciate the grace of the curved staircase, even notice the curling grain of the wood on the newel-post.

The Rectory felt serene. Manageable. She could breathe there.

But could she? Her next recollection was of Mrs Beattie approaching from the gloom of the servants' stairway, striding across and revealing, as she took Mary's hand, the chill underbelly of the Rectory's welcome.

"Miss Bennet." Not a bob, nor a curtsey. The hand swiftly withdrawn.

Thwaite had come to the rescue. "We bring greetings from Pemberley, and from Mrs Darcy in particular, ma'am."

Mrs Beattie had given a twitch of surprise at the word *ma'am*. One did not generally call a housekeeper *ma'am*, however precious she was to the household. But Mrs Beattie commanded respect, and Thwaite had recognised that.

Then to the study, and the much-heralded Mr Hepplecraft.

This recollection began full of fear. Mr Hepplecraft dealt in sermons. Did that mean Mary's sermon-reading, however extensive, would prove inadequate? If he discussed theology, would Mary be excluded? Beside such a weightiness of clergy, would Mary's potential wifeliness be insignificant?

Not at all! The Reverend Mr Hepplecraft whom she now recalled was not weighty, but light and bright: leaping from the study desk, dazzling her with a smile, then disappearing into a low bow. Upright again, with another smile of pearl-white teeth. Mary was glad of the firmness of Mr Needleman's arm in the face of such brightness. Her own teeth were far from white, and somewhat crooked. Yet if Mr Hepplecraft smiled so white and bright, was that not a sign of her acceptance here at the Rectory?

Mrs Hill had used the word *convenient*. She recalled it painfully, then let it slide back into the dazzle of Mr Hepplecraft's smile.

Snuggling down for further sleep, she repeated to herself the sentences with which Mr Needleman had engaged her as his companion and future wife. "Miss Bennet, will you join your future with mine?" Her response had been a shy step forward towards him. "I could scarcely," he continued, "have hoped for one so entirely compatible." And later: "I have made plans. They are as yet flexible. Please make your feelings known. The whole of Europe is open to us, thanks to Wellington's great victories. Paris, Vienna, Florence, Venice... With Mr Hepplecraft as our guide, we will see the best of everything."

She was shamefully ignorant of maps and cultures. Might music feature at all? Could she and Mr Needleman go to concerts in Paris etc., and afterwards discuss the wonders of Mozart and Bach? Was Mr Hepplecraft an expert in music too?

She was dropping back into sleep. Mr Needleman's next comment had been something about who else might accompany them on this marriage journey... She must have a... Oh, that old bother about a lady's maid... It was all too much. She was exhausted.

Birdsong through Pemberley's huge windows. She was awake again, and she had survived yesterday.

Should she arise? No. A servant would knock, enter, stand by the door and give instructions from Mrs

Darcy. She could remain in bed, in luxurious recall.

On their return from Humbole to Pemberley in the phaeton, she had been kept happily occupied by Thwaite's conversation. How charming the trees around the Rectory, how pleasant the tone of the pianoforte, how polished its black and white keys! What friends the Reverend must surely have, as well as the delightful Mr Hepp…

"Oh!" Mary cried suddenly. "Look – over there on that bank – little brown things, chasing about…"

"Rabbits?"

"Rabbits! Of course. Are they not delightful? How they bob! Those little white tails at the back!"

"When I was a child we called them coneys," responded Thwaite thoughtfully. "We caught them, I'm afraid."

"For food?"

"Yes. They were tasty."

"Did you grow up far from here, Thwaite?"

"Up the valley, towards the moors, ma'am. My father worked a mine there. Lead."

"Ah."

"But they get worked out, the mines." Thwaite paused, as if wondering whether Miss Mary would be interested to hear more. "Rabbit pie is common still, even at Pemberley. Only in the kitchen, of course. For the staff."

Mary was not especially interested in lead mines, or pies. "Hepplecraft. His friend. So you think Mr Needleman will have other friends? Some of them with wives, perhaps? Who could become friends of myself? I have not, in the past, been much in the habit of making friends."

"If you are to be Mrs Rector, there will no doubt be ladies to introduce you to the ways of the parish."

'The ways of the parish'. What a helpful thought. Yes, that was where she would make her mark. That would be her contribution. She would tell Lizzy. Lizzy would be happy about that.

However, as they drew to a halt at Pemberley's pillared frontage, Mrs Darcy did not appear at the top of the great steps. A couple of under-gardeners were sweeping untidinesses from each step into wicker baskets at the foot, and they hurried off at the phaeton's approach.

"The nursery," said Thwaite, as she helped Mary down to the gravel. "She goes there at this time to check on how George has been behaving." She nodded to the silent Rectory coachman, who clicked the phaeton round and back towards Humbole. "And Henrietta, of course, and dear William. Let us go to the lower withdrawing room, Miss Mary. In due course, Mrs Darcy will be eager to hear all."

Thwaite had emphasised the 'all' with a conspiratorial little smile. At the door of the drawing room, which proved empty, she murmured that she would check on Mrs Hill, too, and vanished.

Mary had been happy enough to wait. She could spend the time preparing an account of the morning that would satisfy Lizzy. Of course Lizzy would be satisfied. How could she not be? Still, Mary must prepare. How much should she say about Mr Hepplecraft? Anything at all? Oh, but she must, for he was to accompany them on their six-week marriage journey around the art galleries of Europe. Had the Darcys journeyed thus after their wedding? And Jane and Bingley? No, they had not, for the War still raged then, and one could not travel. Even now there were stories of old soldiers on the loose, injured, or pretending to be injured, blaming every decently attired traveller for their injuries or their unemployment, when of course only Boney and his compatriots were to blame. Would that be the case on her marriage journey with the Reverends through Europe? She must not be anxious. She would have two fine men to protect her.

Lizzy had arrived, her hair somewhat awry and her bosom more than usually visible above her gown. Again, Mary sent up a brief prayer of thanks that, due to her new spectacles, she could now notice such things.

"Well! It is done!" Lizzy almost threw herself into a chair. "Thwaite reports that all is well! I can only congratulate you, Mary dear!"

"Thank you, Lizzy. It is indeed a…" She wanted to say *triumph*, but realised just in time that such a word was for others to use, not her.

"Now we must think about protocol. All must be done in a seemly manner. Darcy will insist on it."

Mary relaxed. Lizzy would not wish to know the detail; she was not interested in Mr Hepplecraft, or the bridal tour – only in protocol.

"Mr Needleman must visit Longbourn to ask Papa for your hand. To negotiate the settlement. So you must return home yourself. As soon as possible."

"Do you think Hill is ready for the journey? She has received such delicate care here. The bumps in the roads, in the mattresses of the post-houses... She will suffer so!"

"Mary, my dear! Do not upset yourself! The matter of Hill's health cannot endanger your position, I assure you. Your betrothal is the most acceptable of any I can think of. Your music, your reading of sermons! His kindness over the spectacles! It is a marriage made in heaven. Dear, dear Mary." Lizzy's hand was warm upon Mary's. Sisterly. "And Darcy himself, dear Fitzy, he will be delighted."

Lizzy approved. Lizzy would take charge. Maybe Hill would now rally and be fit for the journey after all. Thwaite was probably making the necessary arrangements at this very moment.

Mary, at this point, had tears in her eyes. She found her handkerchief, blew her nose, and changed the subject. "Did Hill ever tell you, Lizzy, that she had a child, who was sent away? And visited occasionally? How sad, to have a child and then to..."

Lizzy's hand slipped away from hers. "I did know. We do not speak of it. But she will be greatly missed. You will need to look after..."

"After...?"

"Afterwards. The son. The child. He is known to some of us..."

Another silence.

Mary said, "He is Luke, I think."

Lizzy coughed. "As I say, we do not speak of it. At home – at Longbourn – there are Mama's feelings to be taken into account. I am merely saying... You, especially, as Mama's companion so far, must exercise the greatest care."

"Of Luke."

"Of them all. At the time of Hill's… Which may come soon." Lizzy had stood abruptly to ring the bell. "We must proceed. As I suggested. When Thwaite comes, we will compose a letter to Papa to go ahead of you on the way."

⟳

I stared. In RN's terms, it must have looked like I *gawped*.

I said little, for silence is the most powerful weapon in my armoury. When he asked how such a betrothal would appear to me, I answered only with a statement of fact: "You gave me no room, Mr Needleman, to get her to see her mistake."

At which he repeated all the points he had already been making, the points he has already persuaded himself upon, the flummery about conventions, pressures, Lady Manton, the Living, and so forth.

"And has she any feelings for Art?" I asked him. "None whatsoever! How could you attach yourself to a minx" (for I care not to call her a *girl* or a *woman*) "who has no feeling for the Muse? Who has scarce an hour of serious education to her credit? Who, if she were given a month or two at some dusty Dame School, it would be more than her poor small brain could cope with?" I heard the Ulsterwoman in me booming forth, but it did not prevent me. "Who is ignorant of Rembrandt, of Raphael, of Giotto? Whose capacities only reach to… I cannot possibly describe!"

And how did he respond to my justified disbelief?

"Mrs B," came his answer, and it came gently, "you have known, for you possess a far better mind than I do, that there would always come this moment when the three of us would need to accommodate a fourth. Miss Mary Bennet is shy, and has not, I admit, had the advantages in life that we would have wished for her. But she is no *minx*. Lady Manton is adamant. If this latest offer does not suit me, then she will ask one or two pertinent questions. And those questions will be…"

My tongue could stand it no longer. "Those questions will not be forthcoming! No Lady of her standing could ask them! I am the only woman in the county who sees these things clear! She will fluff and she will puff, but Humbole loves you, Humbole respects you, Humbole asks no questions, and Humbole will not put up with such a specimen as Rectory wife!"

At this point he made a gesture about the volume of my voice, and I tossed my head in the direction of the kitchen as if to say, 'Our Patty and our Gladys know nothing, and if they knew it they couldn't find words for it'. I am the keeper of secrets hereabouts, and I know that Lady Manton cannot force this marriage into being. It can only happen with consent of my two men.

Then came the body blow. Again, it came gently.

"Mrs B, I am *fond* of her. Do not deny me the surprise, and the happiness, of finding myself *fond*. She has had so little in her life, and she has made so much of it. She is open to beauty. Her response to my poor little spectacles – you saw it yourself? She is also, bless her heart, quite innocent. She assured me that she enjoys *privacy* as much as I do. We will manage. The three of us will still be three. We will expand, and find ourselves enriched. Lady Manton will be satisfied, Mr Darcy also, and we will be secure. Can you not nod your head, and give us your blessing? Can you do that, dear Mrs B? If you please?"

If silence could indicate consent, then I would give it. And I did give him what he wanted: one very slight nod. But he knew, and I knew he knew, that my consent was reluctant. Entirely and utterly begrudged.

☙

Mary, that evening, prepared for bed with some anxiety. Their return to Longbourn was still uncertain. Thwaite reported that Mrs Hill had rallied somewhat, but might need further care. Mr Darcy was due to return to Pemberley the following day, and Lizzy made clear her preference that Mary and Hill should depart before his arrival. "I know how he is when half his mind resides in the West Indies. It takes him days to settle. However, we shall see how matters stand in the morning." Mary had hoped to put her head round the door of Hill's room to convey her good wishes, but Thwaite advised against it. "She is sleeping. Sleep is what she most needs at the moment."

She was just settling back on the pillows with a volume from Pemberley's fine library when there was a tap on her door.

It was Lizzy, with her hair down. She whispered, "May I?"

Mary set aside her book. Not sermons this time;

she had chosen *A Tour thro' the Whole Island of Great Britain*, by Daniel Defoe, and was searching in it for references to Derbyshire.

Lizzy seated herself on the edge of the bed. This was like the old days, when Lizzy and Jane would flutter in at the end of an evening and regale her with a list of their dancing partners at a ball; a ball which Mary had sadly declined to attend on account of a headache.

Lizzy sat for a while, shifting herself into a more or less comfortable position, and perhaps making up her mind what to say. Mary might have tried to impress her sister by quoting Mr Defoe's comments on Derbyshire, but she had only reached page three. She closed the book quietly and set it to one side. Might she ask Lizzy about the West Indies, which presumably were located somewhere near to the *East* Indies? But, recalling the end of their previous conversation, and still wondering why it was *Mama* who should be given special consideration during Hill's last illness, she thought better of it.

"Marriage is a strange institution," said Lizzy at last, in a tone she might use for 'Bakewell is a strange kind of pudding'. "It is a consummation devoutly to be wished, and yet is full of surprises."

"I am sure it is," replied Mary. She feared that this conversation might be full of surprises too.

"I am happy for you," Lizzy continued. "Personally, I like Mr Needleman. When Lady Manton approached me with the suggestion that the two of you might be introduced, I encouraged the proceedings with a whole heart. Having experienced the happy state of marriage for some years, I felt I had all the evidence

I needed. Yet, as I say, it brings in its wake, as a rule, some unintended consequences."

"I expect it does." Mary had the sense of a weight in Lizzy's hands, a weight which she was preparing to hand over to her. "Have you some examples to offer?"

Lizzy, unexpectedly, laughed. "It may surprise you, Mary, but, looking back, I think that poor dear Lyddy might have had more wisdom than the rest of us about marriage. She wanted a husband, for her own reasons as well as for our reasons as a family. But most of all she wanted to enjoy herself."

"Enjoy? She put herself at risk of universal condemnation, and the family name at risk of slur! Not to mention the eternal aspect! We must always keep the eternal at the forefront of our minds."

"Oh, tosh, Mary. I apologise for descending to George's level of vocabulary, but we must be honest in these matters. On the night of our marriage I was confronted by the more private aspects of the contract between Fitzy and myself, and it came, I can tell you, as a great shock."

Mary did not know what to say. She picked up Daniel Defoe and held on to him very tightly. "That is enough for the moment, thank you, Lizzy. Mr Needleman and I are of one accord about what constitutes companionship and what constitutes privacy. I could not have accepted his offer of marriage had it been otherwise. I recall, moreover, that Mr Darcy had various explanations to make to you about his behaviour and opinions before his suit became acceptable."

Lizzy shifted her position, and Mary thought of

the phrase 'startled as a rabbit'. She had seen rabbits clearly now, and knew what that meant.

"Well! In that case, Mr Needleman and your good self have made better progress in your betrothal negotiations than I ever made with Fitzy. If you are happy with that, I will not pursue the matter." She gave a small cough. "But, Mary, there is this other question. We spoke of it earlier, and I am not sure whether our mutual understanding was complete."

Mary, feeling for the first time in her life that she had the upper hand with Lizzy, allowed a short pause before responding. "About how the condition of our dear Hill might affect the nerves of dear Mama?"

"Exactly. And of dear Papa."

"Why of Papa? I have seen Hill carry his nightcap into the library and occasionally keep him company, but that does not constitute a bond, surely?"

"Oh Mary, are you being deliberately obtuse? Do you not realise that there are other bonds between women and men than those of kinship and of marriage?"

"If there are," said Mary, "I do not wish to know about them."

"Very well. That is your position." Lizzy stood. "I only ask you to remember that Papa may be more disorientated than you anticipate when Hill finally makes her departure. And, when you see it happen, please give me the credit for having forewarned you. Do not expect to lean upon Annie or Luke, either. They will bear the burden of their own grief. I will arrange for a Pemberley maid-of-all-work to accompany you in the coach, who will be instructed to assist you on the journey. Now. Let us await the morrow, and hope that it brings better news of Hill's health. Good night, Mary."

As the door closed, Mary opened Mr Defoe's book at a random page and read the same paragraph over and over again.

6

Clarification?

I N THE EVENT, Lizzy asked Mrs Reynolds the
housekeeper to provide two maids-of-all-work
to accompany Mary and Mrs Hill: both for the
journey, one to return with the Pemberley coach, the
other to remain at Longbourn until the Hill crisis
resolved itself.

Thwaite delivered this information to Mary in the
library, along with instructions from Mrs Darcy that
she, Mary, should stay at Pemberley one further day
and night so as to give Mrs Hill the chance for further
recovery. Unfortunately, Mrs Darcy herself would be
fully occupied in the nursery, preparing the children for
the return of their father, and in her boudoir, preparing
herself similarly. Mr and Mrs Darcy would bid a formal
farewell, together, on the morrow. Mr Bingley might

be in Mr Darcy's company, for business reasons; also to give news of dear Jane, though his visit would be brief and need not concern Mary. Meanwhile, today, the library and the park were at her disposal; even the private Pemberley chapel, should she so please.

Mary saw that Thwaite was waiting for her either to reply or to give the nod and withdraw to other duties. But she could do neither; she simply stood, absorbing the enormity of Lizzy's rebuff. Mary was not to be welcomed, nor congratulated, by Darcy. Lizzy was not to prioritise sisterhood over wifeliness. Mary was to be tolerated until her departure with Hill. Would something further emerge to warm the cold shoulder? No. Even Thwaite could find nothing.

Mary found herself uttering an urgent plea.

"If you please, Thwaite. Before Hill and I travel back together, I would like to spend a brief time with her. Could you enquire of the member of staff who has been attending her as to what time might be convenient?"

Thwaite bobbed a curtsey and turned away.

Mary was alone with a thousand books. Having returned Mr Defoe to his place, she searched for comfort in sermons. Eventually she found a small shelf of collected sermons, mostly quite dated. But *Cattermole* was there. She drew out his stout volume. It was the same small-print edition that Mr Needleman had referred to. That was the strength of the bond between them, she thought: *Cattermole's Selected Sermons*, read by the Reverend Mr Needleman, with Mary's magnifying glass in his own hand.

Thwaite returned. Mary, feeling very small as she

perched her buttocks on a polished chair at one of the many polished library tables, looked up from her reading.

"The staff say, Miss Bennet, that Mrs Hill will be woken for a small cold repast around noon. If it would please you, they will wake her a short while earlier, and you may go in then."

"Thank you, Thwaite. I will cease my reading, take a turn around the garden, then return here to await your call."

"I may be occupied with Mrs Darcy, Miss Bennet. Be sure, though, I will instruct the staff to have you informed."

⁊⁊

She was dying. But she must not die yet. Between here and dying was a long, long journey. She must reach them all: Longbourn. Luke. Annie. The little ones. She must reach them before, before, before.

The crooked little angel came and went. Sometimes Flora was aware of her presence, sometimes not. She could not tell, truly, whether it was a human presence or an angelic one.

Had she, perhaps, already died? No, not yet.

At church they were always on about angels: *angels and archangels continually do cry.* She didn't know much about archangels, but she did know that Annie was an angel. A kind of angel, anyway. She'd never thought to encounter another. There was no *continually crying* about this one, though. Barely a whisper. And even that whisper was nothing that Flora could understand.

Every so often her pillows were lifted gently for purposes of washing (warm water, kind water) and, lower down, some rearrangement that she needn't be concerned about. Sips of balm between whiles. (Maybe Sydenham's, like Mrs Bennet's?) Then she slept.

But her sleeping had a determined boundary to it. She would not die. Not till she was back at Longbourn. In her dreams she could see the narrow alley in Meryton where old Mother Drayton lived. Mother Drayton would have heard the news of her illness. How? Oh, news travelled. Mother Drayton could sniff out any approaching death. She would already be arranging her basket with camphor and bandages, folding the linen strips to bind up the chin, wrapping two coins in a soft cloth for the eyes.

But before that, there was night upon night of a journey.

And, oh dear, there was Miss Mary. Pray God she would be quiet on the way.

༄

The call came while Mary was concerning herself with St Paul's *Letter to the Thessalonians*. "For the Lord Himself shall descend from heaven with a shout, with the voice of the archangel, and with the trump of God: and the dead in Christ shall rise first." Would Hill be one of 'the dead in Christ'? How did one know? Whom could she ask?

A maid she had not seen before bobbed and said, "Miss Mary Bennet for Mrs Flora Hill." Bobbed again, and waited to be followed. Mary returned St Paul to his shelf, breathed deeply, and did as she was told.

It was a long walk along high corridors. When the maid opened a door on the right, Mary could not tell whether the room she was entering was intended for very important servants or for not very important guests. It was large; the curtains were drawn but for a slit of light; the half-tester bed was piled with blankets; a plain upright chair had been placed by the bedside. The maid bobbed and vanished.

In the gloom, Mary was doubtful whether there was a person in the bed at all. There seemed to be no one present, either in the bed or elsewhere. Was that a small movement somewhere? She could scarcely tell.

Then a white hand stirred on the white sheet, and she saw above it a pale, familiar face.

"Hill! How…?"

"Miss Mary." It was scarcely a whisper.

Silence.

A thought came to Mary, very clearly: that one day her mother would be lying like this, and would then die. And that one day, so would she.

There was a slight movement of air behind her. Then stillness again.

She could not bear it. She had so much to tell Hill. So much to ask her, too. About her son, Luke, and so on. She did not have long. She must use this time, or regret it for ever.

"You were right. This will be a convenient marriage for me. Dear Hill, dear dear Hill, I am so grateful to you for accompanying me on this journey! Especially when you are ailing. I could not have done without you! Now, let me tell you what has transpired. A letter has gone ahead of us to Papa, informing him that Mr Needleman will visit shortly to ask for my hand in marriage. And Papa will agree. Lizzy composed the letter on the strict assumption that he would agree. When that is done, we will be wed. From Longbourn, of course. Then away we will go! He was in such excitement, my dear Mr Needleman. His friend – you remember, Mr Hepplecraft? Mr Hepplecraft is artistic. He will guide us. There will be many galleries! I am to become educated, Hill, after my years of ignorance! The capitals of Europe are open to us, now that Boney is safely put away! Six weeks! I will need to find myself a lady's maid, will I not? I am to be quite grand. I must get used to it somehow. It is a dream, Hill. Dear, dear Hill." Her voice, which had started in a hoarse whisper, had gradually risen until it was almost a cry. "A dream! Oh, I should not have bothered you…" She stumbled, and returned to a whisper. "I knew you would be glad for me. But I am sorry to burden you, when you are…"

She paused. That minimal movement of air occurred again behind her. Was it a sign? Should she stay? Should she go? If only Thwaite were here to instruct her. Hill might not have wanted to hear about her marriage plans? But it was what they had come to Pemberley *for*!

"Thank you, thank you," she murmured once again. "And when we are back home at Longbourn, I will thank Annie, and Luke, for their, and your, devoted service. Your faithfulness. You are all so very, very dear. You have looked after Mama so well. Papa too! How would he have managed without your nightcaps and conversation?"

The movement behind her became a small cough. It was as though Thwaite, though absent, were giving her the signal: it was time for her to leave.

She stood. Her thighs hurt, as though they had been held very tight and did not know how to release themselves.

She managed a sideways step.

A croak came from the bed. "No!"

Mary heard it first as *Oh!*, then again, repeated in her head, as *No!*

"No!" Now it was clear as a bell. An instruction, too. *Don't go! Not yet!*

Mary reached for the chair and perched again, half on, half off.

Hill was a white half-figure emerging from a white sheet, with a dark elbow protruding as a prop: she was trying to sit up. Now a small grey shadow slid in from the side, making a slight shuffle as it came. It sat beside Hill and leaned in to support the elbow. Mary scarcely saw it. She gazed at Hill's dear face. It looked somehow like half of Hill and double Hill at the same time.

When Hill's voice came, it was wonderfully familiar and strong. "You need no galleries an' stuff. No Mr Hepple-thing. Get wed in 'Umbole. Afore the congregation. Then, wi' travel, just you an' him. Couple o' weeks. Nearby, somewhere. Got to be wed right. Marriage is f'you two. You two only." She paused, breathing heavily. "The parish, it *sees* things. Needs to see you 'n' him, as Two. Tell him. Not

Hepple thing. Just 'Umbole. Then you two an' a maid go off. A couple o' weeks away only!"

With that last emphatic *Couple O' Weeks Away Only*, her elbow started to slide. Mary watched as the shadow leaned further in, to try and solidify it. She said, "Thank you, thank you. I have no need for more now. Thank you."

Hill kept on slipping. But her face, round and white with the dark of the drapes behind her, became stronger, more rounded, more alive as she slid.

"Look!" she said.

"Look again at the plans? Yes, I will tell Mr – "

Hill said the word again, and Mary heard it differently.

"*Luke!*"

"Luke?" Mary was suddenly back in the stables, the smell of leather and horse-flesh and hay in her nose, gazing at the sheen of Bradwell's flank behind which Luke was hiding.

"Is. Your…" Hill's head was completely back on the pillow now, and the small shadowy figure was shuffling away. "Is your…"

The sheen and the horse-flesh vanished. There was a banging in Mary's ears. The chair was hard under the one of her buttocks; her other buttock was not supported at all. Mary wobbled, and felt a kind of hiccup rising in her throat. She could not speak. She felt herself about to fall.

Over in the gloom of the bed, Hill coughed, then lay still. Had she…? The clatter in Mary's ears faded. Was Hill…?

And here was Thwaite, taking her arm and guiding

her back across the room, through the door and, blinking, into the light.

⊙⊙

Time for *doovus*. The two of us.

Esther worried that there might be no space for it this evening. There had been a time when, on Mr Darcy's return from London, Mrs Darcy would dismiss her with a laugh that was almost a cry, so close was she to her Fitzy and so eager to be alone with him. Since the babies, and especially since the tearing from little William (so huge a baby), Mrs Darcy had needed Thwaite beside her for longer and longer to arrange her wifeliness exactly as Darcy, fresh from fashionable London, would require it. This evening, with Mrs Darcy as tight as a bowstring from not getting rid of her sister and the poor sick woman as soon as she had hoped, and with all the arrangements she'd been obliged to make with Mrs Reynolds about the servantry, she would be more needed than ever.

But no, Thwaite was dismissed, and could become Esther again.

Milly, though, would surely be occupied with her sickly patient, leaving Esther alone in the bed, waiting, pausing for each memory, imagining the two of them sharing it, until at last they could chuckle and snuggle and, with a nose-rub and a "Back i' day? Back i' day!", pour out all the memories and treasure each one? *Milly, Esther, Joel, Ma, Da?*

But Milly came. The patient was stilled, the towel dressings were in place. At Thwaite's request to Mrs

Reynolds, a laundress had been set to scrub the soiled towels so that it wasn't all left to Milly with her bent-back hand.

So Esther lay, a smile on her face, listening to Milly as she washed at the bowl, waiting for her to settle down, knowing they could have their *Doovus* for an hour or so before they slept.

༺༻

Yet another strange maid came to wake Mary, fling back the curtains and bewail the slashing rain that beat against the fine clear glass of the windows.

Mary sat up abruptly. "But we have to take ourselves and our belongings out to the coach today! They will be soaked! The roads will be all mud!"

The maid was at the door already. "Missus says you do your own stays?"

"I do, but... Is Mrs Hill – ?"

But the maid was gone.

Mary's head throbbed. As she laid out her stays on the bed with their single lace loose, she longed to have Cattermole's commentary on *Thessalonians* beside her to help her meet the day. Cattermole was far away, in the library, down hundreds of stairs, along miles of corridors. Maybe there was another copy sequestered in the vestry of the Darcys' private chapel, but that was even farther away.

Wriggling the stays around her chest and into a reasonably comfortable place, she felt herself relax. She saw in her mind's eye, not Cattermole's incisive commentary, but the actual text of St Paul's Epistle to the Thessalonians. *For they that sleep, sleep in the night; but let us, who are of the day, be sober, putting on the breastplate of faith and love; and for an helmet, the hope of salvation.* Her stays would be her breastplate. Her spectacles would serve for a helmet. Yes, here they were, lying on the bedside table with a napkin and a pretty little vase of flowers from Pemberley's exquisite gardens. She could see with them. Whatever the day should bring, they would carry her through.

And her prayers were answered. There was no news of Hill. The rain did not cease to pour, so there was a token farewell from Mr and Mrs Darcy in the vastness of the entrance hall. Lizzy scarcely looked at Mary; her eyes were all for Darcy. Darcy, a full head taller than his wife, leaned politely towards Mary, and she wondered for a quick moment whether he might offer her a peck on the cheek. She saw his square jaw approaching; the deep purple of his lips; the close-shaven chin with a line of dimple in the centre. Before his face reached her, with a stir of the air between them, he withdrew.

There followed a swift raising of umbrellas by Thwaite and other servants for Mary and her accompanying maids to run to the coach, followed by more umbrellas for the stowing of the luggage. Finally, at a funereal pace, with three umbrellas sheltering her on either side, came Mrs Flora Hill, lying on a thin horsehair mattress and heavily covered, like a corpse. Mary assumed she had been dosed with balm, and would continue to be so for the duration of the journey.

Inside the coach, the two maids on either side of Mary pressed themselves against the leather upholstery and drew in their feet as Mrs Hill on her mattress was lifted in and placed on the opposite side by liveried coachmen. She took up the whole space. Whoever had designed this luxurious coach could not have conceived of it being used to allow a dying servant to travel for three days and nights with a modicum of comfort and decorum; to be decanted each time they stopped, with men and maids shouting to each other over the patient's head about every detail of how it should be accomplished, then repeated in reverse each morning for every stage of the journey.

No doubt the maids carried out their services in the post-house lodgings efficiently each night, but Mary was too exhausted to notice. The post-house walls were thin, and let through every possible sound. Mary did not listen to what was going on. She knelt in prayer before sleep every night, begging Mrs Flora Hill to arrive safely home before she finally departed to meet her Maker.

∽

At Longbourn, soon after midday, Annie settled Mrs Bennet in the drawing room and Mr Bennet in the library, and told each of them on no account to move from where they were put. No doubt the coach would be delayed on the way, she told them, and might not even arrive till evening. "Highwaymen!" cried Mrs Bennet, and needed reassurance. "Fetch Doctor Morgan!" cried Mr Bennet, but had his demand denied. Dr Morgan was known to kill as many of his patients as he saved.

Having silenced those two, Annie divided her time between the kitchen and the attic room. In the kitchen she prepared broths from vegetables and boiled capon, made small moulds of sweet white-dish flavoured with cinnamon, and buttered the lightest of breads in case that was all her mother-in-law could manage to eat. She hardly bothered to cook for the Family; they could subsist on leftovers. Up in the attic she smoothed the sheets again and again, and checked that her mother-in-law would have every available spare pillow at her back. Then she dashed around for an extra chamber pot to put with the two already beneath the bed.

Luke wandered up and down the stairs, offering to help, trying to make the time pass. Annie sniffed, buried her face in his leather jerkin, then told him to go and take comfort in the horses.

She had opened and shut the dormer window for the sixteenth time when she heard the sound of wheels. She yelled, hoping that Luke would hear it from the stable. Then she threw herself down the stairs and landed in the hall. Luke was there, waiting for her. So it was hand-in-hand that they came out to meet the travellers' return.

 ᐧ⌒ᐧ

On the last, long, fortunately rain-free day of the journey, Mary wondered if the two maids on either side of her had been starved at Pemberley, because they stuffed themselves at each of the post-houses and became more corpulent and bulky by the day. Even more irritatingly, they succumbed to sporadic fits of the giggles, which were provoked by some indeterminate trigger and impossible to control.

It was in the midst of one of these giggly outbursts that Hill, without preamble or warning, rose onto her elbow and demanded air.

"Up the blinds!" Her voice was hoarse, but viable. "Make the wind blow through!"

The girls, wide-eyed, did as they were told.

The coach was negotiating one of the bumpier sections of the route, and Hill looked unsteady on her elbow. Mary leaned over to prevent any dislodgement from the mattress to the floor.

To her horror, Hill recoiled. "Do…not…touch…me!"

Mary flinched and fell back.

"I…will…not…have him!" Hill's eyes flared. "Tell him, I will not!"

"Of course. Dear Hill, there is no need for anxiety. Annie will do everything exactly as required."

The eyes flared again. "And who, may I ask, is doing the requiring?"

Mary had no answer. But Hill gave her own. "Who?" she croaked. "Mr B, that is who! And no, I say, and no and no and no!"

The stout maids, terrified, clung to the grab-handles of their nearest doors.

Mary made an effort. "How so? What, no?" What nonsense was she speaking? But Hill was also talking nonsense. What could it mean?

Hill flung herself back on her mattress. Then she spoke again, this time in a mutter to the air above. "Silly girl. You wonder who, still, do you? Wonder?

109

Only need to look at 'm, don' you?"

Mary thought that if she followed those words carefully she might find some way to make sense of them. But did she want to reach that sense? No. She only wanted to reach Longbourn, and not to be responsible for Hill any more.

Doubtfully, she said, "We are near to Meryton, I am sure of it."

She was right! There was Meryton Church! And the next church they saw would be St Bride's, Churchtown, where she had been baptised and confirmed in her faith, where she worshipped faithfully each Sunday, and often during the week too!

"Home, Hill!" she exclaimed. "We are almost home!"

A moan issued from Hill, and Mary was silenced again. She tore her eyes away from the familiar view and, leaning forward, heard the two maids consulting anxiously behind her back. "Worn off. Needs more. 'T'would look bad if. Should we? No! But..." Mary eased herself down more comfortably between them. First one of them, then the other, stopped muttering and bit their nails.

There was only one thing to do. She must pray.

She rose and knelt down sideways; there was no room otherwise. But, finding she was facing away from Hill's head, she must struggle to her feet in the tight space, turn, and kneel again. Now, properly positioned and with her eyes closed, she longed for one of the tapestry hassocks from St Bride's to be under her knees for comfort.

Mercifully, she remembered the words that she

must say.

"O Lord of all grace and blessing, behold, visit and relieve this Thy servant."

Was Hill 'the Lord's servant'? With her pregnancy out of wedlock? But she had cared wonderfully for all the family. Surely the Lord would forgive.

"Look upon him, er, her, with the eyes of Thy mercy. Give her comfort, and sure confidence. Keep her in Thy perpetual peace and safety."

She kept on praying till the carriage juddered to a halt. Opening her eyes, Mary glimpsed the frontage of Longbourn as it shuddered and then relaxed. A breeze blew in through the rectangle of the coach window: it held the face of Luke, like a portrait. He looked both frightened and reassuring, anxious and relieved, all at once. But most of all, he looked like Luke.

Another portrait slid out of her childhood memories and covered Luke's face. It was her father. After Jane's and Lizzy's marriages, Mama had engaged a portrait painter to do a likeness of Papa; it was to hang on the stairs, as Darcy's and Bingley's portraits hung on theirs. Mary had privately thought the result to be a true likeness; but Mama was outraged by it, and demanded its removal and disposal.

That portrait flashed into Mary's memory now, and the two portraits alternated: Luke, and Papa. Papa and Luke. The one was here now to help her out of the coach and into the safety of Longbourn; the other was waiting with Mama in the house, ready (she hoped) to greet her and be told the news of her splendid engagement.

7

Confusion

ISARRAY. THE WORLD OF Longbourn, thought Annie, was turned upside-down. Mr Bennet sat as if pinned to the floor beside Flora's bed up the attic stairs, while Edie and John-James, wearing whatever clothes she'd snatched up off the cottage floor, played hide-and-seek in the drawing room and out along the corridors, happy as the day was long. For food they begged from the kitchen. Meals around the table were a thing of the past. Mr Bennet ate his plateful slouched in his chair – his library chair, which Luke and Annie had hauled, sweating, up all those stairs – and Annie shuffled Mrs Bennet along to the parlour, where she dozed and moaned, and periodically shouted for Mr Bennet. Or, if what she needed was a visit to the necessary house, for Annie.

Mr Bennet had ceased to speak to his wife. Or even listen to her. He only had eyes for Flora.

Luke, disconsolate, drifted in and out of the house. He begged Annie – "Can you not shift the bugger from her side, so we can have our time up there?" – but she shrugged, helplessly. Once he disappeared entirely for three hours, returning flushed with a sort of triumph. Later, in bed, he confessed to have ridden Bradwell out through the broadleaf woodland and up onto the Beacon. The horse needed it, he said, now Mr B's morning constitutionals were no more. Annie nodded and held him close.

Meanwhile the floors continued to be polished, the laundry hung out to dry, the crockery and china washed and wiped, the chamber pots emptied and scrubbed. Even the necessary house was kept in the cleanest condition. Both Pemberley servants had stayed on, at Annie's request to Mrs Darcy. They kept themselves to themselves, and indulged in whispered gossip that ceased the moment Annie came near. Annie didn't begrudge them this. They were far from home, and they worked hard. Annie blessed Mrs Darcy for the relief that all this cleanliness brought with it. She suspected Miss Mary would bless her too, if she wasn't so busy in the drawing room, composing the speech that she and her Reverend would (hopefully) deliver to Mr Bennet on the morrow. Annie watched, sporadically, as Miss Mary wrote, crossed out and rewrote.

෧෨

During three nights of fitful sleep on the way home, Mary had imagined the look on her mother's face when she made her announcement that she and the Rector were to be wed. Rector! So much more august a title than Vicar! Of St Michael and All Angels – *all* angels! Humbole was not *humble* at all. She was to be The Rector's Wife. In her mind's eye she saw the pleasure spreading over Mama's face: an initial smile of astonishment, then a rosy flush on her soft round cheeks, and finally a gasp of true pleasure at the news. Despite their thousand hours of pained companionship, Mary did so wish to be a pleasure to her mother. Fate had denied it so far. Now was to be the moment when disappointment gave way to approval; when the unfortunate past gave way to a glorious future.

The parlour, generally reserved for visitors rather than for family occasions, felt a strange place to stand before her mother to deliver her announcement. It faced south-east and should have been drenched in sunlight. But the curtains were more than half drawn. A sickly smell filled the air. Its origin sat in a large brown apothecary's jar by Mama's right hand: *Sydenham's Liquid Laudanum.* She could administer it herself; there was no need to summon Annie for each dose.

Mary coughed, then began her speech. "You will be gratified, I am sure, Mama, by the turn of events at Humbole. You have always been concerned for my wellbeing. So I am happy to share with you this simple fact: I could not have had chosen for me a more kindly...genteel... He really is the most..."

Her mother barely opened her eyes. Mary ran out

of adjectives, and realised that this speech was getting confused with the speech she was preparing to give to her father the following day. "A suitable match in every way. Not more suitable than Elizabeth's or Jane's, of course. So, if you and Papa could give your consent…"

Would there be a settlement, a dowry, to induce Mr Needleman to set aside any doubts about herself as his wife?

Oh why, she wondered for the hundredth time, had there been no education, no instruction book, no dress rehearsal for this crucial moment in her life? Her voice trailed off. It was pointless. Her mother was embalmed in the world of Sir John Sydenham's potion.

But she was desperate to evoke that smile, that flush of maternal pleasure she had dreamed of. If she leaned over and took her mother's hand, might she persuade her to become happy at last?

She slipped her hand underneath her mother's. The hand she held was her mother's left hand, and one of the nobbled fingers was adorned with rings: a wedding band, with diamond-set keeper rings on either side to protect it. These rings symbolised exactly what she wanted to say to her mother. "See, Mama – this is what I will wear. Mr Needleman will slip this gold ring…"

Her mother stared glassily at the two hands entwined. "Ring? Ring?"

"We are to be wed, Mama. Mr Needleman and I. If I just slip this off" – the joint was arthritic, it took Mary a tug or two to release the outer ring before she could reach the simple gold one – "I will put it on my own finger, to show you…"

"Never! Never! You shall not have it! No one shall!"

"I do not mean to *take* it, Mama!"

"It will go with me, unto the grave! To my death!"

Hastily, and with more of a tug for each, Mary returned first the wedding band – tug! – to its knotty finger, then the keeper ring – *tug*!

"Never! Ever!" Her mother's tone reached a high-pitched squeal. "Help! Help! Thief! Look at her! Comes back to this house and starts thieving! Annie!"

"Mama, I am Mary! Not a thief! It was simply to show you!"

"Hill! I must have Hill! Mr Bennet! Where is Mr Bennet!"

Annie swept into the room, with "There now, there" on her lips, as if to a child.

Mary was weeping. "Annie, she called me a thief!"

"I heard," shouted Annie over Mama's screams. "Don't fret. She calls me all manner of things. It's the pain, or the Sydenham's, or both of 'em together. I'll sort her. You go and have a lie-down. You've had a shock. Take yourself upstairs, now, and recover."

෴

Luke knew that Mr Bennet, in ordinary times, was very particular about his chestnut Suffolk Punch, Bradwell. Rosie, or Blossom's lively replacement, were anyone's, but on Bradwell Mr Bennet had exclusive rights. Now, though, Mr B was not in his ordinary mind. And neither was Luke. All those hours he'd spent in grooming, feeding Bradwell, soothing him and bedding him down, gave Luke a right to ride him now. If he couldn't shift Mr B from beside his dying mother's bed, then he would take Mr B's seat in the saddle.

On the way past Meryton he was too intent on the question of property (as in: might this extended ride of his, in a court of law, constitute theft?) to feel anything but the reins in his hands and the pommel between his knees. For years he had watched his every move in case it could be construed as a crime; he had been on the run all those years, and the stripes on his back wouldn't let him forget it. But, as he steered the horse between the gaudy yellow of gorse and the milder yellow of broom, he heard the voice of the wind, and as the yellow gave way to the ochre of summer couch grass, it became the voice of his mother.

Only once had he asked her what it was like to carry him and then to give him up to a stranger. He was not a man of detailed memory, but her reply to this was something he could repeat over to himself whenever the pain in his back stopped him sleeping.

It was the time of the visit of that pudgy-faced clergyman – the one who was after Miss Lizzy but went for the less fancy girl instead. Between the hectic comings and goings and feedings and cartings-around of those few days came a moment in the kitchen when Luke and his mother were alone together. She was squeezing the juice out of the final lemon for her citrus tart. This was his chance.

"What was it like?"

The look she gave him was part conspiratorial, part warning. "Wi' what?"

"Wi' me."

She didn't miss a beat. Just gave the lemon a heartier squeeze, as if tearing the pith away from the peel. "You were mine, and I were yours."

"And?"

"You are still. I am, still."

He and Bradwell were at the top of Beacon Hill now. The Beacon itself was empty of fire; it had last been lit for the mad old king's death and the start of Prinny's proper reign. Luke could see for miles: beyond Meryton, round over other villages and farms, and back to Longbourn. Always, back to Longbourn. To Annie, and his mother.

She'd asked: "And for you?"

Luke couldn't answer.

He'd not known his mother for most of his childhood; he'd known her by the loss of her. She, as well as knowing the loss, had always known of his first existence. She could hold it in her flesh and bone. He could not.

He wanted to say this to her now. *Now I know you, you will be mine and I will be yours. Even if I lose you, you will be with me still.* But Mr B was in the way.

He clicked the reins and edged Bradwell slowly back down the hill between gorse and broom.

⁂

Mary surprised herself by not actually going up to her room and continuing to weep. She did go upstairs, but headed for the bedchamber that had been occupied, years ago, by Jane and Elizabeth. She entered, closed the door behind her, and began to walk in a small circle, round and round and round. When dizzy, she turned and walked the opposite way, round and round again.

The room was full of Jane's touches: a small hand mirror placed strategically on the tallboy below the larger mirror on the wall, so that she or Elizabeth could view the back of their hair; the inlaid Japanese box that held her folded handkerchiefs so that the embroidered initial could be seen in its perfection. Reminders of Lizzy were more haphazard. Three pairs of unused shoes lay abandoned in a corner as too poor for Pemberley but too quality to go to the servants. Lizzy's bedside prayer book was untouched, where Jane's was thumbed and dog-eared. They had each received new prayer books as wedding presents from the local Vicar, Mr Jennings, a family friend.

By the time Mary had stopped walking, and stopped being reverential to her older sisters, she began to calm down and realise something very immediate.

She had lost her Mama. Though had she ever, in fact, *had* Mama? Her mother was always distracted by something else. What that something was, Mary had no idea. But she could find no memory of her mother focusing upon her, and just upon her.

She was not only the product of her birth. Now, with this offer from Mr Needleman, she could change. She could emerge into a different Mary. For instance, she had her spectacles now. She could distinguish between the unusedness of Lizzy's prayer book and the usedness of Jane's. She had learned from Thwaite about rabbits ("coneys") and the mining of…what was it, in Derbyshire? Iron? No, lead. A weighty, flexible metal. She could be flexible, and have weight. She had claimed her right not to listen to Lizzy on the question of married bliss. She had even managed to steer Lizzy's conversation away from some family secret that she, Mary, did not wish to know about. She could make up her mind about what she wanted to speak of and what she did not; what she wanted to discover and what she chose to see. Or not.

Hill, too, tried to press some sort of knowledge on her. After she was married, might knowledges of a further kind be in store? And if so, how could she bear them?

She must pray. Pray to be led: to discern what she should do, and what sort of a person she should become.

"Jane!" she begged, inwardly. "Return to me, from wherever you are! We all, we five, were and are members of this family. How can we know what should be known, and yet live contentedly on? Why must our father sit endlessly beside Hill's bed? And why did Hill have anxieties about Mr Needleman? What does she know?"

Jane's form rose from her bed, hovered, and spoke. "We must all know," she said. Her voice was sweet. It was a sweetness that Mary missed so much. "And we must all live."

Jane's head was bowed. Mary bowed her own head in response, begging for instruction. *Please, Jane, please!*

Perhaps her inward plea was not enough, and she should say it out loud. "Dear Jane, what should I do?" She held her breath for an answer.

Now Jane gave forth syllables. They were mostly th's and s's, and incomprehensible. Mary blinked again, and prayed again. Then, without thinking, and in a somewhat surprised tone, she said, "I beg your pardon?"

The vision said: "Think of Thessalonians."

"Think of?" Suddenly she knew. She spoke the words of St Paul, the ones that came before the words about helmets and breastplates. "*For they that be drunken are drunken in the night.*" That was her father! And so to the next verse: "*Let us, who are of the day, be sober, and put on the breastplate of faith and of love.*" That was herself!

Jane had spoken truth. Her father was of the night, while she, Mary, inspired by saintly Jane, was of the day, and sober. She must put on her breastplate, and act.

She opened her mouth to tell Jane that she understood. But the vision had vanished. Mary was alone, standing between the light of the sash window behind her and the darkness into which dear Jane had disappeared.

In that darkness, Mary knew what she was to do. She must go to the attic room and remove her father from Hill's bedside.

She turned on her heel and walked out of the room towards the attic stairs.

☙

Annie came upon Mr Bennet shuffling towards the parlour. He seemed to be propelled by something from behind. He did not give her a nod of acknowledgement, as was his custom; he was in motion, and would not, could not, stop. Annie pressed herself against the wall to get out of his way. When he was past, she saw the energy that propelled him. It stooped, and was Miss Mary.

Mr Bennet shuffled on, and Miss Mary kept moving behind him. Miss Mary nodded to Annie, and said: "Chair by Hill need swiping."

Baffled, Annie watched the joint silhouette disappear through the parlour door. As it banged shut, she heard a shriek from Mrs Bennet inside. It sounded like a mix of dismay and satisfaction. She turned her gaze towards the main stairs and then the servants' stairs, and felt her lips repeat Miss Mary's words:

Need swiping. Chair by... Needs...wiping!

She raced down the servants' stairs, through the kitchen and into the scullery. Ignoring the astonishment of the Pemberley maids, she snatched the nearest cloth, dunked it in a bucket of tepid old water, gave it a squeeze, snatched a dry cloth with her other hand, and raced back upstairs. Up, again, and again, until she reached her mother-in-law's side.

There stood Mr Bennet's library chair. It was damp, whether from weeping or from other excretions, she could not tell. But it was vacant.

Slowly, carefully, she wiped it clean and wiped it dry. Then she turned towards the pillow, and her mother-in-law's face. It was ashen as the fire in the morning grate. "Just fetching Luke," she said, and paused.

The face moved fractionally towards her and gave a sound like *Oh.*

She paused again, and another sound came: *Ye-e-e-s.*

Annie gave the soft cheek a touch before leaving the room.

She ran down again, flung the two cloths in through the scullery door, ran across the courtyard, past the cottage where she heard the children playing, and in through Bradwell's stable door.

Luke opened his arms to her, and she fell into them. Within seconds she'd struggled out of them and blurted out: "Go! She's waiting! Chair's wiped and ready!"

⊕

Mary did not count the hours she spent sitting in the library. She stood up to replace one book of sermons and take out another; her father, she knew, had bought these volumes as a job lot. One of the Pemberley maids came with a query about food; she accepted a cup of tea and some buttered toast, but consumed only half of each. She went twice to the foot of the servants' stairs, up which Luke and Annie had vanished as she intended; she listened for sounds indicative of change, heard none, and went back to the library. She read a commentary comparing St Paul's *Epistle to the Thessalonians* with another epistle; afterwards, to her great concern, she could not recall which epistle that was, and in which way the two differed. When she lifted her eyes and looked out of the window, she saw sun and cloud-shadow alternating across the lawn, and an occasional fleeting curve of rainbow. In her mind's eye she saw the Humbole Rectory garden with its handsome borders and its lively little eruptions of mole-hill. She recalled some conversation she had overheard in the stables, long ago, between servants, concerning contact with the mole-catcher who would "string up a pile o' the divils". She resolved that when she was Mr Needleman's wife she would persuade him and his stable-boy towards a kinder method of dealing with moles. With her new-found sight, she would describe the moles to her short-sighted husband in such a heartfelt way that he would... Oh, no. Moles never appeared over-ground. Oh, dear.

On the morrow, Mr Needleman was due to arrive and ask her father for her hand in marriage. She had words ready for her father to use in reply; she had made notes on paper. Here they were, on his desk: that very paper, those very words. She reached out and put her hand on them, to keep them safe.

But she could not allow Mr Needleman to arrive unprepared for the disorder that now pertained at Longbourn. She must find a way to warn him. She would need help in this task, and the only soul she could think of as her confidant in such an emergency was Luke.

Luke was now sitting, at Longbourn, in the same position as she herself had sat beside Hill's deeply curtained room at Pemberley. She had known that she must sit there, half on and half off her chair, and listen to what might be Hill's last words about her life and her future. Her thigh muscles had ached with the tension of sitting.

"Don't go!" Mrs Hill had croaked. She was trying

to wrench herself up onto her elbow.

Had she meant *Don't go now*, or *Don't go on that marriage journey?*

"Galleries and stuff."

Ah! It was about the marriage journey.

Then – yes, she remembered now – Hill had been precise. "Be wed right there, in Humbole. Before parish and congregation."

She imagined it now: herself and Mr Needleman waving goodbye to the parishioners outside the church, and them cheering her on the way: cheering her marriage, and her marriage journey. Then....

"*No* Mr Hepplecraft!"

Hill had said that, most specifically.

What did she mean? No friend? No guide around the *galleries and stuff?* Must she persuade her husband to part from his beloved colleague, and be alone with her, his new and tender wife?

"You two. An' a maid. An' *two* weeks *only!*"

Hill had thundered those words, *two*, and *only*, as if her life – Mary's life – depended upon them. The memory of those hammered words engulfed Mary now.

If, as Hill had commanded, their marriage journey were to be only two weeks long, then they could not travel abroad. There would be no Paris, Florence, Venice. Their travel must be to somewhere near, somewhere already visited by Lizzy or Jane and their husbands. Somewhere like the Lake District.

That was it. A public marriage, at Humbole rather than at Longbourn. A modest honeymoon. And no Mr Hepplecraft.

That was Hill's dying message to her.

No Continent. No Mr Hepplecraft.

What a mercy that would be. No canvases to admire when she had never even heard of the painter. No gleaming teeth of Mr Hepplecraft to compete with her crooked ones. No competition for her husband's attention, with Mr Hepplecraft winning that contest every time. No breakfasts with theology. No sermons, in Italian or French or who knows what other languages to befuddle her.

A simple marriage ceremony. Not from Longbourn, but from Humbole. A simple marriage journey, with no boats, no Grand Tour.

Hill was right. But how to bring about this change of plan?

At this moment, Mr Needleman would have covered two out of three nights of the journey so recently covered by Hill and herself. She must interrupt the last stage of his journey, the last change of horses, at Meryton. She would have two purposes: one, to warn him about the discombobulated person Mr Bennet had become and how best to make his bid for Mary's hand; and two, to persuade him to marry at Humbole and abandon the notion of six weeks in Europe and his cultured friend in favour of two weeks, not too far away, without either.

But she needed the coach to be taken out early, and in secret. Only Luke could arrange that. But Luke sat with his mother, sharing the last hours of her life on earth. How could he possibly be persuaded to listen to her needs now?

8

Permission

LUKE WAS AFRAID FOR HER, for Miss Mary. In there, in the coaching inn, she'd get shoved. If not groped. If not worse.

Miss Mary hadn't a clue. It was his personal opinion that none of those five young women had a single clue to rub between them. The only reason Miss Mary seemed more clueless than the rest was that she'd no clue how to pretend. Pretending was how Miss Lydia had ended up with her lot in life, Mrs Bingley with hers, and Mrs Darcy with hers. Bless 'em, how they'd triumphed. And how they suffered now.

Yet Miss Mary did have one clue, if Annie's suspicions were true. She now understood about him and his mother, and even about Mr B. Her knowing those facts, and him knowing that she knew, was why he'd agreed to the ridiculous request that she be taken out in the coach this morning. His mother was gone now, and he could leave her mortal remains to be laid out by Annie and old Ma Drayton. He had said his goodbyes.

To Miss Mary he'd said no at first; he couldn't do that; the coach would rattle and echo around the yard and wake everyone up; if she needed to be so secretive about this plan to interrupt her Reverend at the Blue Boar she'd have to walk; the fresh air would rosy up her complexion ready for the gentleman in question, surely?

But who could be against it? Her parents were the only ones who mattered, and they were past caring. So, in the end, he'd nodded and gone to set up Rosie with the coach.

Now, while he curled Rosie's reins between his fingers and listened to her gentle harrumphing as it merged with those of the other nags outside the inn, Luke thought back to what he'd said to Miss Mary, that she might *rosy up her complexion*. He might have overheard it in the chat between her and Annie as he passed through the kitchen; it could have related to Mrs Bennet after her extra dose of medicine, or be a backhanded reference to one of the Pemberley maids who was prone to blush whenever Luke came near. Or had his mother put that sort of idea into his head?

His mother. How seldom had she been able to be just that.

How little he'd been able to know her in that way.

Thank God he'd sat at her bedside at the end, and said what he needed to say.

His eyes remained dry, but his mouth filled with tears. He swallowed them away and let his head fall towards his chest to avoid betraying himself amid the clang of tack and heaved luggage. A portly old ostler chafed him: "Too much brarn ale the night, yer nobby!" Luke raised his head, swallowed again hard, and pulled himself back to this morning's task.

He should go into the Blue Boar and protect Miss Mary.

But he couldn't, because he was under instruction to remain out here and watch for the arrival of whatever post-chaise or stagecoach or hackney carriage this stranger, her Reverend Intended, might be travelling in.

Miss Mary must surely have taken heed of his advice to go in and immediately turn to the *right*, into the lounge bar where the gentlemen gathered? Now she'd got those spectacles from Reverend Intended, she could read GENTLEMEN ONLY on the door-glass, surely? The lounge bar would be, though smoke-filled, relatively clean and quiet. She couldn't have turned *left*, into the *public* bar? Where the stink of unwashedness would hit her in the face, and the sight of tables scattered with gobs of spittle would induce the vapours?

Surely. She wouldn't? But she might.

~

My dearest – you will be anxious to hear of my progress.

Yes, I am here at last, transported to Hertfordshire, the county which contains (if all goes to plan) my future family-in-law.

The journey has been straightforward, if somewhat bone-shaking, until this final stage. Here I was apprehended by a coachman who seemed to be expecting me, but whose purpose, it seems, was to catch hold of me before my arrival at my final destination, because...

I pause here, cherished friend, as I am still bemused by this turn of events.

I could not immediately comprehend the coachman's attempt at explanation; only that it concluded with the statement that I might find my bride-to-be in the lounge bar.

"I told her straight, turn right into the lounge," said the man. (A perfectly personable specimen, if a little awry in his musculature. He must have been in the soldiery in the late War.) "But she might of turned left, as she is somewhat uncertain in her bearings."

I understood. I had already seen my fiancée 'uncertain in her bearings'.

"She said, twice, I was not to follow her," fretted the coachman. "I should stay with the coach and horse, to watch for your arrival."

I nodded to him, entered the premises, and glanced into the lounge bar. My eyesight is poor, I confess, but there was certainly no sign of a woman there.

Of course, I have never before entered the precincts of a public bar. Why might I? But there I stood, the excellent leather of my shoes paddling through beer-swill, the cavities of my nose assaulted by sweat and stale piss, my ears bombarded with the curses of market day in this pretentious little town.

I saw her immediately, a burst of bonnet and primrose-coloured muslin amidst the muck-spattered buffs and russets. She did not see me; her eyes were staring into some other world between her and this foreign land.

Swearing inwardly in a language that would be familiar to the coarse strangers around me, I strode through, pushing ruffians away to right and to left, until I reached her side.

"Miss Bennet! Miss Mary! You must not... simply cannot...!"

I seized her, allowing my arm to take her weight as she fell onto it. "Come. This is no place for you." The ruffians, startled no doubt by the contrast between my gentlemanly appearance and my ungentlemanly shoving, parted like a latter-day Red Sea, and let us peculiar Israelites pass through.

My principal feeling, as the doors swung behind me, was relief that I had secured the small box with the ring inside it in my waistcoat pocket, where no thieving hands could sneak. It was my mother's ring, a gold band, Indian, with a rose-cut diamond in the centre. I have never shown it to you, have I? I had hoped to offer it to another.

(You may guess to whom.) But that would be impossible.

So I continued on, on towards my necessary marriage.

☙

Mary was sure that she would faint. But she allowed herself to be upheld by her affianced groom and propelled into a safer space. She even found her voice.

"I trust there was no impropriety in my forestalling you in this way, Mr Needleman. My purpose was simple: to describe to you some unusual circumstances before you become emb—"

"No matter at all, my dear. I trust your instincts implicitly."

"—broiled in them."

"Embroiled?" He manoeuvred her into a corner of the lounge bar. "I think, perhaps, here?" The room contained a series of curtained enclosures, each of which offered a degree of seclusion.

When they were seated, Mary felt impelled to press ahead with her prepared speech in case she lost track of it in this strange and confusing environment.

"There is important information I must offer you, before—"

"No!" He put up his hand as if making an announcement from the pulpit. "My dear, your nerves must be in shreds. I shall order refreshments before you lay your burdens at my feet." And he was gone.

Mary took off her gloves and laid them on the cushion beside her. The only other occupants of the room were two men deep in their own business, banging emphatically on their table or exclaiming at each other's stupidity. This was a relief: it meant that her revelations to Mr Needleman would not be overheard.

What should she say next? That her father was *distrait* (she remembered this word from French classes with Mlle What-was-her-name). *Distrait*, because of a bereavement in the household. Mr Needleman had met Hill and knew of her illness. He would be saddened to hear that this had resulted in her death.

But Hill was a mere servant. So why was her demise so significant?

Come, come. Her main point was this: that Mr Needleman should not expect Mr Bennet to be seated ceremoniously in the parlour or the library, alert and ready to hear his request to become a son-in-law. Papa might, in fact, be upstairs; *upstairs* in every sense, clinging fast to the bed in which his housekeeper had spent her dying days. If he were on the ground floor he would be fending off the shrieks of his unruly wife, or behaving to her with unspeakable rudeness. He might even be wandering around the corridors of the house, bawling. Whichever was the situation, it would leave no space for Mr Needleman and their marriage settlement at all.

Yet he, Mr Needleman, must demand that attention, and hold it for long enough to make the necessary arrangements. How was this to be achieved?

Mr Needleman returned with a small glass in one hand and a large one in the other. "Elderberry wine," he said, offering her the smaller one. "Most fortifying,

I find." He took a sip from the larger one, which he did not identify. "My dear. Now. Take your time, and tell me what lies so heavily upon your mind."

⟲

It had been easy for Luke to identify Miss Mary's Reverend among the men who stepped down from the stagecoach. Stocky or skinny, ancient or innocent, gaudy or modest, most of them stumbled blinking into the sudden light. In contrast, this one was slim, silent, and alone. He paused on the top step and turned his eyes slowly to right and left, a half-smile touching his lips as if the good Lord was blessing his arrival.

The man looked unsurprised when Luke approached him and addressed him by name. He was taken aback only by the specific news that he would spend a little more time in this establishment than he had expected. For he would find his lady-love waiting for him, not at home at Longbourn, but here, inside the inn.

Now Luke must wait. It would not be long, he thought. Miss Mary would be tongue-tied, would fall into a trap of her own innocent making and emerge in tears, possibly hanging onto the Reverend's well-cut sleeve.

He stood by Rosie's warm head and leaned into it. The damp of her saliva slipped into his sleeve, but he was used to that; he liked the intimacy of it. Horses accepted themselves and accepted you likewise, if you loved them as he did.

No Miss Mary. No Reverend Intended.

And for him there would be no mother when he

134

returned to Longbourn.

How would they bury her, and where, when she was both servant to the Bennet family and lover to the head of it?

Still no Miss Mary, or her man.

He watched the comings and goings at the inn, leaned into the warm horseflesh again, and continued to wait.

There he was! The Reverend Intended! He emerged from the Blue Boar and glanced to right and left, much as he had done on the stagecoach step.

After him emerged Miss Mary.

She took his arm! They were together! At ease!

Luke pulled himself away from the horse's side and nodded to them.

"Ah! My man," said the Reverend.

Luke, patronised, tried not to flinch. He moved forward for instructions.

"Miss Bennet and I will proceed together for the remainder of the journey."

Part of Luke's mind still held the puzzle around the question of his mother's burial, and he did not jump immediately to fulfil the instructions.

"The luggage, man!"

Luke, mortified now, leapt into action. The baggage was to be stowed first, then Miss Mary helped into the coach. That redness around her eyes, that dampness on her cheek – were they from tears? The Reverend stepped up after her, settled himself, and waited for Luke to climb up in front. "To Longbourn!" Miss Mary, with a weak smile, gave her assent. Luke went forward and climbed into position, and the Reverend tapped his cane for Luke to click the reins and set off.

They had barely gone a half-mile before Luke heard another tap-tap of the cane. But it was not the authoritative tap of the Reverend. Could Miss Mary have seized control? She must have! Tap-tap, tap-tap! He reined Rosie in and turned. Miss Mary's bespectacled face was leaning out of the window.

"Please, Luke, if you could? The lane, to the left – do they call it Stakes Lane, or Stooks? Might we turn in, and pause?"

The Reverend's voice, from inside, was impatient. "Might I ask why, Miss Bennet? Are we not adequately prepared for our arrival?"

Miss Mary kept pleading. "There is more. Please? Luke?"

Should he do as she bade him? Or wait for the Reverend to decide?

The Reverend must have opted for good behaviour. "Of course, my dear. These are important matters. The day is still young."

Luke clicked the reins and they turned into Stakes Lane. This was where he had turned Bradwell in the direction of the Beacon the other day. He knew the very oak tree under which he could settle Rosie, climb down from the coach, stand at a short distance, and wait for whatever else Miss Mary needed to get clear with her Reverend before they arrived home.

He did not mean to listen; he meant to return his thoughts to his mother and the right placing of her mortal remains. But both Miss Mary and her man immediately stepped down from the chaise, and their voices became raised.

The Reverend, the Intended, was trying to calm Miss Mary. He understood, he said, the difficulties in which Miss Bennet's parents found themselves, especially with the death of this dear person. He, too, found that servants could be so much more than servants, almost equal to friends, in fact. His own dear housekeeper Mrs Beattie was another example of such. What the Reverend could not quite grasp, though, was how Mrs Hill's situation should affect decisions about the length of their marriage journey and who might accompany them? Miss Bennet could surely arrange for a lady's maid to bring with her? Since he himself would be satisfied with the company of the Reverend (Luke did not catch the name) who was expert in everything concerning art, and Europe?

No, no, insisted Miss Mary. She thanked him most heartily for agreeing to their marriage taking place at Humbole, not from Longbourn. (That would be a relief to all concerned. Especially to Annie.) But she could not possibly…

Rosie gave a little snort at this point, and Luke could not hear what Miss Mary could not possibly do.

When his ears next picked up Miss Mary's voice, she was heaving great sighs. She could not tolerate… She was unaccustomed to travel… Might two weeks in, say, the Lake District, suffice? And could they be more, more *alone*? Please? His friend being so very *expert*, and Miss Mary herself so very *modest*… This marriage, he must understand, was a great change in her circumstances. She had hoped that Hill would accompany her. Now, with this woman's illness, she needed to find someone *different* to be her lady's maid. But who?

Her voice dropped off, and the Reverend's, too.

Luke heard no more. But what he had heard already was enough to renew his rage. This 'special' person, as Miss Mary called her: how she'd been treated! Spurned, deprived of her son, overworked, always at the beck and call... *Special?* When the Family, even now, demanded *special* consideration over and above the actual matter of his mother's *death?* Annie and himself were offered no consideration at all! It was always the Family, the Family, the Family!

He gave the reins a tug and moved Rosie a step forwards. He would speak. He would let these people know the sorrows of his furious heart.

He turned. But when he opened his mouth, all it could manage to produce was a paltry servant's plea. "Miss Mary, your family, if you please! They will be wondering mightily about your absence!"

The Reverend looked up, startled. "My man!"

Luke kept his eyes trained on Miss Mary. "Can I beg you? We must go."

"Do not give us orders, man!"

Luke felt a small but satisfying moment of power. He reached for Rosie's head and gave it a long, slow stroke. "Just, one, moment."

He took a few stolid paces back to his post under the oak tree, and stood while they continued their murmurings. After judging that time enough had passed, he turned back. The Reverend was nodding. "Of course, my dear. If that is what you need."

Miss Mary stepped up into the coach and settled herself. "Thank you, Luke." She adjusted the bonnet on her head. The Reverend followed her and made himself comfortable in similar fashion. And there the two of them sat, in as dignified a posture as possible.

Once in his seat Luke called over his shoulder, "You'll be in haste, then?" He flicked the reins and turned Rosie back towards the road. Veering left, he clicked again, urgently. Rosie picked up the message, and they rocketed along the last couple of miles to Longbourn.

ᖇᖇ

The moment had passed, and Annie noticed its passing. Luke had been present for his mother's last breath, then hurried away to collect Miss Mary for this strange intervention.

Biting back tears, Annie installed Mother Drayton in the attic room with all her appurtenances, and closed the door. Mother D had requested bowl after bowl of ice-cold water on account of the sun on the attic roof and the length of time it might take for the body's removal. There was so much to be done. Annie knew there was no time to grieve just now.

She found Mr Bennet groaning his way up the narrow stairs and blocked his way. "No, sir. The midwife must be left to her work. Your task is a different one today." She was two steps above him; it gave her height; she was in charge. "You've to go down, Mr Bennet. To the parlour, to your wife, and await Miss Mary and Mr Thingummybob."

"Mr What?"

"You know. The Rector man. Down. You've to go to Mrs Bennet. Now."

His face crumpled, but he shuffled his feet around on the stair and laid his hands downwards on the rails. He was a child, thought Annie. Younger than John-James, a little older than Edith. Though she wasn't even sure about that.

She steered Mr Bennet in the direction he must go, first at the foot of the attic stairs and then at the foot of the main stairs. She could hear Mrs Bennet wailing. As they drew near to the parlour door there came a shout: "I must have *Hill*! Bring me *Hill*! Mr Bennet, do as I say and bring me *Hill*!"

Annie dodged in front of Mr B, opened the door, and stood there with her hand up in command. Mrs B's wailing ceased, her mouth open at Annie's authority. Mr B shuffled in, and Annie gave him a further little shove from behind. He paused for a confused moment, taking in Annie's rearrangement of the chairs.

"Sit there, Mr B, if you please. I'll get glasses of water. One of the Pemberleys will bring sweetmeats when they arrive."

"They?"

"The man Miss Mary's to be wed to!"

"Needling!" shouted Mrs Bennet. "Marry that one?"

"She is! So you're not to move from here, the pair of you, unless it's for your hygiene or comfort. From what the message-boy says, they're not far from the gate. Not a word about nerves, now, nor medicines, nor laying out. Miss Mary has waited years for this day. She should get what she deserves. What it's about is arrangements. And her reputation. And, most of all, money. There'll be some handed over? Right?"

Mr Bennet pursed his lips, but sniffed and said, "I expec' so."

For heavens' sakes, thought Annie, this slurring is no good. Will Mr Needling think his proposed father-in-law is drunk? Is he, in fact, drunk? In all the rushing up and down stairs she hadn't thought to check the corner cupboard with the gin. Well, if this Reverend Needling were upset by a little bit of squiffiness, he didn't deserve Miss Mary's hand in marriage anyway.

"Now," she said. "You stay put. I'll be back in two shakes of a lamb's tail."

Having closed the door on the two old reprobates, she stood for a moment to calm herself and listen to the sounds of the children on the landing. Were they giggles, or shrieks? Giggles. Good. Off to get glasses of water from the kitchen, and to give orders to the Pemberley maids for coffee and fruit cake. They were still taking slices from Flora's home-bake while she lay cold upstairs. How could that be?

Some small voice in her head made her fling a request back at the Pemberleys as she left the kitchen: "When you hear the coach in the drive, go to the front door for meeting and greeting, can you? I'll be busy with them in the parlour."

Which was a mercy, because she didn't get as far as the parlour. Edie, small in size but battling in nature, had pushed John-James from the top to the half-landing, and he was bawling his heart out and needed a cuddle.

∽∞

Mary and Mr Needleman spent the last ten minutes in the coach in silence. Luke seemed to be steering them over every pothole in the dry summer road and made far more speed than was strictly necessary. Either from the potholes or from fear of the scene to come, Mary felt nauseous. Mr Needleman's silence was ominous compared with his usual benevolence. Had she been over-demanding? Was she now a hysterical girl with whom he could not possibly spend the rest of his life? Might he let her dismount at Longbourn, then order Luke back to the Blue Boar to await the stagecoach back home?

Luke pulled up at the gates and climbed down to open them.

The house looked handsome, Mary had to admit that. Mr Needleman might be impressed. But if he were impressed by the house, then what a let-down would her parents be! Her nausea waned and waxed.

When Luke came to hand her down from the coach, her head began to spin. Luke was their faithful servant, but also her brother. Papa was her father, but also a sinner…

Let her not be sick. Please. Not now.

Surprisingly, it was not Annie who met them at the door but the two Pemberley maids. She hadn't noticed before, but through all their months away from home they had continued to wear their crisp, pressed, Pemberley uniform. What a blessing, to have maids who simply did what was needed and required no attention otherwise. Mary's nausea vanished.

Mr Needleman climbed down and came to her side of the coach. He looked with approval first at the house, then at the maids. He turned to Mary. "My dear," he said, "we are here at last. What a delight. I have heard so much about Longbourn from Mrs Darcy."

The maids flushed with pleasure and led them inside.

"We are instructed to take you to the parlour," said the older maid. "Mr and Mrs Bennet will be expecting you."

Mary found herself starting to smile. There was some scuffling from behind the curve of the staircase, and she released herself from Mr Needleman's arm to go and investigate.

"Annie? Is one of the children unwell?"

"Not at all, Miss Mary. Just a little accident at play."

Mr Needleman was at her side; he had not retreated to the Blue Boar.

"Your parents are eagerly awaiting you, Miss Mary," said Annie. "And you are very welcome, sir." She nodded towards Mr Needleman, but he was already on his way to the parlour door.

Mary hurried after him. "Dear Annie is the daughter-in-law of dear…"

"I believe," said Mr Needleman, turning, "that the protocol is, in due course, for me to have time alone with your father. But do not be anxious about such things, my dear. I will manage it all."

That was it. That was the point of it. He would manage it all.

After a backward glance towards Annie and her children, Mary allowed her arm to be taken so that she could be led forwards to her future.

9

Wedding

CONCERNING THE arrangements for the wedding, Mr Needleman was all acquiescence. The ceremony would take place at Humbole. As to the honeymoon: Europe vanished, art galleries ceased to exist, Mr Hepplecraft returned to his place in the shadows. Their destination was to be the Lake District.

With the advent of their betrothal they could spend time together without impropriety. They went for walks together. Mary watched with delight the way the horses in the field frisked their tails to and fro, performing as if entirely for her entertainment. Then she noticed the fleas that fled the action of the tail. So *that* was the purpose of such frisking!

Now, seated with her fiancé in the drawing room during his extended stay at Longbourn, she looked at Mr Needleman's hand as it drew a rough map of England. Here was Hertfordshire. There, roughly in the middle, was Derbyshire. Up here on the left was the north-west, and here was the Lake District. As Mary saw and absorbed it, she noted at the same time the veins standing up from the flesh of his hand as he drew. That was a sign of age. Her fiancé must have more years to his credit than she had assumed. He had mentioned his deceased parents, especially his admirable mother, but she realised how little she actually knew of him at all.

He set aside his map and began extolling the glories of the Lake District. "Natural expanses, streams, woodlands, mountains. And the celebrated lakes themselves!" To make up for the lack of art there were plenty of poets. And churches: she and Mr Needleman would worship there, and over meals they could discuss the architecture, the organ music, the sermons. And no sea journeys were required. It was all in England.

"Grasmere?" suggested Mr Needleman. He retrieved his map, and nudged his chair closer to hers.

The syllables *Grass-mere* sounded soggy and cold. But Mary was anxious to please. "Are there hostelries to suit?"

"Surely, surely. The poetry-followers have ensured such facilities. Of course, we may not actually *see* Mr Wordsworth. He and his family moved to Rydal some years ago."

"Wordsworth! Lyrical Ballads! Rustic bards! 'The frost performs its secret ministry Unhelped by any wind'!"

"That was Mr Coleridge. The Lucy poems…"

Mary, startled at this sudden wave of remembered verse, cried, "'O mercy! If Lucy should be dead!'" Then the crest broke. Her eyes stung. "Was that Mr Coleridge too?"

"No, indeed." Mr Needleman's hand took hers. "Lucy was very much Mr Wordsworth. Now we will, as you say, need to consider hostelries, the details of our rooms, etc. There will be your own maid? I guess you will choose one from Longbourn?"

The warmth of flesh on flesh was reassuring, but her hand trembled at the question, yet again, of one's personal maid. Please God the trembling would not communicate itself to Mr Needleman. "They cannot spare one, following our housekeeper's unfortunate demise."

"I understood that Mrs Darcy sent staff, especially to solve this difficulty?" He put his other hand firmly over hers. Further trembling was not to be allowed. "When travelling, one must have assistance. Even my mother, who was always so independent, insisted on it."

Ah. The previous Mrs Needleman. So fine, so self-reliant. But, like Hill, so very dead. Mary murmured, "Will you be taking your man?" She remembered his man: the silent, leisurely character who had driven her and Thwaite in the phaeton. Mr Needleman had explained that his name was Harry, but for some reason everyone called him Hurry. Maybe that was a jest? Leisurely, Hurry – a witticism?

"Of course. He will share my room, as your maid will share yours. And we could arrange for another room for us to be together." There was a fractional pause. "During the day."

Mary knew there were other questions she must raise, but could not recall what they might be. Tears sprang once more. Pulling her hands from his and nervously adjusting her hair, she accidentally wrenched off her spectacles. "I cannot... I have always... There will be maids at the hostelries, surely? Oh, I wish your mother were here to advise me! You said that she was of independent temperament, and so can I be, if allowed!" She retrieved the spectacles from her unruly curls and wiped them on a muslin fold.

"My dear." Mr Needleman coughed, as he tended to do when his mother was discussed. "Let us set that aside for the moment. Would you like me to request a further room, where we can take our meals and be waited on by Hurry and whoever? In private? Or would you prefer to dine among the other worshippers?"

"Worshippers? I beg your pardon?"

Mr Needleman laughed uneasily. "I mean, Wordsworthians. He is much revered, you know."

"Oh."

She fell silent. His lively mind so often tripped her up like this. Of all the unspoken anxieties that weighed upon her, none concerned Mr Wordsworth. She was anxious about how she might appear, how many strange bodies might be pressed against hers in the coaches on the way, how many clothes she might need and on what basis she should choose them, how she and Mr Needleman would behave towards each other as a couple, whether they would continue to enjoy each other's company when their proximity was so great. And so on.

If only she could take Annie! Annie, like Hill, knew about the world and understood its mysterious ways. What did Mary know? Nothing. Where had Mary been? Nowhere.

Yet she could learn. As with the piano: dear Mr Prendergast had praised her occasionally. *The Scarlatti is coming along nicely*, he would say. *Slowly, steadily: that is your way.* She could learn, slowly and steadily, how to be a wife.

Lifting her head, with her spectacles still in her hand, she gazed with blurred eyes at her husband-to-be. He would be her marriage tutor. He was a patient man, as Mr Prendergast had been. She had made her needs known about the length and scope of the marriage journey, and succeeded. She had even dismissed Mr Hepplecraft from the honeymoon plans. Now she must negotiate the question of her lady's maid.

She put her spectacles back on, adjusting their position on her nose and behind her ears. There sat her husband-to-be. His hair, grey at the temples: she had noticed that before. His frown, which came and went, but always left a little shadow of itself behind: that was a new observation. "Please, Mr Needleman. Tell me. What should I do?"

"I propose we take Mrs Beattie. She will help us, as she always does. But mainly, on this occasion, she will attend upon you."

Mary assented immediately. "Thank you so much. I agree."

෬෨

Charity baskets. This was Mama's contribution to the plan for Mary's role as the future Mrs Needleman, and demonstrated an upturn in the state of her nerves during the few weeks between the betrothal and Mary's departure for Humbole and marriage.

"A Rector," Mrs Bennet gloated, giving Mr Needleman's status its full capital letter, "is a much larger receiver of tithes than a mere Vicar."

"Is that a great deal, Mama?"

"Ask your father!" Her father was nowhere to be seen. "He will tell you! Such and such a per-cent of the... Ask him! A Rector has other powers in the parish, too. Humbole will bow to you as the wife not only of the Rector, but also of the Magistrate, and the Regi..."

"Registrar?" Mary had heard of such a dignitary, as she had heard of the Magistracy, but did not know what either involved.

"They will look up to you on account of his status! And you must live up to his great height! As Lizzy looks up to dear Darcy! She lives for him! Oh..." Mama's voice faltered. "My last chick departs the nest! How will I survive it?"

Mary studied the work in her hand and let her mother's tears pour for a while. She was embarking upon a small embroidered sampler. Its words, pencilled carefully upon the fabric, were simple but profound: BE NOT WEARY IN WELL-DOING.

"How can I live up to Mr Needleman, Mama?" she asked when the weeping abated. She was contemplating the top curve of the *B*. "He is too good for me!"

"Baskets! Charity baskets! Charlotte Lucas declared

149

they were the saving of her in the early days of her marriage to Mr…"

"Collins."

"Exactly. Miss Lucas, of course, had nothing to fear over her suitability for that man! He has designs on our dear Longbourn still, I fear! Where were we?"

"How I might live up to Mr Needleman. Be a Rector's wife."

"Charity baskets!"

Throughout their childhood, the girls had made scathing comments about the vicar's wife from St Bride's, who paraded herself around the hamlet laden with basketfuls of wholesome items for the cottagers. Baby mittens (knitted by herself), rock cakes, a few eggs (deemed too small for the housekeeper's own recipes), cast-off clothes from her own offspring: all these must be gratefully received by the poor. Now Mary, when she became Mrs Needleman, could do the same. She could bear her neighbours' possible scorn; she was more concerned with spiritual gain than local esteem. As her needle successfully bridged the gap over to the letter *E*, she concluded that the spiritual gain would be in direct proportion to the lowliness of the hovels she visited.

Then her mother's tears returned, and wailings at the prospect of her impending loneliness. Mary wept too, though she was unsure whether her tears were from trepidation at the change that loomed or from relief that her entrapment at Longbourn would soon be over.

Yet more tears issued from Mama when she realised that she would not see her dear Mary given away by her father at the church. Mary said gently, "You are not well enough, Mama. Either of you. It was to relieve you of the stress of the ceremony that Mr Needleman and I decided upon a modest event in Humbole."

"Dear Jane will not be present, either! Her children have dragged her down so! Melancholic! My poor Jane!"

So what might have been joy turned to sorrow, and Mary must call for Annie and yet more balm.

Mr Bennet also wept. He wept on the stairs, he wept in his library, and most of all he wept in the courtyard, especially where the cobblestones were worn to a track leading towards the stables, and to Luke and Annie's cottage. There must be a reason for the copiousness of his tears. Mary wished they might be connected with her own departure, but a flutter around her heart made her doubt it. Those two portraits, of Luke and Papa, hung in the shadows of her mind, alternately hidden in gloom and out in the open, fully lit.

෴

Annie composed another letter in her head. It was to her departed mother-in-law, for whom her heart ached.

Look favourably upon me from where you now reside, I beg of you, in the matter of Mr Bennet. Do you hear him? Do you see, now that you are no longer here, how he repents his folly, his cruelty? Can you witness his agony as he freely passes that agony on to myself? And, worse, on to Luke?

Mr Bennet wishes the children to come out and speak to him, Mother. They do not know why he paces up and down outside our door. They are frightened of him.

They ask to see their grandmother, and I take them to the soil under which you lie. They cannot hear your voice there. They ask, "Why did she want to go away from us?" I reply that dying is not about what people want; that she longs to be here with us still, but is not able. I do not take them to the far part of the churchyard, where their brother and sister lie namelessly buried.

Meanwhile, Luke's daily life and work is vastly upset. For he must peer around each time he needs a meal, or a visit to the necessary house, or simply to ask me a question about his boot polish or the time my cooking in the house will require him to come and eat with us in the kitchen. His whole mind is taken up with avoiding his... I can scarcely write it: his father. This father who, even in the face of death, gives no thought to the feelings of anyone but himself. I want to shout at him, "Luke needs to weep too! And he cannot, because you are in the way!"

Mother, dear, can you speak to him from where you lie? I would like to think you can. But I fear it may not be possible.

I miss you so.

Your loving daughter, Annie.

Again, she did not write it down. She merely sat, gripped by grief, until it rested at a level where she could shrug, give a small brushing-away gesture with her hands, and heave herself back to her duties.

⚬⚬

Afterwards, Mary's chief memory of the honeymoon was this.

On one of the reasonably rain-free days, Hurry had driven them in a hired brougham over the county boundary into Lancashire to visit a priory said to have a particularly fine organ. As they entered the priory portals, an ancient stooping man muttered facts into their ears about monks, tracery, misericords, and the remarkable story of…Dissolution. Pilgrimage, Grace… Something like that. Mary had difficulty following his thread. Then, as the bent old form stood back to allow them to move forward, the organ started to play.

Robert (as she had begun to call him in her own mind) walked directly to a nearby pew and knelt to pray. Mary, awed by the music that filled the vast arched space, followed suit.

For her prayer of Thanksgiving, she prayed:

Thanks be to God for this uplifting music. Thanks be to God for enabling Mr Wordsworth to leave the area for a while, so we need not commit the idolatry of worshipping at his shrine. Thanks be to God for telling Mrs Beattie not to protest at my fastening of my own stays. Thanks, oh great God Almighty, for my husband, for Robert, and for the fact that he appreciates my curiosity rather than condemning my ignorance.

For her Intercession, she prayed:

Bless Mama's nerves, if that is possible. And *God rest the soul of Mr Johann Sebastian Bach, whose music I think this is.*

As for her Contrition, she had so many possible sins to confess that she hastened through this prayer without any itemising. The good Lord would surely know that she was doing her best.

Having relieved her burdened heart, she glanced sideways. Robert's face was hidden by his folded hands. He prayed on, and on.

Mary felt stiff, and needed to get to her feet, but was reluctant to disturb her husband's prayers. Eventually her pressed knees and tense thighs spoke more urgently than the longueur of her husband's devotions. Carefully, she stood. She felt tall above him. He was very still, though she could hear his breaths quite clearly. He did not move as she slid out of the pew.

The music continued as she moved up the aisles and round the smaller chapels. From the light trills of the Swell manual (thanks be to Robert for his description of the organ's workings), through the warm harmonies of the Great manual, down to the rich bass of the pedals, the sound engulfed her. Indeed, at a point when the pedals played heavily beneath the melodies, a deep throb made its way through her entire body.

I could sing, she thought. *Somewhere between the trills and the throb.*

Of course she could not. There were no other

visitors to the priory, but she must not, ever, sing. She had always been told that she had no voice.

Still, she thought, she would name this piece *Cantata*. Whether Bach had named it so or not, it would be for her a Cantata. A song. Her song.

She found herself in a familiar aisle and realised that she was going round in circles. What childishness, to lose herself with such abandon. Robert must surely have completed his prayers by now. She must return to his pew. The organ was sounding its final resounding notes, and she let them slip by without returning to her earlier throbbing condition.

She passed a battered-looking pew door – oh, bullet holes! The parishioners had shot at Cromwell's troops in 16-something or other!

But Hurry was waiting for them outside with the hired brougham and its horse. Mrs Beattie (who had kept her lips pursed throughout their stay so far) and their brusque landlady both insisted they keep to the meal schedule and not be late. And Hurry could never *hurry*. She must alert Robert immediately.

There were his shoulders, low over the pew in front. He was, even now, deep in prayer. She approached, uncertain as to whether she should cough or shuffle her feet to convey her presence.

His shoulders were moving. Rocking. Shaking.

Alarmed, she moved to his side. His fists were upon his eyes, and she could see on his knuckles the shine of tears.

He must not know she had witnessed his weeping.

Hurriedly she tiptoed back a few feet and scraped her feet on the ancient stones.

Still no movement from her husband. She moved farther back, picked up a prayer book and leafed through it noisily before striding back to his pew.

"My dear!" he said, only half-turning at her approach. "I was deep in my devotions. Was the music not divine?"

She nodded, careful not to stare at his face in the gloom. "We must away. Luncheon awaits us, and Hurry must not press the horse too hastily along these rough lanes. Come. You look quite pale. I am sorry to have left you alone for so long."

Interval

Blood and Thunder

MARY WAS WOKEN by the roar of thunder. It was not the first thunderstorm of her life, but it was the first that she remembered in every detail. She was thirteen years and eleven months old.

If there was thunder, she thought, there must be lightning too. How exciting! Might she see it zigzagging across the sky? Surely, such an awesome phenomenon would not be blurred, like everything else seemed to be?

Her bedchamber faced north, so its window took the full force of every gale and slashing rain; while Jane and Lizzy's room faced south and was sheltered by the corner of the porch. Her parents' room lay on the far side of the tall landing window, and Lyddy's and Kitty's room was round the corner from there. Were they, all four of them, at their windows now? And even their parents? All gazing out at the storm? Might she join one or other pair of sisters? Was she allowed? Would she be laughed at? She so wanted to be in company while seeing such a sight.

But no sooner had she heard the clap of thunder, and wondered if there had been a series of thunderclaps while she had slept but she had missed them, than she felt something much closer, and more alarming.

She was leaking.

More thunder! It came from the direction of Jane and Lizzy's room. So close that it rocked Mary with its fervour.

She heard a small shriek. Two shrieks!

Or might those noises be part of the storm's array of cries?

Leaking! It was not painful. It was just wet. No, not *wet* as such – she had not let any water out, she was sure. It was *sticky*. Somewhere unmentionable. Her legs. Her thighs. Between them, where one didn't go, except for a light glance of the cloth during one's night-time toilet.

If she were to tell someone about it (though she must not, of course, tell anyone) should she say *leg*, or *thigh*? Was it some liquid from the flesh of her leg (or thigh) that was issuing forth onto the sheet underneath her (though she had done nothing to cause such a wound)? Or... Horror! Did it come from *inside* her, like the liquid and solid that passed regularly into her chamber pot and down the hole of the necessary house? Was there a third aspect to that region, to the nature of which – or even to the existence of which – she had not yet been introduced? Yet, by whom could she possibly have been introduced to such a thing? Small children, she knew, learned where to put their bodily extrusions at the same time as they learned not to mention them, ever, and certainly not in polite company. Anything *down there* came into the same category: unmentionable, and so unquestionable.

She must look. She must lift herself from the bed, slide out, make her way in the dark across to the fireplace, light the small candle from the embers of the fire that little Annie had banked up the night before, and take it to the large candle on the chest. That light would show her the truth of what was happening. But – more horror! Worse horror! On lifting the back of her nightgown, and on bringing the back of it round to the front to examine it, she would then see – would then realise – that she was *bleeding*.

She was wounded. Wounded inside. Was dying, most likely. She did not want to know that! At the same time, she would rather die than tell Jane and Lizzy what was happening to her: that she was in a filthy, bleeding situation and did not know what next to do.

But what next *could* she do?

Another thunderbolt! Massive, louder by far than the others!

Or was that noise the noise of her heart, beating with fear? Sounding out its last beats before they stopped altogether because she had died? Bled to death?

There! Lightning! It flashed through her heavy curtains, and through her eyelids too! She was now standing in the middle of her room. It was pitch black again, but she could feel the texture of the small rug that lay there, far enough from the fire not to catch sparks. She was standing with the candle in her hand, and she must light it from the fire, and light the large candle from the small one, and then she must – *flash!* – *crash!* – run to Jane and Lizzy and tell them that she was dying, and please would they make her goodbyes to Kitty and Lyddy and their dear parents, as she was going to the Good Lord in Heaven, where, at last, she would be safe... Oh, and say, too, a big sorry to Hill and little Annie and the washerwomen from the village for the mess she had made – she really didn't mean to, and would never do it again.

But of course there would be no more *again*. There would be no more mess, because there would be no more Mary. She would be dead.

By this time the big candle was safely lit, and she blew out the small one.

Now. To her nightgown. She must bring the back of her nightgown round to the front without letting the cloth touch the candle in case it caught fire.

But she did not even do that. She stood stock still, because she realised that things were worse than she had feared. She was leaking all down the insides of her legs. (Yes, she would say *legs*, not *thighs*. She could not say *thighs*.) Onto the floor. If she walked over the landing to Jane and Lizzy's room, the leaking would happen there too, and there would be a streak of leakage across between their doors.

But she wanted to see the lightning.

Yes, those shrieks *did* come from Jane and Lizzy's

room! They were awake, they were watching the lightning, and Mary wanted to watch it too, before she died. They would see her bleeding, and they would cry bitter tears, and she would say all those goodbyes and sorrys, but she would have seen the zigzag of the lightning first, and the thrill of that would accompany her all the way to Heaven...

She burst through the door.

Jane's and Lizzy's faces, candlelit, shot round and stared.

Between them, a streak of lightning – somewhat blurred, but definitely lightning, definitely zigzag, definitely wonderful and amazing – shot across the whole frame of the window from bottom left to top right.

"Mary!" cried the older girls in unison.

"Were you frightened?" asked Jane.

"Watch that candle!" said Lizzy.

Mary, looking down at the candle to straighten it, suddenly remembered that the most important thing was not the lightning, amazing and wonderful as that was, but the fact that she was bleeding. She was dying, and needed to tell her sisters so.

"It's my nightgown. See, at the back. It, I am not exactly sure, I think that I might be…" The words dried on her lips.

Thunder came again, and then a silence that ended in Lizzy laughing, then Jane laughing, then both of them laughing together.

Mary suddenly thought of the word *witches*. It was a word she didn't understand, but somehow seemed to fit the sound – the *cackle* – of their laughter.

How could this thing with the nightgown and the blood be *amusing?*

"Poor you," said Jane, when she could catch her breath.

"Silly you," said Lizzy. "Don't you know? Take yourself off up the attic stairs and call out for Hill. Or Annie – she started hers in the spring. They'll get you some towelling and sort you out."

Mary stared. She was not dying after all. But she almost wished she was.

"Off you go, silly-billy," said Lizzy again. "And hitch your nightgown up, will you? Between, down there? We don't want your mess all over our floor. Do we, Jane?"

Mary wanted to hear Jane say again, *Poor you*, but Lizzy had given her orders. So, hitching her gown as instructed (*down there*), she fled.

PART II

10

Marriage

SOON AFTER THEIR RETURN from honeymoon, Lady Manton paid a visit. Patty must have opened the front door to her, but knowing that her ladyship required no introduction, whisked her to the drawing room and run back to her chores. Thus was Mary for the first time alone with the woman who had invited her into this new life.

"My dear girl! If I may? So fortunate! My little fancy! Mrs Darcy's little miracle! Mr Needleman's little saviour! Not so little, either. Might be bigger, though? In the due course, if you take my meaning? Bigger around the..." She waved a hand around her voluminous skirts. "Hush hush, says her ladyship! All in good time!" Her ladyship found herself the deepest chair and sank into it. "Abject, oh abject apologies.

My remiss-ness! You would not believe! There was I, before, during, after, your blessed nuptials, which were held – oh commonest of sense! – here in dear Humbole! Not in faraway Hertfordshire, your dear parents acquiescing in my own personal request – or was it Darcy's – I forget? For, immediately afterwards, what could possibly take me away but my dearest of cousins! Such lamentations. Oh dear, a fall from her horse! Wretched beast! I warned her off, but no! Two legs broken, one arm! Gathering up doctors as I went, I arrived and, no surprise, she fell upon me in tears of joy and delight. Leaving you behind, my dear girl. Dear Mary! If I may? Miss B as you were, Mrs N as you are?

"Of course, you should still address *me* as My Lady. We must uphold the conventions. Though I seldom do, aha! I am known around the county for it. No Conventions for Lady Manton! His Lordship feared for me, years before his untimely... I cannot speak of it! My children fear for me still, grown and separated from me as they are. But no, it is my decision. I will uphold or will not uphold the conventions! For I have intuition! Intuition, yes! How blessed are we to have your dear self coming into our community. Our family, as I like to term it. That you should be given unto us, dear girl, through Mrs Darcy's generous mediation. Here we are. Here. We. Are."

Mary's intuition bade her be silent. Indeed, there was no alternative.

"Stand!"

Mary, at this sudden instruction, pressed herself further back in her upright seat.

Lady Manton's plump and imperious face darkened. She repeated: "Stand!"

Mary must rise. She was to be inspected, surveyed, examined. It was like being the lamentable cousin's horse: she would surely be condemned at first sight by the severe standards of Lady Manton.

But no. As the eyes did their penetrating work, the dark cloud that had hovered over the face disappeared and a smile took its place. "A sensible visage," she concluded. "No pretensions. A Bible-reading visage, maybe? A parish worker's visage. Hair with a mind of its own, but chocolate brown, a decent shade for your position. Blonde, whether strawberry or silver, will not do for me. Your sisters have it, but you should not. They have the features conducive to their position. Yours will do for yours.

"Now. No more close-quarters pontificating. You are acceptable, my dear. I knew you would be, from the start. But I must put my stamp on things, you know?

"You will forgive my intruding and ordering! We live in strange times, do we not? The wars are over, of the French type, but wars continue, English wars, in town and country. We must be on our guard. Peterloo! Do not speak of it! But I must not fray your delicate nerves. Oh, I heard about your nerves from dear Mrs Darcy! She denies having those persecuting little monsters herself, hey ho? But, like your poor mother, she will be prey to them. That is a woman's lot. No matter! You will do. Sit down, and tell me all about yourself."

Without a pause, she continued: "Mr Needleman

tells me that you begged mercy for the moles! I do like a tender heart in a woman. Of course it will not win the day. Moles need to be strung up. An example to their fellows! But a little protest from a tender heart is a sweet addition to the Rectory. And to the parish that it serves. Tell me, what other *tendresse* is there about your person? Do you fear child-bed, too? As well you may! The loss of my beloved Gwentholen... I weep nightly for her. I do, I do.

"No need to be shy. I am not the tyrant I seem. Underneath, I am pure butter. Widowhood softened me. You are so fortunate with Mr Needleman. You notice I come on a Wednesday? Alternate Wednesdays to Derby, for Mr Hepplecraft? And every *other* Wednesday, Mr H would come *here*. But no more! For your sake! See, I note things. I hear things. Rumours, from Hertfordshire! Longbourn, the housekeeper? It may be nothing, it may be something... Men cannot control themselves. A tragic fact. Nevertheless, a fact. A secret on the bend sinister? It will stay with me, my dear. Confidentiality is my watchword.

"Talking of housekeepers, as we were... Be careful of Mrs Beattie, my dear."

At the word *confidentiality*, Lady Manton had leaned sideways. Now she leaned the other way, like a metronome. "Too much brain for her own good. And for yours. To compound the problem, her being Irish! A whipper-snapper nation, make no mistake. However, she is excellent in her vocation." A hand rose and waved around, illustratively. "Spotless!" She pointed at the table where Patty had slipped in with a Bakewell tart. It lay ready sliced, with two china plates.

"Exquisite! But!" The metronome swung back again. "Ideas. That will be her ruin, if I am not mistaken. She manages, she controls, she devises for the household. Underneath it all, she *thinks*. Unhealthy, that, in a housekeeper. Not such a problem with yours at Longbourn, eh? But blood will out. Remember this: blood…will…out.

"I have prattled, as my dear late husband would say. He was always quick with the cheerful reprimand. Now. What have you to say for yourself, Miss Bennet dear?"

It took Mary the rest of the day to recover from the whirling, swirling pronouncements of Lady Manton. It was a pleasure, for sure, to be designated as acceptable by the personage on whose generosity one depended. But, as she knelt for prayer, some words and phrases came thudding to her the front of her mind. *Rumours… Men cannot control… Blood…will…out.*

What was "the bend sinister"? A heraldic term. "A little secret…your housekeeper…"

Lady Manton knew.

Those portraits: Luke's at the carriage window, her father's hanging so briefly but potently on the wall.

Hill was the connection.

That was why Papa had clung to her death-bed. At one moment, Mary did not know. The next moment, she knew.

And knew that Lizzy knew, and also…everyone who needed to know.

They were awake to it, aware of it. Now she was awake and aware of it, too.

She prayed, over and over: "*Lighten our darkness,*

we beseech Thee, oh Lord, and by Thy great Mercy defend us from all perils and dangers of this night."

⁓

At the Rectory, now they were married, Mary was in some ways mistress. It was very strange. She would begin to be confident, to feel that she was moving forward step by step, but then she would take a lurch and slide backwards again.

She and Mr Needleman discussed privacy; privacy was what she was given. Her bedchamber was her own. In the Music Room, Bach, Scarlatti, and even a little Beethoven were her own. She and Mr Needleman had together picked out some pieces of sheet music from a catalogue, which were then ordered from a specialist printer in Derby and presented to her by her husband, with shy smiles, as a marriage gift. Gladys or Patty would light a fire for her in the Music Room, by request, now that the evenings were closing in. The room contained a chaise-longue, "comfortable enough for you to recline on, my dear, when you are weary of scales and arpeggios". When she was so reclining, Mary recalled Mr Prendergast's adoration of Haydn and leapt up again to check that the Haydn pieces were amongst her precious sheet music pile. Yes, there was the Minuet in C Major, which was simple enough to play by sight.

One evening, less than a month after they returned from Grasmere – a Thursday, the day after Mr Needleman's mid-week visit to Mr Hepplecraft in Derby – Mary, on coming out of her room with a handful of extra threads for her sampler, happened upon Mr Needleman coming out of his room across the landing.

"Ah! My dear! Mary! – if I may? Shall we? 'Mary'? And might I be 'Robert'? Here at home, if not in the public domain?"

She halted in mid-step, unsteadied by this almost intimate request, and held up her handful of threads. "It is a pleasure to be busy with a proper piece of needlework. Formerly, with my dreadful eyesight, I was only to make rag rugs for the poor. You know, with little pegs to push the cloth through? How I longed to embark on finer work. And now it is possible! Now that I am, you know, bespectacled!"

She was almost tearful with joy, and at the same time embarrassed: she had said 'You know', twice. This was a phrase that had always irritated her mother. "Only *maids* say 'You know'. They do it to pass the time while trying to fill their empty minds." And she had not responded to her husband's request to use Christian names.

Mr Needleman came over to her and, as if he too were embarrassed, tried to take her hand. But the hand he chose was burdened with threads, so he seized her by the wrist instead. Immediately, she knew that this was the first time he had actually touched her elsewhere than on the hand. Flesh on flesh.

He spoke tentatively, while indicating the door to his room. "I wonder, would you care to see...? It is my pride and joy. Simon, Mr Hepplecraft, found it last year in some obscure village up in Yorkshire, in a hidden corner of the church vestry. They had no use for it, so he was able to acquire it for quite a small sum." He let go of her wrist suddenly and said, almost peremptorily, "Do come and see."

See what? She walked behind him towards his door, while he continued to speak of this mystery. "Of course it was not meant to be used for its current purpose. It is so finely carved, with such dedication, in the days before the church suffered its Great Rift. Henry Eight, and so on? And it fitted exactly!" He peered at it closely. "Now I have the four Gospel-Makers at my back, throughout the night!"

Her presence in her husband's room was also a first occasion. At their lodgings in Grasmere he had greeted her each morning at breakfast; neither had visited the other's room. Mrs Beattie had supervised proceedings on their first evening, instructing their landlady that all arrangements would be under orders from herself, the landlady's own duties residing merely in the provision of food. Mary had noticed a truckle-bed being removed from her room by two lanky boys. Mrs Beattie would not be sleeping in rough fashion at the end of Mary's four-poster; she was provided with her own room.

Each morning the two women met on the landing as the clock struck eight. They would nod to each other before going down to join Mr Needleman at table, and Mr Needleman would greet each of them with equal warmth. A similar pattern had pertained at the close of each, mainly rainy, day.

So this visit to her husband's bedchamber, in her own home, seemed a kind of intimacy. Mary wondered what Lizzy might say at this turn of events.

Large beeswax candles were lit on either side of Mr Needleman's bed, with smaller ones in candleholders on the tallboy and the blanket chest, and the shutters were still closed. Mr Needleman fetched one of the smaller candles, drew aside the bed's curtain, and directed the light onto what was she supposed to admire.

"See! To inspire me all night, to better sermons and deeper spiritual peace! Four evangelists! On my bedhead!"

He leaned even closer to the carving, so precariously that Mary became alarmed lest candle and bed-covering would make contact and cause fire.

"Matthew here… Mark… Luke the physician. And, here, the most beloved disciple. John! See this hand, holding the sacred Book!"

Standing back, he made to offer her the candle. But she could not take the risk of accepting it. She stood very still to admire the intricate object that meant so much to this holy man, her husband. The air between them seemed to quiver as she stared. She begged to feel inspired, but failed. Hoping that her pretence would not show, she counted the seconds before she could say, "How wonderful. How truly wonderful, Mr…Robert."

"I am eager for you to know how much I am in his thoughts. Mr Hepplecraft's. Simon's. Like David and Jonathan in the Old Testament? You remember? Such closeness of spirit."

She nodded, but could find no suitable words in response.

"So," he continued in brisker tone, "he – that

is, Mr Hepplecraft – might come to stay here, on alternate Wednesdays? If that is acceptable to you? As of old? We work so diligently together. You will not be inconvenienced in any way. Next week, we thought? That routine could begin again?" He drew back, and Mary saw that the candle-flame was trembling in his hand. "Good. That is settled. I was sure you would find no difficulty." He leaned and peered again, pointing the candle towards the carving. "See, the work is at its finest with John, the beloved disciple."

Mary suddenly coughed. She was spluttering, and could not stop. In a moment when she could at last speak she said, "Water, please!"

"Of course! My poor dear." He abandoned the candle on the tallboy and lifted the jug, took a small cup from beside it and poured a splash of water for her to drink. "Emotion. I feel it too. Sometimes, when I offer a sermon... I am overcome, as you are now. There, my dear...Mary."

He accepted the threads from her hand so that she could take the cup and drink. She was reminded of the sacrament of Holy Communion.

"We will manage, will we not? We will manage very well. Better now? I thought so. Good. Good."

He took the cup, returned it and the candle to their place, gave Mary back her threads, and went out of the room. Mary, following him obediently down the stairs, felt so confused that she could not speak for some time.

☙

There they are: my Mr Robert, my Mr Simon, and herself. At breakfast, silent. Each with their nose in a book. Mr R's held close to his eyes, as always, because his vanity refuses him the necessary spectacles.

My two and the minx! The three of them! And myself sliding in through the door with a jug of extra hot water for their pot like a seal sliding across Strangford Lough, with never a cough to alert them to the presence of me.

She *is* a minx. She manipulates, to get her way. She reads sermons, so as to please.

At the same time – or at other times, I should say – she is, to a small degree, *biddable*. An example. I asked her, would she *not* bring her good self into the kitchen, if she pleased? It disturbs Gladys, it disturbs Patty. I did not also say that it disturbs *me*, for that should be apparent without the saying of it. When she resided at Longshanks, or whatever godforsaken place it is she came from, did she enter the kitchen there, or the other rooms in the servants' domain, without a knock or a *May I* or a *Do you mind*? I expect she did. The shambolic nature of the household in Hertfordshire was reported to me by Mrs Reynolds through the maid-of-all-work who returned to Pemberley after Miss Mary's marriage. That *housekeeper*, whom they treated so tenderly during her illness, had clearly been the master's *mistress*! The offspring of which was still employed in the *stables*! Naturally, I shall keep that information to myself.

As to the minx's behaviour in the Rectory, I let it be known that I am the queen of my kitchen. She slid away at my words, abashed.

Biddable, so she is. But she is present, everywhere. *My dear Mr Needleman*, she needles him all the time. Or, more recently, *Robert*. He responds accordingly. When Mr Simon is here, it is *Mr Hepplecraft, might you explain?* He lays down his own book and politely replies: "That would be the Anti-Nomianist Heresy. The Antinomians hold that obedience to God's law is motivated by an internal principle of belief, and not from some external force. There are connections with Calvinism and Lutheranism, which need not concern you." He returns to his book. She adjusts her spectacles and returns to hers.

Mr N gave me to understand that he had particular Discussions with her, both before and after the marriage sojourn in Grasmere. (A wetter place to endure a 'honeymoon' I can scarcely envisage. The Glens of Antrim would have been drier.) Discussions about how their rooms might be arranged, both at the hostelry in Grassy-mere and also on our return to the Rectory. After he had made the arrangement to stay at the establishment, his words to me were these: "There will be a room for myself and Hurry, who is satisfied with a truckle-bed; there will be a room each for my wife and your good self; and there will be an extra room for whatever other purposes we may, between us, require." In due course it transpired that the 'other purposes' were: for Mrs Needleman to make her morning prayers; for Mr N to write his afternoon correspondence (no doubt directed towards Mr H); and for myself, and them too, to recover in the evening from whatever the day (the drizzling day, the thunderstorm'd day, the wildly unpredictable and

178

windy day) might have offered us. Hurry, of course, made himself scarce during the daytimes, unless Mr N and the minx had planned a day out. In the rain.

So that left the mornings for me to be on my own, to use as the whim should take me. I composed coded letters to Mrs Reynolds at Pemberley, indicating whether or not what was expected of a married couple had actually occurred. (It had not.) I did not anticipate a reply; there was none. She will no doubt respond in kind, upon our return, as to the marital situation at Pemberley. When the sun shone (as it did, on occasion) I took a turn around the lake. In the remaining time I waited upon Mrs Needleman, or, if the extra room was vacant, made use of it to restore my spirits with what, in my own mind, I term 'housekeeper's nap': the kind of light doze during which one remains alert to certain sounds, and from which one can easily be woken if those sounds should occur.

Now we are back, and have settled ourselves. Mr N smiles at me with a question in his eyes, and I nod to him, sometimes with a straight face, sometimes with a grimace. Just once, when he had re-established Mr H's old routine of visitation here on every other Wednesday, he took me to one side when he knew that Mrs Needleman was out on a parish errand and said quietly: "We are still the same, are we not? We are three – two boys and their mother?" I gave my assent to that; he took my hand, gave it a small stroke, and smiled once more.

Mrs Reynolds knows nothing of this. She may suspect. But words have never been spoken. She and I confide what we choose; no less, no more.

Authoritative as the Rectory might be in the confines of Humbole parish, Mary felt all the time the presence of Pemberley. It was compelling. Since the beginning of Mary's existence as the Rector's wife, Lizzy had been in control of their weekly exchange of visits.

Lizzy suggested that she come to Mary one week, Mary to Lizzy another. This would enable them to exchange conversation about tapestries and samplers (Lizzy congratulating Mary on developments in her work), about lace (Mary might surely wear more at the cuff?), about menus (Mrs Beattie's raised pies were admired for their lightness, but Mrs Reynolds' pastry was more elegantly presented), about Fitzy's sister's happiness in her recent marriage, Lizzy's pride in and frustrations with her young, dear Bingley's latest visit, and, of course, beloved faraway Jane.

There were occasional silences from Lizzy. Mary perceived that, while Lizzy's silences were shorter than her own, they seemed more significant, because they were in such contrast to Lizzy's high spirits as a girl. Now the two of them would sit together gazing into different spaces in one or other withdrawing room: Pemberley's capacious and exquisite in all dimensions, the Rectory's brightened by Mary's introduction of cut flowers from the garden and extra book-stands for whatever reading was in progress at the moment.

Thwaite always accompanied Mrs Darcy to Humbole; Mary was driven by Hurry to Pemberley in the phaeton, loosening her bonnet to enjoy the feel of the wind in her hair. At Pemberley, Thwaite would be waiting at the top of the steps to greet her, and would deliver her back to the phaeton at a time of Lizzy's choosing. Lizzy, on days when the children were most preoccupying her, sometimes cut Mary's visit short. On those occasions Thwaite would explain to Mary what George had done to Henrietta (or, occasionally, vice versa) or in which particular way young William had delighted everyone. She would conclude her account with the remark that these occurrences were typical of any family, whether rich or poor or somewhere in between. This typicality included Mrs Darcy's wish that George's behaviour be kept, if possible, from his father.

The sisters were at the Rectory sharing their enjoyment of the autumn colours – "Magnificent throughout the estate! The beeches, the deer grazing beneath, they are almost the same colour. Let me give you a ride around when you visit next week, Mary" – and some gossip about the new King – "Fitzy tells me he is little improved from when he was Regent. There is talk of establishing a National Gallery of Art, which is intriguing", when, as if it were part of the same conversation, Lizzy said, "I have had a letter from Annie at Longbourn. She hopes it is not too presumptuous of her to initiate a correspondence. But you and I have perhaps been remiss, have we not, in not visiting our old home in the three months since you were married?"

Mary could only murmur, "My goodness, does time not fly?"

"She fears that our mother's health is deteriorating. Indeed, Mama's own letters reveal the same, do they not?" Both sisters received fortnightly missives from Mama, which (they admitted to each other with rare bursts of guilty laughter) were so repetitive that one tended to skim through them rather than peruse them properly. "In her last, she mentioned that Lyddy and Kitty had made a joint visit, albeit a brief one. Also that Mr Bennet is 'lax in his discipline of the household, even of himself'. I remember the words precisely, as I expect you do too."

Indeed, Mary did remember.

"Annie writing to me now must surely herald a turn of events. Mama spends so much time alone, Mary. I am sorely disappointed in our father."

Mary nodded.

"Remember your wedding, with not even a father to give you away?"

"Darcy performed splendidly, though."

"It is kind of you to say so. He was most brotherly, given that you – that we – I mean – do not have such a..." Lizzy's voice petered out at the approach of the word *brother*. There was a resonant silence.

Mary, for some unaccountable reason, pictured Thwaite listening outside the door. Surely not? Could the angelic Thwaite be deceitful? She said in a measured tone, "It grieved our mother deeply that the Divine Will did not grant her a son, to inherit." She spoke with eyes lowered, then looked up at Lizzy and saw her flush.

"These things must not be spoken of." Lizzy's tone was also measured, but breathy. Mary expected her to change the subject at this point, but she did not. "I have begun to see our mother as something of a tragic figure. We were quick to despair of her, were we not? Yet now I feel that she could not help herself. That she should be pitied, rather than blamed."

Mary felt words rising in her throat: *Should we then blame our father?* She could not say them – she would not dare… Yet, again unaccountably, she spoke them. "Should we, then, blame our father?"

Lizzy's reply was sharp, but took a different turn. "Indeed, Annie seems to blame him for his present behaviour. Papa has lost control of himself. We must surely go. The two of us, together."

Mary took in breath to respond, but Lizzy overrode her.

"I will find occasion to speak firmly to him, while you stand by in case he finds my behaviour un-daughterly." She sighed. "Such a long journey! Yet Mama may indeed be mortally ill. Maybe this is what Annie is trying to tell us. We must see for ourselves. Fitzy would urge it, I am sure, as a matter of family duty. Before winter descends."

But Mary wanted to return to the question of Hill. Indeed, she wished to mention her in the context of their father. Her voice steady, she said: "The journey will remind us of dear Hill. Her accompaniment of me to Pemberley was the last journey she ever made, and was much affected by her illness. She spoke to me frankly about her unfortunate…"

Lizzie stood up peremptorily. "Let us keep our attention on the declining health of our parents. The circumstances you allude to are best left buried where they lie."

Mary drew breath, but the words she had hoped to

say would not come.

"How are we to travel?" Lizzy's voice was suddenly weary. "Thwaite will accompany me, of course. And you? It would seem unjust for your household to be deprived of Mrs Beattie once again. Shall I provide you with a lady's maid from among the better staff at Pemberley?"

Mary's heart sank. "I can manage without, Lizzy."

"I know that you could manage. But the sister of Mrs Darcy may not manage. Not when she rides in a Pemberley carriage. I trust you may find the answer to this conundrum, Mary. But, for the purpose of our visit to Longbourn, are you willing to leave those arrangements to me?"

Mary answered, "Of course. I am only too grateful."

11

Visitations

MARY UNDERSTOOD. Lizzy could not get away for the proposed visit to Longbourn while Fitzy was at home; she must wait until he returned to London and (as she put it) to the West Indies. "No no, he does not *go* there. What, on that perilous journey across the oceans? He has *people* who go. He has people who are *there*. It is in his *mind* that he goes to the West Indies. When he is in London. But when here at Pemberley he insists upon my full attention. As *I* do, on *his* attention. Especially with regard to the children."

They were seated again in the Rectory drawing room, on either side of the fireplace, where a handsome fire was lit.

"Then, when he is gone, I can return to the consideration of the parts of life which he, dear man, finds difficult. Of which, of whom, the principal is our dear Mama."

Mary, to her own surprise, laughed at this, and Lizzy turned from frowning to plain face and thence to laughing with her.

Mary and Lizzy, laughing together about their impossible Mama! Mary wondered at it later as she lay in bed listening to the doves coo-cooing under the Rectory eaves and the owls hoo-hooing to each other under the stars. It was she herself – pious and respectful Mary – who had this time introduced the laughter. The memory made her feel almost *even* with Lizzy. On a level. As sisters, and as wives of respectable and sometimes mystifying men. There was a difference in their styles, of course. Lizzy could order a tapestry for her walls, an ancient work of art; Mary could order embroidery threads for her sampler. But Mary was as proud of her modesty as Lizzy was proud of her style.

Lizzy, on this occasion, had quickly returned to frowning again. She said, "And Bingley. Dear Charles. He tells us that Jane can barely converse with him now. It grieves him so. He needs the respite that Pemberley can bring. And London, too."

"Was there not talk of another doctor to help her? One who induces bleeding not with leeches, but with some device called a…?"

"Scarificator? Yes. Charles described it to Fitzy, and Fitzy to me. The blade snaps in and out somehow – I cannot express it – the blood oozes… Can you imagine anything so horrible? I asked him, does she not scream? Charles thought so, but such screams are an essential part of the treatment. This doctor apparently questioned him about our 'family history'! How *dare* he! Though admittedly there has always been the question of Mama's nerves. And the difficulty she had in each of her confinements."

"*Mama* did?"

"No, *Jane* did! Yet you may be right. Mama too may have suffered. We never spoke of such things. It was Jane's speaking of it, Charles says, that was the first indication of her decline." Lizzy sighed deeply. "Some women never recover. Oh, my darling Jane. I go as often as I can. But even I can only rouse her for a short time. I miss her so. She was like my better self."

Mary tried to imagine having a better self, and failed. Then she imagined a husband whose preoccupations lay far across the oceans, and there her imagination was more successful. Such preoccupations must be very unpleasant: the sugar plantations – or was it tobacco? The heat, and so on. At any rate her dear Robert was close to her most of the time. It was only on alternate Wednesdays, when he visited Derby to commune with Mr Hepplecraft, that he was absent. Otherwise he was most attentive. Except when Mr Hepplecraft was staying; then she must leave the pair of them alone. But, mostly, Robert was simply her relaxed and silent companion.

"Ah, one's better self," she said, hoping to bring the conversation round to her own life's happenings. "Mr Needleman remarked only the other day about my 'goodness', how it was emerging through my visits to the poor and needy of the parish. 'The poor we have always with us', as our Lord said."

"Though, if I remember a long-ago sermon,"

responded Lizzy quickly, "the true meaning of that text is that the poor can always wait for good things, because they will always be there to receive them. Whereas the woman who poured sacred oil over our Lord's feet – which signifies the finer things of life – was right to do so. Thus do I pour out my love and attention upon my family, and on Pemberley, which benefits the whole community. Including the folk of the parishes all around. Such as Humbole."

"Of course." Mary, reprimanded, sat up a little straighter to defend herself. "I think it would hearten you to hear about my parish visits. Only yesterday I visited a family with eight children. Imagine – eight! I took with me two baskets of good things. I carried one to the door. Our groom followed me with the other, then readily made his escape. For the odour was most oppressive, Lizzy. I had not understood what rigour it takes to make a house clean. Especially when there are infants around who are not yet breeched. There were *three* such! And breeches were there none! One little girl and two little boys, each in their naked innocence, and the mother allowing them to… I felt desperate. I did not know where to walk, even to stand! But I did not falter. I offered my baskets. I bent to put the goods wherever I could. One item was a string of French onions, donated by my sterling housekeeper. Even in the gloom of this wretched household I could detect that there was no fire on which to cook. So how were the onions, with whatever meat accompaniment, to be used up? I was at a loss, Lizzy. The poor are so different from us. I am by no means sure that my charity baskets contain what is truly needed."

"I congratulate you on your fortitude. But, from my longer experience, I would counsel caution. One can easily catch diseases from these places. Infectious diseases. They go flying around such hovels, with no means of protection for those of us who live in more delicate surroundings. You must take care, Mary!"

"I do, I do, but…"

"Has Mr Needleman not upbraided you? His duty is to care for his vulnerable wife."

"I am by no means vulnerable, Lizzy! In fact, I find myself to be quite stalwart. And how can the work be done other than by such visits? 'Inasmuch as you did it to one of the least of these My brethren, you did it unto Me'. How can I resist the Lord's work when it lies so clear, and so close?"

Lizzy rose to her feet and began pacing to and fro. "Listen, Mary. Take Georgiana. Our dearest sister, now so happily wed. She had a companion once, who came to share French lessons with her governess. It was a matter of charity for Fitzy's parents. You recall what models of rectitude were his parents? This was a distant cousin, a girl a little older than Georgiana. She was not robust in disposition. She stayed just once, when Georgiana was perhaps twelve. Immediately upon her arrival Fitzy saw that the girl was unwell. She sickened further, doctors were called, but she died even before they arrived. It was *typhus*! Fitzy tells me they had the entire house washed and fumigated, every single garment scrubbed. Fitzy never forgot it. Never forgave it. One must give to those who are in need, but not – *not ever*! – put at risk those nearest and dearest to us."

She was at the far side of the room when she ended her speech, and strode back to her seat to deliver her final words. "Am I not right?" Then she sat down, breathing heavily, opened up Annie's latest letter, and stared at it without reading.

Mary lowered her eyes too. "Lizzy, I did not mean to upset you. Please forgive me. I will remember what you have said, and discuss it with Mr Needleman. Did I tell you…" she looked up again, trying to elicit a smile – "that he and I are on first name terms? Robert, and Mary? I never thought I could be so fortunate." But Lizzy's eyes remained lowered. Mary said quickly, "Let us return to our travel arrangements. I hope we can make plans which entirely correspond with what is good for Darcy and for yourself, and even for Mr Bingley. I think of Jane all the time. Pray for her."

"Please," said Lizzy, "while you are about it, pray for yourself in accepting the maid I will select for you from among Pemberley's staff, for the purposes of our visit. You simply cannot gad about the country without one."

Longbourn, Herts.
Dear Miss Thwaite

I am not sure how to address you, but that is of little consequence. In any case, you will have another name that is more truly your own? I have been able to retain my 'Annie' because I came to Longbourn as a child, and Mrs Hill needed more and more help as the family grew. I did not replace

190

someone special, like a Lady's Maid, as you did. I wonder if you know of the person originally called 'Thwaite'? She, like you, would know the exact temperature of the water your mistress prefers for washing; and could adapt, as you have done, to the large bath-tub recently delivered, so we hear, to Pemberley! Attention to every tiny detail: that is what makes a true Lady's Maid. Set aside all one's own feelings. Think only of the feelings of the Mistress of the House. I hear that you are expert in doing this. For Miss Lizzy, you can do no wrong.

I hear that you have a sister? That must be wonderful. Sisters have always been much in evidence here at Longbourn. I myself was an orphan. But I have my dear Luke, and my two precious children. I know how fortunate I am to have been able to marry and give birth. Many women in service, especially those who work closely with their mistresses, can never leave, because their mistresses depend on them entirely for their personal care. The servants, in their turn, depend on the small sums dispensed each Quarter Day. Such sums disappear quickly on essentials and leave no way of saving for longer-term needs.

However, my purpose is not to bemoan our lot, but to warn you of the difficult situation here, and to reassure you that when you puzzle over the complex relations between the Bennet family and its servants, you will not be alone. I beg you, bring me any questions that arise, and I will answer them so far as I can.

I nurture a hope that the two of us might sit together in a quiet corner to talk. Perhaps during one of Miss Lizzy's much-needed rests, and while

Miss Mary is reading her Bible?

These thoughts are, as always, not consigned to paper. Those who put words on a page are always at risk from having their words read by others. The owners of libraries, with their ink-wells and their precious paper, are privileged, because they have seals to keep their letters private. Privacy! Oh, the luxury of it. I try to imagine…

The children call, and I must go to them.

Your hopeful friend, Annie.

༄

Mary wrestled all through a long night over what she should do. She must choose for herself rather than have a lady's maid foisted upon her from Pemberley. She would beg Mrs Beattie to accompany her once again.

As soon as she opened her mouth, at breakfast, in the presence of Robert, she envisaged Mrs Beattie coming face to face with her ailing mother – then her dishevelled father – in the current condition of 'lax discipline' at Longbourn.

"No no, of course, I did not mean *yourself*, Mrs Beattie! I wondered if, perhaps, Gladys might be prevailed upon?"

She glanced at Robert, but his attention was divided between his toast and his book. Mrs Beattie had completely free rein.

"Such collusions and confabulations, I have never known the like. To think that Mrs Darcy should not see the solution that is staring her plain in the face." As she expostulated, Mrs Beattie's head rose out of her solid frame like a full moon rising over the hill. "It must surely be plain to all of them. But no, it is as if no one even noticed the poor mite as gave such dedicated care! She would have brought that wretched woman back from the dead if it were in her power! And she being the sister! She would suffice. Yet none can murmur it. Their minds are too small."

There came a ring at the door-bell. Robert and Mary gazed at the doorway through which Mrs Beattie now disappeared. The wind of her exit ruffled the edges of the tablecloth. Robert smiled vaguely before returning to his book and his toast.

Mary, astonished, remembered that in the middle of her troubled night such a solution had come to her, too: that Thwaite's little sister, the silent crippled one who had tended so devotedly to Mrs Hill, might step in. But the idea had faded from her mind. It was up to Lizzy to make such a suggestion, anyway; and Lizzy would never allow such a creature to occupy space in the Pemberley coach.

But the doorbell brought news which demanded a dramatic change to all their plans. Gladys came in with a sealed letter, which she handed to Mary with a bob. "Mrs Needleman, ma'am."

Mary broke the seal loudly enough to drag Robert from his book. "It is from Lizzy. It seems quite long." Seeing she had caught Robert's attention, she returned her gaze to the letter and read it aloud.

"'Mary dear, I know you will stand by me in this difficult hour. George's behaviour has become intolerable. You know how he torments dear William? Now there has come an actual wound. Bleeding, copious bleeding, which has required the doctor, and stitches to the poor dear's forehead. You may ask how it occurred? It was those medieval stirrups that hang on the wall beside the tapestry, the sharpness of their metal. How did George manage to fetch them down, the wicked boy?

"'The consequence is that Darcy himself has become involved. That means – has always meant – the belt. It pains me to report it. I hate to hear my firstborn's cries. But it must be done. Spare the rod, spoil the child. Even the most loving mother must restrain herself from staying the father's hand.

"'In these difficult circumstances I must remain here to keep the peace. Mama and Papa must be satisfied with you alone. And you will surely satisfy, Mary dear. You have ever been a calm presence in time of trouble.

"'Darcy declares that George is for school, without delay. He is acquainted with the processes. I must be here to support him, to care for my little William, to smooth George's path to discipline. I tried to argue with Darcy. I asked if we might bring Bingley and his children to Pemberley, for company, to distract George from the wilder aspects of his character. But no, Darcy's answer is *School*. He himself was sent there at seven-and-a-half. Had any of us Bennet offspring been of the male sex, we too would have gone away at this age. Tradition, together with the current crisis, demands it. It is decided. My tears have been of no avail.

"'As for your lady's maid for the Longbourn visit, I am clear that you should take Thwaite. I shall suffer without her at this sore time, but your need is the greater. She will arrive on the eve of your departure, to give time for the two of you to settle.

"'Dear Mary, what a blessing you are. Thank you so very, very much'."

൦ൟ

They, Esther and Milly, are to be separated yet again. So they must spend the night before Esther's departure on *Doovus*. Nothing, not even sleep, is more important than Doovus. Returning, in their minds, in their eyes, in the gloom, to Da and Ma and Joel.

The pair of them freshly wiped, hair untied and combed and retied, teeth dabbed with soda, first Milly and then Esther climb into the one bed, and lie together as one.

Esther begins. "Joel used-a tek 'is models up and round the 'ouses. Joel 'n' 'is models, they'd sell, Da says. Go try it on, Joel boy. Look at 'em! Thass 'un's an 'oss! Dead right it's an 'orse, our Joel! Outta lead! Old bitsa lead!"

Milly takes over. "Dead right, this 'un's a donkey, and all can see t' diff'rence! An this 'un, li'll old lady, is jus' like Ma Trumbull darn't road! Mek money fra that, our Joel!"

Esther, as Thwaite, knows that if anyone else were listening, they'd not understand a word. They'd understand *her*, but with Milly, all they'd hear would be grunts and mumblings. But Esther understands. She is the one and only person in the world, now, who can do that. She grins in the gloom. "An' Joel, he goes an' does as Da sez. Goes roun' yon villages an' sells 'is stuff. Meks money, 'e does!"

"Folks ken, don' they," takes up Milly, "diff'rence 'tween 'osses 'n' donkeys. They ken who's old Ma Trumbull, or if no', summun 'oo's as like Ma Trumbull as not."

They're quiet for a moment, gazing at each other, drinking each other in, and remembering Joel. Not the Joel whose body threw him to the ground after his accident, whose limbs leapt in seizures and tossed his tiny, intricately-made toys all over the floor. The Joel they remember is the one who crafted those toys, who spent hours each evening – too many hours, Ma had argued, but softly, with a smile – taking each one down from the shelf Da had made specially for them, then creating one more tiny finger on the man, one little tweak of a smile on the old woman; one flick of the donkey's tail to show he was a mardy donkey and would moan raucously about his load.

Then Esther's face clouds over, and Milly's too, as they carry the load of Joel's fate between them: carry his dear burnt body after it had thrown him into the fire.

Eventually they rub noses, come out of that space, and go into the future. They look at the day that is to come, how they'll live it together or separately, and what they'll do to keep themselves together even when they are apart. And, because they know that Something Happened, Milly gazes into Esther's eyes as she strokes her face, to give what comfort she can, and acknowledge the sorrow that it is impossible to give comfort for.

Esther is always the second one to drift off into sleep. As she drifts this night, she turns to her part in the coming day, and recalls Miss Mary, whom tomorrow she will serve. She sees her quite clearly, riding in Mr Needleman's phaeton as they approach the Rectory in Humbole for Miss Mary's first visit. Her plain face is alternately clear and troubled. Most likely today will produce the same picture: part troubled, part clear. As lady's maid, as Thwaite, Esther will console Miss Mary's troubled aspects and encourage her clear ones. What will be her troubles? Is it a trouble or a clarity, being the new Mrs Needleman? *Something* will have happened to her in this process, surely. What might that mean to Miss Mary, Mrs Needleman? She is Mrs Darcy's sister, after all. *Something* used to make Mrs Darcy happy, at first. Exhausted, but enraptured. It was only after the births – successively, one, two, three, growing worse each time – that Mrs Darcy's spirit had become subdued and her troubledness had begun. The fear, the overwhelming fear.

Mrs Needleman: is she enraptured? Folks like them seem to find enjoyment in such a thing, though Esther has no way of knowing how. Maybe their own Ma made a place for it in her life? Not just giving way to what their Pa wanted? The grunts from behind the curtains of the corner-bed had given no hint of what anyone was feeling at the time.

Esther recalls Miss Mary again, and wonders whether the vital energy that possesses Mrs Darcy each time her husband returns from London could arise in Miss Mary, too, as she does her duty as Mrs Needleman. Tomorrow she might find out.

But Longbourn, Hertfordshire, would be a different place from the one she visited this time last year. Mrs Hill, whom Milly had cared for devotedly in one of the upper servants' rooms at Pemberley, had gone to the graveyard beside the church where Miss Mary worshipped as a child, where she would have listened to the sermons and learned the hymns as she grew up, and sat with 'Miss Lizzy' and her other sisters in the locked, high-sided Family Pew, next to the pulpit.

This time, it is she who will be at Miss Mary's side. She will be Miss Mary's lady's maid, not 'Miss Lizzy's'. She, Thwaite, will not need to attend to the anxieties arising in Mrs Darcy about each Longbourn episode as it unfolds. This, she confesses to herself as she falls asleep, will be a relief.

∽

On the evening before Mary's departure for Longbourn, she and Robert sat on either side of the fireplace as usual, reading. It was a Monday; she was to travel between Tuesday and Thursday, to avoid travelling on the Sabbath. Mary was re-reading the sermons of the Very Reverend Dr Pratt Green, and especially that comforting quotation: 'Blessed are the meek, for they offer quiet spaces to the soul'. It felt like a prescription for her: to find a quiet space for her soul. Yet in the darker corners of her mind lay spaces that were far from quiet. She felt tormented by two different questions. One was: 'Will our parishioners miss my visits while I am away?' The other was: 'When I contemplate the commandment to honour one's father and mother, how can that be translated into honouring my Papa, who has dishonoured both his wife and his mistress, and Mama, with whom a calm conversation can never even begin to take place?'

She looked up. Robert was deep in his book. He had showed her its name and told her the subject it concerned, and though she nodded sagely, she did not understand his words. *I cannot ask him either of my two questions*, she thought. *Especially the second.*

Maybe she could start with an enquiry about his reading. She coughed, twice, and at the second cough he looked up.

"Robert, dear," she coughed again, and swallowed. "I know 'Evangelicalism', but am confused by 'Oxford' and 'Clapham'. Those two are place names?"

"That is a very good question, Mary. These are the places where clergy are thinking on the same lines as myself and Simon."

"Where they are contemplating Evangelicalism?"

"Exactly. But there is no need for you to contemplate it yourself. Your wifely support is enough. And your devotion to the parish, of course."

"Ah!" Mary rushed towards one of her vital questions. "You place a value on my parish visits?"

"Of course! How could you doubt it? It is remiss of me not to make such visits myself. But I am much more suited to preaching Our Lord from the pulpit than putting into practice his Sermon on the Mount."

Mary was delighted. *Blessed are the merciful* from the Sermon on the Mount was her favourite Biblical quotation. Each of her baskets, she would remind herself when approaching a hovel, was filled with the

Lord's mercy. A mercy which would, in due time, return unto her.

Robert's eyes had slid back towards his book.

Mary said, "But?"

He raised them again. "Yes?"

"I can give an example, if you can spare the time?"

"Surely."

"I took one of Mrs Beattie's splendid raised-pastry pies to a cottage by old Mr Wormley's farm, near the pig-sties." Robert frowned, but she continued. "I had heard from a parishioner that Mr Wormley had docked the man's wages after an altercation concerning alcohol, so there was need for nourishment in the household. But when I entered the place, a loud argument was taking place between husband and wife. Sensing I had interrupted their privacy, I retreated, but the woman leapt upon my basket and grabbed the pie, whereupon the man leapt upon her, and in the scuffle the pie fell to the ground and was seized by one of their dogs. Large dogs. The children, who were reputed to be many, were not to be seen, though I heard sounds of mirth from behind the flimsy walls. I made my escape, and upon my return Mrs Beattie was most displeased to hear the outcome of her pains with the pie. Understandably displeased."

Exhausted by the telling of this tale, she thought Robert would be exhausted by the hearing of it and return to his book. But he did not. Instead, his face adopted a most gentle expression. He stood, came over and, drawing an upright chair close to her and taking her hand in his, sat down.

"My dear wife, I have been waiting for an

opportunity to open this subject to you. It is one which occupies my mind, and Simon's, during much of our time together. We feel our Lord's love, both of us, as it stretches out not only to ourselves but to every human soul. But, at the same time, there is an image which is very precious to me, and to Simon too. It is the image of the Great Chain of Being." He enunciated the phrase carefully, as a priest educating a parishioner in the pew. "Have you heard of this Great Chain?"

Mary shook her head.

"It is a truth which sets a pattern for our lives. This Chain holds every small fragment of life, every over-arching aspect. Each part is graded, and placed exactly as Our Lord has planned. At the apex is God Himself. At the far end of the Chain lie all the tiny creatures whose purpose is to sustain us, human beings, who are made in God's image. Who are 'a little lower than the angels'. We represent the summit of God's creation. You and I, who worship Him as we do, are set nearer the angels than the more wretched, such as those whom you visited with Mrs Beattie's pie. The task for each of us is to discern our place in this Great Chain of Being, and to live it out as faithfully and as humbly as we can."

He turned, awaiting her answer.

Mary took her time before answering, and felt sad that her answer could only take the form of another question. "I had hoped that my visits might help to raise these poor people to a higher level than their present position. Is that not possible?"

Robert stroked her hand comfortingly. "I fear not, my dear. Their link in the Chain is at a great distance from ours. We can only gain merit by our good deeds, and leave the rest to the Lord."

Further questions now rushed through Mary's mind – so many that they seemed to burst through on her tongue. "What about those poor creatures who have received the mercy of the Lord – say, someone like my mother, or my father – and yet are ungrateful for their place in this Chain? Who instead resort to sin, to… Oh, they are not *kind*! They have not *been* kind, to those who are lesser than themselves! To Hill, dear Hill! How, Robert, could that possibly be Our Lord's intention?" Tears welled in her eyes and dripped onto the lower rim of her spectacles.

Robert left his chair and dropped to his knees before her. "My sweet wife. Do not distress yourself. I understand what you are asking. On the morrow you are set to depart for your childhood home. You wish for your poor parents to gain entrance to Heaven. And is the Lord not merciful? You grieve for your faithful housekeeper; your heart grieves for the burdens that she bore. I do not know those burdens, nor do I wish to know them. The great questions of sin and forgiveness are not for us to understand. They are for Our Lord to deal with in His own good time. Our task is to do what we are bidden to do, in our place, in our time. And to pray."

He bowed his head, and she expected him to pronounce a suitable prayer. Or even, she thought suddenly and wildly, he might lead her upstairs and, instead of bidding her his usual good night, take her into his own room – might even suggest that she lie with him in a close embrace.

But he regained the upright chair, and continued.

"Let me enlarge on the complexities of this matter. My own mother, as you know, departed this life some years ago. In her last will and testament, it emerged that among her properties, bequeathed in their entirety to me, was a single slave in Jamaica, in the West Indies. Such slaves come from faraway Africa, the dark continent, where the trade in slaves is a long tradition. In a letter accompanying the will, my mother wrote that this creature, her possession, was in her opinion a child of God, though a lowly one. Throughout her adult life my dear Mama sent small parcels of useful or decorative items to this woman; she asked me, as her son and beneficiary, to continue this practice. She wished to show that Britain is a civilised nation, and to that end she asked me to support men of God such as Mr Wilberforce, who, more than a decade ago, helped to bring to an end the trade in slaves throughout the world. I have done my best to fulfil my mother's wishes, to the letter."

Mary stared at her husband, who now stood solemnly and breathlessly between her and the fire. He seemed to grow in stature before her eyes. "What was the name of that man again?" she asked him. "Wilber... force? How wonderful must he be, Robert, to achieve such a change! Are the slaves in the West Indies to be freed, then? Will this woman, who through your mother's bequest is your possession, now be free?"

"I fear not." He turned slightly away from her, as if perplexed. "The question you raise is one that Mr Hepplecraft and I wrestle with during our times together. We ask ourselves, would such an eventuality

– the freedom of the slaves – not contradict the central truth of which we have been speaking? The Great Chain of Being? Slaves occur throughout the Scriptures. If a slave is a slave, then surely it is God's will for him to remain so? Or, in this case, her?" He gazed at the fire in perplexity.

Mary rose to her feet. "And how does one determine what might be God's will? Is that not the underlying question that we all must ponder?"

With a swift movement, Robert turned back to face her. "Mary, you are tired and anxious. Tomorrow you will embark on a journey towards your ailing mother. You must not exhaust yourself with matters of theology." He took her hand as if to lead her. "Please, my dear, go to your room and rest. There will be much to accomplish in the morning before you depart."

But Mary was reluctant to let go of this unusual, perhaps precious, moment.

"Robert?"

"Yes? Briefly?"

"I would like to ask: while I am gone to Longbourn, will you miss me?"

His face, so constrained and concerned, cracked open in surprise, then collapsed back into the sad twist of a smile. "My sweet wife! Never doubt me. Go with my blessing. And leave me your blessing to sustain me here."

He kissed both her hands, let them fall, and walked in front of her out of the room.

৩৩

Sisters: how alike, yet how different. Esther, struggling on the journey to be entirely Thwaite and not Esther at all, clutched onto this thread of thought.

Even as the Pemberley carriage sped and rolled and bumped towards Hertfordshire, Mrs Needleman pressed her needle through her sampler with astonishing persistence. Esther could see the final word emerging: 'WELL-D…'. The phrase might be *BE NOT WEARY IN WELL-DRESSING*, or *WELL-DANCING*, but was much more likely to be *WELL-DOING*; Miss Mary would surely never weary in that purpose. Nor would Mrs Darcy, in her own way, weary of her own kind of well-doing. Sisters; the same, but different.

Already she ached at her separation from Milly. Through her body, to her very centre, she ached for her other half. And she knew that she would continue to ache until she returned to Pemberley's servants' wing (east), to bed, and to Milly.

But this mission to Longbourn had no fixed end point. It had come at the summons of housekeeper Annie (who seemed to have her own Other Half, and children too… Now what was *that* like?). They would stay, said Mrs Needlewoman (*WELL-DOI…*) as long as need be. Mrs Darcy, engrossed in matters of the nursery, had generously agreed to forego her lady's maid's services until the outcome of Mrs Bennet's illness became clear. Thwaite smiled her assent and swallowed her ache. The only cure for it was to focus her mind on caring for her present mistress, who was so much the same and so different from Mrs Darcy. And she must press down her Esther self for all that she was worth.

"Hertfordshire!" cried Miss Mary suddenly. "The county sign! My native county! Just as I reached my *G*!" She pressed her needle into its case, wound the remaining threads around it, and packed the sampler back into its cloth bag.

It was at this moment that Thwaite, viewing her charge across the carriage, knew for certain that Miss Mary was in fact virginal, that she was Mrs Needleman in name only, because Nothing had yet Happened to her.

In the same moment her aching for Milly was knocked out of place by another feeling entirely: a wave of nausea.

She ignored it. Thwaite she was, and Thwaite she would remain, through Hertfordshire, through Longbourn, through enabling Miss Mary to fulfil her role of daughter to difficult parents, however that might unfold.

֎

Mary had determined to use this journey as a chance to get to know Thwaite better. After all, if she had a mission to the poverty-stricken members of her parish, she must also have a mission to acquaint herself with the classes in between, of whom the most available were the servant class. Back at the Rectory, she was becoming less nervous of the vociferous Mrs Beattie. Her husband told her that Mrs Beattie, when young, had sailed over from Ulster, in the north of Ireland, with her father, who was bound for St John's

College, Cambridge: a transition that astonished Mary. What about the other servants? Gladys and Patty were impenetrable, but they were sisters, from a 'lamentable' family and had been (in Mrs Beattie's words) 'rescued in the nick of time'. Mary longed to rescue the unfortunate in the nick of time, but felt more relaxed in the company of souls like Thwaite, who behaved in a more amiable manner.

On the middle day of their journey she had laid aside her absorbing sampler and asked Thwaite a little more about her people. She remembered from their previous conversation that her father was a lead-miner.

"Do you have brothers and sisters?" she began, rather abruptly. "Of course, apart from your dear…"

"Milly. Yes, I had a brother."

"Oh. How fortunate, to have a brother! His name was?"

"Joel. He was very good with his hands. He made little toys for children, and ornaments. From pieces of lead."

"How clever!" She did not know how to continue, and paused for a while. Her fingers itched to get back to her sampler, but she disciplined herself into waiting for Thwaite to say more.

In due course Thwaite said, "Unfortunately, we lost him."

"Lost? Dear dear. How?"

"An accident. But, in our distress, we were helped greatly by the master of Pemberley."

"I believe he was a remarkable benefactor. All those alms-houses!"

Thwaite, after a while, spoke again. "My mother had

died some years previously, and my father, too, soon after our Joel. But the staff at Pemberley, especially Mrs Reynolds, whom you will know…" Mary nodded gladly. "She knew Joel from him selling his gew-gaws like a scotchman." Mary felt a little lost here, but leaned forward in the effort to take it all in. "So the staff asked Mrs Reynolds, could we join the household in some way, and Mrs Reynolds said we were worth a try."

Mary joined her hands together in a little clap. "How very, very kind! And you did well? You proved yourself in the work?"

But Thwaite seemed cast down by the telling of her story, which involved such a number of family losses. She had become quite pale.

"But you still have Milly. That must be a great strength to you. She is quiet, but so very helpful."

"Oh, she is, Mrs Needleman, I can assure you! Milly is the greatest help in all the world. Your Mrs Hill remarked as much, when she was so ill. You remember?"

There. She had done it. She had raised Thwaite's spirits by her enquiries. Instead of pallor there came a little blush to the girl's cheeks; she was almost animated. What a blessing it was to have a mission in life. Smiling, Mary took up her sampler once more.

Then came a moment, as she was re-threading her needle, when Thwaite unexpectedly returned to their previous conversation.

"I rose quite quickly, I believe, in comparison with others in my position."

It was unusual for a servant to persist in a personal

conversation, and Mary found it rather irksome when she was pressing so hard on her needle against the jolting of the carriage. But perhaps, she thought, this further talk might yield some opportunity for learning. "Did you indeed?"

"That was on account of Milly. She requires nothing for herself. She simply thinks of others. Mostly, she thinks of me."

"Indeed! That is most fortunate. I know how Mrs Darcy values your qualities. You must miss your dear, er, Joel?"

"I do, Miss Mary. Thank you so much for thinking of that. I do miss him. We both miss him. It is most kind of you to understand that."

She had done it. She had understood.

Thwaite was again looking somewhat pale, and Mary vowed to pay her particular attention in the coming days. Though of course the errant members of her own family would soon loom large, and would probably occupy all her attention for most of the time.

༺༻

Luke, waiting in the stables for the Pemberley carriage to arrive, propped John-James up on Rosie. He held his son loosely. "You steady?" The lad nodded.

Surely they must arrive soon. He didn't want to settle John-James on the mare only to grab him off again at the tinkling approach of the carriage-and-pair: that would only provoke a howl of disgust from his son.

All Annie had said to him was, "Keep 'em, will you?

She's sliding quickly now. I've got to stay by." She'd called Mother Drayton the night before last, just in case. Ma Drayton ate healthily; Annie was wearing herself out running up and down stairs with pies and custards conjured by the faithful Pemberleys. Snobs they might be, the Pemberley maids-of-all-work, but they did what was needed and didn't complain or ask awkward questions. With Mr Bennet wandering as far away from his dying wife as he possibly could, that could only be a good thing.

Luke took his hands an inch away from John-James on either side. "Aw-right?"

John-James nodded grimly. Luke took his hands away completely. John-James sat up firm upon the old nag's back.

But Edie, who'd been clutching at the rough leather of his trousers, now cried, "Me too! I wanna go behind him!"

The scars on Luke's back started to itch, as they always did when things riled him. He knew that the minute he'd got Edie up there she'd cling to her brother like a house-leek to a slate roof, and he couldn't abandon the pair of them on the horse's back to run out when he saw the Pemberley carriage in the distance. He'd posted the message-boy at the gates, to open them when the time came. But still, he himself must be there to bow and scrape before the Pemberley lot on their arrival.

It was hearing those words march through his brain – 'bow and scrape before *that lot*' – which prompted Luke to say out loud: "To hell with them!" He crouched, grinned broadly at his daughter, lifted her up high, and seated her up on Rosie behind John-James. He murmured *Coo-o-o-ome on, coo-o-o-ome on* to the mare, and she snuffled and shuffled and gave the children to feel that they really were riding, like their dad did. Both children roared with delight.

Then, as the tinkling came from a distance at last, he said firmly, "Enough now, we've a carriage to see to," and lifted first John-James down and then, with a final squeal of protest, Edie.

So it was with a child on either side of him that Luke approached the Pemberley carriage as the coachies reined the horses in. He waited a formal moment for the dust to settle over the gravel and for the coachies to gaze at him in surprise. In that moment, his eye caught the whips that each man held up at an angle in the sun, and his back remembered the lash. He remembered, too, the bayonet – the bayonet in his own hands, the bayonet he himself had wielded – and the popping eyes of the man whose belly he was bayonetting; the final push he'd given to the weapon; the light going out of the eyes of the man... And the vow he'd made to himself in that moment. *Never again. Never again. Never again.*

Even though it meant becoming a deserter.

Never again – and he wrenched himself back into the present moment, with himself, his daughter and his son, and the Pemberley carriage before their eyes.

He had no plan for what he would do next. He only knew that he couldn't face Miss Mary just now. She'd realised what he and Mr Bennet were to each other, and it was just too complicated.

Things went *click* in his mind. What he needed to

do was get Mr Bennet, gin-soaked as he was, away from snivelling around the courtyard, and settle him somewhere in the house where he could do no harm. Then he needed to give his children their tea.

Ignoring the affronted looks on the coachies' faces, he shouted up to them: "Would you be so kind as to hand Miss Mary out and accompany her into the house? Her poor dying mother is in need of her. Her father's no good to man nor beast, an' I'll see to him. Then it's the post-house in Meryton for yourselves and the horses. We'll send the message-boy when you're needed."

A couple of cries of "But!" came from on high, and there may have been a flick of one of their whips. Luke, though, was already walking his children across the crunching gravel as they headed back towards their cottage. He did hear one word – it might have been *quick*, or *sick* – but he ignored it. Miss Mary and the Pemberley lady's maid would have to manage somehow once they got inside the house. At this moment he was a husband and a father, and not a brother nor a servant to anyone.

⟳

It's quiet in this dark and curtained room. There are underground naggings in my mind: *How are my Edie and my John-James going on? What's Luke done with Mr B? Will Miss Mary and Miss Lizzy's maid find an empty gin bottle under the chaise-longue?*

Mrs Bennet is part of the quietness. Each breath is slightly rasping, but only slightly. Not like she's near

212

the end, says Ma Drayton. I've sent the old biddy for a lie-down. She's been good. As she was with my mother-in-law. Respectful. (So long as she gets enough to eat.) When the message came that it would be just Miss Mary and Thwaite, I did, I confess, breathe easier. And I felt for Miss Lizzy over the matter of Master George. That's the first of her little chicks to be flying the coop. Not that he isn't a menace, but they can all be menaces, on and off. Not many of them get the chance of going off to boarding school for months at a time. Or was it less like a chance, more like a punishment?

My mind, fastened like a thread to Mrs B's breath, lifts itself away. For I can hear, in the distance, the sound of the Pemberley carriage.

Now would be the moment when, in normal times, I'd have raced down the stairs to gather the maids, including the Pemberleys, and the extra maids commandeered from the village, to stand on the doorstep and make a good show.

But not today.

My eyes drop down again to Mrs B's rasping breaths. I can't summon Ma Drayton: she needs her sleep, ready for when the end does actually come.

I make myself sit still.

I can't quite make out the sounds I'm hearing. There's the hooves, the wheels, there are voices and occasional shouts. Then, do I hear John-James or Edie? From over by our cottage? Are they laughing, or crying?

Where's Mr B? What will Luke do with him? The sounds are muffled. I can't make them out.

Then quiet once more. For some time.

My head lifts again. There are soft footsteps on the stair. Just one. A woman.

Miss Mary's head comes round the door. I've got used to the gloom, so I can see her. She's taken off her bonnet and her hair bursts out every which way. Behind her spectacles, she blinks. Coming from the brightness, she cannot see me yet.

Eventually: "Annie! How is...?"

I lift a finger to my lips. Then I cannot resist a smile. I am not alone any more. "Did you see Luke? Are my babes all right?"

"I glimpsed him taking them to your cottage. Then I think he will deal with Papa."

"Where will he put him?" Then I catch myself. "I'm sorry, Miss Mary. I am very glad to see you. Sit there, won't you, where Mrs Drayton was seated earlier." I put a hand out towards the bed; the blankets retain some of the old biddy's shape. "As you see, we are taking good care of your mama."

"I knew you would." Miss Mary takes her seat. "I think the coachmen had expected to be given accommodation in our servants' quarters, but Luke sent them back to the post-house."

"Oh, I should have made provision in the stables! It slipped my mind – there was so much else to think of!"

"Do not be anxious, Annie dear. I expect the staff at the Blue Boar will see the livery and know that they will be reimbursed in due time."

My oh my, I'm thinking, Miss Mary has become a woman of the world in this short time! I wonder if she knows yet how much her husband takes in tithes? Or how it is that married life involves, well, Lord knows what?

She's speaking again. "Annie, there is something else. Thwaite – you remember? Such a charming maidservant. We have had a delightful journey. But less than an hour into our final day, she was quite ill. I had to hammer on the roof to alert the coachmen. She only reached safety just in time."

"Safety? What sort of safety?"

"Well, if she were to be, you know, ill, and there was an emission, and an odour, in the Pemberley carriage?"

Now I have to get real with her. "Miss Mary, we've been sorting out that sort of mess with your mother here, day in, day out. Before that, with my mother-in-law. We'd have cleaned up the carriage, would we not? Miss Lizzy cares greatly for Thwaite."

Miss Mary is duly admonished.

"No matter," I say. "Poor girl. Where is she now?"

"I almost took her to the drawing room, but then thought again and decided on the kitchen. A glass of water was all that she wanted. She is a maid, after all."

"As Luke is a manservant. Not a member of the Family."

But Miss Mary hasn't quite finished her previous sentence. "Though a lady's maid." Then she hears what I have said, and looks up at me. I can see her flush, even in the gloom. "Annie dear. Life is confusing, is it not?"

I nod, painfully, and the silence into which we fall is full of unspoken things. It goes on, and on.

At last I realise that Mrs Bennet's rasps are

becoming noisier. I wonder if Miss Mary has noticed this. Probably not, because she speaks again.

"I have been thinking of some kind of compensation, Annie. For Luke. For you all. My father took what was not his, and people suffered as a consequence. To think! My brother! Is your husband!"

Should I shush her in case anyone might hear? Mother Drayton in the room next door? – she may or may not be asleep. But rumour has it that such women know everything anyway. As for Mrs Bennet, she is beyond caring.

"And I am the Rector's wife, while you and he are mere servants! Oh, I should not say *mere*. Forgive me, Annie. My mother is dying. My brain is not my own."

Mrs Bennet's breathing now almost crowds out the sound of Miss Mary's words. But I am listening intently; I want to know what she is saying. I wait.

"It was Luke's mother who suffered most, of course. First from his...from how he was related to her, in that way. I have yet to understand it! I thought it was marriage that brought such things about. But it seems not! And dear Hill was, as yet, unmarried? And had her child in secret? And he was looked after by whom? And returned here, how? Oh Annie, when will all this become clear?"

But now the rasping reaches even Miss Mary's troubled ears. I am busy assuming that her next words will be something like *When will all these questions be answered at last?* when Mrs Bennet breaks off, her body gives a sudden wrench from its prone position, and she sits up.

Bolt upright.

Her eyes stare, not to left nor right, not to Miss Mary nor myself, but directly in front, towards some eternal, or ancient, but certainly alarming place. Words come. They are steady, and they come from a place deep inside this dying frame.

"He did! All that time! He denied! I cried! It was true! As I feared!"

After *feared!*, the dying woman coughs, cannot stop coughing, and collapses back onto the bed.

In rushes Mother Drayton. She sees myself and Miss Mary sitting paralysed with shock. She orders Miss Mary: "Shift." To me: "Check there's water. If not, get more." To Miss Mary again: "Get the husband."

Miss Mary and I catch each other's eye. She is panicking. I know it's me who must say it. "Mrs Drayton, I fear… He will not come. I know he will not."

She looks at me sideways. "Then," she says, "you sit there, while I do what's needed." Nodding to Miss Mary: "Take hold of her hand. Speak to her. Say things. Nice things. What she's done. How she's been. Speak, speak. It'll calm her."

Mrs B is now silent. Everything is silent. Then Miss Mary says, in the faintest voice: "Surely she cannot hear?"

"They can hear. Right to the end. Speak!"

Miss Mary speaks. She is the Rector's wife, she knows how to say these things.

"My dear mother, our good Lord knows what you have suffered, and what you have borne. He bears it all with you. He knows, too, how you have showered your affection and concern upon us." She could have been, in this moment, the Rector in person. "Despite your great sufferings, you have loved us. The Lord blesses those who love. He will bless you. He will keep you. He keeps you, dear Mama, this moment and forever more. Our Lord knows it all. Take it to Him. That is where it belongs…"

And so on. But I have long since left the room, for I will get water and bring it to the death-bed. And, after that, I need to be with my children and my Luke.

12

After Mama

MARY DISCOVERED that when a significant death occurred there were consequences which followed almost of their own accord. Not a death such as Hill's, of course, but a death among her own people, the Gentry. The first consequence was the arrival of visitors to her father to pay their respects. Her sisters (except Jane) would come when summoned, but they did not count as visitors.

Mary consulted Annie about how her father should be dressed to receive the neighbours, and together they managed him: nudged, cajoled, and finally ordered him into the black suit made for the occasion of his own mother's death twenty years before. The suit was distinctly shiny, but nothing could be done about that; the neckerchief was designed to be tied in the old style, as though the Corsican Fiend had never existed; but mercifully there were no moth-holes. Thus accoutred, he must be seated in the parlour on an upright chair, cushioned to take account of his lumbago and what Annie called his 'pesky emerods'. The chair had been carefully placed between the fire and the bay window, at an angle which allowed him to sniff alongside the visitors but also, on occasion, to nod off without them being too offended.

She noticed that the arrivals were accompanied by a certain tentativeness on the door-knocker: a 'pat-er-pat', rather than a 'rat-a-tat-tat'. "Ah," said Annie when Mary mentioned it. "We call that 'the mourners' knock'." There were not as many visitors as Mary would have expected, and none stayed long, except poor demented Doctor Morgan, whom she had to show firmly out after half an hour.

The second consequence was that a Man of the Law appeared in a black-lined coach, together with an assistant bearing boxes. Both were to be conducted to the parlour, served with port and plates of sweetmeats on a silver tray, and left alone until sundry documents had been signed. At intervals during these sessions, Mr Bennet would stumble out of the room and totter along to the necessary house to deal with his personal needs; the Men of the Law did not seem to have any such needs of their own, but the level of port in the decanter went swiftly down and the plates of sweetmeats were left clean of every crumb.

A further visitor was the Man of the Church. This was dear Mr Jennings. The girls, when they were children, used to call him Jen-Jen, and when he called to offer his compliments to the dear Bennet family, Lyddy would sit on his knee and pull his moustaches. Sweetmeats were part of Jen-Jen's ritual; Jen-Jen declared Mrs Hill's sweetmeats second to none in all of Hertfordshire. Mr Jennings was long retired (his place taken by a large-boned young curate with no moustaches at all) and the old man remained quietly in his alms-house, unabashed by his lowered status as Perpetual Curate. But he must have persuaded the younger man to allow him this visit to Longbourn to mark a great event – Mrs Bennet's demise.

Seated in the parlour, Jen-Jen began with a trembling prayer. "Dear Lord, who consoled Martha and Mary in their distress, draw near to those who mourn. Thou who wept at the grave of Lazarus…"

Mary, sitting between her father and Mr Jennings with her eyes tight shut, felt a change in her father's breathing. It was not unlike the change that had occurred in her mother's breathing immediately before her death; she gasped at it – a gasp she was sure that Jen-Jen, even through his prayers, must hear. She wanted to open her eyes, but dared not. *Please*, she prayed, *oh consoling Lord, not another death!*

Mr Jennings remained oblivious, and prayed on. "Comfort us in our sorrow. Thou who promised Paradise to the thief who repented…"

Mr Bennet did not die. He simply opened his mouth (Mary's eyes, too, were now open) and howled. Mr Jennings, finding his prayers overwhelmed by the roar, brought them to an abrupt close. "Bring consolation. Through our Lord Je… Amen." He reached for Mary's arm, and she realised that he needed her help to stand up.

When he had gone, Mary provided her father with yet another cloth for his tears and left him alone. Then she returned to the packet of black-edged paper in the library. Now came the difficult task of informing her sisters of their mother's passing and the arrangements to be made for her funeral.

ꙅ

Annie, with Thwaite helping, smoothed each linen sheet and woollen blanket in layers. It was the final stage of reclaiming Mrs Bennet's bedchamber and bringing it into use for the invasion of the family. Which of the Misses Bennet, wondered Annie, would have the courage to sleep in this bed? Not Miss Lydia/Mrs Wickham (disgusted); nor Mrs Darcy (unthinkable); nor Mrs Bingley (regretfully unable to attend). So that left Miss Kitty, or Miss Mary/Mrs Needleman. There was always Mr Bennet, but that too was unthinkable, on account of the long years since he had ceased sharing his wife's bed, or even her bedchamber.

Miss Kitty? Well, she was a strange one and no mistake. She seemed to have no opinions of her own, but simply followed one or other of her sisters. Time was, when Annie herself was a little servant girl following Mrs Hill from room to room, Miss Kitty would be running after her two big sisters, whining, "Me too! Don't be mean, let me in too!" Then, when her little boobies were sprouting – rather late, though Miss Lyddy's two years afterwards were somewhat early – she'd follow in Lydia's wake, whining a dozen different versions of the same sentiment. She would never follow Miss Mary about. No one ever did. Yet it was clear now that Miss Mary would decide about the bedchambers.

Strange, thought Annie, how impossible it was to call Miss Mary anything but 'Miss Mary'. The phrase 'Mrs Rectory' had occurred to her, though of course she wouldn't dream of saying it.

Meanwhile, there were other matters to be dealt with, and smartish.

Thwaite straightened up in the way that an old woman might, putting weary hands on her hips and breathing shallowly. Annie unthinkingly mirrored her stance.

"Listen," she said. "We must have words, you and I."

Any remaining energy drained from Thwaite's face. "Is it that obvious?"

"It is. Come, sit yourself down." Annie went round the end of the bed and pulled up the old nursing chair that always lived in this room, even though Mrs Bennet had never nursed any of her own. Thwaite perched on it, and Annie knelt beside. She could have sat on the bed, but she wanted to be eye-to-eye with the poor girl. It could so easily be herself in this situation. Or any woman.

"So – you've a follower?"

Thwaite looked puzzled. "No!"

"Not one of the gardeners lurking around the rhododendrons?"

Thwaite gave a short laugh. "No, there was one like that, but he got knocked dead in a drinking bout a year back."

"Any other of the indoor staff?" Annie knew there'd be plenty to choose from.

"No, no."

"Then it's one of *them*." No need to explain. The lord-high-mucketty-mucks.

Thwaite slouched. "Can't say. Won't say."

Annie put a hand on the girl's knee. "You've to look after yourself, you know. Lay blame far or wide, but lay it somewhere. Else it's all on you. You've got to name him. Whoever."

Thwaite knocked Annie's hand off her knee with a swipe of her hand. "Never!"

"Never ever?"

"Never ever, ever."

Annie sighed. "Very well. But here's a question. Were there just one?" Doubt shot across Thwaite's face. "I've got to ask."

"One." A kind of terror seized the girl's pale face. "Only one."

"Were it Mr Darcy?"

"No. No no no."

Annie breathed again, got up off her knees and went to sit leaning against the bed-post. "So. You need time. The thing may come away of its own accord. They do, specially first ones. It *is* a first?"

"Aye, it is! What kind of a girl d'you take me for?"

"Just asking. They'll be watching your monthlies. They do, don't they – report to Mrs Reynolds in places like Pemberley. Can you get some other girl to wear your towels once or twice if your monthlies come the same time?"

"Nay." The Derbyshire of her came out in her distress. "We're odd, we two. They don't know what to make of us, and I rose too quick for them. They don't have truck with us. Any case, I'm heaving up me breakfast. And me tea."

"There's other reasons for losing your innards: meat's off at the post-house, or mussels. Mussels, I'll tell 'em! Mrs Hill was sick as a dog with those mussels only a week before she died, I'll swear blind!"

"Oh Annie, you're such a friend."

"We've all been there – or been near."

"I think it was nerves, anyway."

"Was it your first? When you, you know?"

"First ever."

"Nice or horrible?"

"Bit o' both. He was sort of *kind*. I was so scared. I knew from me Ma what'd happen, like as not. But he just wouldn't…"

"Wouldn't stop?"

"Wouldn't stop. Ma told me to watch out for 'em, but not how to stop 'em once they were started."

"Oh Thwaite…"

"Esther, please."

"Esther."

After a pause, Esther said, "Folks talk about ways to get rid of it."

"You can't have Mr B's gin. He'd notice. Even in his state."

"There's women who do it for money, though, isn't there? Them as lay out bodies, they sometimes do it?"

"Don't go that road! Don't ever, please, Esther! There was a maid-of-all-work at Netherfield got that done. It went wrong; it was terrible, and they buried her. Don't *think* of it! Take *care* of yourself!"

"It's all very well saying that! What am I to *do*?"

Annie got up on her feet. "Let's start with you not being sick. I'll get you some ginger and squeezed lemon. Meanwhile, sorry for changing the subject, but we've got this pesky funeral to get through."

∽

Seated at her father's desk in the library, faced with the ribboned pack of black-edged paper, Mary took a sip of water from her glass, pulled at the black bow, drew out a sheet, and decided to write first to Robert.

> ~~Dear Mr Needleman~~ – *My dear husband* – *it is with dismay and distress that I have to ~~inform you of~~ share with you the sad news of my mother's ~~demise~~ passing. I was ~~fortunate enough to be~~ at her side as she left us.*

She could not go on in this way. One striking-out could be overlooked, but this was too much. Lamentable as was the waste of paper, she folded over the errant page, laid it to one side and reached for another.

Her mother's staring eyes rose before her; her mother's shrieks echoed in her ears. *He did! As I feared!*

She shook off the vision, and silently repeated her comforting words. *My breastplate of faith, my helmet of salvation.* Her stays were her breastplate, her rampant curls were her helmet. There was work to be done, and only herself to do it. She took another sip of water.

My dear husband: It is with great sorrow that I
have to impart... I was at her side as she left us...

Then the practicalities, the date and so on.

I am your affectionate and sorrowing wife, Mary.

Then the folding: it must be a neat, straight fold.

Now the seal. How exciting, as a child, she had found the process of sealing a letter! The stick of red wax, was it the third drawer down on the left? Yes, here it was. Beside it lay the seal itself: the Longbourn seal, its design procured from faraway St Albans by Mr Bennet after much nagging from his wife. Mary laid these ready on the desk and, with a swish of dark skirt from her mourning dress, fetched a candle from the mantelshelf to melt a few red drops; they fell like drips of life-blood on the deathly packet. Then she applied the seal: not too much, nor too little; lean it this way, then that. It was a sign of strength, this seal: her own strength, and that of her marriage to the man who would tear it open and understand her bereavement, her responsibility, her need.

Now to the others. She had spent more than half an hour on the first; the others she could do more quickly. Was there enough ink? Yes, Annie had ensured that the well was full.

She wrote them in order of their birth.

My beloved sister Jane: I have the grievous task of

informing you that our dear mother left us on… Please break the news gently to your husband, who, Mary knew, would be the one to read this to Jane – *to the children…*

Dearest sister Lizzy – I hope you have dear Darcy at your side as I impart to you the saddest of all possible news…

She took another sip and gave a nod to her own position: the third, the middle one, alone.

Dear sister Kitty (c/o her sister Mrs Wickham, at the latest of many rented addresses) *The funeral… Reception afterwards here at Longbourn…*

Now Lyddy herself. How would she feel about losing the mother against whom she had rebelled without ceasing? Mary could not answer that question even on her own behalf; still less could she answer it on Lydia's.

Dear Mr and Mrs Wickham: …to be held at St Bride's Church, Churchtown. Our old friend Mr Jennings is on hand to assist, though the main service will be led by… On this occasion of our bereavement, I look forward to meeting you in sombre and sober fashion at the church.

What was it that Lizzy said about Lyddy? That she might in some unfathomable sense have been wiser about the purpose of marriage than she herself, or

Jane, or anyone? That was not possible! Surely?

Would Wickham come? Would Bingley, or Darcy? She must turn her attention to these questions, for Annie had asked her to decide where everyone – family and accompanying staff – should be accommodated. They ran through the numbers and concluded that there would be a bed available for each, but only if Mrs Bennet's old room were used, and if husbands were willing to head back to the Blue Boar. Annie had murmured that the men might appreciate the distance between themselves and the red-eyed mourning of their womenfolk.

Mary was certain that Robert would stand at her side in the church. And she was relieved at the suggestion that the men repair to the Blue Boar. In fact, she would propose taking these letters to Meryton herself today, if Luke and Rosie were available, and while she was there she could call in at the Blue Boar to reserve some rooms. As to Mrs Bennet's bed, she could tell Annie that in her opinion Kitty was the least likely to object if asked to place herself between those old sheets.

‹⁄›

Annie felt dismay, even outrage. Only one of the sisters' husbands turned up for their mother-in-law's funeral, and that was the most recent: Reverend Mr Needleman! However, though Miss Lizzy hadn't managed to drag or cajole her dear Fitzy to Longbourn, she had brought folks with her who would be considerably more useful: two extra maids-of-all-work. And someone else.

Miss Lizzy, on her arrival, bustled past Annie with

a quick explanation: "I have scraped as many staff as I can. Mrs Reynolds was persuaded: your need is the greater." She didn't mention the other someone. Annie only came across this one when Luke nudged her elbow and pointed at the pile of luggage at the foot of the front steps.

"See?" he said.

"See what? I'll help if I can, but I'm needed in the rooms!"

"I know that." He flicked his head. "See there!"

Annie was none the clearer, but took a step sideways. And there, hidden behind the pile of trunks and baskets and assorted hat-boxes, stood a very small person. Neither child nor adult, like a wisp of wind-battered hawthorn clinging to the edge of a moor: a person of twists and turns. She wore a child-size bonnet, and her gaze was lowered to the ground.

Annie knew immediately who she was.

An autumn wind was quickening, and her first impulse was to get the poor mite in out of the cold.

"Luke," she said, nodding to him as he lifted a couple of boxes one on top of another, "I'll take her to Thwaite. To Esther."

Avoiding the luggage, she put out a hand to the mite. "Will you be Milly? I'll show you the way to your sister." The tiny person did not take her hand – maybe she could not? – but followed on.

Annie had to slow down as they climbed the steps, for one of the girl's feet was turned aside and it put her whole gait askew. "How was the journey? There'll have been mud yesterday with that dreadful rain. Now, where is she? Thwaite. Esther."

They stood in the hall for a moment while Annie worked out that Thwaite would now have returned from Mary's employ into Mrs Darcy's, and so was likely to be found in Miss Lizzy's (and Miss Jane's) old room. "We'll go up here." Up the narrow servants' stairs, with their own door, to the right of the wide main stairs.

Annie led, and again slowed, because the small person's tread behind her was so small and so very nearly silent. In the dark of the staircase Annie pictured the small face with its jaw jutting to one side. How the poor child must be struggling at every move! She must trust that this – no, she was not a *child*, she was a *person* – would follow on, and not disappear back into the thin air whence she had come.

Servants' landing. Annie glanced behind: she was still there. Under the threadbare bonnet, every feature of her face showed strain. Below, her body likewise.

Annie tore her eyes away. Mrs Hill had taught her it was rude to stare, whatever station in life was the person before you.

"Through here and we'll find her."

From the main landing it was just a few steps to Miss Jane and Miss Lizzy's room. This girl, like her sister Thwaite, must find Longbourn tiny in comparison with Pemberley. Annie knocked, and after a moment Thwaite opened the door. Annie moved out of the way.

Thwaite's hands leapt to her face. "Mill-...!" She took a step forward, and the sisters were entwined; then, immediately, disentangled.

Annie stood dumbed by the wave of confusion and

joy that had surged momentarily between the two girls. Oh, but she should have taken Milly up the attic stairs and left her on the top landing, in servants' territory! – for, if Mrs Darcy came out of her room now, into this sudden joy, who knew whether she would behave tenderly towards it or be infuriated by it?

But Annie heard Miss Lizzy call across her room towards the door: "Dear me, I should have mentioned, how useful it might be if you had your sister with you, for all that is to be done?"

Thwaite bobbed her thanks to Annie and whisked her sister out of sight and into the room.

At the same moment, Luke appeared, backwards, bearing a small trunk with the Pemberley crest on its side. Annie didn't say a word about what had happened, but skipped out of his way through the door.

◦◦

Despite the fact that pride was the deadliest of all sins, Mary did feel proud of the five of them as they sat in the family pew on the pulpit side of the chancel steps: Miss Catherine Bennet, Mrs Elizabeth Darcy, Mrs Lydia Wickham, herself (Mrs Needleman), and the Rector of Humbole, the Reverend Mr Robert Needleman.

First into the pew, of course, had come Mr Bennet: an aged, shaking man. He leant upon Kitty. Mary, her pride turning momentarily to shame, saw him as an object of pity in the eyes of the parishioners assembled in the nave. Swiftly she reminded herself that those parishioners had, over the years, been grateful to the Bennet family for numerous services: the balls they had paid for in the Meryton Assembly Rooms, the Christmas festivities they had hosted under their own roof, and the occasional year when the sisters had walked amongst their lowly cottages with gifts of leftover fare. Recently, though, the community had seen little of the ailing and nervous woman and her shambling husband, and their absence must have dulled the memory of such delights.

Mary's husband had taken the Mail coach for speed, and she felt that a degree of pride was indeed permitted her in standing here beside him, in his clerical garb, in her own family church. On his arrival Mr Needleman had leaned his face towards one of his wife's cheeks in an almost-kiss. Luke, who had hitched Rosie to the chaise to go and collect him, must have noticed such a thing. Now the parish folk would see that her husband was tall and dignified, and would probably judge him less forbidding than Mr Darcy yet with more backbone than Mr Bingley.

Dear Jen-Jen had been waiting outside the church, his moustaches drooping, to shake her hand and be personally introduced to her husband. "Ah! The *Rector*! May I congratulate you on your good fortune, sir, in capturing the heart of such…" He waved his hand towards Mary. "Such a *spiritual* young lady." 'Spiritual'. She had never heard the word used for a mere human being like herself.

More important to Mary was a fact no one else could guess at: that in order to make the journey to Hertfordshire for this melancholy occasion, Mr Needleman must have sacrificed his regular midweek sermon-writing session with his friend Mr Hepplecraft.

The service, devoid of fulsome eulogies, devoid (on the advice of Mr Jennings) even of a long sermon, ended with a simple homily on the theme of death being the gateway to eternity. The final act was a relevant hymn, recommended to Lizzy by Thwaite, about God moving in mysterious ways His wonders to perform. Mary was particularly struck by the lines: *He plants His footsteps in the sea And rides upon the storm.* Pondering on Thwaite's recent lapse into illness and the arrival of her minuscule sister, she hoped that God did not have any particular storm in mind. Maybe it was the storm of tears that affected the youngest Bennet daughter during that last hymn. While Miss Kitty's face was impassive throughout, Lyddy, who little realised how hard her family had struggled to change her from Bennet to Wickham, was the only one who wept her heart out for the loss of her poor mother.

☙

Esther could breathe again. It was not the ginger and lemon infusion that settled her stomach and her soul. It was Milly. It was being *Doovus* again.

Before clambering into one of the two large coaches provided by the undertaker to take family and staff to the church, she'd tucked Milly up in bed to recover from the three-day battering of the journey. Then she knelt beside her for a few precious moments, murmuring small questions and receiving small answers.

How had she managed it? Milly had stood at Mrs Darcy's door, relentlessly, repeating three words to the mistress as she moved graciously to and fro: *come*, and *Fwaite*, and *please*.

What had induced Mrs Darcy to give way? No notion, murmured Milly. Just, at the last possible moment, without pausing in her movement, she'd said, *You are small, and those two are not plump, there may be room. Make haste then.*

"I'll tell one of them maids to bring you up supper," Esther promised as she tore herself away. "It'll be broth and bread, they're that stretched wi' the funeral tea, but Annie'll slip you a slice of the ham. It's a good ham, almost as good as Pemberley's. They've splashed out."

Now, with the crumbs swept from parlour and drawing room, the remaining food saved for the servants' meal tomorrow, the dishes washed, the grates scraped out and re-laid, Mrs Darcy settled at last, and her own face wiped and her teeth rubbed, Esther climbed in beside Milly and snuggled close.

"Doovus."

"Doovus."

Together: "Esther-Joel-Milly-Ma-Pa-all-ov'us."

Then they unpacked their special memories. Over the years these memories had worked themselves into stories they must tell; those had expanded into the pictures they must embroider, and that in turn gave over into every detail of what they knew and felt about their family; and so they created a history of what they had possessed, and what they had lost. Each time they told and embroidered it, and paused to feel

235

their feelings again, they stroked one another, held one another, breathed in time to one another, asking and responding in little murmurings and reassurances, giggling often, and nestling into each other until they were one again. Spiralling round and around in this way, they finally came to this day, and what it might hold.

Esther: Talked with Annie. About…about.

Milly: Mmm. Good?

Esther: Goo-ood. She says it may come away.

Milly: An' if not?

Esther: She says, tek things day-be-day. Tek care. Not too hasty.

Milly: Mrs D'll've wondered why I begged to come. You've bin away afore an' I've not begged.

Esther: Mebbee. But she's busy with her Pa, an Kitty an' Lyddy, an' all that. Mebbee she's too busy to think owt about me.

Milly: Mebbeeee…?

Esther: C'm on, Mill. What're you thinking?

Milly: This 'not be hasty'. You gotta be hasty. Iss gotta come away, or else.

Esther: She said I can't go at the gin. An' she knows a woman as did that other thing an' the girl copped it.

Milly: There's the towels. Laundry maids'll've noticed yours aren't there.

Esther: Annie said I should borrow soiled uns from some other maid.

Milly: An' you canna.

Esther: So Mrs Reynolds'll most likely get to know.

Two joint sighs.

Esther: Ah, Mill, what's to do?

Milly: We'll do as wiv allus done. Even after Ma, even after Joel, even after Da. Allus, allus done. You an' me, Essy, we'll do. You see.

∽

The embarrassed neighbours were gone at last, and the extra servants from Pemberley thanked for their services and conducted to their low-ceilinged attic room. Annie had scarcely had time to lay the sheets, dust the floor over and put a fresh bowl of water by the window. At the last minute she'd run back down to warm up a bottle and put it in one of the beds. They'd have to share it, but that was a maid's life.

In her first moment of the day on her own, on the servants' landing, she leaned against a door jamb and gave herself the chance to turn from being housekeeper-cum-maid-of-all-work to grabbing an old cloak, treading the cobbles over to the cottage and becoming a mother again. Luke would have mopped the children's faces and popped them into bed, but she knew they'd lie awake until she came to kiss them goodnight.

She went through the sisters in her mind, in no particular order, one by one.

Mrs Darcy: exhausted, and grateful to Thwaite for attending to her every need. But she did manage to say to Annie, "You are a dear girl. You have done my mother proud. I am sorry to end the day such a limp flower. I little knew how one's mother's death would weary one. I think back to you and dear Hill, and wonder how you kept yourself upright through it all.

Thank you."

Mrs Wickham. Coming out of church, her face had been surprisingly tear-stained. But she bounced back soon after, and tucked into a good ham tea with plenty of raisin bread to follow. She and Miss Kitty had put their heads together about who should sleep where and told Annie that, as Kitty had chosen their mother's room, it would be a mercy for her, Lydia, to have their old room to herself at last. She undiplomatically proclaimed how much she missed dear Wickham, who was at the present time offering his many talents to the citizens of Bath; she would set off to join him immediately in the morning. Annie knew for a fact that Lydia had not consulted Luke about the use of the Longbourn coach, which Miss Mary needed for use by her dear Rector. Maybe Miss Lyddy thought it a neat fit, that Luke should transport her and her luggage to Meryton for her journey to Bath – unescorted! – then do a swift turnaround to collect Mr Needleman from the Blue Boar for spending the day with his wife at Longbourn? Mrs Darcy's eyebrows had shot up to hear of Miss Lyddy's plan, for she (and Mary with her, willy-nilly) were to stay on here at Longbourn for at least a week and maybe even ten days. Together with Miss Kitty, the Pemberley staff and her indispensable Thwaite, but without help from Miss Lyddy, they would deal with the many and various matters arising from this lamentable death.

Miss Kitty, now. This young lady was comfortably settled between her mother's sheets. It seemed Miss Kitty had no susceptibility to ghosts. In fact, Annie concluded that she was impervious to any outside intervention whatsoever. She had asked one of the Pemberleys to help with her stays, but in other ways she could cope quite easily, thank you all the same. Miss Kitty had approached Annie to make her intentions known. "I will remain at Lizzy's side, and my father's. I am willing to be at the family's disposal for as long as it takes to become adjusted to the new situation." Annie's eyebrows needed to be kept firmly in position when she heard this. Miss Kitty was making play for the post of Senior Sister.

Now, given this brief moment of reflection, she slid into Miss Kitty's viewpoint and saw what advantage she might be hoping to gain: it was nothing less than residency at Longbourn as its new mistress. Yes, Mr Bennet was irksome, but he was becoming increasingly helpless; if she could persuade Lizzy to let Longbourn keep those extra Pemberley maids, the old rascal's need for care could be accommodated. That would leave Kitty with a home of her own, an independent if modest income, and a social circle she could re-enter without too much effort. If she were willing to work at it, she could cut quite a figure in Meryton.

That left Miss Mary. She'd been the queen of the day so far as Annie was concerned: the one to help Mr Jennings to the door when he was stumbling, the one who caught Annie's eye and pointed at the half slice of raisin bread on the floor that would stick to somebody's feet if it weren't picked up this very minute. Miss Mary was happy. That was clear enough. She was visibly 'Mrs Rectory' on her childhood turf.

But this man, this Reverend Mr Needleman. Flora, before she died, had been frank with Annie about her opinion of the marriage. Miss Mary might think herself happy in the first instance; but in the long run, this Rectory chalice would likely turn out to be a poisoned one. Flora had warned Miss Mary as honestly as she could, but Miss Mary had made her choice. Now she must take what came to her as a result.

Right. That was the Bennet sisters taken care of. Now she was free to go and kiss John-James and Edie goodnight.

She grabbed the cloak and clutched it around her as she crossed the yard, and had a quick thought about the morrow. Poor Rosie was lame with all this to-ing and fro-ing. Would Luke think the old nag was fit to take the coach to and from Meryton for the purposes of Miss Lyddy and Mr Needleman, especially if it looked like rain?

∾

Luke was furious. Furious with Mrs Bennet for dying, and in so doing, taking up everyone's time and energy. Furious with Mr Bennet for letting himself go to pieces in the face of an event that could, after all, have been easily predicted, but prevented Mr B from doing business – like signing off the money for a fresh horse that would allow poor Rosie to go out to grass. Most of all, he was furious with himself for pushing Rosie between the bars of the coach and even giving her a touch of the whip to keep her going against the wind and the rain.

His fury bounced with the bouncing of the coach through ruts and puddles, and blew gusts through him like the ones blowing through its flimsy roof. He didn't mind Miss Lyddy. Miss Lyddy was predictable, which was a mercy among the Bennets any day of the week. The one he did mind was this Rector fellow with his poncy ways. 'My man' indeed! A man of the church should show respect for all levels of society, should he not? No, that was only the Mr Jenningses of this world, and there weren't many such as he. Most were dandies like this Needle fellow. Luke hoped there'd been bedbugs in the Blue Boar to keep him company last night.

Annie had been up for a cuddle, and it was lovely. They'd to be careful about the time of the month, as she was anxious about getting caught. They mustn't fall for any more babbies, or Annie wouldn't have time to be a proper housekeeper; she'd be back on maid's wages and acting as underling to whoever Mr Bennet took on as new housekeeper. What's worse, if Miss Kitty got the chance to pitch up here at Longbourn and throw her weight about (as Annie had hinted she might), neither an incoming housekeeper nor Miss Kitty would take kindly to an erstwhile superior breathing down their necks, and the whole family might be thrown out on their ear.

He pulled his cap further down, wiped the raindrops away, and slowed Rosie down so Miss Lyddy, inside, wouldn't notice. Though Miss Lyddy didn't notice anything much.

Think on… How many years had Miss Lyddy been Mrs Wickham? Year upon year! So why had she not fallen for a babby or six? Was something wrong with her, or did she know something the rest of the world didn't? Mind you, Wickham being Wickham, he'd know all the tricks. Word was that our Wickham'd had more ladies than the rest of them'd had hot dinners. And he'd not got enough of the ready to pay off those lasses he likely used if they got into trouble. So whatever tricks he employed must be worth the price of rum.

Well, here was Meryton, and the Mail Halt where he must tie up Rosie (whose breathing he did not like the sound of) then hold the umbrella over Miss Lyddy till she was safely installed. Then he must go and see if Mr Needle-me was in the lobby of the Blue Boar ready to brave the rain and be driven back to Longbourn and into the arms of his recent bride. Or not, as the case might be.

ᏻᏅ

Mary sat on the piano stool in the small upstairs room. This was her dear old pianoforte, tinny in tone compared with the Viennese piano at the Rectory, but it was the one on which she had learned to play, and it resonated with memories of dear Mr Prendergast. Today her fingers were like pale half-cooked sausages blundering over the keys. Her head seethed like a whirlpool: with irritation at Kitty's assumption of a senior role, though she was a full two years younger than Mary; with repulsion at her father sneezing his snuff all over the drawing room; with anxiety about Luke and the coach's lateness in returning from the Blue Boar, and with frustration at the rain which prevented her from walking towards Meryton in search of her strangely present, yet alarmingly absent, husband.

In her letter to her husband inviting him to the funeral, had she actually specified that he was welcome to stay on afterwards and play his part as her husband under this roof? Surely, yes? Or had these words resided only in her head and not made their way onto the page? He had not replied. He had simply appeared in the church; stood with the family around the gaping rectangular hole in the churchyard; taken his turn to throw a trowel of soil over the coffin; and returned to Longbourn for the funeral tea. She recalled him standing aside to let her go before him through the front door; then she had been too busy with the neighbours and their ham teas to think where her husband might have got to. Luke told Annie later, who told Mary later still, that Mr Needley had had no need of the coach, thank you, but would walk back to Meryton to take his lodging, as reserved, at the Blue Boar.

And hoped to see her on the morrow.

Had Annie said that? Or had she, Mary, invented it because she so desired it?

The piano keys clashed. Her sausagey fingers refused to stretch to a wide enough chord. The shade of Mr Prendergast was nowhere to be seen. Mr Prendergast had left the area quite suddenly. There was talk of a scandal. But the Bennets did not listen to scandals, still less ask questions about them.

Oddly, she needed Mr Prendergast now almost more than she needed her husband. She wanted him to teach her how to play the piano truly well; to try out some Couperin and Clementi as well as his beloved Haydn. That was all she wanted: to play the piano, and to play it well. And everything conspired to prevent her.

Down below, outside, she heard crunching. Feet on gravel.

Feet? Not wheels? No horse, no coach? Two feet, not four?

She ignored it, returned her fingers to the keys, and played the first piece she had ever learned by Bach: dum-diddle-diddle-dum dum dum. It came out perfectly.

Why? Why could she at some times be perfect and at other times miserably fail? Our Lord had said, 'Be ye therefore perfect, even as your Father which is in Heaven is perfect' (Matthew 5:48). She could never obey that command.

Then there was her husband's philosophy of a Great Chain of Being, from God at the top, through the angels and the saints, on and on, down to the smallest of creatures. Like the tiny spider she could see up on the wall there, an inch away from the brocade curtains.

What might be her particular link in that Great Chain? And, if there was one link for Miss-Mary-now-Mrs-Needleman, how was that link to be found, and lived? And what of dear Jane, so achingly absent from Longbourn at this time of her mother's death and burial? She had been, in her bloom, a saint, and perfect, ready to become, in due time, an angel. But where was she now? In limbo? Purgatory? Mary had heard those terms and, fearing they might be Roman in origin, shied away from them in terror.

Here were footsteps. Outside the piano room door. Odd-sounding footsteps.

The door burst open. Annie appeared, pink and flustered. She looked at Mary as if she didn't know what to say, then turned to someone behind her. "You shouldn't've come up! *I* could've told her!" Then, to her: "It's Rosie, she's in trouble!"

Annie came fully into the room, and Luke pushed in after her.

He had no boots on, and Mary saw there were darns – Annie's neatly woven darns – in his socks. His cap was in his hand, and he was drenched everywhere except on parts of his socks.

"It was after I'd done with Miss Lyddy, she just fell in upon herself, did Rosie, and I ran into the Blue Boar to get a man who knew about 'osses, and there was Jack Anfield who does, so he comes out and, straight as a die, he takes one look at her…"

Annie interrupted: "She doesn't need to know all that, Luke."

Luke overrode Annie, and continued. "But I need to tell it! Her belly was sunk to the ground beneath her, her head uplifted, her mouth open. Her rump up in the air an' all, and the stink was summat else. Jack Anfield said Sorry, old mate. In that tone, you know, when someone's done for. Rosie, she were my friend, she were. An' I were her friend an' all." He sniffed a huge sniff.

Annie took his hand. "Then Mr Needleman came out?"

"Ah, then Mr, um, came out, and he looked, and he said that's a dreadful sight, my man, and not to worry about him, he had his bag packed and could walk to the… And Jack Anfield went to get some of his mates and a cart, for she needed to be taken to the knackers', and I said I needed to go with her. You can't just leave 'em, not when they've served you like Rosie's served us!"

Annie again: "And Mr Needleman said that he…"

"Oh, your Mr Needley. He said he had a sermon to write in Derby, or some such. Some person was in need of him or summat. I couldn't tell; I were weeping. Don't call me daft, Miss Mary! I think that's what he said. He weren't coming back to Longbourn, anyway."

"And he said," Annie concluded, "please to convey his apologies to his dear wife, he was sure she had much family business to do, and he would await her return to Humbole, entirely at her convenience."

13

Longbourn to Humbole, Again

EARING THE GRANDFATHER clock strike seven (now that Luke was winding it regularly instead of Papa), Mary experienced a moment of sudden clarity. She wished to return home as soon as was feasible.

Her husband had left peremptorily; she would leave peremptorily too. In fact, she would leave this very day. For today was a Wednesday, which meant that she would reach home safely before the Sabbath.

Home was now Humbole, not Longbourn.

Her room here, she realised, had scarcely changed since she had left it in June. The shabby Turkish rug lay a little farther out from the bed, and when she lit a candle in the night to use the chamber pot she noticed that her own pot, the one with the blue spiral design around the rim, had been exchanged for one with a square jade-coloured pattern around its curves. That jade pattern had been Jane's favourite; its home was under Jane's bed. Longbourn had made changes almost without her noticing, or, indeed, caring. She was weary of being here.

She imagined another day – worse, another five days, or ten – of inhaling the stale lavender from her mother's wardrobe as they sorted her clothes. How repellent were the smells of both her parents. Worst of all was the sickly smokiness of Papa's snuff. How she loathed the coughing and spitting, the pipes and pinchings around his perpetual snuff-sniffing. She could not bear it.

Instead of waiting for Lizzy to announce she was ready, Mary decided that she would return home alone. She would no longer strive to be a perfect daughter. She would be imperfect. Lizzy and Kitty would have to manage the rest of the work without her. Annie had arranged for Mama's unmentionable garments to be collected today by the more respectable of Meryton's rag-men, and Lizzy was to pack the gowns and petticoats into a spare trunk and distribute them around the staff at Pemberley. When Lizzy enquired whether any of the sisters wished one of Mama's dresses as a keepsake, there had been a collective shudder they recalled poor Mama's girth.

She rose, used the chamber pot again, and dressed herself.

Lizzy's insistence on her having some sort of lady's maid from among the Pemberleys had vanished entirely in the fluster surrounding their mother's death. Thank the good Lord for that, she thought, contemplating her stays. She had married a clergyman who cared not a whit for women's fashions. Though, now she thought about it, Mr Needleman was very particular about his own clothes. The day she left for Longbourn he had set off in the opposite direction, into Derby, with a complaint about the fit of his latest suit. As for Mr Hepplecraft, the lace cuffs alone must have doubled the cost of his shirts.

Life was complicated. She had never expected to understand this institution called marriage. Though her husband's departure without a word had been a shock, she would take life, and her marriage, step by step, day by day.

She made herself ready to go down for breakfast, wondering how she should announce to Lizzy her intention to depart. Then she remembered that Luke was in mourning for poor dear Rosie, and that the Longbourn coach still lay abandoned outside the Blue Boar. Such factors would be cited in any argument about her leaving today.

Lizzy and Kitty were already seated, and Annie whisked in and out of the room. Papa was never up this early, as he needed Annie to help him dress and must wait till the rest of the family had broken their fast.

Mary, shaking open her linen napkin, enquired of Annie: "How is Luke this morning?" As she watched Annie's hand replacing an empty milk jug with a full one, she heard Hill's dying voice inside her head: *Luke. He is your brother.*

Lizzy looked up and said, "The poor old mare.

How upsetting."

Kitty was staring out of the window – rain again – and said nothing.

Did they also think: *We are talking about our brother?*

Annie said from beside Mary's shoulder, "He's not had much sleep. Tossing and turning, brooding over how he'll find another. Which reminds me, Miss Lizzy. Might you get your father to sign off a payment?" *If things had been done differently...*

"Of course, Annie dear. It shall be done today. Tell Luke to have no anxiety on that account." *... differently, Luke would have had authority over us all in matters of family finance.*

Kitty said, "I hope we can afford a better nag than Rosie."

At that, Annie disappeared away through the door. "Toast?" called Kitty. But Annie did not return.

"I enjoyed riding Rosie," said Mary. "She was slow, and kind."

"You cannot use the word *kind* about a *horse!*"

"I can, Kitty. And I expect Luke would agree with me." *If he were known as our brother, he would have reprimanded Kitty for such a remark.*

Lizzy said sharply, "Now. Today's tasks."

Mary seized the moment to announce her plan. "I must proceed in the direction of Derbyshire today. I apologise if this should inconvenience either of you, but the Festival of All Souls approaches and I must be at St Michael and All Angels in Humbole to support my husband."

Lizzy stared. "We are not yet finished with our

work! How will you go? I will retain the Pemberley coach and the services of Thwaite. How can you possibly go?"

"I can take the stagecoach."

"On your... All *alone*?"

"Lydia travels unescorted. If it is good enough for Mrs Wickham, it is good enough for me."

"Mrs Needleman," said Lizzy, "is not to be compared with Mrs Wickham."

Kitty coughed into her tea-cup.

Mary took no notice. "I wondered if Thwaite's sister might accompany me. When Hill was ailing, she very much proved her worth."

The door opened, and it was Thwaite rather than Annie who returned with more toast. Mary took the piece offered her and continued to address Lizzy. "I could arrange a hackney carriage to take us to Meryton, and after that the journey would be much as before." She reached for the butter and then for the cherry jam.

Lizzy looked dumbfounded.

"Milly, I think she is called, would stay beside me at the various post-houses. Given her particular needs, I would expect our fellow travellers to treat us with especial respect."

Lizzy found her voice again, and spoke to Thwaite. "But did I not, Thwaite, expressly bring your sister here so that she could be a source of strength to you in your illness? And are you not feeling strengthened, and more able to fulfil the tasks which Miss Mary, I should say Mrs Needleman, seems suddenly prepared to relinquish?"

Thwaite's voice was low. "I am strengthened, Mrs

Darcy; thank you for asking. But of course, if you should choose otherwise…"

"I do not so choose! Mary, I think you could give some attention to my feelings at this time, given that poor George is to embark on his first steps in the outside world while I am away from home!"

Mary felt a wave of guilt at this accusation. Another wave followed it – that of inadequacy in the face of Lizzy's superiority to herself in every way. At the same time, she could hear her mother's plaintive voice echoing through Lizzy's: *Nobody considers my poor nerves!* She spread her butter and her jam very carefully, and waited.

But the silence, and the clinking of knife against dish and plate, was so loud that she finally said, "For Thwaite's sake, then, I will not ask for Milly's services on my journey. I shall simply continue with my original plan, and return to Humbole by stagecoach, alone. The Meryton hackney carriage will suffice for the first mile, since we have suffered the loss of dear Rosie. Give my sympathy to Luke, would you, Annie?" She looked down at her toast, and before her next bite said, "This is excellent cherry jam. It was our mother's favourite, I recall?"

෴

Now that the minx is away at her original home, and my RN is doing duty at his wife's side, and *moreover* (as they say for emphasis here in England) the season of All Hallows requires us to honour the spirits of the departed, I give due honour to my dear Father and Mother. I lay the books and texts for All Hallows beside my bed, and morning and evening I open them at familiar phrases: *I beheld, and lo, a great multitude, which no man could number, of all nations, and kindreds, and peoples, and tongues, stood before the throne.*

I honour my Father, who brought myself and my Mother with him over the water, together with Reverend Mr Prunty. I shall mourn my Father's loss until the day that I too am called to meet my Maker. He was a man with thoughts so deep I scarce could fathom them, but with words that I could mostly understand; a man with a care for his wife and only child, and a sorrow for the loss of the former that could not be repaired until he joined her at the feet of the Eternal Divine. I honour my Mother, whose nurture and schooling in the ways of the world enabled me to learn, and work, and progress in my profession of housekeeper, without the necessity of compromising either my principles or my faith; albeit with the necessity of remaining on this side of the sea, far away from County Down.

The words 'multitude which no man could number' remind me of the news which I recently received from Mr Prunty: that he and his dear wife have added to their family. A fifth daughter, whom they will call Anne. He chided me for forgetting, yet again, the revised spelling of his family's name, and gives the postal address of the parsonage in the community of which he is now Perpetual Curate. I trust that their new home is large enough to accommodate this burgeoning, and that his hard-worked weaver neighbours will gather the family to their hearts. Reports reach us about rebellious northerners in general, and cloth-makers in particular. I have no doubt that Mr Prunty (yes, I will retain that name in the privacy of my own thoughts) will serve them faithfully, whatever odours are emitted from the effluent that runs, he tells me, darkly down their cobbled streets.

Here in Humbole we are more blessed. During RN's absence, Mr Hepplecraft has ridden over here twice, and I have had the pleasure of his cultured discourse without interruption. He introduced me to the work of some Continental artists beyond the main-stream, which he has encountered through the aristocratic circles on his mother's side of the family. One, to whom he takes a particular fancy, goes by the name of Caravaggio; he has seen several of this man's paintings. (Copies, of course.) How tragic, he said yet again, that he was deprived of the sight of the originals by Mrs Needleman's impudence in abandoning the Grand Tour of Europe for the mere Lake District, where, so he has heard, only peasants live. Apart from Mr Wordsworth, of course. Even his verse is said by some critics to be of the inferior kind.

I warned SH, yet again, that this marriage must now be robustly accommodated; that the household depends on Lady Manton's influence with the Darcys; and we must support RN in his efforts to let the minx have her way. SH's response, I fear, was the ominous glint in the eye that I know too well. This glint, in the past, has given way to explosive interludes, when I have had to effect a rescue and return him to an aghast RN. SH, though devoted to RN, is an evangelist, and fiery; his inspirational aspect is of great attraction to other men. It is my task to be his wise mother and draw him back into the Rectory fold.

However. For now we are free of the minx. RN has sent word that he will return early, alone; SH is to ride to meet him, and they will have the freedom of the house for several days before Mrs Needleman manages to escape her Hertfordshire imbroglio. I shall give Hurry leave to pursue his interests in our neighbouring spa town, and issue instructions to Gladys and Patty as to their work and their movements. For myself, I will be busy tidying my kitchen garden, hidden from all that may transpire (though keeping my ears alert for inquisitive parishioners). My beetroots look splendid this year, my leeks grow tall, and I shall cut back the soft fruit bushes now that the jam is all in jars, their paper lids each neatly labelled in my own hand.

⁜

Annie knew that Miss Mary would be panicking about her lone journey, and caught her on the half-landing to offer to help her to pack.

"Miss Jane and Miss Lizzy, when they journeyed with the Gardiners," she said, "they each had a larger reticule for their overnight needs. Hers will still be somewhere in there, I'll be bound."

"But we must not disturb Jane's things, surely? Lizzy forbids us to do so!"

"Miss Lizzy is occupied with your poor mother's effects. She'll be there for a while yet. We can have a rummage?"

"Oh Annie, thank you. I am such a nuisance. And

there is the mourning aspect to consider. I may have to leave my beige muslin behind."

Annie led the way, with Miss Mary chattering anxiously behind her as she creaked open Miss Jane's wardrobe. "What should I wear for the journey? Should I persist with the black, for dear Mama's sake?"

Annie laid out a possible dress on Miss Jane's bed. "This lavender grey. It'd count as half-mourning. And you'll have the black-and-beige cape; it's dark enough, with the black in your bonnet. You'd not want to look like a widow, would you?"

Miss Mary went pale at the thought. She held up the lavender-grey against herself. "But what if Jane...? When she recovers?"

"You're both of a size," said Annie firmly, "and would she say you nay? As for your other things, you leave them to me. Anything left over, I'll slip into the layers in Miss Lizzy's trunk when she gets ready for her own return, and Thwaite can get them returned to you."

"Would you, dear Annie? Won't Lizzy notice?"

"No, it's maids' concerns. If there's any bother, I'll get her going on her George. That'll distract her. And Thwaite will always be on hand to help."

As she spoke, Annie's mind hopped over to the little creature in Thwaite's belly. There'd been no sign that it had come away. How would she fare when she was back under Mrs Reynolds' eagle eye? As she began to show? God help her.

"Annie?" Miss Mary had her head in the wardrobe, and her voice was muffled. "Is this the reticule?" She brought it out and flourished it. "What a splendid size!

And stout linen! Bless you. If only I had an Annie at Humbole!"

Annie took it and unfurled the gathers on the string. "Best check for moth holes. You can't have it falling apart in your hands."

"Never mind," Miss Mary went on, oblivious. "Married life is suiting me very well. Mr Needleman was so affectionate at the funeral."

Annie glanced up. Miss Mary had paused, as if someone had walked into the room. Was it the ghost of Miss Jane?

But Miss Mary wasn't thinking about Miss Jane. She said suddenly, "Luke!"

"Luke? There's no moths."

"He was so kind. Years ago. When I wished to ride Rosie. He did not insist I ride side-saddle. He seemed to understand my wish for the more adventurous type of riding. As if..."

Annie saw where this was heading – *as if he were my brother* – and would have none of it. "There's no need to fret about my Luke. He's content with his stables like we're content with our wardrobes. I'll put your overnight needs on the top. Now, off you go."

Miss Mary, thank the Lord, took the hint. "Back to my Rectorial duties. You are right as usual, Annie dear." She held up the reticule. "To the journey! Alone! I will manage splendidly, I am sure. God willing."

⁊

As Esther and Milly snuggled into each other that night, Esther broke off at the end of their Ma-Da-Joel-

Esther-Milly ritual and burst out: She said your name!
Mrs Needy did! Asked if you'd go wi' 'er! Spoke o'
you as if you were her own!

Milly (giggling): Nah. She didna?

Esther: Honest, Mill. She did. *Might she come...?*
Then, *No, no, course not, you need to be together, you
two.*

Milly: She kem in t' kitchen. When I were polishin'.
That new Pemberley were chivvyin' me cos I were
slow, an' t'other Pemberley were saying nah nah, leave
off, shiz jus' an extra, she gets nowt in 'er pocket, oney
bed 'n' board. So t'other left me, but kick me later,
she did.

Esther: Lemme stroke yer. Comfort yer.

Pause.

Milly: Shiz off, then?

Esther: Aye. Wifey stuff.

Silence between them.

Milly: Essy?

Esther: Nah. Nowt 'appen. Nowt come away.

Milly: So it's the gin, then? An' t' 'ot bath? Or a
poke wi'...?

Esther: Canna. Canna risk it. I'd be iller, then Miss
Lizzy'd really ken what's up.

Milly: God, Essy. God save us.

Esther: God save us an' all.

Milly: What gives, then?

Esther: Ah, Mill. You's 'one wi' brain. You tell me.

Milly: Am thinkin' on, Ess. Thinkin' on.

෴

Mary was on her way. Her heart hammered in her chest. She could not tell if her nerves were the product of her heartbeat or the other way round. Her parents' childhood exhortations were all about the outward: "Do not bury your head so, Mary!" "Straighten your backbone, young madam, or they will think you don't possess one!" And, to encompass all their strictures in one: "Look what you are *doing*, Mary!" It was this last which drove her to despair. How could she *look* at what she was *doing*? Might someone walk backwards before her, holding a mirror? In any case, her picture was always *blurred*!

But her vision was no longer blurred. She could see, and judge, and decide for herself. She was discovering, too, that her heart had an indicator of its own. Her head, her brain, could manage quite well, even while the beating of her heart made her want to scream. She did not scream; she had been brought up to resist such an urge. But her heart screamed for her. It thumped rhythmically, like a giant version of the metronome on top of the piano.

For instance, take the hackney cab driver on the first stage of her journey. She recognised him by his gait; she had forgotten his name, but his features, now sharp in her vision, told her that he was the one who had brought the Meryton lawyer to see Papa about the Entail. Now she was alone with this man, inches away from him, through the flimsy rear of the cab. He might whip the horse into the undergrowth and… And what? Who would protect her? She was without maid or chaperone. Without a maid, she must do all the work that a maid would do: remember the man's name, not be repelled by his badger-like unshavenness or the remains of his dinner that were splashed down his jacket, give him the correct instructions, and pay his fee.

Her heart beat out that metronome motion: *His name is... His name is...*

Samuel Monk! She recalled her father commenting, "Never was a moniker less apt! *Monk*, indeed!"

God be thanked for her memory. Her heartbeat eased. She gave the man an outrageously large gratuity when they arrived in Meryton, all because he had not taken her into the undergrowth and she had remembered his name.

On it went, all through the journey. For each of the services on the way, she proffered far too much money. Her largesse gained her a comforting level of appreciation, and her dark dress of mourning elicited respect from other passengers. She was both ashamed of her misplaced generosity and proud of her unexpected courage.

The post-houses were by now quite familiar, and she settled into her third strange bed with no nerves at all. Then, just before dropping off to sleep, she realised that she had failed to alert the Rectory of her intended early arrival. Her husband and Mrs Beattie must somehow be told to expect her on the morrow.

In the morning she requested from the innkeeper's wife paper, pen and ink, and a message-boy to ride ahead with a letter. But she was soundly rebuffed. Friday-cum-Saturday was the very worst of times to make such a demand! Could she not have asked last night, when the smallest message-boy might still be free to ride on one of the carts that hung about for that purpose? Mary ran after the woman, pleading with her in the most undignified manner. But the answer did not change. Message-boy there was none. Carts: all gone. It was pointless to repeat her request for paper and ink.

When the stage coach put her down near Humbole, she found that the equivalent of Samuel Monk with his hackney carriage was out on another errand. But it was mid-afternoon, a fine day, and the late October sun was bringing out the glorious colours of the beech trees. She would manage the mile and a half to the Rectory on foot.

How fortunate she was, she thought as she walked. She had been able to leave her family home in the capable hands of her sisters and return to the marriage into which she had entered of her own free will. Nevertheless, she still prayed for Papa, who had wept at her departure and exhorted her to "obey your husband in all things, as the Good Book says". And, inwardly, she committed her mother once more to the mercy of God, repeating the words of the Old Testament reading for All Hallows: "The souls of the righteous are in the hand of God, and no torment will ever touch them. In the time of their visitation they will run like sparks through the stubble."

Sparks! They were all around her. She gazed up at the sun streaming through the branches: crimson, ochre, gold, she could see every spark of colour, every shadow out of which the sparks shone. She was indeed blessed. For sure, there were poor and unhappy people in some of the cottages she passed; she knew just how poor, and how unhappy, from her charitable visits. But she, as Rectory wife, was able to alleviate some of that distress and return home with a sense of achievement.

The Rectory gates were open. Ah! Had someone told Hurry to open the gates in preparation for whatever vehicle might convey her from the staging post?

From the start of the gravel drive, she saw, beside the stable building, a horse, tethered. There was no sign of Hurry. The horse was a fine bay stallion. It was Mr Hepplecraft's. Today was a Saturday, when Mr Hepplecraft never visited.

She mounted the steps, remembering the anxiety with which she had encountered them, on that first occasion, many months ago.

From down in the kitchen there were sounds of clattering. That would be Gladys and Patty. No doubt Mrs Beattie too would be hard at work.

Heart pounding again, she came through the doors, closed them behind her, and paused on the pattern of the hall tiles. Unidentifiable noises were coming from the drawing room. The door was ajar.

Mary knew she must not approach it. She also knew that she must. She put her reticule quietly down on the antique bench and tiptoed towards the drawing room door.

There was a long strip of light, a foot or so wide, through which she could see carpet, furniture, ceiling. Between these, figures moved. Naked figures. It appeared to Mary as a scene of some violence, yet no one was resisting. Everything moved. Everything breathed. Breathed with a depth that she had not known existed. Breathed, moved, heaved, within that narrow canvas.

She stood, paralysed. Swayed to the right, to the left, instructing her feet to move silently one way, then the other, trying to find some meaning in the constantly moving tableau in the drawing room. The figures, strangely child-like in their exposed state, were entwined in ways she could not make sense of. She glanced down; caught a glimpse of familiar lace, of leather. Her eyes, her mind, could not accommodate it.

She closed her eyes, but could still hear. The sounds grew, until they felt like an assault on her ears. Surely they must stop? Must give way to the bursting of one or more of the actors out of their slit of tableau, through this door, and onto the floor where she now stood? But no, the sounds went on, and on: dipping, rising, dipping, rising. There was no end to them.

She must move, but could not.

Then she had actually moved, even before the intention to move had arisen.

Treading lightly as before, silently, moving first backwards then turning to move forwards, she tore herself away from the tableau, retrieved her reticule from the bench and forced her feet to make for the kitchen stairs.

Half-way down the stairs she became the opposite of silent. She coughed. She stamped her feet on the twisting wooden treads. She called "Gladys! Patty!" before she became visible to the two she was summoning. "I am returned! Get fresh water from the pump!"

Their two faces turned towards her, one from one end of the table, the other from the opposite end. Gladys was kneading bread, Patty was chopping carrots. Each face looked like a plate of bread-dough with carrots of horror, staring.

Mary's mind registered that Mrs Beattie was nowhere to be seen, but did not have an explanation for that phenomenon.

"Patty!" Mary heard herself shouting. "Do you hear me? Water! From the pump! With that cup there!"

Patty obeyed.

Mary pointed at the measuring-jug that Gladys was using.

"Leave that, wipe your hands" (she pointed at a limp cloth lying over a kitchen chair) "and proceed up the stairs to the drawing room! Knock heartily upon the door, and shout that the mistress is arrived! Then come back down here and minister to my needs!"

Gladys still stared at her, dough-like.

"Go! Drawing room! Knock, announce! Then back! Here! At once!"

Gladys moved her bulk at last. She almost knocked into Mary as she shifted herself across the kitchen and into the darkness of the narrow stairs.

Mary slumped into a kitchen chair and waited for the water that Patty would bring.

Out of the tumult of impressions of what she had seen, she perceived one necessity: that what mattered now was outward behaviour. She would behave as if she had seen nothing. This would lead the actors in that drama to behave as if nothing had happened. All of them would continue as before. She had known nothing before; she would continue to act as if she knew nothing still. That was the way the world worked.

Interval

A Revelation

MARY, ALONE AT BREAKFAST (it being a Wednesday and Mr Needleman having ridden off early to Derby), waited until the Bath buns before instructing Gladys to fetch Mrs Beattie in, if she pleased.

Mrs Beattie did not please until Mary was well into her second bun. Her prepared speech hovered in the space between her plate and her mouth, removing itself as she took each bite and reasserting itself as she chewed.

Now here was Mrs Beattie, dark and thunderous, and she must assert herself. The Lord, in the middle of the night, had told her to be assertive.

This was her time of the month. Not for bleeding, but for the time between her bleedings. She had noticed this phenomenon ever since the thunder had brought on her first, and so memorable, Monthly. But, since her marriage, it had grown stronger. It was a feeling of *urgency*: she must *do* something, *be* someone. *Become*, mysteriously, in a way that could not be denied.

During these times she would wake in the night panting, and clutch her knees, and rock. She could only return to sleep by recalling her favourite Prayer for the Day: *O Almighty Lord, grant that the stewards of Thy mysteries may make ready Thy way, by turning the hearts of the disobedient to the wisdom of the just.*

But that left her with a question: did she herself belong to the disobedient, or to the just? Surely this panting, this *urgency*, threw her into the disobedient category? It seemed, at these times, that her body was ruling her mind. Which could only brand her as a sinner, bound for hell. Yet the urgency was irresistible. So it must surely be propelled by, and be a movement towards, a version of wisdom and justice.

"Mrs Beattie," she said now, "I am aware that November storms are brewing. But I am also aware that the Custance family have Mr Custance out of employment, and so have no means to put food on their children's plates. I wish to fill my basket with nourishment from the kitchen and deliver it to the Custance family today. Remnants will do. I saw a plate-full carried towards the meat-safe last evening, and some of the suet pudding besides. Those will do. Thank you."

Mrs Beattie's lips pursed, and her eyes glared full into her own. It was in the face of this glare that Mary felt a revelation occurring deep down in her belly. It took only a fraction of a second, but it was a whole world in significance.

Ever since Lizzy had left Longbourn to take her place as Mr Darcy's life companion, Mary had wondered where this took Lizzy in terms of the private happenings at Pemberley. How Marriage, in its detail, played out. There must be some sort of private behaviour which led to the swelling of Lizzy's belly, not once but twice, thrice, and thence to a birth being imminent. Once, twice, thrice, Mary had approached in her own mind the question of how the birth of a child was linked with what must happen in the secrecy of the marital relationship: the Mr meeting the Mrs of the Darcy-ness. But she always retreated from this question; closed her mind to the awe-inspiring hugeness of it.

Now, facing Mrs Beattie's glare, then lowering her eyes so as to muster the courage to continue, she felt the blaze of revelation: there was a *something* from the man that must transfer itself into the space of the woman in order for the belly to swell and the child to grow; for the inheritance of Darcy-ness to be apparent throughout the world of Pemberley; indeed, throughout the whole wide world, from the smallest Derbyshire alms-house to the vast West Indian sugar estates.

What came to Mary now was even more unexpected. As with the bodily urgency, it came so truly that it must have come from God. It was the knowledge that *she would like to have a child*.

Not as Lizzy had her children, though. Lizzy had tried to explain things to her: something about *the more private aspects of the contract between Darcy and myself*, and it being *a great shock*. At this point in the conversation Mary had silenced Lizzy; she had, astonishingly, forbidden her to say more. Even now, she wished to hear no more of this *marriage contract*. But she did wish to have a child.

Her body wished it. The Lord God willed it. It must happen. She was a woman. She would be a mother.

Eyes still dropped to the level of her plate, which was now empty of all but the last bite of buttered bun, her speech to Mrs Beattie continued. "And please would you ask Gladys to go across to the stables and speak to Hurry." She almost lost the thread at this point, but caught it again, as one did with a stray thread in one's sampler. "And convey to him my orders for the day: that the phaeton be tackled up for my venture, and blankets of the picnic variety be taken from the blanket chest. The Custances are not the only cottagers I shall visit this day. I shall take those cradle blankets, which Lady Manton sent by her manservant the other week, for charitable distribution. I have not yet decided to…"

But now Mrs Beattie's intake of breath was so loud as to draw Mary's eyes up to level with hers.

The housekeeper spoke. "Well! It is to be hoped that Hurry will respond as his master would wish! You would be best left safely by the fire, not venturing out at all!" The Irish richness of her voice came over in every syllable. "However! I will convey your wishes out to the stable. And we shall see what transpires!"

She turned on her heel, fury still visible in her rustling black rear, and Mary was left in a strange limbo between triumph and doubt.

But the revelation remained intact within her, and she determined to press on, moving towards becoming a mother, towards producing and possessing a child.

PART III

14

Thunder and Blood

"TACKLE UP THE PHAETON, Hurry," she says. "If you would be so good," she says. "Do not be as you are, Hurry! Be as your name, I beg of you! Hurry! I must be on my mission and back before the storm breaks!" she says.

Takes no notice when I say I'll not tackle up nor hoss nor phaeton for her, nor any, on a day such as this.

Takes no notice when I interrupt her with, "You can go begging all you like, Mrs N, but I'll not do it. It's the north-easterly, an' what it's carrying. I cannot be responsible for the life of you on a day such as this," I says.

"Them parishioners!" she says. No, not *them* – "*My* parishioners!" she says. "They need my *baskets*, Hurry! And my *blankets*! So, *hurry*!"

I stand there, stout. "Fragile nature of the phaeton," I says. "It's no carriage, there's barely a cover for your good self, Mrs," I says. "Blow off in a second, will that top, in the wind already starting up. Blow your good bonnet away," says I.

But: "I am the lady of this house, and you will do as I command!" says she.

I, having known the man of this house a full ten years longer than her, and knowing (to boot) where he is this day (and what he may be up to) says, "But the man of the house leaves you in my care, an' I will not tackle up nor hoss nor phaeton. Not for nobody." Nor for my good self, neither, is what I bite back.

But, do you know, she wears me down.

I'm weary enough with my own self, truth be told. But I look at that little jaw of hers pounding up and down 'neath her spectacles, and I've a kind of respect for her. Because she *will not* sit at the hearth and eat shortcake and drink sweet lemon tea till she's as tight about the waist as her bonnet is now tight about her head. She *will* go out and get there to The Poor (as she will call 'em) come wind, come weather.

Even to the accursed Custances, that the folk of the village wish to send to perdition and beyond. She'll plague The Poor with her butties and her shallots and her nourishing scraps of old bacon wrapped in the last fragments of ham: luxuries that 'her' parishioners, specially folks like yon Custances, haven't clapped mitts on in all their born days.

So I dose myself up, tackle the fragile phaeton, and slip the poor hoss between the bars. And off we go. "If it be God's will, the storm will pass by," she says.

But does God will? He does not. Rain starts flat in our faces while we're going forward, slices into our cheeks when we're rounding a corner, runs down our chins and our fronts and round the backs of our necks. Her skirts are every which way, and my britches cling to my knees like dirt. While I'm bouncing us around pot-holes, she's clutching the side of the phaeton. One of me hands holds the whip up high while the other hangs onto the reins for dear life. We sway and we holler (oh yay, *she* hollers a' all) while I try to find which one of the hovels she'll first set upon with a blanket or a shallot.

Still it's "Go, Hurry!" without ceasing.

An' yay, we're now heading for yon Custances.

But, like I warned her, the top flies off and lands in a ditch, and I'll have Lord knows what trouble finding it when the storm clears. Her bonnet, miraculously, stays tight upon her head. As do those spectacles of hers.

As for the nor-easterly, it's swerving to the north, is black as sin, and worsening. The good Rector's wife is still heading to the Custances', and I'm aching in every muscle in me body. She'll do it, she shouts, if it's the last thing she does. Which, given what light there is is fading, given the thunder issuing forth from that there cloud looming, it might well be.

That's before what happens next.

∞

Hurry reined in the horse, for there was some sort of obstruction in the lane. Mary called against the wind and the wet: "What is it? Must we stop? Can we not continue on our way?"

There was a curious roaring sound in the midst of the storm.

"Indeed not, Mrs N!" came Hurry's reply.

Mary peered out and saw, at an angle to the side of them, through the slashes of rain in the gloom, a shape of humps and rectangles and outcrops, which in due course resolved itself into the form of a cart. A cart with an unidentifiable burden on board. The chief outcrop emerged as a man at the reins: a stout, seriously dishevelled and wildly roaring man. His visage was fierce, and the whip in his right hand was lashing his poor mule. The mule had locked itself deep into the mud, and though the whip whirled and swirled against the mule, and sometimes against the burden that lay in the cart, it could not be budged.

A bolt of lightning now shone upon the man, the burden, and the whip. In that flash, Mary recalled another vehicle: the one she had seen on her return from Humbole after Mr Needleman's almost-proposal. She remembered the bedraggled horse, the broken-rimmed cart, the half-dozen children on board cowering as if against everything that life could throw at them. That vision had provoked her to ask how many such carts and children and nags or mules she might have missed seeing during her earlier, purblind condition. This present wild scene came as answer to that question.

Hurry shouted, "'Tis a pesky beggar of the mischievous kind! Take no note! I'll whip the hoss on past!"

Mary, barely hearing his words, leaned forward and stared at the lumpish burden on the cart. Even without the lightning, she could still see that this particular lump consisted of two parts: one part, tangle of cloths, the other, exposure of naked flesh. Human flesh.

As she watched, the flesh heaved, and rose up, and sank again. Meanwhile the whip came down on the mule, flew back up, whirled around over the cloths and the naked flesh, and came back down. On the flesh. And up. The wild man hollered. Round swirled the whip once more. Meanwhile, the skin-and-bone mule tried again and again to lift a leg and start itself up, but was prevented again and again by the mud.

Hurry was now silenced; he must have seen what Mary saw; and the two of them watched, transfixed, as the carter brought the whip to fall finally upon the heap of human flesh. Then he dropped the whip, heaved himself towards the flesh, and started using his arms and the strength of the rest of his body to hoist it towards the edge of the cart.

It was at this point that Mary, despite the rain running down her spectacles, forced herself to witness the detail of what unfolded before them.

She saw, in turn, two human legs, with a space between them, and within that space an object emerging. The object appeared in the centre of the picture, then stilled itself, then moved out from the surrounding flesh again, stilled itself again, then moved outwards once more. It was propelled by some force inside the flesh that surrounded it: propelled by jerks, each time further and yet further forward, towards the thunderous world. A moan accompanied each heaving movement of surrounding flesh.

Mirror-fashion, Mary felt herself propelled forward in order to grasp, and in some sense pay honour to, the force of the propulsion that was taking place.

At the same time, another propulsion was taking place: the movement of the man who had now dropped the whip, had stopped hollering, and was trying to shift the entire burden of cloths and flesh over the rim, out of the cart and into the mud.

He failed in the attempt, tried again, fell back, tried yet again. Just before he succeeded, the child being born from the woman (for this, Mary could now accept, was what was happening) slithered out and became, apart from a snaking cord that joined them, a separate human being. Then the burden of flesh and cloths submitted to the action of the man's lifting, and fell onto the rain-lashed verge.

The impact of his action relieved the struggling mule so that it could pull its hooves from the mud. There was more struggling, but the man had the whip back in his hand now, and the mule felt the sting of it and howled a strange howl. Then the mule and the cart, amidst more hollering from the man, were freed, and lurched off and away into the storm and the gloom, leaving the burden that had given it its freedom splayed on the sodden, slithering turf.

Mary, sodden to the skin herself by now, heaved herself out of the phaeton.

Hurry shouted, "Let it alone, ma'am! Mind yourself! Come back!"

But Mary could do no other than approach the bodies. She crouched down. The foul frame of the woman lay open for all the world to see, and Mary reached for the coverings to try and provide some decency. But the wind and the rain defeated her, and the flesh remained open to the gaze of Hurry, who was down from the phaeton and breathing heavily behind her.

"Don't you touch it!" Hurry's voice was a croak. "Leave it be!"

But she could not leave it be. They were human. A woman and a child.

The woman moaned frightfully, then fell silent.

Hurry pulled at Mary from behind, but feebly.

She could not tell whether either of these beings was now living or dead. She stared, and felt Hurry staring over her shoulder, and for a while there was a cocoon of silence between the turf and the storm. The woman was still, and she and Hurry behind her were still, and most still of all was the small creature that had issued forth from the woman. Between those two human beings there lay the cord, which pulsated weakly. Mary watched as it, too, became still. Then she realised that she had been witness to two events: one of life, the other of death. The life part must be how her own mother had given birth to her. But her mother had been in a comfortable bed, with doctor and midwife beside her, and hot water brought, and servants to clear the detritus away afterwards. This woman had only the whip, the mud, and the storm. The death part, too, her mother had finally undergone. She, Mary, would also undergo that, when her time came. *Oh God. Dear God.*

She's praying, of course. That's what they do, these folks, when there's nothing else to be done. I can't shift her while she's praying.

I know the words, too. I've heard them often enough while waiting for His Rectorship to finish the service and I've to take him back home or, again, often enough, to a different destination. *Lord, now lettest Thou Thy servant depart in peace, according to Thy Word. For mine eyes have witnessed Thy salvation...* She needs to do summat, I can see that. And praying's all she can do. I'm aching so bad, I leave her to it.

Yet we've to be back home. Smart-ish. I've to get back there for my own purposes. And we've to get ourselves cleaned up and back to normal, somehow. And how's that to be accomplished?

Let's hope this is her last prayer: "*The Lord bless thee and keep thee, the Lord make His face to shine upon thee, and give thee peace.*"

෧෨

She heard Hurry's words: "Mrs N. Get yourself back in. Let's be off." But she could not. Would not. There were procedures. Those procedures had carried Mama and Hill on their journey to their Maker. These here – these lumpen pieces of human flesh – were of the same ilk as Mama, as Hill, as herself. The proper procedures must be gone through, so as to carry them to their Maker, too.

She heard herself barking in a way that was not

unlike Mrs Beattie on one of her bad days. She pointed at the human burden: "Lift." Hurry did not move. "This is to be lifted. We must take them."

Hurry's response was like a wail into the storm. "Where? Where to?"

"The churchyard. I will take this side" (the infant) "and you will take that."

"Mrs. Mrs N. I cannot."

"But I can. So you will."

"Churchyard? The paupers' end?"

"The end matters not. We must lay them on consecrated ground."

"How?"

"As best we can. The churchyard. They must be laid there."

A moment's thrill shot through Mary when, after a fractional pause, Hurry leaned towards the burden and actually touched it. Touched the filthy cloths. Not the flesh itself, just the cloths, but he leaned with the purpose of lifting those cloths to cover the nakedness of the bloody mother and the blood-stained child.

Neither body resisted as he did so.

The awkwardness of the task of transferring them to the phaeton was exacerbated by the fact that the cord slipped out of the cloths; it fell, it swayed this way, and that, with the wind and the carrying motion. Mary, making a gesture of help at the burden's far end, prayed that they might get the whole burden up into the phaeton without either herself or Hurry letting loose the contents of their stomachs.

Her prayer was answered, and for that she gave fervent thanks.

When she finally faced her own task of climbing the phaeton's step, she realised that the cloths, together with the bodies of mother and child, entirely filled the floor, and there would be no room for her feet. Her flimsy shoes were, in any case, caked in mud. Hurry held her elbow while she climbed the step, and drew the burden to one side with his gloved hand so that first one foot, then the other, could get a purchase on the phaeton's floor. She eased herself up, balanced herself, and found that she could sit down. Hurry strode to the front and leapt into place. His whip must have fallen into the mud, for he drove off without it. The only place for Mary's feet was to be wedged, toes down, firmly against the mud- and blood-soaked burden. Except if she took her muddy shoes off. She must do that. She pressed one shoe off with her other, then pressed the second shoe off with her shoeless, stockinged foot, and her feet – stockinged, yet feeling as if naked – rested on the mound of the deceased.

She sat, the living with the dead, rocketing along, borne by righteousness, exhaustion, and a mysterious surge of authority. And by the erratic steering of their agitated driver.

When they reached the churchyard gate, Mary perceived that it was not the paupers' gate but the main, official, Sunday parishioners' gate.

No matter, she thought. We will dispose of our burden, and after that, make our way back to the Rectory, find some explanation for what has occurred, and order Gladys and Patty to fill a bath.

⌒⌒

The clocks tick round: the ormolu clock on the mantelshelf, the Viennese in the dining room, the grandfather clock on the stairs. I hear them over the storm.

The minx is late back. She is seldom late back from her parish visiting. She talks of the hours to be spent with Her Poor, while in truth I suspect she hurls a basket through a door and calls out a prayer before hastening back to the safety of the phaeton.

Yet I will do her justice: she perseveres. Like today, she goes out in all weathers. More dedicatedly so since RN has increased his hours away with SH, first by inches (one hour extra, or two), more recently – daringly – by an extra night. These changes are made on the excuse of the weather or the condition of the roads. I warn him: if she can go out in all weathers, why cannot he? I murmur about my friendship with Mrs Reynolds, hoping he will grasp my meaning: the danger of gossip flying over to Pemberley, then along a few more miles to the luxurious gardens of Lady Manton.

These lengthenings of the weekly absences, together with the cancellations of SH's regular presence here in the Rectory, tighten up the minx's little jaw. She knows that she must not complain; nevertheless, she grants herself an allowance of breakfast-time queries to her husband. "How difficult will your work be on this occasion, my dear? Is Mr Hepplecraft an expert scholar in this field? Are our congregations becoming well-known for theological enquiry?" RN's answers range from the perfunctory to the bland. Dissatisfied, she renews her missionary zeal with the charity baskets. I feel her dissatisfaction floating around the Rectory like a miasma.

At the same time, I find myself leaning slightly towards the minx in terms of sympathy. She does not detect precisely what is amiss, but her frame, her manner of being, reveals her awareness that amiss is how things are.

And things will become yet more amiss, I fear, when she reads the sealed missive that came today from Pemberley. I have no need to wait for Mrs Needleman to break the seal. Mrs Reynolds has conveyed the situation quite clearly in our regular, carefully coded correspondence.

However. Today. This afternoon. The storm.

She is late.

The rain lashes the windows; the chimneys become trumpets for the roaring of the wind. Gladys and Patty waddle from room to room with pole-screens. As time goes by, my anxiety turns to fear. I order Gladys or Patty to put a warming-pan in the mistress's bed. Never have they known me offer such indulgence before.

"The roads will be rivers of mud," I declare finally. In truth, my imagination is getting the better of me.

Me? Fearful? For the minx? Yes! And for Hurry. He has his needs. I am privy to the nature of those needs, and know that they can become urgent. "Patty, put the largest pan on the fire. Gladys, fetch the tub from the back kitchen in case the mistress needs herself to be warmed through. Brace yourselves for the carrying of jugs."

Yet more than an hour more passes till there is sound

of them, and a full half-hour since Patty declared the largest pan was full-boiling on the fire and begged for Gladys to come and damp the fire down against the output of steam.

‡

A blazing fire. A tub. In *her* room. Screens around, for privacy. Cloths and towels passed discreetly round the screens from Gladys's or Patty's rough hands. Mrs Beattie whispering orders to them, and queries to Mary herself: too hot? Not hot enough? Might she cease that dreadful shivering?

Mary had paid no attention to the phenomenon of shivering and was surprised to have it pointed out on her arrival. Her concern was more for the mud that she was spattering on the clean tiled floors and the shuddering of Hurry – yes, Hurry was not *shivering*, he was *shuddering* – before he took himself off to his home amongst the horses. Mary submitted gratefully to the maids' ministrations and, when she glimpsed Mrs Beattie hurrying to and fro, tried to explain to her the nature of things out there in the wild. *Shush*, commanded Mrs Beattie. *Shush. Shush.*

Mrs Beattie enquired whether a further towel might serve as a mat when she was ready to climb out of the tub? She replied, "I have no wish to climb out, thank you very much, Mrs Beattie. I wish to stay in the water for some time." Mrs Beattie retreated a little way away and, by the sound of it, sat down for the duration.

Mary's body slowly returned to her as a properly feeling entity; the stomping of the maids' feet with fresh jugs of hot and cold water slowed, then ceased. She began to realise that she was naked, and alone in a bedchamber with Mrs Beattie. Which was in itself an astonishment, even though there was a screen between them. She gently splashed herself with water and then lay still against the slope of the tub, absorbing the unusual sensation of creaturely pleasure. Oddly, the presence of Mrs Beattie on the far side of the screen gave her no embarrassment at all. Hearing her housekeeper's steady breathing made her own breathing-space feel more, not less, private.

"Did I tell you?" she began tentatively. "Might I have already related to you, Mrs Beattie, on our arrival earlier, the circumstances in which we found ourselves? The cart? The tragedy? The task? I must apologise, you must forgive me, my mind is unclear."

Mrs Beattie left a considerable pause before responding: "You may remember, Mrs Needleman, that while the maids were in the business of helping your good self into the house, I had the duty of care towards our coachman, and so was absent while you gave your explanation."

"It was a death, Mrs Beattie. Perhaps, even, a death brought about by someone. Though whether or not deliberately, I do not exactly…" She could not continue.

"Of these things we need not be the judge. Hurry will know the name, the type. It need not concern us."

"Oh, but it did concern me. It was most terrible. I have never seen the like. She, the woman, was in the process… I cannot describe… There was a mother, there was an infant…"

"There is no need for description, Mrs Needleman. It would be a favour to me if you would erase the scene from your mind. The question is: what must be done? Where did you find to dispose of the poor creatures?"

Mary swished the water as if attempting the erasure that Mrs Beattie begged for. It was not effective; the scene was indelible. "When we reached the churchyard, Hurry said the paupers' end, I could not see which end that was... We must lift it. The burden. Entirely. Carry it. The wind... The cloths, scattering themselves... The smaller of the burdens fell... *Leave it!* cried Hurry. But I could not!"

She heard a slight change in Mrs Beattie's breathing, and swished the water again. She did not wish to imagine the emotions on her invisible companion's face.

There was so much to say, and it was her duty to insist upon it, whether Mrs Beattie wanted to hear it or not.

"They must not be abandoned! They should receive a Christian burial! They were souls in need of God's mercy! Two souls, Mrs Beattie! However lowly they may have been in this life! We should inter them with due ceremony!" She coughed, and paused. "Might a message be got to Mr Needleman, please, that he should return from Derby at his earliest convenience, and officiate?"

The wind gave an answering roar down the chimney. Mary had made a ridiculous request, and should withdraw it. But she must be obedient not to convention, but to the voice of the storm. She said,

"When he returns? Mrs Beattie? Will you support me in this?"

"Your concern is admirable, Mrs Needleman." Mrs Beattie's voice was low, but her Irishness struck Mary afresh. Did those of a Catholic faith, she wondered, have the same respect for Christian burial as us, the Protestants? Though now she remembered that Mrs Beattie was, in fact, a Protestant like herself.

Mrs Beattie stood up. The screen between them wobbled at her motion. "My first priority must be your good self. Mr Needleman would reproach me powerfully if the drenchment you have suffered – and the shock! – should result in an infection of the lungs. I will inform him of those other requirements in due time. But first, let me tell you, I have put a warming pan in your bed."

Mary tried to over-ride her. "My concern is for the deceased woman and her child!"

Then the words *warming pan* reached her ears, and her anxiety for the souls of those poor wretches started to weaken. Her eyes were opened, like Adam and Eve in the Book of Genesis, and she saw that she was naked.

Her hands made vague waves at the tub's edge. "You are most kind. Pass me the towel, if you will."

She stood, and a towel was transferred into her hand. The fate of the two souls in the churchyard must be decided by others. Mary must take care of herself.

❧

My beloved, my soul -

As I creep away from you into the weary dawn, I ask just one question: How could you?

But I have always known how you could. That you could.

I could never. My heart is yours, my body is yours. My soul, too.

I have known from the beginning that, for you, the triumvirate of heart and flesh and soul take flight, and dance, and depart from each other with no constraints at all.

I know, too, that this constraintlessness is the first of many reasons why I adore you.

As I ride back home to the Rectory, I observe all around me trees woefully damaged by the storm. Fields awash. Roofs holed. As for the lanes and bridleways, they are pitted and puddled and ridged to destruction. My poor horse must pick his way around the debris and wade through the soaking ruts.

The landscape can scarcely bear it. Yet, this is what winter does to us. It arrives, and we must bear it. "Bear it out, even to the edge of doom". Thus does the Bard insightfully advise us about the nature of love.

As I give the horse to pause, I take a moment to stare around me in the growing light and see that the destruction is of an average kind for the time of year. Only the branches of trees are down, not the whole beast. See that ash? It has lost half its branches, but the trunk stands firm.

Is this a metaphor for my loss of you? Does it say,

you are only partially lost to me?

No! For you have breached our unwritten contract.

You have renewed the C...m connection.

Do you remember how, as we lay in one another's arms that first time, I asked you softly about your needs of the C...m variety, and you promised me that your need for such variety was all in the past? I pressed you... I needed your reciprocal vow that it was indeed over, and you replied – oh, with your body as well as with your words – that though there might be occasional strayings from the fold of our love, none of them, ever, would be in the direction of C...m?

So I now demand: how could you?

It is, I fear, a rhetorical question. For I know the answer already.

Ah!

The anguish in his cry alerted the horse, who mistook it for the instruction to proceed. With a hefty jerk, they were in motion and away.

And Robert was grateful for it. He must stop this ranting, this endless round of how-*could*-hes. He must continue this all-too-familiar journey, arrive back at the Rectory and listen to his wife's reedy little voice grow strong as she relates to him the earnest goodnesses of her lonely days. He must wait patiently for the hour when the house falls quiet, and there can be tiptoeing from one room to another, and sitting by the side of his would-be mother, and the spilling out of his terrible pain into her understanding lap.

Seated at the piano and staring at the notes of Scarlatti on the page, Mary heard the return of her husband's horse, and wondered if Hurry had ceased his shuddering and could deal with the horse and its rider as efficiently as he generally did. Whether, indeed, after she had climbed between her beautifully warmed sheets, Hurry had received a similarly comforting gesture from Mrs Beattie in his turn.

But Hurry soon vanished from her thoughts. Robert, Mr Needleman, her husband, must be the sole object of her attention now. How was his journey through the last blusterings of the storm? When could he listen to her tale? Would he find it heroic, or foolish?

She played a line of Scarlatti over and over again, played it fast and played it slow, picked it out in staccato, then laid her hands on her knees and stared again at the page of notes. Normally Mr Needleman's return from Derby was accompanied by a rush of glowing sentences towards a sermon, a fresh insight from the Concordance, an enthusiastic reference to Mr Hepplecraft's outstanding scholarship in the field of Manichaeanism or the intricacies of Mosaic Law.

But when the door of the Music Room opened this time and her husband stood before her, his stance was diffident, his face pale and quiet. He had taken off his riding boots and put on his buckled house shoes, but she noticed splashes of mud up and down his attire.

There occurred then a certain suspension of time, like a minim's rest on a page of music: a moment of significant silence before the next theme began.

In that interval, Mary heard some birds cackling in the garden. She was gradually learning the names of common birds: the wren with its little stand-up tail; the robin of the red breast; the blackbirds with their delightful song. This cackle, she knew, came from the handsome magpie that strutted about the lawn and flew off at her approach with a string of unmusical squawks.

Had her husband felt this suspended moment?

Perhaps. He shifted his body awkwardly, drew up a chair and placed it not far from her piano stool. Then he said, frowning as he did over Cattermole's sermons: "Tell me, my dear, how your time has been spent since I departed for Derby. Mrs Beattie tells me there was some kind of fracas, and there may be consequences with which I might need to deal."

So Mary unburdened herself of the story about the Custance visit, the ramshackle cart, the man and his whip, the woman and her disarray, the infant emerging, even the cord and its pulsating, until at last she came to the transfer of the ejected woman and her child, as reverently as possible, into the churchyard, where they lay (she prayed) in the arms of Almighty God. "I can only hope," she concluded, knitting and un-knitting her fingers, "that, as I have done my duty by these remnants of humanity, others in their turn might carry out the necessary ordinances and give them a decent burial."

She did not expect Robert to accede immediately. But, wearily, taking her cold hands between his own warm ones, he said: "My dear and ever-surprising wife, you are a woman of courage and of faith. You set an example to us all. I will arrange for the sexton to dig the grave."

"In which section of the churchyard, my dear? Hurry was in doubt as to whether it should be the paupers or the..."

"Do not fret yourself about such minutiae. The sexton will be told of the circumstances, and he will follow the usual custom."

"Thank you, thank you."

"But..."

"But?"

Her husband coughed, and withdrew his hands. "I fear there are other matters for you to deal with. Please set all questions concerning this burial to one side until I acquaint you with the developments to which you must now give your attention."

"My dear? Developments?"

"Mrs Beattie says that there is a missive from Pemberley, from your sister. She fears that some important happenings may be under way."

Mary was astonished. Lizzy? What could she possibly require just now, in this weather, when there were so many other matters that she, as Rector's wife and as an example to the parish as a whole, must attend to?

"There, there, my dear," said Mr Needleman. He patted his knees, stood up, and brought the conversation to a close. "Mrs Reynolds has indicated to Mrs Beattie that there is a domestic matter of some sensitivity to be confronted. No doubt Mrs Darcy will welcome your view on the matter, when you are ready."

15

Married Life

MARY SAT UP IN BED when Patty came in with the usual jug of warm water, thanked her briefly, but then called her back: "Patty dear, I am so grateful for your hard work with my muddy clothes yesterday. I must apologise for causing you so much trouble. There may be more such incidents in the future, I fear. I am led by the Divine Spirit to do this work."

Patty stared at her, bobbed, and left the room, leaving Mary with the remnants of a dream. She had been dreaming of the infant; but this child was not the product of the storm, but a child of stained glass on his loving mother's knee. The mother was herself, Mary; she was clothed in Madonna's robes of the deepest blue. She felt a surge of power throb through her. Yesterday she had accomplished the Lord's will in tragic circumstances. She would continue on that path in times to come, when others, following her example, would feed on her inspiration.

However, Lizzy's letter lay uncomfortably on the bedside cabinet. It was brief, and suggested she visit the Rectory that morning.

Patty reappeared to light the fire when Mary was almost dressed. Mary forbore to remind her that lighting the fire should come *before* one's mistress was ready to dress. No matter. She was above such pettiness. Proud as she was of managing her own stays, she resolved to do without stays altogether quite soon. Though, for the funeral of the tragic woman and her unbaptised infant, she would of course need to dress respectfully, including stays. They were her breastplate, after all.

She imagined the funeral ceremony: she would stand in the pew while the coffins were carried past, the tiny one containing the infant lying poignantly alongside the larger one for the mother. A small circle of parishioners would gaze in reverence, first at the procession of coffins and then at her, their Rector's wife, in admiration. Her husband might even allow her to deliver the final words of committal: *Dust to dust, ashes to ashes*. She would be the first to cast a handful of soil into the darkness of the grave.

Downstairs, she found her husband in conversation with Mrs Beattie. She took her seat modestly, and Gladys put her bowl of porridge in its place. Mary took up her spoon, but held it in the air for a few moments while trying to find an entry point to the discussion between her husband and the housekeeper.

"...without your wisdom, Mrs Beattie? I should have known myself, of course."

"If you had attended Cambridge University, rather than Oxford, that wisdom could have been yours, Mr Needleman."

"I acknowledge that Oxford is intensely theological. These practical matters, parish boundaries and so on, seem trivial compared with the fate of the human soul in eternity."

"But we live in Humbole, do we not, rather than in eternity? The Parochial Church Council and the Poor Laws regulate our lives down here."

Mary, taken aback at Mrs Beattie's peremptory tone, brought her spoon down on the side of her bowl with a clang.

"Mr Needleman. Mrs Beattie. May I interject?"

Her husband and Mrs Beattie turned, as if they had just noticed her arrival.

"My dear. Do eat your porridge while it is warm. There have been some adjustments to the day's proceedings. But they need not concern you overmuch."

Mary tried to look eager to hear more, and took a mouthful of porridge.

"With reference to the wretched woman of yesterday, together with her infant. It has been pointed out to me that this family belong to the far side of our parish boundary."

"The farthest corner of our parish?"

"No, on the far *side* of our *boundary*. So the disposal, et cetera, of the remains, and so on, are the responsibility of the curate and sexton of Little Mossley-in-the-Vale. Not of this parish, of Humbole, at all."

The remains of a mouthful hardened in Mary's throat as it went down.

Mrs Beattie gazed at her in expectation of a reply, while her husband rose from his seat. A glance at Robert's plate showed Mary he had finished eating and was ready to leave the room.

Mrs Beattie pursued the point. "Our sexton could instruct their man to dig in the paupers' section, and payment be made so that our parish accounts do not suffer the loss incurred. It would not be a large sum. However, to quote Scripture, he who is faithful in little is faithful also in much."

"Exactly. Thank you, Mrs Beattie." Robert had reached the door and taken hold of the handle.

"Is there not some way in which I may assist?" Mary could not abandon her vision of the coffins and the committal. "Might I be party to this proceeding? As I was the one who was present at the demise of those poor unfortunates?"

Mr Needleman took a step back into the room. "My dear. You did splendidly. Far beyond the call of duty. But you have done enough. You must rest now. Recover from these events, put them behind you. Have no fear: matters are in hand! In Mrs Beattie's hands!" He gave a small cough. "I must away to Derby. I will see you on my return? Report on progress then, as to your nerves, and so on? Yes?"

Mary's dream of power plummeted, and vanished. By the time she looked up, both husband and housekeeper had left the room. Presumably Mrs Beattie was now to take command of the arrangements about which Mr Needleman, the Rector, had made such a regrettable administrative error.

But Mrs Beattie returned almost immediately and said briskly: "Mrs Darcy will be here within the hour. Some haste is necessary, is it not, Mrs Needleman, if Gladys and Patty are to clear the space and arrange a modest plate of fruit bread?"

'Thwaite' is slipping from me. Slipping as a stone slides down the clough, lower and lower, in the path of the storm, till it reaches the river and is carried away. Each averted eye, each small change of plan, is one more slip. It comes with the giggles in the third kitchen that cease as I enter, the eyes of the stable boys that fall to my belly, that ginger-knob girl who hands me back Mrs Darcy's muslin gown: "I goffered it specially, just as Madam likes it done." Most of all, it comes in the little cough with which Mrs Darcy heralds a change of subject whenever a future plan comes up.

I don't show; I make certain I don't show; but word is out. They've seen it all before. As I have myself.

But there is something new in this contempt towards me. For I am not only lady's maid to the mistress of Pemberley; I am also the upstart lead-miner's daughter with the grotesque little sister whose face no one can bear to look upon, however immaculately she behaves. No one will mourn our departure. They're already laying bets on which of Mrs Darcy's personal staff will leap to occupy the valuable vacancy as her lady's maid. When they're not speculating whose prick caused the scandal in the first place.

What no one is betting on is the fate of the upstart and her crippled sister. That is all too clear. The workhouse. The ditch.

Our *Doovus* sessions last longer and longer. We need each other more than we need our sleep.

I murmur: We cud go back up t' valley.

Milly: But there's none there for us now.

Me: Joel'd be there.

Milly: Ghosts, Ess, ghosts.

Me: I'd sooner die 'mong 'em 'n die down 'ere.

Milly: Us 're no die-ers, Essy. We med it 'ere, we cun mek it elsewhere.

Me: None'd let us, Mill. King Darcy rules. He's ranting at his missus; he'll rant at anyone as tries t' 'elp us.

Milly: Then we muss...! You know, Ess! You muss! Get rid!

Me: I willna. Willna.

Milly: Willna?

Me: Na. Na!

So we go back then, back to Joel and our Da, back even to our Ma. To "Back i' day? Back i' day!" To cuddles and snuggles.

And, with a nose-rub, to sleep.

Milly sleeps, yes. Her breath moves warmly over my throat.

But do I sleep? I do not. I, and the small living stone inside the clough of my body: we lie still, but wide awake.

The shower passed over. With the chance of sunshine, Mary decided to go through the front doors and stand on the Rectory steps to welcome Lizzy.

The garden gleamed. The lawn, scattered with leaves and twigs from the storm, stretched out on either side of the path. Jackdaws cackled overhead. At the far end of the drive, the gates lay open. The deciduous trees (for Mary's reading now extended to horticulture and arboriculture) had shed their final leaves. The open structure of trunks and branches made the scene look like a room with the curtains opened, ready for winter. This must be a message from the Lord: she must open the curtains of her disappointed heart, and accept whatever the future had to offer.

But why this sudden visit from Lizzy? Had Mary erred? Was there a reprimand in store? Maybe word had reached Lizzy about her overstepping the charity basket routine – her over-reaching of the role of wife, her straying into the sacred territory of church law? Yes, that would be it: Lizzy, in her Darcy incarnation, would be repulsed by Mary's handling of the bodies of those deceased wretches. Her behaviour had been quite unsuited to her station as Mrs Darcy's sister. On its journey to the Pemberley domain, the story would have gathered gory detail and heavy blame.

Mary, blown by the wind as she waited on the steps, felt once again cut to the quick. How she had longed to enunciate the words that would ring out over the open grave: "I am the Resurrection and the Life, saith the Lord! He that believeth in Me, though he be dead, yet shall he live!" Could her husband not have acknowledged that she, by her action, had saved the souls of mother and child for eternity? Rather than allow some footling aspect of parochial law to forbid her presence at a ceremony?

Here came the Pemberley carriage.

Knowing that the coachman would hand Lizzy and her maid out of the carriage, she did not come down the steps. The maid, Thwaite, would be handed out first, so she could be in attendance on her mistress to guide her round puddles.

Mary, though anxious about Lizzy's arrival, recalled Thwaite very clearly. What a pleasant young woman; how careful of her poor little sister; what a distance they had travelled from their lead-mining village in terms of status in life. What a blessing it must be for the sisters to be safely together at Pemberley.

But the coachman handed Lizzy out of the carriage and led her towards the steps. There was no sign of Thwaite.

Lizzy shook off the man as she approached the steps. "That will be all. I shall send my sister's maid for you when I am ready to return."

Lizzy's feet on each upward step seemed weighted, reluctant. And Mary's heart felt suddenly eased. She need not be nervous. Lizzy had a difficulty to discuss. This was a Lizzy who might even need Mary's services in some way. Though in what way she could not for the moment imagine.

∽∾

I place my ear a few inches away from the drawing room door.

The minx and Mrs Darcy have seated themselves in their usual wing-back chairs. But, soon after I close the door on the scene, I hear the sh-sh-sh of chair-legs across the carpet. One or other of the sisters has moved; I cannot tell which. One of them has something private to impart.

As is my custom and skill, I lean in to hear what might transpire.

Mrs Reynolds, in her coded missives, has already laid out her anxieties. "I have asked that our staffing difficulties be answered within a sen'night, so that replacements can be put in place before the December festivities. There is a fervour in the air which requires resolution. My dear Mrs B, answer me this: why can the ways of the world not operate smoothly, and according to my, and your, carefully laid plans? And according to the needs of the head of the household?"

"The needs of the head of the household": that is the nub.

This is the picture as I see it. When Mrs Darcy entered the Pemberley portals at her marriage, she was under the illusion that a shared headship, together with her adoring Mr Darcy, would fall from its corniced ceilings directly onto her shoulders. Now she sees the remnants of this illusion lying in tatters at her feet. When the needs of the dynasty are at stake, adoration gives way to the exercise of power. At this moment, we two housekeepers are watching Mrs Darcy as she stands at a fork in the road in the journey of her marriage. If she makes the wrong choice, danger will be lying in wait like an adder in the tall grass of a summer day.

Aha. Mrs Darcy's tone is raised. Now I can hear more than murmurings. I am offered detail.

I lean in closer. "I cannot, Mary! I *will* not! I forbid him! Unless he changes his mind, he must leave me be! If he presses me, against my will, it would..."

Her voice drops back. I press my ear more firmly. I feel the door vibrating with her passion. "It would *break* me."

My mistress minx replies slowly in her prim, tight voice. "I am not sure I understand you, Lizzy. At the time of your marriage, did you not discuss with Darcy your occasional need for privacy? For separateness?"

I almost smile. I can imagine Mrs Darcy sitting back and wondering what world this sister of hers lives in. *Scarlatti and Bibles.* Those were RN's words to me. *So long as she has her Scarlatti and her Bibles, she will leave us alone.*

"Can you make such bargains with your husband, Mary? Surely not! Has he no passion? But then..." Mrs Darcy attempts to grasp Mrs Needleman's point. "You have no dynasty to carry forward. No imminent knighthood to prepare for."

There is a pause, during which any listener other than the minx would respond: *Is Darcy expecting a knighthood? Lizzy, how delightful! And you a Lady! When can we expect to offer congratulations?*

But Mrs Needleman has no interest in knighthoods; she would not know her baronet from her earl.

"Naturally, Mr Needleman and I wish for a child of our own. In due course. In God's good time." Her voice fills out on the last phrase, then grows thin again as she continues. "I reject a coarse term such as *bargain*. We respect each other's needs. Surely, for you, after three offspring, there could be a significant pause? 'A time to give birth, a time to refrain from giving...'? *Ecclesiastes* Chapter 3."

Just as the minx has no time for knighthoods, Mrs Darcy has no time for Ecclesiastes. She can employ a different story from the Good Book. "And it needed twelve sons, did it not, for Jacob to create the tribes of Israel? Children are frail creatures, Fitzy reminds me. The more we have, the more secure the dynasty. But I am so *frightened*, Mary! How torn I was with Henrietta, and again with George, and yet again with William! I have no wish to transmit my fear of it onto you, Mary dear. But it is *horrible*!"

I am confused. Mrs R gave me to understand that Mrs Darcy was withholding herself from conjugal duties in an effort to keep the lead-miner's daughters at her side. Whereas this confession of distaste for the whole experience of childbirth exposes a more fundamental danger to the marriage. "Who knows, you may let slip a child as easy as a cow does a calf!" Her tone is close to nervous laughter. "But there are ways..." Now it changes to one of confidentiality: "...ways, are there not, to subvert the inevitability of the event? You must be familiar with such ways, Mary? Having not, as they say, 'fallen' for a child as yet? I beg you, how is it done? How do you achieve your result: doing as a wife should, yet not becoming *enceinte*?"

I am on tiptoe with anticipation. Has the minx, in fact, any information to impart? I should be most surprised if she did.

And indeed, all I hear from Mrs Needleman is silence.

Mrs Darcy continues. Her impatience with her sister is increasingly apparent. "There is another story entirely which we must discuss."

Ah. Now we come to the lead-miner's daughters.

But it is during this next pause, while Mrs Darcy is near to what must surely be the most difficult decision of her married life, that I am suddenly aware of my own personal needs. These, unfortunately, are preventing me from concentrating on this exchange and interpreting it in proper fashion. I must *see to myself*, as we say in Ulster. And just when I might discover how the field plays out with the lady's maid and her sister.

☙❧

Mary felt a trickle of cold sweat down her back. Thwaite, that delightful young woman with the afflicted sister, had fallen into sin! No wonder Darcy had responded with immediate condemnation.

Yet did our Lord not say, *Let him who is without sin throw the first stone*? Darcy himself must be without sin. Not sin of *that* kind, of course. But he had surely committed the sin of greed, to have acquired such immense wealth?

"Mary! Are you listening to me? He demands they be thrown out! Without a character! With the workhouse as their fate! Separated, inevitably, from each other, she to the able-bodied, the other flung into the company of wastrels! It is unthinkable! Yet he, whom I love and adore, can not only *think* it, but be adamant to make it *happen*!"

Make it happen. The words detached themselves from Lizzy's meaning, and reverberated in Mary's head.

Lizzy was still speaking: *believe* it, *imagine, happen...*

Mary withdrew into herself to consider this question.

What made 'it' happen? How, for instance, had Hill the housekeeper become the mother of Luke, the half-brother of herself and Lizzy and Jane and Kitty and Lydia? What was the actual process of the married situation? An Event surely did happen. Lizzy had come close to asking whether such an Event had ever happened to *her*. Which it had not. (To her relief.) Yet everyone expected it. As a result of such an Event, a woman often became sick, as Thwaite had been, in the carriage. This was one of the signs that the woman was *enceinte*. Like the young woman in the storm; the pulsating cord; the infant emerging in fits and starts, breathing, then breathing its last and becoming dead flesh; the flesh under her feet, the soul on its way to its Maker. A soul born, a soul dead, all within an instant. And her own feet upon the corpse.

These dramas were precipitated by that Event to which Lizzy kept referring. About which she was still speaking. "Even the workhouse might refuse them! Turn them back into the night – the open road – to die in a ditch!"

Mary burst out: "Lizzy! Tell me! What is it? What *makes it happen*? What has Thwaite done, what do *you* do, what do *I* do or *not* do? What does Mr Needleman do or not do? What, please, makes it *happen*?"

Lizzy shot to her feet. She stood before the fireplace, staring at Mary. Behind her the logs on the fire sparked, shuffled themselves and slipped into a different shape.

Mary could not bear the silence. She had asked a question, and now wished to take it back. But taking it back was not possible. The air around her heaved with it. She drew up her knees and grasped them so that her ankles pressed against the edge of the chair, and hurt. She let them go again. One of her light leather morning shoes – replacements for the abandoned pair full of mud – came off as this happened, and gave a little flutter as it fell on the carpet.

Lizzy, erect between Mary and the fire, still did not speak, but simply stared.

Mary, her throat full of those words that should not have been uttered, tried to speak so as to cover the utterances, and failed. She tried again: "What was your purpose in coming here this morning, Lizzy? Thwaite, of course. Your fear for the two devoted sisters. You are devoted to Thwaite. You lean upon her, rely upon her. Thwaite's sister, the poor soul, also relies upon her, upon Thwaite. They are devoted to each other. You cannot tolerate the notion of them being thrown out, into the ditch, to their doom."

She was getting there. She was getting to where the Lord was leading her.

"So. Why, this morning, did you need to come *here*, to see *me*? Without Thwaite? What question do you have in mind, Lizzy?"

Lizzy still stared at her. Minutes seemed to pass

before she even blinked.

Mary had no more words to say, and waited.

Finally, it came. "You. You are my hope, Mary. My possibility."

"Lizzy, I am not always in possession of the facts that you assume I am in possession of. Please explain. Your possibility? How? And please be seated. Away from the fire. I recall dreadful tales of women whose skirts catch fire when they lose sight of their own safety."

"What? Oh!" Lizzy turned abruptly, removed herself from the vicinity of the fire, and sat. "Is it not obvious? And please, Mary, please erase from your mind whatever I might have spilled out about…"

"About?"

"About Darcy. Our dynasty. The possibility of knighthood: that you may retain. Even murmur it to Mrs Beattie, if you wish. Fitzy and I, we are supremely happy. Our happiness will be complete when that honour is bestowed. I have said all that I have to say on that subject."

"Why did you come here this morning? Was it about Thwaite and her condition?"

"Yes. That. She begins to show. Servants talk. Darcy is informed. The moral condition of Pemberley, which is central to his position. *Our* position. However, my reliance upon Thwaite is not a factor in his thinking. It is the appearance of a child out of wedlock… Oh, Mary, think what happened at Longbourn! If you know nothing else, you know *that* story!"

"What?" Mary reeled. "You mean, *Luke*? What has *he* to do with it?"

Lizzy carried on as if Mary had not spoken. "Please

try to employ your native intelligence in this matter, Mary. Thwaite and her sister. I have withdrawn from Darcy for several reasons...for some time...to help him focus on my needs. I cannot bear that he throw those two poor sisters into the ditch. The *ditch*, Mary! Please! Tell me, how many servants' rooms you have in the attic here?"

"Rooms? Servants' rooms? How should I know how many?"

"Have you never even been *up* there?"

"Why should I? It is Mrs Beattie's territory."

"Does Mrs Beattie herself sleep there?"

"Of course not. She sleeps on the first floor, along the corridor above the kitchen. Lizzy, please, why are we talking about where Mrs Beattie sleeps?"

"And your coachman – he sleeps above the stables?"

"Yes. I mean, no. I think he sleeps beside, in some kind of addendum to the stables. Lizzy, you are surely not suspecting our coachman of any misdemeanour? Thwaite? What about Thwaite?"

"So," Lizzy said in sudden triumph, "there will be a spare servants' room in the attic, will there not! They will be keeping it for a nursery maid. You have an extra servants' room, Mary!"

Mary, in the hope that the floor would hold her up better than the chair had done, now stood. "Are there not rooms a-plenty at Pemberley for whatever it was you have in mind?" She had stepped forward, and realised that only one of her two feet had on a morning shoe.

"But Pemberley cannot *keep* them!" Lizzy was shouting. "Are you *mad*? You, Mary, you with your charity boxes, you with your forgivenesses and your righteousnesses, you surely must realise that—"

There might have been more words from Lizzy, but Mary did not hear them. At the moment she heard the words *realise that*, the truth behind Lizzy's visit hit her quite suddenly, with complete clarity.

There was a way forward, and Lizzy was trying to show her that way.

But she, Mary, must say it. Must offer. Must open her heart – and of course, Mr Needleman's heart – and, oh dear, Mrs Beattie's heart too.

She opened her mouth, and spoke.

ೲ

Feeling a deal more comfortable after my visit (with towels) to the necessary house, I take up my place again silently at the drawing room door.

As ever, I fear that my presence might be detected. But to neither of the women on the far side of this door is it important, at this moment, whether someone is eavesdropping on them. The pitch of the voices, the pain, the mystery of what is at issue between them: the naked needs of these two women, the one God-bound, the other God-forsaken: those needs pierce the mahogany and flow straight into my ear.

"Your forgivenesses and your righteousnesses..."

The minx now cuts across her sister in a way that, on any other day, I guess would be unimaginable.

"Lizzy, dear. Please think it possible that I have a mind of my own. I see the signs, as you do. As soon as the situation revealed itself to me, I knelt down in prayer, as is my wont, and asked Our Lord whether I might be of assistance to His abandoned ones. His answer came most clearly."

I gasp. The minx *could* not? *Would* not! Surely?

There follows a silence in which I hear a gasp from my own mouth. Or perhaps it is a gasp from Mrs Darcy that I hear. Or the two intermingled.

Yet still they do not detect me. There are no footsteps towards the door.

I hear Mrs Needleman's breath heaving between the points she is anxious to make. "Do not be afraid, Lizzy. There is a solution to the dispute between yourself and Darcy. I will take them. They will come here, to the Rectory."

She is making *arrangements* without consulting *me*!

"The sisters. Both. Yes, even the crippled one. Thwaite, despite her fall from grace. If I am able to help in this way, I may choose to address her by her other name? Her baptismal name? And her sister? Is she called... Is it Tilly?"

Mrs Darcy, it seems, can barely speak. "Milly! But Mary, what will Mr Needleman say? Or his housekeeper?"

The minx carries on as if uninterrupted. "They will follow my lead. My husband is at present away from home, but he has confidence in my life of prayer and the decisions that arise from it. The sisters will be accustomed to sharing a room. As I say, I have never explored the Rectory's attic. Come, let us go upstairs. Let us do it together."

The minx's decisiveness has paralysed me. When I hear the word *Come*, my ear is still fixed to the mahogany. But it takes the crescendo of accompanying footsteps across the Axminster to force me into leaping backwards.

In the split second before the door opens, my hands clutch each other upon my chest. I take up an awkward stance to the side of the door, and watch my mistress and Mrs Darcy sail through. As they walk towards the stairs, I see that Mrs Needleman wears only one of her morning shoes. Mrs Darcy, whose face radiates what may be fear and confusion but might also be relief from despair, does not seem to have noticed this fact.

"The attic stairs," says Mrs Needleman to me over her shoulder. "A room will be needed. Shall we?"

"Needed, Mrs Needleman?" I almost snort with laughter at my alliteration.

Mrs Needleman stops, and tries to look me straight in the eye. She cannot, so instead she looks back at her sister. "Mrs Darcy and I are considering an adventure in the provision of care. We propose taking someone in. Two people, in fact. *I was a stranger, and ye took me in*. It is God's work, is it not?"

෨

As Mary led the little procession up the servants' stairs, she felt her feet to be slightly unbalanced, and remembered with a shiver of embarrassment that one of her shoes had slipped off during that astonishing exchange with Lizzy. But she straightened her shoulders and did not falter. The Lord had led her on this journey; He did not fret Himself about shoes.

At the top of the narrow wooden stairs she was

challenged yet again. What if there *were* no spare room on the servants' floor for the unfortunate sisters to share? She would be shown up for a fool. Folly, surely, could not be part of the Lord's plan?

As she reached the servants' landing she stepped aside, and put out a hand for Lizzy to step aside too, so that Mrs Beattie could go ahead of them.

"The spare servants' room, if you please, Mrs Beattie."

There was some shuffling, as the space was tight, but the housekeeper did as she was told: she opened one of the two unvarnished pine doors and called behind her as she went in: "Our own maids-of-all-work share the other room, Mrs Darcy."

There was a room. The Lord had provided for his forsaken ones.

Mary stood aside for Lizzy to go in, and followed her.

The two beds on either side of the door were unmade with sheets or blankets. Each bed held a thin horsehair mattress on which various sizes of lump were visible.

Mrs Beattie turned in the narrow space beyond the beds and addressed them. "As you see, we do not expect our servants to share beds. There is even a night-stand for their comfort." Mary felt abashed at the way Mrs Beattie was taking over the situation, then grateful for her diplomacy in addressing Mrs Darcy rather than herself. Mrs Darcy's comfort was what mattered most.

"Is there no provision for warmth at all?" Mary asked. "No fire?"

Mrs Beattie gave a short laugh. "Our maids have no time for basking by a fire, Lord love them! Nor myself! Up with the dawn and on with the working day, is my motto. As you will appreciate, Mrs Darcy?"

This was too much for Mary. She said briskly, "Thank you, Mrs Beattie. Let us not detain you from your duties. I will inform you of my plans in due time."

Mrs Beattie fired back: "Then I will return to the drawing room, Mrs Needleman, and retrieve your missing shoe. No doubt you will be needing it later on." With a turn that stirred the air, she manoeuvred herself past them and out of the door.

"Oh, Mary!" As they listened to the housekeeper's stout feet descending the stairs, Lizzy's laughter reminded Mary miserably of the mockery of their girlhood days. "You really must be careful. I fear Mrs Beattie has the upper hand."

"Perhaps," said Mary, mortified, "I should withdraw my offer to take in those who cause Mr Darcy so much offence. My only purpose is to do God's work in the world."

"No, no! Mary, please, I am so grateful. I cannot express just how grateful! When might they be brought from Pemberley? I dread the prospect of Thwaite's tears at leaving. But they will be kept together! Shall we expedite this new arrangement as soon as possible?"

16

The Other Sisters

MARY WAS DETERMINED to assert herself with the housekeeper.

"Mrs Beattie," she said.

"Mrs Needleman."

Those vowels of hers! The *ee* was almost an *a*, the *a* was definitely an *ah*...

But the housekeeper's accent was not at issue. Mary's task was to open up a new dispensation. During a long night, she had prepared her words for it.

"I thank you for your co-operation in this matter. There is no question of my intruding on your authority in the kitchen. However, I have made this decision about the two maids from Pemberley" – at which she heard a suppressed *harrumph* from the housekeeper – "under the direct guidance of answered prayer. *He leadeth me in the paths of righteousness, for His name's sake.* Can I rely upon you to arrange the practical necessities? The change may be a difficult one, I am the first to acknowledge that. It is all the more important for me to have your assistance for it to run smoothly."

That is enough, Mary, said a clear voice in her head. *Do not overdo it.*

Mrs Beattie was making some sort of statement. "I am employed not by yourself, but by the Rector. Is *he* not to be consulted about this decision of yours? Moreover, are you not concerned about the *time*? The fact that your husband is quite *unusually* late back from Derby?"

"It will be the storm, the condition of the roads... I and my husband have developed a mutual respect for each other's spiritual explorations." Mary knew there was no logical connection between these two sentences, and again Mrs Beattie *harrumphed*. "He will see, when he returns, the great need of these two souls. I anticipate his approval."

"What about Gladys and Patty? The affront to them, to have their habits undermined, is it fair? And what will be the fate of the crippled one? Then there is the issue of the arrival, in, would you say, around three months' time?" Mrs Beattie did a half-turn towards the kitchen stairs. "Will the good Lord deliver His answers to those questions by messenger-boy, or by what other means?" And she swept away down the stairs.

Within a few moments Patty shuffled by with a steaming bowl and a scrubbing brush, and soon afterwards Gladys thumped across the hall muttering something about the lack of heat in the flat-irons. Mary stood in the fading light and let it happen around her.

In a while she found the confusion of small questions settling into one big question. Where was her husband, and why was he so late home?

Could Hurry be despatched to ride towards Derby and retrieve him? When Mary enquired this of Mrs Beattie, she snapped out a few syllables without even pausing in her busy flow about Hurry's being "down with a head cold" which had to be "dosed through".

So. Absent her husband was, and absent he remained. Mary retreated to her room and reflected on the situation she had brought about.

She could not be certain that Robert would approve of her offer of sanctuary to the two maids. One was disgraced, the other a grotesquely twisted presence. The latter could be rejected on grounds of financial probity, the former on grounds of Sin.

She could quote Scripture in her defence! *Except the Lord build the house, they labour in vain that build it...* But her husband would quote Scripture in reply, and with years of scholarship to shore it up. *Except the Lord* rule *the house*, the Rector could argue. Then she, the unschooled Rector's wife, would stand accused of Misrule. Of allowing the Lord of Misrule into the House of the Lord God.

All Mary could do was wait. She fell to her knees in prayer beside her bed.

⚬⚬

If Thwaite is to disappear, thinks Esther as they travel the short distance from Pemberley to Humbole, she must recall the last hours of the lady's maid's life for later memory. For she now carries a hope for the future, as well as a small creature yet to be born.

The coach rattles and sways. Milly is nestling her body against Esther like a bean in a bean-pod. Her eyes are closed, but Esther knows she is not sleeping; she too is reliving the last few hours and imagining what the next hours and days might hold. Milly has never visited the Rectory, but because of *Doovus* she will have as vivid an image of the place as if she'd accompanied Esther there; only now it will be bathed in a golden glow, because the Rectory is to be the place of their salvation.

Yet Pemberley was the place of their earlier salvation. Which, after an interval of threats (expulsion, abandonment, workhouse, death), has come now to an end. No salvation was ever permanent, secure.

Thwaite. How had Thwaite died?

"Thwaite, dear." It was Mrs Darcy's kindest, most considerate of tones.

"Yes, ma'am?"

"You are saved. I have found a solution. My dear sister..."

"Mrs Needleman, ma'am?"

"Indeed." There followed a brief description of the attic accommodation at the Rectory, followed by a formal expression of thanks for services rendered in the last few years. Then a reference to her sister Mary's godliness, which guides her every move. And that, Esther knows full well, could go one way or the other, depending on the mood of the God concerned.

She and Milly spent the morning under instruction

of Mrs Reynolds, scrubbing out their room from top to bottom. Esther, on receiving these orders, looked Mrs R straight in the eye in the hope of acknowledgement, but gained none. Mrs R stared back, let her eyes fall to the level of Esther's belly, and said: "You know my expectations. Perfection. You may present yourself in the sub-housekeeper's office in two hours' time to receive a small closing disbursement."

Milly stirs now as the coach shudders over an especially rutted stretch of road. Esther tightens her hold.

It was ten days ago that the explosion took place. Mr Darcy's return from London was preceded by the usual beautification of Mrs Darcy's face, hair, clothes, and night attire. But Thwaite perceived a significant tension in her mistress: there were frequent sighs, gazings into the distance, slumps into half-sentences or the sudden cutting short of an exclamation. Thwaite made sure that every gesture of hers was exactly in line with how she had always been. But The Matter stood between them. The growth inside her, which could no longer be disguised.

Gradually, Thwaite sensed the existence of another Matter entirely.

"Mr Darcy will expect" was Mrs Darcy's usual form of words, but, little by little, it was changing to "Mr Darcy makes his wishes known" and in due course settled on "Mr Darcy has begun to demand".

Esther, as Thwaite, remembers precisely when this word *demand* entered her mistress's vocabulary. It came in the bedchamber. Mrs Darcy was choosing a variety of nightwear, as she always did, but this time she threw aside in exasperation one of the more exquisite of her nightdresses. "But will that not give precisely the message that I wish to avoid? The demand that I should always be ready, always be beautiful, always be...?" And here Mrs Darcy had paused, empty-handed, and gazed into a scene to which Thwaite could not be privy. The blood drained from her mistress's face; her beautiful skin turned to alabaster.

Then she came to some inward resolution. She tossed her head.

"Oh, Thwaite, why do I ask *you* what is to be done? You who are surely the last person who should know the answer to my dilemma? I might as well ask that useless *Mary*!"

Thwaite was dismissed, and not recalled until an hour later.

Esther recognises from a turn in the lane that they are nearing the Rectory. She moves to alert Milly. But, in the fraction of a second before she does that, some words of Mrs Darcy detach themselves, and repeat.

"Some Greek women managed to accomplish it! In story, in legend... The men would not do as their wives bade them, so the wives took the action of last resort. They would no longer *be* wives. In the fullest aspect of that term. There, Thwaite! I'll wager you never counted your worth so great, did you? I told him... I even found the reference in his library. Lysis...-is-trata!" She stumbled over the pronunciation. "I *will* not have my maids cast into the ditch! I *will* maintain my distance! I will *not* give way! Until he accedes!"

Esther, threading her mistress's words back carefully through memory, wonders at them. She does not understand why Greek wives should be held up as an example to English wives. But she does recognise the marital transaction that Mrs Darcy describes.

Can she believe that Mrs Darcy has valued her services so highly as to deny her husband his marital rights on her account? And on Milly's?

She gives Milly the tiniest of nudges. "We're 'ere, Mill."

Milly is ready on the instant for what is to come. As is Esther.

The horse rears as they come to a halt in the Rectory drive. Esther does not wait for the coachman to open the door; she knows he will remain up top. She and Milly are vagabonds, to be taken in by charity. They are safe, but bereft of their Pemberley status.

Status be damned, says Esther to herself. They are alive. They have a roof over their heads. Thank God. Mrs Needleman's God. May He be a kind one.

The minx is up in her room in prayer. She cannot face the consequences of her precipitate action. She is contrite. She begs for forgiveness.

Or perhaps she begs for the Lord to make it all come right? For RN to come home wreathed in smiles and ready to welcome the waifs, as if they were honoured guests?

The woman is naïve to expect it. She uses the Lord as an instrument of her own will, to be bent accordingly. If I know the Lord – and I have known His rigour from my earliest years in County Down –

His Will cannot be so bent.

Yet the two wretches are on their way. And, so long as the Rector fails to return to his Rectory, I must swallow my pride and take them in. For sure, they cannot be returned to their previous home.

Where *is* my RN? How *goes* my SH? How fares that unspeakable love, which we have all three cherished at peril of our lives? My heart beats with terror at what might have occurred. For SH is a whirlwind, and a whirlwind can rip up a landscape.

Here are the carriage wheels. I must go and receive the lead-miners' daughters.

I move through the hall and open the doors; the wind gusts in my face, up my skirts. I hold them down, my skirts; modesty has ever been my first concern. I close the door behind me, move to the top of the steps, and stand.

Here comes the coach. It is the oldest of the Pemberley coaches, used only for transporting staff around the estate.

The coach door creaks. A crack opens, closes with a gust, opens again, and as the door bangs outwards, the young harlot who was once Mrs Darcy's Thwaite descends, almost falls, from door to gravel drive. For there is, of course, no assisting step. She waits a moment, then turns, presumably to extract the second occupant. Thwaite – ah! her name is *Esther* – her hand goes back into the doorway as she puts up her arms for the other. Lifts her, in one light gesture, down to the ground.

It is a child, or a midget. I could fell it, if I wished, in a single kick.

They link arms and shuffle towards the steps. I have a sudden vision of other arms, linking to other bodies, other faces; others who have brought these two beings to pass; unknown men and women by whose means these two have been created. *In His image created He them.*

I blink it away. I am no Irish visionary. I must keep my wits about me.

The pair, linked so inextricably, move in little jerks across the space. The small thing blows in each gust of wind, rights itself again with the help of its sister, and their progress continues.

I watch it: its left foot stepping forwards, followed by its right foot stepping sideways, half-dragged. Yet it can move quite readily. It almost floats.

Now the wind blows her tattered cloak and I perceive an arm. The arm, right arm, comes out to hold the cloak, just as my arm holds down my skirts against the wind. The hand is bent back, almost at right-angles to its arm.

She is so tiny.

I feel my mind, under instruction from my heart, transfer its language from *it* to *she*.

Oh, my rebellious heart! Mr Prunty saw the heart in me, because he had the same trouble with his own heart. Under his control, yet not under his control. As is mine.

Here they are. I must, at any rate, be civil to these two.

As my feet carry me down the steps to acknowledge them, a small weight in my housekeeper's pocket reminds me that these emanations from Pemberley bring with them a task. It is a letter, and a task assigned to me therein by Mrs Reynolds: *chercher le père*. Mrs Reynolds is in great perturbation around her failure to establish the *paternité* in relation to the *enceinte*. She who knows everything about everyone knows not this essential fact; and so, now that the *enceinte* has become my responsibility, she pressures me into filling that gap.

But oh, my far more immediate task! To find my beloved RN!

There has been no message! Is there an accident? Does some filthy ditch hold his injured frame?

The two figures are three steps below me. Two. One.

I will obey my rebellious heart and take them in.

☙

Milly, now their attic door is shut, flings back the blankets of one of the beds, counting in whispered breaths: "One – two – three!" Then we see a large lump under the sheet and she flings that back: "Bott-le! Hot bott-le!"

We hug, and chuckle, and dance a little jig of delight.

I explore the other bed. It too has three rough blankets. Three is generous for a maid-of-all-work. But in this bed, no bottle. No matter! We only need one bed and one bottle between us, and we'll have six blankets to see us through the winter. *To see us until...* But I will not think about that.

Milly clambers up onto the warmed bed and, with a

feathered motion of her bent hand, strokes the bottle. Gives a tiny shriek and licks her hand: hot hot hot! She giggles, I giggle, we giggle together. We are together. Not in a ditch. We are warm.

I am Esther now, and can shake off Thwaite. I do not have to be two; I can become one. And, even more, one with my Milly. She flings her cloak onto the floor. I do the same, then retrieve it and wrap it round the bottle. We leap into the warm bed and, with a cry of *Doovus, Doovus*, arrange ourselves around it.

In a moment she throws back sheet and blankets and leaps out again.

"Hung-ry hung-ry! I saw summat!"

She's right. On the night-stand are laid two plates, each holding a slice of bread, lightly buttered, and two quarters of an apple, faintly brown from awaiting our arrival. We fall upon them, and with giggles still on our busy lips, devour them.

We are just licking our plates when there is a knock at the door. We freeze. Who could it be that *knocks*? On *our* door?

I stand, stiff, find Thwaite again, and retrieve her manner. "Come... in?"

The door opens. It is Mrs Needleman, the Rector's Wife.

It is strange that she did not greet us downstairs but left that task to the fierce Irish housekeeper.

Mrs Needleman does not come in. She stands in the doorway. Her hands are folded on her belly and, oh! she cannot help it: her eyes fall to *my* belly. She cannot tear her eyes away. And she cannot find words.

The lady must speak first. The Lady of the House

even more so.

My heart beats, and Milly's behind me. I can hear our two hearts beating.

Mrs Needleman continues to stare. I close my eyes, so as to stop looking at her looking at my baby.

There are breadcrumbs on my chin, I know there are. But it would be impolite to brush them off onto the floor, here in this room, which is so newly ours.

At last she speaks, as from some gravel at the bottom of a pond.

"I cast my mind back, and thank you most sincerely for your care of my sister, Mrs Darcy, and also…your sister…for her care of our dear Hill."

I remain silent, for I am now but a maid-of-all-work, and new, and her eyes still flutter between my belly and my face. Also, her eyes seek out my other half, my Milly. I make a tiny step sideways. Milly takes the hint and does a tiny bob before disappearing back into my shadow.

"Ma'am, that was our duty. And our pleasure, to care for such fine women."

Then I am tongue-tied, for I realise I have made some equivalence between Mrs Fitzwilliam Darcy and the humble housekeeper of Longbourn.

At last, Mrs Rector pulls her eyes away from me and, with the energy of that pulling, pulls her own self together.

"I see you have enjoyed the food that I ordered. Was there jam?" Puzzled, I shake my head. "None. Now. You will in due course be introduced to my husband, the Reverend Mr Needleman, who is unfortunately detained on a mission to the city of

Derby. Nevertheless, you will take your orders from myself and Mrs Beattie." I could not grasp where *nevertheless* fitted into the scheme of things. "Mainly, of course, from Mrs Beattie. You will respect the work done by the other maids, Gladys and Patty. Excellent, both. I expect them to give you...instructions, and so on." She speaks with much blinking, as if she cannot see very well behind those spectacles.

I have a desperate need to giggle. I suspect Milly feels the same. We must not. We absolutely must not. Please let this talking be finished very soon.

"My husband has sermons, and great business to accomplish. It is about the Great Chain of Being, you see? But that is enough for today. You may stay upstairs until first thing in the morning, when you will rise and... When you will rise. There are chamber pots under each bed. You may check?"

Check? What?

Ah, she means *empty the chamber pots*. I bend to see them. I sense that, while I am doing this, she is staring at Milly. Accustoming herself to the twistedness of her, the handicaps she bears. People do. We are used to her being stared at.

The chamber pots are white, old, with cracks in their glaze.

I stand up straight, and Mrs Needleman and I meet each other's eyes for the first time. She is flushed. She knows she has stared at Milly, and she knows I know she has stared at Milly. It does not matter to me. But it does matter to her, to Mrs Needleman the Rector's wife. She may be wishing that she had not done God's duty and taken us waifs into her home after all.

It was one of Scarlatti's simplest sonatas, but she could not get her fingers round its demi-semi-quavers. "Five hundred and fifty-five sonatas in his lifetime!" Mr Prendergast would exclaim. "We shall aim for, say, seven?"

Mary lifted her disobedient hands from the keys and made them into a little hammock on which to rest her forehead. She had spent an entire night not knowing whether her husband was alive or dead, and her only solace was the keyboard. The ghost of Mr Prendergast bid her to master the Scarlatti. But Mr Prendergast also loved Bach! The whole family of them, especially the one called Johann Sebastian. J S Bach wrote such simple pieces. Pieces that could have been designed for people like her: simple, yet ardent. Like *Air In G*.

She loosed her hands and searched for the *Air in G* among the sheet music on top of the piano. Here it was! Octaves, mostly, with a slow, simple tune above. She picked out the tune with her right hand, then picked out the octaves with her left.

But there were *three* staves! How could that be, when the player had only two hands to play with? Octave oct-ave oct-ave oct-ave...

Her eye caught the title at the top. *Air In G for the Organ*.

The *organ*! She was supposed to play these octaves with her *feet*! Her dear husband, when presenting her with his marriage gift, must have added some pieces from his forlorn attempts at the church organ!

She collapsed with a shriek, knocking the music off

its stand and herself almost off the stool.

Retrieving the *Air In G* from the floor, she caught sight of her feet in their morning shoes and remembered how the loss of one of those shoes had recently humiliated her. She was hopeless. She was clearly no good at the piano. She was no good at being the Rector's wife, or her husband would now be at her side rather than with Mr Hepplecraft in Derby.

But *was* he in Derby? Might he be lying on the sodden pitted road, injured by a fall from his horse? Hearing the wind and the rain beating on the windows, she saw that he was most likely lost to the storm, or to Mr Hepplecraft, and she could do nothing to save him.

Mary leapt to her feet. She must have her husband back! He would lead her into paths of righteousness! He might even celebrate her courage in taking on those two poor waifs whom Mr Darcy was set on throwing into the workhouse or the ditch!

She strode out of the music room door and ran down to the drawing room, where she placed herself by the fireplace and rang for Mrs Beattie.

The weight of the woman's footsteps could be heard ahead of her presence.

Mary said, "I rang to enquire how the new maids are settling in."

"I set them to the chamber pots," replied Mrs Beattie stiffly, "followed by a thorough clean-out of the necessary."

"Was that really...?" She could not use the word *necessary*. And she must not challenge Mrs Beattie on her own territory.

"You will not be familiar," continued Mrs Beattie, "with the training of staff. They must start with the basics. Gladys and Patty are glad to be relieved of such tasks. In times like this, with such changes afoot, it behoves us to keep our regular staff as content as can be managed. Will that be all, Mrs Needleman?"

"By no means. Has there been word from Derby?"

"Not a one." The housekeeper's voice dropped into a lower register. "Mr Needleman has a mind of his own. He can send information if he wishes."

"But he has never remained longer than the stated time! Not during the whole of our marriage! Where is *Hurry*?" Mary began to shiver. "Could he not ride out along the road normally taken by Mr Needleman, in case there has been an accident?"

"Hurry is unwell. He cannot ride."

"That is news to me. Why was I not informed of his illness? He might be infectious! Mr Needleman may have caught some disease from him!"

Mrs Beattie did not dispute this. Mary saw that her housekeeper had no more fight in her. This was so unusual that she was lost for words.

Mrs Beattie swallowed, then coughed. She said, croakily, "He has to take a nostrum. For a condition that he has."

"I do not understand? Please explain."

"The laudanum. It is a compulsion for him. Addiction. He asked me not to tell you, but maybe it is needful for you to know now. He has times of being unfit to mount a horse."

This was the first straight answer to any of the difficult questions Mary had faced since her marriage, and, though still shivering, she was set free by it. "Is Mr Hepplecraft also afflicted? My husband, even? Mrs Beattie, you are a woman of the world. You must see how protected I have been from everything that a young lady could be protected from. Please, tell me! What is at issue between my sister and Mr Darcy? Clearly there is the matter of the two maids. But, grateful as Mrs Darcy may be for my taking them in, it is only a measure of what is afoot. I know that the bearing of a child is a dangerous proceeding, but what is it that occurs beforehand? What is the practice that my sister constantly refers to, to which she is bidden by contract, and from which there is no escape? It seems that everyone is aware of this practice except myself! How can that be? And how may I accommodate – ?"

"Stop!"

Mrs Beattie's single syllable left Mary's words hanging in the air.

In the silence, the image came to her of Robert, her husband, weeping at the throb of organ music as he knelt in the Priory pew. Then a second image: the storm and the cart and the man with the whip, the woman splayed, the infant dead, the life pulsating between them and, at last, like a candle blown, going out.

Mrs Beattie had started to speak again, and Mary blinked away the images.

"...must cease forthwith. We cannot be having such talk. Please return to your piano."

"I will, Mrs Beattie. But not quite yet. I need an answer to just one more question."

Mrs Beattie hesitated, then nodded.

"What were the circumstances under which Gladys and Patty first came to the Rectory?"

Mary was surprised to hear herself ask this question. It had not occurred to her before the words left her mouth. But, as she listened to Mrs Beattie's reply, she realised that there was a third image – that of Gladys and Patty, very much younger, and, perhaps, still innocent – that she could add to the other two, and begin to grasp the essential truth that she had missed so far.

Her shivering gradually eased as she listened as Mrs Beattie gave her answer. It was as clear an answer to this question as her answer had been about Hurry's condition. Later, Mary could not recall her exact words, but they made sense at the time. In response, she was able to ask: "So those two faithful women were ill-treated in that way by a man? Like, perhaps, the man in the cart with the whip? By what should be an act of fidelity?"

Mrs Beattie lowered her head and murmured, "I regret to say, Mrs Needleman, that such is the way of the world."

She and Mary looked each other in the eye, and more silence followed.

Then came a banging at the door. And Mary ran, and Mrs Beattie ran after her, out of the drawing room and through the hall, where Gladys, with Patty holding on to her from behind, was undoing the heavy doors and letting in the evening, and the wind, and the rain.

"The master!" shouted Gladys. "It is the master!"

17

The Other Marriages

MARY SAT ON THE SMALL upright chair in her bedchamber, and wept.

Ever since Mrs Beattie and Gladys and Patty had enfolded her husband in a tripartite embrace and borne his bleeding body up to his room and out of her sight, it was as if she had never arrived at the Rectory. Never married her husband, never taken up residence, never sat at breakfast with one or two clergymen discussing questions of salvation, nor arranged daily menus with the housekeeper, worn the Rector's spectacles, sat in the handsome Rectory pew each Sunday to listen to her husband short-sightedly preaching, from Mary's notes, the Gospel for the Day.

She knew nothing of his wounds, their origin or severity. Nothing was said about Hurry, whom she had glimpsed hunched in a half-run-half-limp over to the stables, grabbing the stray reins of the horse as he did so and dragging the poor animal in out of the rain. Had he returned together with her husband, or separately from him? Had he rescued Mr Needleman despite his (what did Mrs Beattie call it?) condition, medicinal disability? *Addiction*? She had caught Mrs Beattie's eye for a moment then, and enunciated over her husband's groaning body the single word, "Hurry?" But all she had received from the housekeeper was a grunt of "He knows what is best for his self." The servant threesome and the rescued gentleman had lurched off up the stairs, guided by shouts from Mrs Beattie: "Mind...! Do not trip! No matter, we will see to it later." Mary had followed disconsolately in their wake, heard her husband's moans echoing up to the ceiling as they reached the door of his bedchamber, and found herself wishing she were a maid-of-all-work and could take part in his care. Fetch a bowl herself, and kneel to scrub his blessed blood off the stair carpet.

This last thought flew tearfully around her brain until it took over and propelled her into action. Hearing the splash and clatter of Gladys for the sixth or seventh time, she ran out to meet her on the landing. "Please. Allow me." Ignoring the maid's bewilderment, she took careful hold of the bowl of warm water and, seeing the brush, declared, "This one is mine. I shall busy myself on the stairs. Fetch a further bowl for yourself."

It took Gladys several minutes to let this instruction sink in, but finally she did as she was bidden. On her way back she dropped a dishcloth into Mary's hand for mopping up the dirty water after she had scrubbed her stair. So, Mary thought humbly, there was a brain in the maid's head after all.

꩜

Esther and Milly huddled together uncomfortably in bed. Whatever the racket and palaver going on down there, the mystery of the master's return and whatever it signified either for poor Mrs Needleman or for their two selves, Esther knew that the only policy now was to keep out of the way.

And no *Doovus*.

They held tight to each other, but there was a ballooning layer between them called The Question. It quickened. It kicked. It felt sore as a wedge, forcing them apart however close they lay. The outside noises came and went. The barrier between them hurt with every breath. It was about Saying His Name. Accusing.

Esther whispered, "I willna, Mill."

"Yer muss, Ess. It's stren'ff an' 'elp. Fer us. Us all."

Silence.

"Ess. I askit. Why d'yer wanna *save* 'im? Yer din' luv 'im, did yer?"

Esther felt choked. What was her answer to that? "Na. I couldna, cos 'e wouldna stop. Only if 'e'd stopped could I've felt it as love."

"So? Then?"

"Don't *Then* me! I willna *use* it! Willna be so bold, so bad!"

"Ess! Yer bein' Fwaite agen nah! Liss'n t'yer! Yer juss Fwaite! Where's Ess gone?"

She was silenced by how completely Milly knew her, heard her, saw what was happening in her head and her heart and what they should do about it.

But still she resisted.

Milly's forehead was against hers, tapping gently.

Esther knew what that meant. *Why, why not?*

She had no answer, but opened her mouth all the same. And out it came. It came not from Esther but from Thwaite. "It's Mrs Jane. I cannot do it to her. She has suffered enough. I cannot bring disgrace to her, atop of all that. I canna, Mill. Canna."

Milly's forehead tapped. Tap. Tap. Each tap meant *Yer muss. Yer muss. Yer muss.*

അ

Dear Mrs Reynolds - I have your letter of the 10th inst. and am grateful for sentiments therein expressed. The Rector regains a little strength, though is still silent on what caused the accident. He speaks again and again about the fall from his horse. It is clear to me, by the way he turns aside when asked about church affairs during the Christmas season, that the Rural Dean should be apprised of his illness so that substitutes may be found. When I enquire after the health of Mr Hepplecraft, his face turns further from me, tears drenching his pillow. I conclude therefore that the Rector will be making no more journeys to our county town and that, henceforward, he will be composing sermons with the help only of his library here at the Rectory.

Lady Manton has sent a message proposing an imminent visit. I will believe that when I see it. It is she who must alert the Rural Dean of a change in parish requirements.

All this, you will understand, comes with consequences for my good self. About these I must remain silent.

But silence is my long-time companion. The skill of it has been with me since I was a child in County Down. My father taught it me; I was a ready pupil. Mr Prunty was envious of my skill at it, freely admitting his own failings in that regard.

You enquire about our newly accommodated members of staff. Surprisingly, both of them are fully functioning, one despite her girth, the other despite her gait. This has taken the sting from fears of competition between them and our existing staff.

The mistress, as you know, has a fondness for lost souls, and reminds me of the role of the small creature in nursing the now deceased Longbourn housekeeper. So I allowed the small one to shuffle into the master's room, first to do the chamber pot, then to attend to his clothing and so on. She cannot reach very far, poor mite, but she borrows a stool from the kitchen in order to complete some tasks over which I, personally, have felt tentative. She moves at a pace that compares well with that of Gladys or Patty.

You mention again the matter of paternity. With dismay, I have to report no progress. Esther, whom you knew as Thwaite, remains tight-lipped as ever. The other has no language that any normal being can comprehend.

She, the crippled one, has a way of disappearing from view. An instance. Yesterday I was with the master, the small cripple assisting, when, on the chime of the clock on the stairs, I remembered that the loaves were due to be retrieved from the oven. In shock at my unreliable recall (which is normally impeccable) I must have cried out, "Bread!" In a trice, she vanished. A disgruntled Gladys told me later that when she stumbled along to see to the loaves, she found them neatly arranged on the wire rack to cool and the hot oven already damped down. It was of course impossible that the child had done these tasks. Yet, unless it be elves, she must have done them. I admit to feeling quite discombobulated.

As ever, I am composing this letter solely in my mind. I will convert the main import in our specially devised code and send it by the trusted messenger-boy when next he comes from Pemberley.

Meanwhile, the mistress busies herself in the parish during this welcome spell of winter sunshine. She seldom speaks of her husband; her visits to his sick-bed are a brief glance from the doorway: "My dear? All well?" And she backs away again.

I look forward to your next coded missive. Surely Mr D will not tolerate further prolongation of his wife's denial of marital rights now that the offending question has been resolved? But I knew from the moment I laid eyes on Mrs Darcy, née Bennet, that she would fail in her duty of obedience. I must admit, however, that poor Mrs

Bingley, to whom obedience came so naturally, has scarcely seen benefit from that stance.

∾

There was, against one of the walls of the Rectory drawing room, a two-seater sofa of the bergère type which Mary was in the habit of using for the pursuit of needlework. She would place her small bag of fabrics, needles, threads and thimbles down on the floor beside her and use the wooden arm of the sofa to rest her work on as she sewed. One day, when Esther, having completed a task, bobbed and said, "Will that be all, ma'am?", Mary had the impulse to reply, "Esther dear. Sit beside me and keep me company a while."

Esther looked hesitant, but Mary waited in the hope that she would interpret the request as an order. She did, and sat.

"Might you hold my threads for me? See, there are five colours in this creation. I tend to muddle the beige with the cream, and with you holding them out, I will be able to tell the difference."

"Glad to be of service." Esther held out her hands, and Mary laid her threads over one hand so that the maid could use the other to arrange them neatly. Esther arranged the confusing colours at opposite ends, so that Mary could more easily distinguish them. What a sensitive young woman, thought Mary. No wonder Lizzy was so attached to her.

Then Esther took a sharp in-breath: a thread had caught on a rough bit of skin.

Mary said, "Dear dear! I hope Mrs Beattie has

not set you too many tasks of the coarse variety. At Pemberley, your duties will have been of a more delicate nature?"

"No matter, ma'am, I assure you." Esther recovered, and continued arranging the threads.

Mary threaded her needle, popped the thimble on her middle finger and started to sew. She felt Esther's eyes upon her, and hoped that the quality of her sewing matched up to Lizzy's. Though did Lizzy still sew? Surely not. The mistress of Pemberley would long have ago left samplers behind.

The silence deepened. Mary found it uncomfortable. "I am embarked upon this pretty little thatched cottage. My theme is Home. It is a concept that much preoccupies me. Most likely it comes to your mind, too? I hope you are feeling quite at—"

She stopped abruptly. As she spoke, she had become aware of Esther's belly in the corner of her eye. It had moved.

Mary's hand stilled in mid-air. The far hand of Esther's, the one that held the threads, moved down to the far side of the belly, while the near hand, the one holding the single thread ready for when Mary needed it, stayed in the air. The quietness continued long enough for the hand with the single thread to become tired; it sank into the space between Mary's skirts and Esther's. During that time the belly moved again. Twice.

A word came into Mary's mind: *quickened*. A biblical phrase: *quickened in the womb*. That sparked another thought: *the quick and the dead*. The infant in Esther's womb was *quick*; the infant that had lain between the legs of the young woman tossed out of the cart was *dead*.

Between Mary's hands lay her own belly. It was thin, flat. It was neither quickening – moving with new life – nor dead; it was inert. Empty.

There was a little cough. "Ma'am." Esther spoke. "I see the two colours clearly now. They are quite different."

With effort, Mary pushed her hands back into the movement from which they had been interrupted. After a few minutes of sewing she felt at ease enough to say, "You had a home, I think. Further up the valley? Where the lead is mined?"

"Indeed. It feels a long way away now."

"Your father, did he make a good living? Delving into the earth and bringing forth its fruits? As the psalmist says, 'fruits in due season'?"

"There are no seasons in mining, ma'am. He must work both winter and summer alike." Esther paused, then said, "The water in the dark there, it went up to his waist. But he must dig on. To get money from the lead, to feed us, his family."

"That does sound hard."

"Life is hard, ma'am."

"Yes." Mary wanted to find more words, but could not. She wanted to feel akin to this young woman, but she felt no kinship, only a desperate kind of awe, and envy.

Envy? How could that be? She, who had everything: a safe roof over her head, a husband who cared for her... And for whom she must be caring! And be seen to be caring!

She pointed her needle into her work and flung it down towards the bag. "Tidy that up for me, will you? I had almost forgot my dear husband. I am late for my caring duties upstairs."

◌〰◌

Ess, Mill, *Doovus*. There's space here, there's time. No Mrs Darcy demanding Thwaite come down and sleep in the truckle-bed to ward off Mr D. No last-minute orders for hot milk with a drop of balm stirred in. Just Ess n Mill.

Ess is telling about the missus and the sewing. Mill hides her laughter in the sheet (they're still fearing getting overheard by Glad and Pat) and trying to imagine what happens between Mr and Mrs N.

Course, says Mill, Mr N does it wi' Mr Heppyhoo. Till that bites dust wi' a big bang, eh?

But do Mrs N try n mek 'im do it wi' 'er? asks Ess.

Never, sez Mill.

Never, sez Ess.

Mill sez, Mrs N's done nowt in 'er life, eh? Watch 'er, Ess. Shiz goin' to try n get our babby.

Get…? Ess canna believe.

Ah, sez Mill. *You* got what *'er* wants.

Ess weeps then.

Mill strokes Babby. Their four hands go travelling around it.

Tell, sez Mill. Tell it me again.

So Ess does. She can't tell it as Ess; she can only tell it as Thwaite. If she's Thwaite, not Ess, she can stash it away in a tin trunk in the back of her mind. Like

344

that trunk as sits in Mr Darcy's dressing-room ready packed for his trips to London: shut, lock, strap. So the pain won't spill out into her main mind.

Thwaite, dear, says Mrs Darcy into the darkness. Thwaite had known by her tossing and turning that it was one of those nights again.

A small milk drink, with the usual, ma'am?

If you could, my dear. It does soothe. Only one drop, though. Remembering my poor Mama.

So Thwaite goes down to the kitchens.

The house seems to continue its life in the dark of the night: continue by the clocks. From the grandfather of all clocks on Mrs Darcy's landing to the third-kitchen clock where the dairy door goes off to the left: that's a walk of seven minutes. Thwaite had counted.

In the kitchens, the ovens are damped down, even in June.

Occasionally, on these trips, she meets a maid on some other errand. They let their candles nod at each other, but their eyes do not meet.

Once – it was three nights before, the time was twenty-past-three by the third kitchen's clock – Mr Bingley was there. Whisky glass in hand. Empty.

Strange, that, as the butler's rooms were miles away.

He smiled his sad smile at her, stood, and walked off. Her heart went out to him. *Poor Mr Bingley.* All the maids spoke of him like that. *What a thing to befall to such a sweet-natured woman and her husband. So boyish, he is, so curly-headed. You could scarce believe the good Lord would let it happen that way.*

This night, now, he's there again. Perched on the edge of the table. Whisky glass half full. He looks up, nods at Thwaite sadly, looks down again at his glass.

Thwaite goes through the doorway into the dairy and makes for the dairy night-safe where the milks are kept. All the time she feels: *This is a man, I must take care.* The care that every one of the maids, be they high or low, must take. Though she also feels: *But not with poor Mr Bingley?* Yet, Mill would say, *Allus. Wi' all o'em.*

She fetches the milk into the third kitchen, then the pan and a cup and saucer. (Mrs Darcy is not fussy about which cup – not for her night-time drink.) She pours the one into the other, places the pan on the oven, wonders at the keeping of the ovens on all night even in the summer; remembers her parents, their search for wood and coal; and is aware of Mr Bingley sitting on the edge of the table.

He seems not to be looking at her, or even peering at her. Yet he is there.

She does not want to pass Mr Bingley to go the place where the small wooden steps lean against the wall for reaching into the high cupboard where the medicine bottles are kept. For her own sake, and also for Mrs Darcy's, she does not want to step into Mr Bingley's space. For Mrs Darcy would not want her husband's closest friend to know that her night-time milk drink has a drop of balm in it.

She has her back now to Mr Bingley. He is still... still...perched on the edge of the kitchen table. The milk twinkles at the edge of the pan; she takes an oven cloth to lift the pan by its handle and pours the milk into the cup. At the same time, she hears his breath take a heave.

She cannot help it: she turns, puts the pan down on the side of the oven, then the nearly-full cup on its saucer. Yes, she turns, as Milly would say she *muss'na*. And says, "Oh, Mr Bingley."

She knows it could be her undoing. Yet he is *poor Mr Bingley*.

He tosses back the whisky, puts down the glass, and starts to sob.

Men do not do this. It is women who weep. Men must not so upset the natural order of things. *Please, Mr Bingley*, Thwaite says inside of herself. Outside of herself, she freezes. One movement, and she is trapped.

But he is only weeping, says the Thwaite inside her.

No such thing as 'only', responds the Milly inside her.

He puts out his arms, and she steps into them. *I am his mother*, she says in her mind. *He is a child, a golden-locked, gentle-tempered, Darcy-instructed child. He is my child, he is every woman's child.*

Make it better, Mamma, he is saying. *Make it not hurt any more.*

She rocks him.

Then, at the moment when she thinks *The milk is cooling in the cup and I must get the balm from the cupboard but I do not know how to get the steps to reach it*, he grasps her by the shoulders and half-lifts, half-drags her upwards.

"The library. Come. Please. It will not take long."

As he sputters out these pleas, he is pulling her. The two of them are sideways to each other. She is struggling, but helpless.

But she *should* not have been helpless! It was her

fault! She knew what 'the library' meant; it was code for 'the room that no one goes into at night and has a surface upon which a man can lay himself and one other'. She *knew*. So she must have led him on. She could have been brusque: *Excuse me sir but I must trouble you to move out of the kitchens. Yes sir, thank you, but you have no business, I have Mrs Darcy to see to...*

She does struggle. But she is helpless.

Because she is his mother? No, because he is strong.

Stairs first, up from the kitchens. Then passages shimmer with low lights high on the walls. Then doors, turnings, more doors.

She has never been in the library, even in the library corridor. Her brain says, *I must know the way back: back to the kitchen, and milk, and balm, and Mrs Darcy...*

Now he is hauling her up. "Please!" He is a child who knows how to be polite while hauling.

Inside, she screams: *No! She will be waiting!*

But she does not scream outside. He knows what he is doing. She does not.

...It did not take long.

...Mrs Darcy was sitting on the bed, anxious, irritated. "You have been an hour, Thwaite! What in mercy's name could have happened? You what? Spilled? But the maids-of-all-work could have cleared it up in the morning! Oh, you are too good, too helpful. No balm? It is a lesson to me. I must not take the balm. I must not become like Mama. Thank you, my dear. Try not to let it happen again."

෨෧

Mary knew she must talk seriously with Mr Needleman. So much had happened since his departure for, and return from...how should she refer to that place, that person, those unnamed, unacknowledged, unspeakable events?

She must ask Mrs Beattie's permission to speak to her husband.

But that was nonsense. She, Mary, was *Mrs* Needleman to his *Mr*, wife to the Rectory; she was 'Mrs Rectory'. (Where had that moniker sprung from? Was it from Annie, dear Annie, far away at Longbourn?) She was his wife; she needed no permission from anyone, least of all a servant.

But Mrs Beattie was more than a servant. Mary had understood, from the beginning, that this was so. Now, in the ten days since Mr Needleman's rain-soaked return, it was clearer than ever. She was like a mother to him. Mrs Beattie often spoke to her, Mary, but without full eye contact and without full attention. Her attention was always on Mr Needleman. She had none to spare for Mrs N.

But then, no one, from childhood on, had given her their full attention. But (she continued to wonder, while warning herself against the sin of Self-Pity) there had been some who paid her heed. Not in her childhood; more recently. Hill, for instance: on their journey back to Longbourn from the introductory visit to Humbole, when she, Hill, had been desperate to make clear to Mary the likely reality of her prospective marriage. And she was right. How had she known? Mary had no idea. But Hill had known, and did not want her, Mary, to suffer.

Yes, there was another occasion when she had gained full attention. It was from Mr Needleman, when he explained to her about the Great Chain of Being! In his need to explain to her about the Divine Order, he had gazed at her, begging her to listen to him and understand!

But the Great Chain of Being had to manage without her just now. Her task was to speak to her husband. And she must do it without calling on Mrs Beattie.

She knew the time to do it. Every day, for an hour or so after breakfast, Mrs Beattie would go across to the stables to tend to Hurry. He was still unwell, but (said Mrs Beattie with her eyes cast slightly skywards) he was beginning to be 'more like himself'. That was the time when Mary could knock on her husband's door and go in.

There were flurries of snow. From her window, Mary watched Mrs Beattie carrying items over to the stables: a basket of food in one hand, a heavy object wrapped in towelling under her other arm. (That would be a hot-water-bottle.)

To her husband's room.

She knocked. It sounded too much like a rat-a-tat-tat, and she wished that she could withdraw the sound. But she could not; the sound had been made.

Was that a "Come?" from him? Whether or not, she must go in.

He was sitting up in bed, a small white figure between the drapes and below the great dark carving given to him by Mr Hepplecraft. She remembered his ecstasy at being given it. The four Gospel-Makers. One of them Jesus's special disciple: the *beloved* disciple.

He saw her, and his face fell. He had expected Mrs Beattie.

She stood by the open door. She could not find words. But nor could she retreat.

Duty. She must remember her duty. She had a duty to him as his wife, to visit him on his sick-bed. Likewise did he have a duty to her, as his lawful wedded wife. They had no need of each other, but were bound together.

She stepped forward. "Robert... Mr Needleman."

"My dear!" He seemed to pick up his face from where it had fallen. "I have asked myself, where is my dear wife?" The words sounded rehearsed, but they were the right words. "Mrs Beattie is splendidly attentive, but your presence is welcome. It has been a wretched time."

She turned to close the door. Mrs Beattie must not be allowed to interrupt the discourse between husband and wife. "Are you recovering? I have been afraid for you."

"It was such a fall. You must understand. The situation was..."

She did not understand the Situation, but was unwilling to say so. She would wait. It was his duty to explain. She, too, had A Situation which she must explain to him. But his explanation must come first. He was The Husband. *Wives, submit to your husbands*, ordered St Paul.

He drew breath and spoke again. "I had, as you know, a fall. To be clear: two falls. One in Derby. Mr Hepplecraft was not kind. He is... I am no longer..."

There seemed no ending for this sentence, and no end to the wait for it.

Mary found herself suggesting: "You are no longer the beloved disciple?"

"My dear!" His face lightened. "I almost forgot how understanding you can be."

But Mary was embarrassed. This was beyond Duty. She could only cope with Duty.

"And your second 'fall'?"

"Ah! That was on the return home. Weather was atrocious. Road, equally so. The horse staggered. I slipped; fell. No bones broken. Bruising, though! Everywhere! There is no need for me be precise. But, as I say, Mr Hepplecraft will no longer be my, um, theological companion."

As he adjusted his position on the pillows, Mary realised that she was in the presence of a man in a nightgown. She realised, too, that the bed was large, with plenty of space for another occupant. Her bed, in her own room, was smaller, and with no such extra space. Why was this so?

Oh! His was the marriage bed. That space was where the wife might sleep.

But that wife, that occupant, could never be herself. On that she was perfectly clear.

She could see, above her husband's head, the carving of the Gospel-Makers: Matthew, Mark, Luke, and John the Beloved Disciple.

"I see you understand my difficulty," said her husband. "That gift." He gestured with disgust towards the carving. "It must be returned to its place of origin. Some hamlet in the wilds of Yorkshire. I must make arrangements."

Mary burst out: "No. Yes – if you wish! But, Mr Needleman, please. May I? Now? Be your spiritual, if not your theological, companion?"

Her husband, his drift into Yorkshire interrupted, stared at her like a startled animal. "How can you, my dear? I know you take an interest, but no schooling in these matters..."

"I understand, though! That day, when you explained it to me! Not about the Beloved Disciple, of course. That is for men to ponder, not for women like myself. But The Great Chain Of Being! The Divine Personage at the top, and we, a Little Lower than the Angels!" She felt the capital letters spilling out of her mouth. "We are the Summit of Creation? While other creatures, and some poor wretches, lie below. You could teach me more, and I could respond! For I have a question, Robert, husband dear, about how the Chain of Being might be for us? Might it contain, say, the servants? Even the slave woman, to whom your mother was so kind?"

Mr Needleman's expressions responded to her speech in a number of different ways, none of which Mary could interpret. No matter. She had said the words. They now lay on his counterpane.

Slowly, he began to speak. Mary felt her heart in her breast, beating, beating.

"My dear, I am not entirely clear as to your meaning. You make an interesting point, if theologically quite mistaken. After this fall of mine, we may have more time to spend with one another." His lower lip trembled. She felt a prayer rising in her throat: *Not tears. Not now, Lord, please. Not here.*

And her prayer was answered. Her husband gulped and said: "We shall, yes, we shall find time for these matters. Thank you for this suggestion. But, for the moment, we should look at practicalities, should we not?"

"Such as?"

"Mrs Beattie tells me there has been an augmentation of our staff here at the Rectory. In order to resolve some difficulties at Pemberley? There will be serious matters to attend to in that regard, it seems? My dear?"

It took Mary a few seconds to realise that he was talking about the matter which was lying heavy on her own mind: Esther and Milly, and Esther's child.

"Indeed!" she said. "It came to me in prayer that this was a time for us to practise our Lord's direction on the forgiveness of sins. To offer hospitality? 'I was a stranger, and ye took me in'?"

She was startled to hear the audacity of her words. Had she been too audacious?

Mr Needleman frowned and folded his arms over his nightgown. "You did well, my dear. Your action was a response to Mrs Darcy, as well as to our Lord. As to the future, no one can divine it. Let us see, shall we? The child might not even..." He sat up straighter. "Shall we see?"

"See? In what way?" What did he mean, *might not even*? This child would live!

"I am weary now," said Robert firmly. "Let us return to this subject on another occasion."

And indeed he looked deathly pale. She must leave him now. Feeling the swish of her heavy winter skirts as she turned, she opened the door and closed it behind her.

Out on the landing the clock ticked intrusively. All was a wintry gloom. Mrs Beattie was normally responsible for lighting the lamps, but she must have been too busy because of her nursing roles here and in the stables.

Mary's heart beat in time with the clock. Tick. beat, tick, beat.

And there was another sound. A rustle.

Mary closed her eyes, then opened them again in the hope that she could see better.

Here came that rustle again. Then a breath, then a mumble. Someone had emerged from the darkness of the stairs.

It could only be the invisible one, the one who seemed to shuffle along, an inch or two above the floor. Milly.

"Milly? Is that you?"

There came some sort of reply, which Mary did not expect to understand. She said, "My husband and I have been discussing..."

She paused in case there might come another word, another mumble, from the girl. Her small frame was beginning to take shape in the gloom.

A word came. A long word, garbled. "Thankyoukind-mistress."

"I beg your pardon?"

"Thankyoukindmistress."

"I beg... Oh! Kind! Mistress!" Mary understood, and in response she found words of her own. "I am glad you feel comfortable here. We are bidden by our

Lord, are we not, to show kindness to each other? I must go to my room. We need to have the lamps lit. The days are so dark, so very wintry and dark, are they not?"

She must stop gabbling. Or go to the kitchen and find Gladys or Patty to light the lamps. Yet she did neither of these things.

She said breathlessly: "Milly? I have wondered. I am in need, you see, of a lady's maid. Like Thwaite – Esther – was, until recently, to Mrs Darcy. I wondered whether... Esther could not, in her condition. So, might you be, might you take on, the responsibility of being my lady's maid?"

Had she said that? Had she been so reckless as to ask that? Yes, she had. Her husband had rejected her company. So she needed the company of another.

"I need help with my stays, you see. No need to say anything just now. I will go and find Patty for the lamps. We will return to the subject another time. Thank you, dear. You are a kind soul. Thank you."

Interval

Another Revelation

THE PATTERN OF THAT Sunday was normal. Mary dressed in simple garb to accompany Robert to Early Communion, to give the maids and Mrs Beattie an extra hour in bed. Robert, fasting as was his wont during his morning of prayer and preaching, remained at the church, while Mary returned home through the wicket gate and fetched a cup of milk and a pippin from the kitchen to take back to her room. She read through the day's Petition and Intercession from her Book of Common Prayer as a reminder of what was to come later, at Matins. Then she sat in her chair by the window, looking out across the brightening churchyard and going over in her mind the harmonies of today's hymns, preparing to make her contribution to the service through the medium of contralto singing. All the while, she was waiting for Milly to come silently into her room and help her into her stays, her petticoat, and her soft, cream, woollen, many-buttoned Sunday dress.

When she heard the click of the door latch and sensed Milly in the room, for some reason she did not stand as usual and come round from her chair. She simply sat and watched a blackbird pecking at the frozen grass under the cedar at the edge of the lawn. But she was aware of Milly waiting for her in the space of the carpet just behind her.

The blackbird and the cedar and the frosty grass faded, and she stood, turned, and momentarily opened her palms to indicate that Milly might begin her duties as lady's maid.

Milly went to the mahogany wardrobe to fetch the Sunday dress from the rail, then the stays and petticoat from the drawer. Her movements were precise despite her curvatures and her shuffle; the wardrobe door did not creak as it did under Mary's ungainly hands. Milly's tiny claw pushed the soft cloth of the Sunday dress into position on her good arm, then moved to hold the drawer steady while the good hand located the petticoat and stays. In all things, the bent-back claw acted as companion to its straight and more agile partner.

Today, instead of removing her old two-piece outfit herself as usual, Mary stood as she imagined Lizzy would stand while being dressed by her maid: helpless, but observant.

When Milly had reached the basic layer, the chemise, it was time for the stays. *Today*, Mary thought, *I shall*

*let my stays be done for me. After all, I am 'Mrs Rectory',
and I have a lady's maid at last.* She closed her eyes.

Milly moved slowly, with pauses. There was one
awkward moment when the stays slipped and Mary
feared she would have to bend down and retrieve
them from the floor. But no, the small hands somehow
caught them just in time. The lacing? How would she
manage the lacing? *Do not fear. Let her do it. Breathe.
Do not hold your breath; breathe deep while it is done for
you. While it is done. Well done.*

She remembered a sentence from the Book of Job.
The breath of Almighty God hath given me life.

Now they came to the many-buttoned Sunday
dress. Mary moved in harmony with Milly: stepping
over, stepping into, standing straight for all the tiny
actions which combined to create, from an indecent
woman, a fully-dressed Rector's wife.

She closed her eyes again.

The buttons. Small, neat, each one covered in tiny
rounds of identical cloth.

It was a slow, slow process. But there was plenty
of time. The church clock had not yet struck the half-
hour.

One button. Two. Five. At seven – knowing there
were nine buttons – she opened her eyes, but quickly
closed them again.

Milly's hand, the straight one, paused, and instead
of continuing the buttons, carefully unbuttoned the
one she had just completed. Then did it up again. The
same with the next – the eighth. And with the ninth
– the last – she did it again: let her hand rest on the
fabric, under which Mary's skin lay. Then returned to

the task of doing up the button. And rested her hand.

Deep in the firmament of herself, Mary felt a bubbling.

She remembered the courtship of owls.

She had heard them at Longbourn in the spring, high in the large blurred trees, the *twit* and the *twoo* bubbling separately, then together. She would give thanks to God for her hearing, a gift which sometimes compensated for her dismal sight. Maybe, she thought, she would hear them here, too, around the Rectory, in the spring. Now, here, in the winter, she could recall it. Feel it, that inward bubbling.

Breathe. Breathe deeply. *The breath of Almighty God hath given me life.*

"Thank you, Milly," she heard herself saying. "In a moment, that will be all."

PART IV
1821

18

A Sermon, a Visit, a Light

IT RAINED, AND IT STILL RAINED. Mary's skirts were drenched even by the short walk from the Rectory to the church; other Vicar's or Rector's wives, she knew, would have insisted on the carriage, but Mrs Beattie had let slip that the parishioners nicknamed her 'Simple Mary', and she must keep up that reputation. In any case Hurry was still on light duties; he had not regained his old strength since Mr Needleman's accident.

Nor, indeed, had Mr Needleman. He fulfilled his duties, especially in regard to the sacraments, but his sermons were re-cast from earlier ones, or versions of *Cattermole's Selected*. Probably only Mary realised this was the case. And Mrs Beattie, who would never breathe a word of it.

Mr Needleman muttered from the pulpit through the readings for Candlemas, and Mary, alone in the ornate Rectory pew, shivered. She had rehearsed him through each Collect, Epistle, and Gospel. They had agreed, happily, that Candlemas was one of their favourite times of the Church Year, because it was when Mary mother of Jesus had presented her Son in the Temple; soon would come the celebration of Mary's Annunciation, when she encountered the Angel Gabriel, and the truth became known: Mary would have a child, miraculously.

Mary knew that this applied only to this one, and very specific, occasion. Nevertheless, her own name was Mary.

Then they had searched for a sermon. *Cattermole* only offered two sermons for Candlemas, and one of these focused vividly on the uncleanness of a woman after childbirth; how she must be secluded, for a short time if she had borne a son, a longer time if it were a daughter. That left the sermon about the blessing of the infant Christ in the temple.

Mrs Beattie had hinted that the parishioners were impatient for the Rector's wife to produce a child. It was, of course, impossible for Mary to mention this to her husband, in case he should connect the subject of their childlessness with the stray child that was soon to be born up the attic stairs.

But he made this connection anyway. For, in the midst of discussing the Epistle for Matins, Robert burst out fretfully, "There is talk!"

"Talk? Of?"

"An immoral child! An illegitimate child. Here, in

the Rectory."

"But Esther is never seen! Neither of the two is seen. They are under my care. Under guidance. The Lord's guidance."

"My dear, such arguments reach only so far. Old Blake" – the sexton, who had made a fuss about the parish boundaries in the case of the tragic woman on the cart – "reports that the common folk wonder why the Rectory had to intervene in this matter."

Mary had prepared a reply to this allegation. "The Lord will provide an answer in His due time. Be not anxious for the morrow. Sufficient unto the day is the evil thereof." She was astonished at how confidently her words flowed. Robert's fragility had revealed a strength in her that was quite unexpected.

Yet his fragility was becoming all too public. This was more than short sight. Now, delivering his sermon from the pulpit, he was mumbling rather than preaching. Only ten minutes in, and already there were snores from the pews. He stumbled on his words: "Our Lord Christ was to be a light...a candle. Hence, candles."

Mary held her breath. *Dear husband, do not fail. We cannot have that hectoring curate stand in for you yet again.*

But her prayer was not only unanswered, it was rebuffed. Mr Needleman lost his words entirely, collapsed onto the little seat in the pulpit, and let his head fall into his hands.

Mary stood up and ran to him. Heedless of the murmurings from the parishioners in the nave, she flew across the stone floor and up the pulpit steps.

Robert looked part-shocked, part-roused by her sudden appearance.

With one hand on the notes for the sermon, the other on his brow, she whispered, "This is the place!" Then she took his elbow, raised him to standing position and spoke the words into his ear: "'Simeon declared Our Lord a Light to lighten the Gentiles, and gave us the pure light of His Mother, who is sent to bless us all.'" All the time guiding him round until he was facing the congregation once again.

"And now, in the Name of the Father, the Son, and the Holy Spirit..."

The congregation, startled to their feet by these familiar closing words, shuffled and coughed and straightened themselves up. Mary stood behind Robert as he led the final prayers. "Go in peace; be of good courage; render to no man evil for evil; hold fast to that which is good."

By the word *fast* Mary was back in the Rectory pew. Mr Needleman, though leaning on the pulpit edge, could be heard above the common people: "Strengthen the faint-hearted, support the weak, help those who suffer..."

As his words drew to a close, Mary emerged from the pew to join her husband at the pulpit foot, and the two of them walked down the aisle to the west door ready to greet the parishioners as they came out into the weak February sun.

෧෮

Dear Thwaite – though I think your proper name is Esther:

It seems a long while since your visit here at Longbourn, and the conversation we had while putting fresh sheets and blankets on Mrs Bennet's bed. (God rest her soul.) I write to you now on account of the imminent nature of your confinement, for I remember my first confinement in every detail.

I have written to you on previous occasions, but owing to the lack of letter-writing provision for such as myself, have never set pen to paper. Now, in some triumph, I am writing this on actual paper, with actual ink. For Luke and I have much more freedom now than formerly.

Mr Bennet, as you may recall, was pursuing our small family, begging forgiveness of Luke for his previous neglect, trying to capture the attention of our children and generally interrupting the happiness of our home life.

Now Mr Bennet can do none of these things. He is sadly reduced in himself. Shrunk. He spends most of the day curled up under his blankets. I can bribe him out with inducements like whipped cream on his breakfast porridge, but he would rather not walk about at all. So I take his food up to him. He slobbers his way through it, then I stand beside him over the chamber pot. My dear Luke takes him to the necessary house once a day and endeavours to clean him up afterwards. It is a pitiful end to the life of a once-proud man.

But the result of Mr Bennet's diminution is this:

we now have access to the whole house! John-James and Edie slide down the banisters and create dens under the stairs. Luke lounges in the drawing room of an evening, prodding the fire with the poker as if he owned the place. I remind him that, until bastardy acquires some legal status, we do not, and will not, own Longbourn, and one day Mr Collins and his growing brood may come and take possession. (Or even Miss Kitty and her new husband, if they can pay for a clever enough lawyer. Mrs Darcy will have written to Mrs Needleman about Miss Kitty getting a husband? How, lacking a responsible parent, she did it on the quiet, special licence and all, without telling a soul?) "Well," says he, "let them come. I shall enjoy myself at the master's table while I may." So we play Master and Wife, seating ourselves at the refectory table and hurling the salt cellar along the length of it with gales of laughter.

I take to thinking, "This is his birthright. He is of Mr Bennet's blood, of Mr Bennet's loins. He should claim it." But it would not make him happy. We are happy as we are. This freedom offers me also the freedom of the library, and of paper and ink. Hence this letter.

May I ask how you are? Whether your pregnancy has been a steady one, seeing you are settled and safe at the Rectory? Is Mrs Needleman a good mistress? And does Mr Needleman accept your situation, as a Christian should? I too can quote Scripture: 'Let him who is without sin cast the first stone'. (My dear mother-in-law told me of her suspicions regarding Mr Needleman and his friend. I have no suitable biblical quotation for that situation.)

At some point I may take leave of the written page and continue this line of thought on a separate, and private, page. That last sentence, about my dear Flora's perceptions, may also belong to the private page.

For I come to the question of your child's paternity. As you know, my Luke has had the shadow of such a question looming over his whole life. Your child, too, will feel that shadow.

I have heard from Miss Mary about Pemberley: the multitude of corridors, the warren of the servants' quarters, the lofty Family wings, the myriad of Visitors' quarters and Visitors' servants' corridors. I know, too, how visible every quarter must be to every other quarter, and how little space there is for private moments to occur. I ask myself, "How did a man take advantage of this dear girl and hide the fact of his advantage from those who wish to know the truth of it?" The 'tight ship' run by Mrs Reynolds is renowned, and her friendship with Mrs Beattie of Humbole is also well known. Their suspicions, surely, will have travelled to and fro, for there is always a message-boy, who has no reading, yet is trained in the art of passing a folded page from one hand to another, undetected. The incident which led to your indisposition must have been brief, and the other party well-versed in hiding both his desires and their manner of accomplishment. So he must be a regular and welcome visitor to Pemberley.

There is not a long list to choose from. I think I know the name?

Do you wish to keep this knowledge secret? You will no doubt feel as I do about protecting Mrs Bingley from yet more pain. Protecting Mrs Darcy is another matter. Yet the person who most needs protection is yourself. I feel that most strongly. Have no fear. I will keep your secret safe.

- I hear Luke's voice, and must attend to Mr Bennet. I will continue later.

༄

Doovus. It gets harder. The bigger Esther gets, the farther away Milly seems.

Mill, says Ess. Closer. Come closer.

Canna. Babba kicks me if ah do.

Come round 'im then.

'Im? Wha if 'e's an 'Er?

'S'a Him. I ken. Come *round* him.

Ess shifts so that her bulge faces (through the blankets) the ceiling. Milly lies alongside, facing the ceiling too.

Ah' be goin' soon, Mill says.

Goin? Where to?

Ah've a plan, Mill says. Truss' me.

Truss *me*. Tell. Where to?

Mi' not work, says Mill. Le' me be. Lemme go.

Mill, ar't angered wi' me? Wi' me not telling 'em who's the Da?

Nah, Ess. Ah ne'er angered. We Doovus. We truss. Truss, if ah go?

Ess pauses. She must trust, for what else is there?

Listen, says Mill. I been thinken. 'Bout when 'e's born. Missus, you seen 'ow she's toughened up? An' Mrs B, she's right rankled? It be war tween the two o' them, innit?

Mill giggles, down in her throat. Warrr, warrr, she says.

Ess giggles with her: That shoutin' o'er the fricassee?

Mill: "I neeeer cud abaaaaade the Fricassey!"

An', says Ess, Fricassey is phut! Off 'menu.

Ne'er t'appear agen.

She won. Missus won. Mrs B loss.

Soooo? says Mill. Mrs B willna' 'ave a bastard unner '*er* roof. Missus will, tho. An', way things goin', Missus 'll win. Bastard *will* be unner 'er roof.

Silence falls.

Then Mill says, I *will* go.

Go an'...?

Silence. Then, again: *Truss me.*

A curled finger touches Ess's lips.

Oh Mill, says Ess. Tek care. Tek great care.

Will. Will. Milly breathes into Ess's skin. *Will.*

࿊

When Mary went to bed that night, she allowed Milly to undress her. Not completely, just down to her chemise. She closed her eyes as usual, but opened them when they reached the chemise.

"My dear," she said without thinking, "this chemise is ready for the wash. Fetch a clean one, could you?"

She closed her eyes again as Milly shuffled away to

the drawer. On Milly's return, she raised her arms to indicate that Milly's help was needed to remove the old chemise. But Milly was too small for the task. So Mary, eyes open, assisted her, their four hands moving in a sort of dance until the garment lay in a little heap at the side. Then Milly came round to the front, the clean chemise over her good arm. Mary took it, and Milly's hand. Together they reached as high as Milly's hand could reach; then Mary's hands took over, till Milly's came back to assist, and they shared in the smoothing of the chemise, from her shoulders to her knees. All the time, Mary's eyes were alternately open and closed. She felt Milly's breathing, and her own. *The breath...of God...hath given me life.*

When she opened her eyes again, she felt as if she had been in prayer.

She looked down. Milly stood before her, head bowed.

Mary said, "The Lord be with thee."

Milly responded: "And also with thee." It was a mumble that would not have been understood by any other person in the church congregation, but Mary heard the mumble as if it were the perfect response.

Milly looked up, and into Mary's eyes.

Mary bent and took each of Milly's hands in hers, the good one and the palsied one. The difference between the two, one doubled back on itself and the other a small but ordinary hand, caused a slight shock.

"Thank you, my dear," she said. "Now you may return to your sister. Have a good night's sleep."

Milly withdrew her hands and, after an extra moment of gaze, withdrew her eyes also; then picked up her candle and left the room.

When, in the middle of that dark night, she heard the click of the door and a slight rustle indicating that Milly had come, without a candle, into her room, Mary found herself not at all surprised. She lifted the blankets and drew her in.

Maybe an hour or so later, Milly slid out of the bed again and away back to her attic room.

⟳

Intolerable, she is. Did I say *minx*? *Minx* is the least of it!

First it was the fricassee.

Explain and explain as I do, how the fricassee is the lynchpin of the entire weekly menu (Sunday roast, Monday cold slices as we do the wash, Tuesday pieces in sauce as fricassee, Wednesday mince the rest, Thursday an egg-dish if the hens are laying, Friday – of course – fish) she will stick to her point. The *texture* of the sauce, she declares! "Never could *abide* it. And I will not, Mrs Beattie, brook any further discussion on the matter. I am happy for any other way of serving the leftover meat except fricassee."

Eventually (for I am not to be defeated) I turn to the well-thumbed pages of my Raffald, my precious *Experienced English Housekeeper*, for Tuesday alternatives. I am appeased to find several. If they are good enough for Raffald, they are good enough for me.

That is only the first of the ways in which the minx confounds me. She invokes the name of RN to subvert me. "My husband would want it *this* way. *That* way. The *other* way."

I go to RN in his study and place the buttered halves of scones on his desk. The study has been his retreat from combat since his weakness began. But, when I have told my tale, he turns away from me. "I cannot fight her, my dear, any more than you can. She will do it her way."

I move towards him, indicating that I am his Mother In The Lord as I was in former days. Yet – and this is the pain of it – he will not hearken to me. He waves me away.

And so to the other matter. The child. When it appears. *What is to be done?*

The Wednesday after my Tuesday experiment (lamb 'ragoo' with mushrooms), I approach my mistress at the piano.

"This matter, Mrs Needleman," I say.

Her fingers finish a little trilling phrase high up on the keyboard. It is irritable to my ears. "Mrs Beattie?"

"The matter of Esther the maid," I say.

"What is to be done?"

"In what sense *done*?"

"By the look of her there will be need of some kind of layette, and a crib. Very shortly."

"Indeed," she replies. "I have ordered a rocking crib from Dewhurst the joiner. And a variety of infant's needs from Mrs Blake senior. Mr Blake's mother being such an excellent seamstress. It is so helpful to have tradespeople one can trust."

"You have ordered them? But the cost!"

She turns back to her piano.

I realise that I have overstepped my station. I have questioned her household expenditure. The Mistress holds the purse (on behalf of the Master); she dispenses housekeeping to the housekeeper. Housekeeper has the management of that sum, and no more.

In the long-ago time before the minx's arrival, RN and I would choose menus together in preparation for my weekly orders in the town. *Crème caramel.* His favourite! I still bake it, but he does not comment. "Sirloin?" I would say. "That will stretch the budget!" "But Baslow's sirloin is *so* good," he would respond with a smile. Thus did he and I share responsibility for the budget. But those days are gone.

What the parishioners will make of this joiner-crafted crib and specially-sewn baby-wear for the bastard child of unknown parentage, I cannot imagine. But I must bite my lip.

༄

Dear Esther – here am I, Annie, continuing later.

Luke and I have fed and watered Mr Bennet, then shared our own meal. The children played around us while we ate, and demanded bites at will. They are so happy. We will bask in this happiness while it lasts.

You may have heard from Miss Lizzy, during your time as her lady's maid, about the history of Miss Jane's marriage to Mr Bingley: his fervent attentions to her, their troubled courtship, then their joyous reunion and eventual happiness at the marital altar. Who could have predicted that such bliss could turn to such horror?

I will not return to speculations as to how your present situation came about. If you wish to confide in me, please do. In your own time.

As for this letter, I hope to tuck it into a bundle of infant clothes which I shall parcel up and send. Oh, how I wish to steal a little of Mr Bennet's scarlet wax, so I could be sure that none but yourself would read this!

With every good wish, for yourself, your confinement and your sister.

Annie.

PS. Even as I fold this, I unfold it again. Luke called me, urgently. Mr Bennet has fallen. Forgive me if the ink is blotched. I must run.

ꙮ

There was a strange light in the room as Mary awoke.

Everything was different. The shutters, the shafts of light through the cracks in the shutters, the carpet, the counterpane, the sheets, her nightgown, her skin, her whole body. She felt transformed.

She remembered hearing – probably from Mr Hepplecraft, who was much absorbed in things esoteric – about the concept of *electricity*: it being an invisible force that could move energy from one place to another. Which could create sparks of fire. Could even, in some notorious fiction, the name of which she could not recall, enable life to rise up in otherwise dead material.

Had she, Mary Bennet-turned-Needleman, been in some way sparked by electricity? Transformed from a humdrum life into a life that was infused with, well, *Life*? She hummed. Not in her throat, in song, but in her whole body, from head to toe.

Another word came to her. *Touched*. She had been touched.

Yet, as she knew from childhood, the word *touched* also meant something quite other. Something derogatory. Something one would not wish to have ascribed to oneself at all.

Derogatory it might be, but she cared not a jot. She was elated. Treasured. Awakened.

This light in her room, though, was very strange. Maybe it was not just herself that had been transformed overnight, but the whole world?

No! If the light was so strong, on a morning in the depth of winter, it meant that she had overslept, and it was late! Must she arise, and dress?

No, she would not. She need not move. She had been touched by angelic wings. Stroked. From to head to… From head to…*womb*.

'Womb'. She had never used that word except in the context of Mary's – the virgin's – womb. Now she knew that she, Mary, had a womb. She would never enunciate the word out loud, but she could feel that it had been *touched*.

Her mouth opened at the knowledge of it. She smiled.

Meanwhile, outside, the day would wait for her. She would wait for Milly to come and help her dress.

Milly.

Normally, Mary told Milly there was no need for her to come and dress her on weekday winter mornings, as there was so much work to do, clearing the fires out, laying and lighting them and so on, with Esther not being so capable now, and Gladys and Patty being glad of her help. What about her stays? No need to worry, she would manage her own stays.

But today was now different. Today she did, after all, want Milly to come and assist her with dressing. Their hands would move, as yesterday evening with the chemise, in harmony with each other, throughout the process.

She lay, aware of her transformation, her lateness; the fact that she did not care about her lateness. Even the possibility that Mrs Beattie might wonder why she was so late for breakfast did not bother her. Even Robert, if he should be stirring on this leisurely weekday morning.

If she had, in fact, experienced some sort of inner electrical movement, surely it would show on the outside? Might others perceive it? Might the parishioners, in church on Sunday, gaze at her and ask themselves what could possibly have happened to Mrs Rectory? *She must have been touched by an angel!*

Did it show? She must look in her mirror.

She leapt out of bed, ran to the chest and lifted the hand-mirror to her face.

To her dismay, she looked precisely the same as she had done yesterday. Wild hair, small nose (her spectacles not yet in place), pale cheeks, receding chin. Her eyes? Yes, they gleamed. Cheeks – yes, they might possibly have been touched with rouge. But when she put her spectacles on, her eyes would be hidden. And no one would ever ask themselves whether Mrs Rectory had used rouge. Like a…like a woman of the world. Of the common sort. Of the street.

She must dress herself!

But with one difference: she would not wear her stays. What a nonsense they were! She would be free of them. Her little breasts – oh, those beautiful little, sensitive little breasts – had they, too, been *touched*? Do not ask it, do not think of it.

They were too small to need artificial upholding. She would be free.

She put on yesterday's dress, with no stays.

Was she ready now for her entrance into the world? She quivered, not knowing whether she was or not.

Before opening the door, she said her names – Mary Bennet. Mary Needleman. Mrs Rectory – and wondered which one of them she now was.

She was each of these women. All of them. She was *Mary*.

Out onto the chilly landing, down the chilly stairs.

The strange light persisted.

She heard sounds from the Music Room. Scraping sounds.

One of the maids must be scraping out the clinker from the fireplace. Esther was now confined to her room. It would be Gladys, or Patty. Or maybe even Milly, on her knees with the poker and the fire bucket and the shovel.

It could be Milly.

Breathless, Mary went in.

It *was* Milly. Her small hunched back, her awkward

hands, were hidden, busy with the tools. Scrape, clatter, brush. Scrape, clatter, brush.

Milly must have heard Mary's entrance, but she did not pause.

"Milly!" said Mary. "Thank you so much! For your…work!"

Again, not a moment's pause.

Mary went to sit at the piano. But she could not play, not while this clattering went on. There were noises in her head, too. She could not tell what the noises were, just that they clattered and prevented her from thinking. Her breath seemed caught, snatched from her. She could not even lift the piano lid.

She stood again and watched Milly dragging herself to her feet.

A sudden desire to help her stand, to hold the fire bucket, to relieve her of the burden of it, surged through Mary. At the same time she knew she must hold off, be good, hold tight.

Milly, leaning with the fire bucket's weight, shuffled past and away.

Mary had taken several steps forward, and now needed to step back.

She must step back. She made herself step back.

The door closed behind her.

She thought she might weep.

Then she heard Mrs Beattie outside the door – "Get it laid and lit, now, will you? Sharp-ish!" – and turned away. She could not face the housekeeper yet. She walked to the window.

The shutters were open. Every single thing – the cedar tree, the bare winter shrubs in their beds, the lines of the paths – were covered in white.

It had snowed.

So *that* was why the whole world was different! The lawn, but for a few footprints of birds, was brilliant with it. The early morning shone with its light. It was just that. Snow.

Behind her the door opened, and Mrs Beattie came urgently in.

"Mrs Needleman, I beg you. There is news from Longbourn, and Mrs Darcy's message about it too. It seems to be your poor father. The snow will impede travel. I beg you, please attend. I regret to say your breakfast is cold upon the table."

19

To Longbourn...

There he lies, the bugger. Day, after night, after day. As if he's dead already, but he's caught us up in the dying of him. Captured us in his deathly prison. Locked us up along with him; thrown away the key.

Luke, standing in the darkened room, regarded his father as he would a horse. This was the kindest thought he could lay hand upon. If his father were old Rosie, for instance, Luke would walk around him, pat his yellowing skin, gaze at him, his hide, his flank, the places on his body that twitched, the places that hung loose, the lie of the nose, the slant of the eye in the skull. He'd gaze deep, so as to understand the beast, to learn what went on in the being of the beast, discover what the beast needed, whether it be soothing words or a sharp shout to gee it on its way.

But none of this gazing changed the situation: that his father (damn him) *should* be dead, *needed* to be dead, but was still *alive*. The bugger was dragging all of them along with him to the place where no one's alive, no one's dead, but they're all in this limbo from which there's no escape. He'd last forever, drain the very life out of all of them. With Annie and Ma Drayton visiting hourly to dab his grey lips with a moistened cloth.

How could life be sustained for so long on so little?

He wanted to feel the warmth of Annie's body approaching him from behind, her firm hands against his arms, the pressure of her breasts and belly leaning against his back. *Out*, she'd command. *You said your farewells. Leave it to me and Mother D. So hop it.*

He would not touch his father, no, but he could lean forward a little. Just to make sure. The bugger might actually have snuffed it with no one noticing. Luke could just lean over, then accidentally lean a bit too far, lose his balance, fall on his father's face, and – oh, the shock of it, it'd paralyse him, and he'd lie there on top of the dying man, helpless, until ah! – he'd hear his last in-take and out-come of breath... And the bugger would cease! His life snuffed out! Like the snuff he was so partial to! Snuffed out, forever!

Except that he couldn't.

Just as Luke started to lean forwards, a voice came from behind him. A familiar voice, one which had been with him for as long as he could remember.

"Let – him – go!" The voice caught him in the act of leaning, and forced him to reverse it. "It's you as hangs onto him. You'll never get what you want from the man. Let him go. Let him come to me. I'll deal with him."

Luke wanted to argue with the voice, but he could not. It had the authority of his mother's life behind it. Such an authority could make him believe what she said: that she, who had loved the man for a brief time, or at any rate put up with him and forgiven him, would, from wherever she was now, deal with him.

Still he stood, paralysed, as he'd been a moment before, when he'd wanted to squeeze the last ounce of life out of his father.

"Let him go, son. He is who he is. He was who he was. A man of his time."

Still Luke stood. Then he felt a sharp nudge in his back to gee him on his way. His mother was treating him like he would treat a recalcitrant horse. *Gee up! Gerron with yer! On yer way!* He was out of the door before his feet had a chance to decide against it.

And old Ma Drayton, with a damp cloth in her hand, had to skip to one side to avoid him. "Watch it, there's another o' them sisters is come!" she called after him as he tumbled down the stairs.

☙

Lizzy swept into the Rectory and threw her cape over Mrs Beattie's out-stretched arm. Her high lace-up boots clanged across the tiled floor and into the drawing room, and the air throbbed with her movement. "I trust your maids are busy packing all that you require," she said to Mary as Mrs Beattie closed the door behind them.

Mary, following her breathlessly, said, "Do sit, Lizzy."

"We have no idea how long we will be there. Even if the end is soon. Kitty's message was brief. 'The last phase', were her words."

"*Kitty's* message?" Mary sat down, hoping that Lizzy would follow suit.

"Did I not say? The dear girl rushed there. Husband alongside. It appears he cannot do enough for her. Come, Mary. No pondering. There will be plenty of time to ponder on the journey. Darcy is waiting." She still stood, as if waiting to scoop Mary up.

"*Darcy* is?"

"Do not keep repeating my words, Mary, please."

"Did you not say that Darcy awaits? Please – sit."

"Very well. Just for a few moments." She perched on the edge of the nearest chair. "We cannot be surprised at this turn of events. I agree with Fitzy – it is only surprising not to have happened earlier. The poor old soul."

"The?" Mary stopped herself just in time. "Will Darcy not come in?"

"He has much on his mind. We have no knowledge of the Will – whether it has any bearing on the matter, what the future holds for our family home. Whether there has been word from Mr Collins, or his lawyer. Of course, this necessity has interrupted the business that he himself was already taken up with. He has papers with him, to send notes to his agents while we are on the road."

Lizzy paused at last. Mary found herself staring at

her in a way that had always irritated her mother: *Do not stare, Mary! In that rude manner!* Yet how could Mary see unless she opened her eyes wide?

Words tumbled in her mind. *Snow, roads, sheets, night, electricity, light, dustpan, kneel, stays, bound, confined, emerge, free.*

Then just *snow*, and *light*.

The right words came to her lips. "Shall I call Esther for you? Thwaite?"

"Thwaite? Why? Have we need of her? She will be confined, surely?"

"Her confinement is the reason you might wish to see her. Given your previous closeness? To enquire after her? And the child?"

Lizzy coughed. "I have put all that behind me, Mary. There is enough distress in my life at the moment without it. It is an unkindness in you to raise it. Especially now." She put her hand to her throat and rearranged her collars.

"I only thought..."

"Cease your thinking, Mary, I beg you. Our father lies between life and death. Hard on the heels of our previous bereavement. What is needed now is action. You had my message. How long will it take for your luggage to be ready?"

"I have not asked my maids to pack." The words were out of her mouth before she could consider them. "I shall not be coming with you. I need to remain at home in Humbole." Her heart was beating hard with anxiety, but at the same time she was happy with the resonance of those two words: *home*, and *Humbole*. She belonged to the Rectory, not to Longbourn.

"That is not possible! We sisters must all be there!" Lizzy turned sharply on her perch. "Together! For our dear father. For the future."

"Will Lyddy be there?"

"Of course not, Lyddy never..."

"And Jane, also not." Her words grew in strength. "Lizzy, dear, you and Kitty are much the most worldly-wise in our family. You know what to say, what to do. My role has always been a spiritual one. I can continue that role at a distance. Besides, you will have Darcy with you for the business aspect."

"Only for a few days! Then he will proceed to London!"

Mary had said what she needed to say. Now she waited for her words to seep into Lizzy's consciousness and settle, like snow settling into the curves of the landscape. The word *snow* repeated in her mind. Then *snow* beget *ice*, and she recalled her childhood when they had watched the village children sliding over the frozen pond in their clogs. She felt like one of those children. Carried along. Refreshed, anew.

Lizzy was repeating herself. "You *must* come. Our father may not have led a blameless life, but he is our father."

Might Luke have been among those children, sliding in his clogs on the pond? The image of Luke hovered in the room now. She blinked, and he disappeared. She said, "Lizzy, I cannot. My husband needs me. He is by no means recovered from his accident. I must be at his side, assisting in his church work. Our father will not be concerned at my absence. He has taken little interest in my thoughts or actions over the years. This is where I must be. I am grateful to you and Darcy for taking up the reins in the present circumstances."

"Our father on his final journey, and only two of us to see him on his way? You cannot relinquish filial duties just like that!" Lizzy stood up again now. "What a shock for dear Darcy! He has always admired your steadfastness, your commitment, your quiet..." She lost her thread, and repeated: "Your steadfastness."

Mary tried to imagine Darcy admiring her, and failed. "It is my steadfastness which keeps me here in Humbole, Lizzy. With my husband. Last time, with our mother's demise, I served the family well, I think?" Lizzy could not deny this, and gave a small nod. "Now I give way to others. If these days are indeed the last of the Bennets' at Longbourn, then Darcy's fine mind will be more useful than any of my biblical quotations. Yes?"

Lizzy let her eyes fall, defeated. The two of them sat, each breathing heavily.

There came a knock on the door. It was Mrs Beattie, asking for instructions.

Lizzy rose to her feet. "My cape, if you will. We must be on our way."

She turned back to face Mary. "I need hardly repeat, Darcy will be shocked. Mr Needleman may also find your decision incomprehensible. I trust he will not suffer any setback when he hears of it. Please give him my regards."

∽

Annie was startled by Miss Kitty. She had changed. She made every appearance of deferring to her older sister, but ended by having the active tasks in her own list (alerting the family lawyer and the stonemason, checking the available space in the churchyard) while consigning the tedious tasks (ordering more black-edged paper, planning the eventual funeral) to Lizzy. Kitty had brought her own maid with her; the two of them worked together, while Kitty's husband (whose name Annie could never quite catch) moved around after them, shifting a chair towards his wife or carrying items in her wake.

So here was Annie standing over Miss Lizzy in the library while she drafted black-framed letters and left them undated but ready for the moment when they could finally be sent.

"What a mercy it is," said Mrs Darcy with a sigh, "to consign these moments, these intense events – life, death, and so on – to something *orderly*. To words. Ink, paper, sealing wax."

"Indeed, it is," replied Annie.

"You find it so too?" Mrs Darcy turned with a frown. "I have always known you as a keen reader, Annie. But writing? Is that another of your skills?"

"I write in my head, ma'am. As if there *were* paper and ink. I can see my thoughts unfolding onto a page—"

"So, in your imagination, you write – what? Stories? Fairy-tales?"

"No, ma'am, not stories nor tales. There's enough of them around in us lives already. Just letters. To explain things. As you say, to sort out the muddle of things. These long days with your father, well, they're almost over. You can write, 'Sadly, he...' And that is it. He will be no more."

She wanted to say, but didn't: "And what about Mr Bennet's own son? What would Luke write? About the death of his father?" It was daring enough to actually speak of Mr Bennet's death, and, in any case Luke could neither read nor write.

Mrs Darcy said in a clipped voice: "Sealing wax. Such reassuring stuff. One knows that only the recipient will read one's letter; no one else. Bring over the taper, would you? For my letter to Mr Darcy in London." She drummed her fingers irritably on the desk. "The writing of letters is the easy part. When the whole Bennet inheritance is at stake."

Annie, fetching the taper, knew that Mrs Darcy was referring to the Entail. Mr Darcy, impatient at his father-in-law's reluctance to make his exit, was in London already. Luke told her he'd heard the word 'Hunsford' on his lips; 'Hunsford' meant Kent, the county beyond London; it meant 'Mr Collins'.

She opened her mouth without thinking and said something quite unrelated to the Entail. "Might I borrow the seal, on occasion, Mrs Darcy, if you please?"

"But why would you need to seal a letter?"

"I have a friend," said Annie. "Who needs my advice."

"Really? How pleasant for your friend to have your support."

"We servants have our difficulties, just as you in your turn have yours." She stopped, shocked. That had been intrusive. Rude.

But Mrs Darcy sat back and smiled wearily. "I am sure you do, Annie dear. Recently, for me, there has been Thwaite and her troubles. Now that dear Mary has found a solution, I can cease being anxious in that regard. Yet I do remember her." She sighed. "I must tell Mary that! Yes, I will scribble a message on the back of my letter." She selected one of the unsealed letters and pulled it towards her. "*Please give my good wishes to T, for her future.* I will say that, and Mary will understand. Thwaite's time is coming very soon. I can pray for her. Yes, I will say a prayer for her, next Sunday, in church. For her, and her child."

The taper in Annie's hand trembled slightly. There was a pause.

"Shall you seal the letter to Mr Darcy now?"

"Of course."

Mrs Darcy held the folded page. Annie put the taper close enough to let go its droplets of treasure, and Mrs Darcy pressed the seal carefully into place. Back, and forth, and up. Then the two of them returned to the black-edged letters, and Annie checked the ink-well and refilled it when necessary.

It was peculiar, Annie reported later to Luke, how Miss Lizzy leapt from the question of privacy and sealing wax straight to Thwaite, to Esther. Miss Lizzy had read her thoughts. She had turned holy, too. Almost as holy as Miss Mary.

"What that means, I think," said Annie, in conclusion, "is that if I should take it upon myself to creep into the library and write a letter to Esther in her predicament, then it can be sealed. Private. No one else shall see it. And Esther will know that I am thinking of

her, and hoping the baby will be born soon, and safe.
I will have sealed it, just like a member of the Family
would seal it. That is something, is it not, Luke?"

And he agreed that it was indeed something.

෧෬

My dear Mary, wrote Lizzy. *This extra missive
is to extend to you a certain degree of apology. I
can now appreciate your reluctance to return to
Longbourn on this mournful occasion, and to
put your husband's needs over and above those of
your original family. I, too, yearn to be back at
Pemberley, at my husband's side, with my dear
family around me (excepting of course George,
who is settling at school after a somewhat turbulent
start) and the familiar faces of my own staff in my
own domain. Longbourn, I fear, is a place which
has been for too long unloved. Annie does her best;
in the summer she will have placed flowers in the
drawing room and a posy beside one's bed; but in
this dreary month of March there are only a few
dried flowers on the landing windowsill. Luke keeps
the mud mostly at bay, the clocks wound, the horses
exercised. But the aura of death is over all, Mary.
We have had too much of death, have we not?*

*So you will understand our decision – my own
and Kitty's – not to summon you all to the funeral
when the time comes. Our father, if we take an
eternal view, was a modest man, and we will see
him to his grave modestly, alongside his wife and
the Bennet ancestors.*

Now that I am alone with Kitty, I admire her more than I can say. Her energy and enthusiasm are remarkable. She seems to feel none of the weariness of our family burden. I am certain that she knows nothing of our father's errors of judgement in the course of his life, nor that there were actions for which we as his descendants might feel shame.

To business. What are Darcy's hopes for these journeys that he makes on behalf of our family?

Firstly, in London, he will consult dear Charles, who, as Jane's husband, is also concerned for the future of Longbourn; then with some lawyers of his and Bingley's acquaintance who are experts in the matter of Entail. With that expertise in hand, he will proceed to Kent and to Mr Collins, whom he will try to persuade towards the simplest option: that he remain in his present position, under the benevolent surveillance of Lady Catherine (whom, as we know, he reveres as much as he does Almighty God), rather than uproot his family to Hertfordshire and take possession of Longbourn. I have given Darcy a letter from myself to Mrs Collins, my oldest and dearest friend, in support of this decision, and feel confident that it will do its work.

If Darcy manages to accomplish a good outcome, Kitty and her husband can be permanently installed here. Then the Bennets – though under a different name – may remain at Longbourn in, we trust, perpetuity.

Perpetuity. Does such a thing exist, Mary? The

events of this past year would argue against it.

I trust that your husband, under your tender care, is emerging from this unfortunate period of ill-health. Mrs Reynolds gave me to understand that his reverend colleague Mr Hepplecraft is no longer a visitor to Humbole, even implying that there has been a rift between the two men. I sense that this may constitute a benefit, rather than a hindrance, to your interests. Mr Hepplecraft seemed a creature of fashion rather than a solid presence in the clerical arena. Perhaps Mr Needleman will now find a more congenial colleague. Or he may come to rely more on your companionship, Mary? Even your scholarship? I am impressed by your increasing knowledge and understanding of matters theological. They are quite beyond me.

So it is with affection and respect that I will close this page. I fear that further weeks may pass before Darcy and I can return home.

⌒⌒

Mary had come into the habit of tiptoeing into her husband's room each morning. A slight tap on the door, a call from the bed, and she would put her head round the door. He would nod, and she would enter. It had begun on the day she had received the news of her father's death, and had since become a daily ritual.

She did not go to his side; did not wish to touch him in any way. She merely went to open the shutters and let the cold dawn enlighten the room. She would say: "Mrs Beattie will bring fresh water shortly. Followed by your milk and your toast or a small slice of pound cake. Did you rest well, my dear?" And he would answer, "Quite well, thank you." Or perhaps, "A little restless, I fear. But that is in the nature of things."

He never complained. She never exhorted or cajoled him to be active or brisk. She simply opened the day and left the rest to Mrs Beattie. Downstairs Gladys would be taking breakfast into the dining room, while Patty did service in the kitchen, laying trays and preparing Mrs Beattie's porridge. Mrs Beattie's porridge was also something of a ritual; she dressed it with a pinch of salt and 'top of the milk' (not milk, not cream), and ate it with a soup spoon rather than a dessert one. After seeing to Mr Needleman and eating her porridge, Mrs Beattie would go over to the stables with a tray for Hurry, who was still no more recovered from the day of accidents than was Mr Needleman.

Esther did not appear; she was confined to the attic; that was what 'confinement' meant. The infant's necessities which Mary had ordered from Dewhurst the joiner and Mrs Blake senior were stored under the eaves, awaiting The Event.

Milly moved around the house like a wraith. Mary tried not to wonder which room she might presently be cleaning. Every time they almost met, they did a side-step of avoidance. Mary took this as their acknowledgement of what went on in secret during the night.

At first Mary lay quietly after Milly's formal departure from her room, awaiting her return. More recently, though, she had edged her nightgown upwards in preparation for Milly's visit, and had alerted her body to the delights that were in store. She had been awakened by Milly's intervention, and now she began to take that awakening into her own hands. It became part of her transformation; her growth not only into a new and more confident Mary, but also a growth into a new Mrs Needleman, and a new Mrs Rectory.

〰

Lizzy's letter was so long that Mary needed a break in her reading. She now read on:

Meanwhile, your household is soon to have an addition to its ranks. My gratitude remains for your prompt action in this regard. What the future holds for those two sisters and their new arrival, I cannot imagine.

Learning from your deep spirituality, dear sister, I say fervent prayers for all, both high and low. My most sorrowing prayers are, of course, for our darling Jane. But will you please pass the message to the maid who was Thwaite that I pray for her, too.

Your affectionate Lizzy.

P.S. I was about to seal this letter when Mrs Drayton appeared at the door with a bland announcement about our father: the end came a few moments ago.

My dear Mary, it is over. We can proceed. I shall send my letter to Darcy by special delivery. In the circumstances, he will not begrudge the cost that is payable on receipt.

20

In the Attic

FOR THE FIRST TIME, Esther had to move over to the other bed if she were to get any sleep.

Milly: Do that there kid e'er get to nod off?

Esther: Sleeps in 'day. Livens up in 'night.

Still they do *Doovus*. Yet, thinks Esther even as they do it, there's more than a kicking babba that lies between them.

Esther: D'you need to go to 'er, each n ev'ry?

Milly: Shiz strung up as a hanging ham. Needs settlin'.

They stroke each other's cheeks before separating for the night. Milly murmurs, *Come easy, babba. Come easy, easy.* Esther imagines opening up so that the babba listens to her words and comes easy. Then, with a sharp intake of breath, she imagines the babba coming not so easy. Or not coming at all, but getting stuck, and they're stuck for ever, bleeding and not coming apart, instead going far, far, into the long night of never coming apart. Milly, feeling those imaginings, sets up a long moan and a long murmur. *Easy! Easy!* Then she murmurs Esther back from the breathlessness, back from the long night and the fear, into ease, and an easy coming.

In those moments, Esther is somewhere else. She's back home with Ma an' Da an' Milly an' Joel. She can't see Ma an' Da, but she can see Joel. He's bendin' over his work, he's mekkin' summat, but she can't see what he's mekkin' juss yet. Then he shifts hisself, an' his shape is clear in the not-quite-gloom of the doorway. *Le'ss see*, she sez to him. An' he holds it up. The figure he's made; it's Joel; it's hisself. The little lead figure is bendin' over, an' yes, it's hisself, bendin' over and mekkin' another Joel, tiny in his hand.

As she gazes, the Joels go on an' on: one Joel meks another Joel, tinier, and the next one is tinier again: tinier an' tinier they get, one Joel mekkin' another Joel mekkin' another mekkin' another, for ever and ever, Amen.

She thinks: so will my babba be. I'll mek him, an' he'll mek another, an' that one'll mek another. An' so it'll go on, through this King's time, and the next King, and the next. An' just as Mill an' me came from the lead-mine to Pemberley, an' then to Humbole, an' then to God alone knows where else, so each babba'll go from God knows to God knows.

The mistress seems to think she knows what God wants. And Mill seems to know what the mistress wants. She, Esther, must let Mill go to the mistress.

Milly says, of a sudden: She wanns it.

Esther: Wanns the babba?

Milly: Aye. 'Ungers after it.

Esther: Well, she canna.

Milly: But, them folks, yer know? *'Ey* reckon as tha' can 'ave *enny* fing, cos *Ey've* got *Money*.

Esther: Well, ee's not Money. Ee's Babba, an' ee's *mine*.

Milly: *I* ken so, *yee* ken so. *She* ken so?

Esther cannot speak. Her breath is tight again.

Milly: Truss me, Ess. Ah can settle 'er.

Esther laughs. A high titter of a laugh. A scared laugh. Then: Wish yer cud settle this 'un, get 'im to sleep!

But as she heaves herself over from one bed to t'other, she knows she wishes no such thing. The way this baby's kicking shows he's alive. So alive that he can come out in his own good time, and live his own life, through all the reigns till there's... Well, till there's another queen, like Elizabeth. And that'll never happen, will it? Now that poor Princess Charlotte had took everyone's hopes, and her own babba, down into the grave?

Esther was sleepless most of the night; heard Milly go, heard her come back; heard the owls cry; tiptoed to see the last snow fall, and melt as it fell. And, all the time, Babba kicked and said, *Me soon, me soon, me soon.*

ஓ

Mary saw that they were all, in different ways, confined: by the slushy remnants of winter lying across fields and roads; by Hurry's indisposition; by Mr Needleman's slow, sad pacing around the house in search of something that was worthy of his notice. There was no companionship to be had at Pemberley, either. No Lizzy to visit or be visited. They were all waiting: waiting for a settlement on the Longbourn question, waiting for the spring, waiting for the birth.

She felt sorry for the horses left unexercised in their stalls. Hurry gave them the minimum of care, throwing hay towards one end and removing the worst of the detritus from the other, but no more than that. If a pale afternoon sun peeped through, Mary would trudge across and stroke their noses. She didn't mind if they slobbered over her hands. She was accustomed now to bodily secretions; her own were becoming increasingly familiar to her, and she tucked small handkerchiefs in her pockets and waistband in case of necessity. She murmured to the horses: *Milly, Milly, why does she, why do I; it is so beautiful; what is it; it is pure essence; I do not understand it; I await it; I long for it; will she continue to come to me; will she come forever?* The slobbering of the horses seemed an appropriate response to such primitive verbal effusions.

The news from Longbourn was brief. Lizzy and Kitty had been so long preparing for the end that matters were now proceeding steadily. There was no question of Mary coming to the funeral on account of the dreadful weather; Lyddy would not come either. Kitty's husband was being most attentive. There had been no word from Mr Collins or his agent, but Mr

Darcy had already spent some useful time in London on longstanding business in the Caribbean.

This particular morning, Robert surprised Mary by leaving his door ajar and presenting himself seated against his pillows with candles lit on either side. Had he even opened one of the shutters himself?

Mary walked over and opened the second shutter, then gasped. Her hands leapt up to adjust her spectacles. For the window-glass had been transformed into a miracle of beauty. A forest of leaves and flowers had grown in the night and entwined themselves with each other, and the easterly light caught and illuminated them.

"Oh! Robert! Look, my dear, look at this!"

"Frost flowers, yes. They are pretty. Please, come; sit by me awhile."

Mary could not tear herself away. "The windows of my room attract only blotched patterns. These glories seem more beautiful than ever before!"

"Dear wife, do not catch a chill, I beg of you. Come. Sit."

It was like tearing herself from heaven and coming back to earth. Reluctantly she returned to her husband's bedside and sat on the upright chair.

Robert said, "You are becoming over-excited, my dear. I fear that my melancholia has been too demanding of your good will."

"Do not think of it that way! You have suffered, and must take time for a full recovery. Water?" She waved towards the tallboy with its tray of cup and jug.

"Thank you, no. I would like you to sit down and take heed. There are matters on which I seek to consult you."

It was not her husband's practice to consult her.

He leaned forward. "It is the carving." His voice was husky with emotion. "It hangs above me like some sort of guillotine. I cannot bear it."

Mary's hearing stumbled over the word in the middle: was it *guilt*? No! He meant the sword that fell on French necks during their long-ago Revolution! *Guillotine*!

"Surely not, my dear? Those are the Gospel-Makers! Such exquisite carving!"

"But what it signifies, its place in my life; that is now gone. Forever."

"Robert, dear, you must not trouble yourself." She rose from the chair and went to get him a drink. "Please, compose yourself." She came back with the cup. "Take; drink." No, those were the words of the Holy Communion. "A sip. And another. There."

When she sat down and looked at her husband, the extent of their present relationship was clear to her. He needed her. She was Eve to his Adam, as written in the Book of Genesis. "Explain, my dear. Why should this beautiful carving cast a shadow upon you?"

"It should not have happened! it was my failure! My...*sin*."

"That is not so! Surely? You mentioned David in the Book of Kings, how close he was to his friend Jonathan!"

"But mine was not like that. How can I explain?"

"Not *sin*, my poor husband! I will not hear such a word! Such friendship, surely, is a gift from God! Otherwise, why should it exist at all? Why should

Mr Hepplecraft have been led to this carving, if it were not to give it to you, to be yours forever? We are all, each of us, sent angels... Surprising angels, on occasion... Angelic presences, which we could not possibly summon by ourselves. They arrive, we know not why!"

She sat back and gazed at her husband, beseeching his understanding. But all she could see on his face was confusion.

Her purpose suddenly became clear: she must renew her husband's vision after the loss of his friend. Now she saw how to express her spiritual point in a practical way.

Behind him stood the carved figures, dramatically displayed in the light and shade of the candles: Matthew; Mark; Luke the physician; and there, the Lord's beloved disciple, John, holding the sacred Book in his right hand. "Did you not summon Dewhurst the joiner, with his young assistant, for the careful hanging of its great weight? Did he not insert pegs, for the safety of it, to hold it in position? So, if you should relinquish the piece, it would wreak havoc on the entire wall! That work of art is surely intended to remain above your head eternally!"

Her husband's confusion seemed more intense than ever. She was failing him...driving him deeper into sadness by the effervescence of her enthusiasm...

Ashamed of herself now, she made to stand and leave the room.

"No, my dear wife! Do not go! You may be right. Your simplicity may have greater truth in it than my theological convolutions." His voice became warm and gentle. "You are so good to me. You are so good *for* me. What a wise point to make. To remove the carving would be folly. How would I explain my actions to Dewhurst and his boy? And what would be the destiny of this work were I to dispose of it?" He sat up straighter and looked more directly at her. "You have lifted a weight off my shoulders. What a dear wife you have become." Freeing himself from the embrace of his pillows, he folded his hands decisively. "I must honour it. There must be a gift for you. Though the nature of such a gift I do not yet know."

"Do not trouble yourself. My role is to serve. Yet – there may be something?"

He brightened. "Yes? Is there a gift that would fit the moment? That would console you in the loss of your dear father?"

"Not quite that." Mary did not wish to think about her father. "It is about Esther."

"Esther?" He seemed momentarily to have forgotten who Esther was.

"Thwaite, Mrs Darcy's maid, the sister of..."

His face cleared. "Ah. There are questions there, are there not, which remain to be resolved."

"Indeed there are. But I have it. The solution."

"My very dear wife, you always reach for solutions, even to the most intractable of difficulties!"

Mary smiled. In the chill of the bedchamber, with the fire not yet lit, she was warmed by his praise. "Esther. When she is, er, delivered of her child, I see a plan. A wholesome approach."

"Which is?"

"To welcome the arrival. Give thanks for the advent

of new life under our roof."

Her husband leaned forward to interject, but she overrode him.

"Clearly, the question of legitimacy will arise. But, as I was led by prayer to take the two waifs in, when their very being was in danger, so am I now led to plead on their behalf." Mary ignored her husband's bewilderment. During the night, in the quiet hours after Milly had left her, she had prepared the words for this moment.

"You, as parish priest, should offer a baptism for the child. Not a perfunctory one: a celebratory one. With myself as godparent." Her thinking had not included this last suggestion, but it seemed in keeping with her argument. "There is no need to discuss this now. The child is not yet born. We can put these thoughts aside. Take your rest, and come downstairs later to break your fast. I will inform Mrs Beattie accordingly."

☙

I am ill at ease in every particular. I look back to my early suspicions of this young woman and congratulate myself on that early insight. She is more than a minx; she is a taker-over-er; she will dominate; she will have her will.

And I am weak! How can that be so? Day after day I am weakened by the over-turnedness of things. This place has been invaded by sinners, with herself as standard-bearer. The sin grows, and the outcome of the sin grows nearer. And the minx warms to it! Rubs her hands before the fire of it! Draws my RN into the fascination of it! Glorifies the new life of it!

Meanwhile, the crippled one manoeuvres herself into every nook and cranny. I had her down as a saint, but saints are often akin to witches, and I recognise her now as a witch. She scrubs everywhere to so bright a shine as will ingratiate her with the household. Gladys sees the morning sun fall on each dust-free surface and smirks. Patty, sitting for her mid-morning drink, takes an unheard-of fifteen minutes, knowing I will not call her to repeat the scrubbing of the scullery, because the crippled one will have been on her twisted knees there half the morning. Meanwhile, in the attic, the darning will have been done to perfection by the one whom Mrs Darcy used to call Thwaite. There is no argument against them.

The minx has taken up *crochet*.

There will be tiny boots, which she names *bootees*.

There will be jackets, that she names *matinée jackets*.

Yesterday I enquired of her whether she would return to her practice of charity baskets; whether I should prepare items for carrying in them. "Indeed not," she replied with lofty air, "for my charitable energies are fully taken up with aiding the poor who are sheltering under our own roof." With a dash of glee she added, "I thank you, Mrs Beattie, for extending the receipts for every meal with such tender care, so as to include these waifs in our generosity."

Huh! Did she expect me to *starve* the sinners? Has she not read the Gospel in which it exhorts us to *turn the other cheek* to those who *despitefully use* us?

I submit. There is no option. My lip is bitten almost to bleeding.

A further source of discomfort is this. It is several weeks since I last had a missive from Mrs Reynolds. Normally not a week would go by without some confidence passing between us. Have I fallen out of favour? Is there some other ear into which she now drops her gems from Pemberley? I fear she is displeased with my failure to *chercher le père*. Of course, I have my conjectures. But I will not say the word.

And now comes dread news from another quarter.

Mr Prunty – whom I shall now honour with his chosen name, on account of his courage in the face of misfortune – Mr Brontë writes to say that his wife had scarcely recovered from her most recent confinement when she showed symptoms of a more threatening sort. No child will emerge from what he describes; only pain, death, and grief.

∽

The sound awoke Mary. Like mice, or rats.

No, they were human sounds, and purposeful. Purposeful persons were at work in the night, alerting her to the fact that *it was beginning to happen*. She knew not how. But the other Mary, Mary in the stable, long ago, mysteriously, did not know how either. Hers, now as then, was an angelic Happening.

Milly was an angelic Being, too. She appeared only at night; never in the day. The day was for forgetting, for secrecy. But each night this heavenly Being awoke her, breathed over her, touched her, awakened her. Scarcely a sound accompanied what the two of them were doing. Perhaps a moan? Though whether the moan issued from her own mouth above the bed-clothes or from the quick-breathing mouth beneath them, she could not tell. All this was a Mystery, given by God. She, Mary, knew nothing, understood nothing, except that this nightly hour, from its appearance to its disappearance, was sent to her from Heaven.

And now began the next Act in the Mystery Play. Here would emerge the small frail Being that would change all their lives. The fragile would become strong, just as the other Mary's child had grown from fragile infancy to strong adulthood, long ago. This child, the one that had nudged and bumped in Esther's belly, would arrive in this world a bastard (and was not the other Mary's child a bastard, too?) and, by mysterious means, become her God-child. Her child of God.

Now: the noises up the stairs.

She slipped noiselessly out of bed, located her spectacles with her hand and her slippers with her feet, heard the landing clock sound the quarter but knew not which quarter it was, slipped on her night-cape, and clicked open the door.

Her husband's door was, as usual, tight shut.

The scuttering noises were loud in the attic. Candles had been lit, for she could see her way in the gloom. She must follow the scuttering, become part of it.

She had reached the top of the attic stairs when she heard sounds behind her.

Purposeful sounds; heavy sounds; loaded.

Mary paused, and called down behind her: "Thank you, Mrs Beattie, but I will do what is necessary here."

The heavy steps paused, and in their place came heavy breathing. Then the Ulster voice said: "I have towels from the cupboard, and warm water. In thirty minutes' time I will bring more."

"Oh! Thank you!"

The footsteps were already retreating. With their retreat came the realisation that Things were needed for this Event, and Mrs Beattie knew what those Things were.

Mary tiptoed back down the attic stairs, bent to lift the pile of towels, returned with them up the stairs, put them down at the top, and did the same for a jug of steaming water. Held her breath in case the weight might be too much for her and cause her to slip, and she would go head over heels, hot water pouring over her, step, after step, after step... But she reached the top. Breathed. Steadied herself.

Now she must enter the Room of the Event. The Event that would bring Life instead of Death, and expunge the image of that other Death which had been expelled from the tormented woman in the storm. Mary, in her turn, as the one who had rescued the two sisters from their storm, would be the one upon whom this Mystery of Life would be visited.

There came the click of a latch, and an opening. A small, twisted face gazed across the small roof-space, and into her eyes. The biblical word came to her: *transfigured*.

"I have brought towels," Mary said, "and warm water."

Milly nodded, and her eyes flashed behind her towards the bed. "Towels, water. Thank you." Mary heard the garbled words perfectly, and went back to the landing to fetch the other things. Another biblical word came to her: *helpmeet*. Her task was to be Milly's helpmeet in birthing Esther's baby.

The baby. Her baby. Her God-baby.

၈

What is her intent? The minx has no shame. Here she is, with roof, with home, with husband to boot, and now she has another scheme in her uneducated little head. I see it now. She will have it all without paying a groat for it.

Oh, how I long for my father, and Mr Brontë, and the company of scholars in St John's College, Cambridge! I was not made for these bloody occasions, these birthings and dyings, these earthbound exigencies which occupy small minds like Mrs Needleman's. Mine is the life of the mind, the book, the library, the impact of intellect upon ideas. I was not born to be a woman; I was born to be a man. To do a man's work in a man's world. To inhabit the mind of a man.

Yet, as I awoke and heard what was afoot, I knew immediately (and far better than the minx) what to do. For I have been trained in the profession of Woman. Mrs Needleman has not had an ounce of such training. She has no more skills than she came naked into the world with. In a world that was governed properly, she would not be worthy of a moment's notice.

But, as my father told me in his last illness, we must live in the world as it is, not in the world as we think it should be.

I will guard my tongue and keep my peace. And I

will act, when necessary, as I did with the towels and the water. I will continue to serve faithfully, for so was I trained.

᠙᠙

There was nothing for it but to do exactly as Milly ordered her. The crooked finger pointed, and Mary went. Her barked commands were imperative. Mary obeyed, and was glad to do so, for it kept her eyes from straying to the bed, where Esther's form bulked huge against her shadow: first in the gloom of a single candle, and later, as the dawn light from the window increased, hunched on the bed above the workings of her belly.

It was rhythmic, this process. There were moments of intensity, followed by expanses of breathing, and recovering, and waiting. Milly dipped a towel in the water and transferred it to Esther: dabbing her forehead, her throat, her heaving body. The sisters scarcely spoke. How did Milly know so precisely what to do? Mary did not understand; she accepted it as part of the Mystery. When Milly demanded more water, Mary knew that if she went down to the main landing she would find another jug; she knew that the water would be precisely the right temperature, and she should leave the first jug there to be re-filled in its turn. The jugs, the towels, were part of the rhythm, just as she and the invisible Mrs Beattie were part of the rhythm too.

Until everything changed.

Then the panting began. Esther lay back, eyes

411

blank, face white and sweating; she leaned forward and groaned, her dark hair falling to hide her pain; lay back again, forward again, and so on, and on. Mary, hands to mouth, with nothing to do now, could only watch, turn away, watch and turn away, in a rhythm of her own.

"Wa'er and tarls!" commanded Milly. This time Mrs Beattie appeared at the top of the stairs, towels in her arms, jug of water by her feet. And a pair of scissors.

Mary grabbed the scissors and the towels first, then returned for the jug. As she grasped the jug handle with both hands, she caught sight of her reflection in the housekeeper's eyeball. She glimpsed herself as wide-eyed, wild, heroic.

Later she asked herself, could that be possible? Was it a trick of her spectacles? No matter. She saw herself as she was.

Back to Milly, who was bending over her sister and murmuring syllables low and loud against the moans. Mary could not bear to hear it, and turned away to gaze at the shimmering of the candle on the table in the window. The candle stood tall and proud: someone – it could even have been herself – had taken a fresh candle from the drawer, removed the old one, lit the one from the other, blown out the old wick, and set the new one in its place. Of the Mysteries, Mary thought, there was no end.

Behind her there came a great gasp, an in-gulping of air, and Milly's voice rose in a high, ululating song.

"Shall I?" asked Mary, breathlessly. But her offer went unheard. Milly, in this moment, had become part of Esther, just as Esther was separating from the child that issued from her belly. Mary leaned in to see this moment. But Milly leaned further and obscured her view.

What came next was a high triumphant call. It could have come from either of the sisters, Mary could not tell which. Then another. And another.

"Is it there, is it come?" called Mary, trying to make her voice heard over the calls from the bed.

No response. Silence. What...?

Then she remembered the pulsating cord she had seen emerging from the woman in the storm. How it had emerged after the child was born; how it had swung before her eyes in the dark and winter wind.

"Scissors! You will need the scissors!" Where had she placed them? On the bed, or on the table?

Milly's voice came harsh. "No' yet! Outer t'way!"

Her twisted foot, coming out in a kick, bruised Mary's ankle.

Mary scarcely felt it. She was putting out her arms for the child whose wet and slippery form would surely slide from Milly's arms and fall to the floor. "Give it to *me*!"

Milly's sideways-jutting jaw, glinting with sweat, was illuminated by a sudden shaft of light from the window. It was dawn, the break of day.

"Ah, bu' yer *willna*!" she declared, and swung the baby round and back towards Esther, whose arms were stretched out to greet her baby. Her breasts were huge and ready to be covered by his dusky, slippery form.

As the baby passed before her eyes, Mary saw it was a boy.

She felt the movement of Milly and the baby away

from herself, and realised that Mrs Beattie, standing in the doorway, was holding the scissors. She came forward to use them on the cord.

Behind her stood more figures. They might have been Gladys and Patty, and even (still in his nightshirt) Mr Needleman – Robert. But, on the other hand, they might quite easily have been angels.

21

Inheritances

URING THE FOLLOWING WEEK, Mary had a biblical quotation running through her mind as her feet ran up and down the stairs with food, water and other necessities: "Jesus answered, Verily, verily, I say unto thee, Except a man be born of water and of the Spirit, he cannot enter into the Kingdom of God." She found herself arguing with it. It seemed so negative. Could our Lord not have answered, "*Because* thou *art* born of water and of the Spirit, thou *mayest* enter the Kingdom"? Or even, "thou mayest *joyfully* enter the Kingdom"?

Henry (for so, Milly told her curtly, the infant was named) was a candidate for Heaven, surely. For he had been born both of water, brought by Mary and others, and of the Spirit, conveyed by Mary through her prayers. Yet the Church decreed that, without baptism according to the specified ritual, none could enter the Kingdom of Heaven. And could a fatherless mite like Henry be baptised in the parish church, here in Humbole? By the Rector?

Surely, he must be baptised. There was no other way to secure his future in eternity. She had already broached the prospect to her husband. She must take it up with him again.

Meanwhile she would continue with the practicalities.

Run as she might, up and down all four sets of stairs (kitchen, reception, upstairs, attic; attic, upstairs, reception, kitchen), Mary had been afforded only an accidental glimpse of the baby. The glimpse revealed a surprising head of dark hair and a few pink creases; these being mostly hidden in the folds of the nursery blanket that Mary had provided. Esther, spotting her leaning in Henry's direction, would whisk round towards the window, bury her face in his tiny being, and wait for Mary to leave the room.

And Milly?

Of Milly, Mary saw only the small skewed backside as it bent over one or other of the Rectory's fireplaces. For she seemed determined to prove herself as maid-of-all-work as well as Monthly Nurse for her sister on the top floor.

Of nightly visits there were none.

Then there was Mrs Beattie. Mary had expected the housekeeper to huff and puff at Mary's devotion to the illicit mother and child. But no: Mrs Beattie's attentions were elsewhere. Hurry, having failed to recover his usual languid level of energy since the accident on the road from Derby, had now taken a turn for the worse, and Mrs Beattie strode to and from the stables, caring for him with the same degree of devotion as Mary did the family in the attic.

Mary was confused. She knew nothing of the nature of Hurry's complaint except that it concerned laudanum. What did it mean, that word *addiction*?

But questions about Hurry's health must stay in the realm of Mystery. All she required of Mrs Beattie was for her own meals to be placed on the table at the same time as her husband's, so that even if she did not join him at the time, she might have a brief word with him as they passed each other *en route*.

One morning Robert caught her sleeve as she came out through the dining room door. "My dear, it has come to my attention... We must speak with each other." Mary, assuming he meant to return to the question of infant baptism, accepted the wave of his hand inviting her back to the table.

They sat. Mary waited. The confidence she had felt when launching into the subject on the previous occasion vanished. Could she really have suggested a 'celebratory' occasion for Henry? With herself taking on the sacred role of godmother?

Robert ignored the porridge that lay before him; his fine hands played with the folds of his napkin. At last he said, "What a blessing, my dear, that this birth has occurred safely. Mother and child are doing well, I hear. You have been brave, and helpful. One wonders, does one not, how events might have played out had that not been the case?"

"I am happy to give service."

He laid down his napkin and adopted his preaching tone. "With all life's changes, there are rituals to bring one period of service to an end and to move forward into another. In this instance, there is the matter of *churching*."

Mary was familiar with this term, but was not sure precisely what it involved. She had seen heavily-veiled women walk towards St Bride's accompanied only by their mother and a member of the clergy: they were to be 'churched', that is, returned to the community after giving birth. "Does that take place with a woman who...where there is no, or no known...in these circumstances?"

"In such cases, the aspect of churching which signifies *purification* most certainly enters in."

"And baptism?" Mary picked at the toast crusts she had cut off earlier. "Would it follow soon afterwards?" *Please, Lord, do not deny my Henry his baptism, for that is his gateway to Heaven.*

"That presents us with a difficult question. Mrs Beattie has brought the dilemma to my attention."

"Mrs Beattie? Why should she be concerned?"

"She is splendidly well-versed in church affairs. Did she mention her father's degrees from Cambridge University? And coming from Ulster, too! In Ulster they keep most faithfully to the dictates of Mother Church. Especially on such matters as the Sacraments."

"I did not know that," murmured Mary. "Do we not, here in England, keep faithfully to the dictates, and so on? It is, after all, the Church of England?"

"We do, my dear. But we are apt to lapse from the path. To err and stray like lost sheep. Mrs Beattie is

418

concerned lest this child – who, let us remind ourselves, is a bastard – should be afforded the rites of Mother Church. As if he were like you, or me. It is a question of *shame*."

Bastard…shame… Mary shuddered. She tried to speak, but her mouth was dry.

"It would set the wrong example to the parish." Robert was bringing their conversation to an end. "No doubt a solution will emerge. And then, my dear, your part in this most unusual drama will be over."

Mary burst out: "Surely not! My invitation to Esther and Milly, together with the expected infant, was not a perfunctory one but a whole-hearted welcome. My next task is to write to Lizzy at Longbourn, anticipating her return, and telling her the good news about the birth of—"

Her husband's response came in like a knife.

"My dear! Your mind is disturbed. You have confused *our* affairs – the affairs of those who are only a little lower than the angels – with those of the lower orders." He threw down his napkin as if disposing of all worldly confusions. "Let us postpone this topic till a future time, when your mind has readjusted itself. I am weary all of a sudden. The Sunday's sermons are such a struggle."

☙

From Lizzy: *My dear Mary – I sense that I may be writing to you from Longbourn for the very last time. I can now relate to you the final episode of these momentous events. Matters have moved at* such speed that they may take more time to write about than they took actually to unfold.

Fitzy has returned from Hunsford with the best of all possible news. Backed by legal opinion in London, he and Charles set off for Kent with the aim of persuading Mr Collins to remain in Hunsford, rather than transferring himself and his family to Hertfordshire. In this he was entirely successful.

So the Entail is no more! There will be some financial adjustment, but for a man in Darcy's position that is simple to arrange.

Apparently Mr Collins was all smiles; he sends his humble regards (and those, he is sure, of her Ladyship) to Mrs Bingley, Mrs Darcy, Mrs Needleman, Mrs Wickham, and of course to the new residents of Longbourn. I am sure you can imagine his satisfied tone as he itemised these names.

Fitzy then returned to London, where he signed the necessary documents, with Charles as witness. They returned in haste to Longbourn to convey the good news, and the two of them are, as we speak, celebrating in the library over a bottle of excellent port.

Dear, dear Mary, the shadow which hung over all our childhoods is removed at last!

The news was of course most important to Kitty and her husband. It is remarkable how easily the decision was made that they should take possession of the house. Fitzy has arranged substantial adjustments for each of us, in order to balance out

Kitty's gain; you (along with Lyddy) will feel the benefit in due course. Naturally, the major part goes to our precious Jane for medical expenses.

Kitty's husband – I really must begin to call him Timothy – appears satisfied, as well he may be. He has a passion to fill the house with servants from his own family seat (somewhere in Buckinghamshire; I forget where). How Annie and her family will respond to this development remains to be seen.

So Darcy and I can return to Derbyshire in triumph. I hope our Mama and Papa will rest in their graves more peacefully now. Each of us has fulfilled their hopes. The family line, if not the Bennet name, will continue, and we five daughters are safely wed and housed.

There remains the eternal concern for poor beloved Jane. But she has her dear Charles beside her, and financial security. Money does not mean cure, but it is a boon.

I will write more, Mary dear, but on a separate page. You will have been concerned about the confidences I have shared during our recent visits, and I am eager to allay any fears that might remain.

༄

Esther sometimes feels that they have conquered the world.

Mill says: Doovus!

Esther replies: Doo-vus!

Milly: Thee-vus!

Esther: Threevus!

Their ritual has changed to accommodate the expansion of their universe. From being sisters, they are now a family.

Henry lies in an open drawer at the side of Esther's bed. Each time the mistress comes up on some excuse, she gazes down at the drawer and says sorrowfully, "The crib awaits him, you know? Downstairs?" Or maybe, "He will be ready for his crib any day now?" Esther stands over the drawer, the baby blanket, the peep of Henry's precious head: stands over him like an ogre over his lair.

When the mistress has gone downstairs to contemplate the empty crib, Esther picks Henry out of his drawer-bed and snuggles her nose down into the unspeakably beautiful softness of his cheek. The new-born darkness on his head has all but disappeared now, and a layer of pale down is taking its place.

Three-vus.

Us three.

Like it was them two and Joel. Only now it's them two and Henry.

Three of them agin the rest.

At the same time, Esther knows that the future will come, and no one knows how that will turn out. Now is now, and that is enough. Milly does the worrying while Esther does the feeding and bottom-wiping; Milly labours up and down the stairs with chamber pots and monthly-wipes-turned-bottom-wipes while Esther throws open the small window to welcome the spring sunshine and give her son a great mouthful of it after his burp. He is a great feeder, is Henry, and a great burper too.

The mistress heard the burp once, and took a step back. Esther found the nerve to say, in her own tongue, "Ent heard a babby burp afore, ma'am?" and for a moment they gazed at each other, blankly, in mutual incomprehension.

At night there's their Doovus ritual, and Milly's new warning: "Them's talking up *sin*."

"Tell us summat new."

"Pullin' at 'Master. This way, that."

"Ma'am, or Beattie?"

"Beattie. Ma'am's all for flickin' watter round 'church, Beattie won' 'ave'."

"Let 'em fight t'other. Stop 'em fightin' us. *Talking up sin* indeed. They shud tek 'eed to their own."

Milly grunts.

Esther does not speak of Milly's nightly absences, how they ceased the moment Henry came into this world. But, while she accepts Milly's warning about *sin*, she cannot let it enter into her inner self, or it might leak into her milk and curdle it for Henry. He is such a quiet baby. Such a good baby.

She takes Milly's hands in hers and strokes them gently. They are rough with scrubbing. But she cannot complain to the mistress, for the mistress does her share of working, too, in her own way. And, most likely, for her own purposes.

෧෧

Torn as I am between the two sickly men, I do the best I can. I fear for Hurry. Every symptom I have read of, he suffers from. I have known worse cases of laudanum poisoning; what woman of the world has not? But this bodily racking, these sweats, this lassitude so great that even when his beloved horses need his care he cannot lift himself to accommodate them: all this drains my heart of sympathy. My protestations are unavailing; all I can do is borrow the services of Mr Blake's stable-boy for an hour each day so that the poor creatures get some exercise.

And I have news of parallel enormity from Mr Brontë. The dear man has at last taken the course of action that I feared he might: he has summoned his wife's sister from Penzance to care for his brood of children. Only thus can he ensure their proper care; the woman could not travel in the winter months; now, in April, she is on her way. What will become of those unfortunates? I hoped that he might summon me instead of the aunt, who, I understand, is something of a termagant. In consequence, I might have been relieved of my duties here, diminished as they have become, alongside the diminishment of RN and the sundering of his great love with SH. Thus might I have been drawn back into the esteem in which I was formerly held by the Ulstermen of old.

But the greater sorrow is his. Saint he may be, Mr Prunty-turned-Brontë, yet he cannot save himself from being visited, by God or by Fate, with tragedy.

Whereas, upstairs in this very house, the child of sin sleeps the sleep of the righteous. They behave as though there were nothing amiss with his begetting. God Almighty, is there no justice in heaven or on earth?

⟲

Mary read the bulk of Lizzy's letter, trying to take in both the momentous news and the change in Lizzy's tone. She had expected at least a token sentence about *Dear Papa*, his *long life*, be *sadly missed*, and so on. But, read it as she might, with her spectacles on or with her eyes close up, she could detect no daughterly bereftness at all.

But Papa had sinned. And Luke was the living proof of it.

Luke! Annie! What was that sentence buried in the flurry of pages? Kitty's husband Timothy "has a passion to fill the house with servants from his own family seat. How Annie and her family will respond..."! What consequences might follow from *that*?

Lizzy wrote also that Annie would send, packed between the layers of Lizzy's own luggage, two pretty little gowns for baby Henry, and two sealed letters for her previous maid Thwaite, namely Esther; please could Mary deliver them directly? Of course, however puzzled Mary was, she would do as she was asked.

She turned again to Lizzy's opening words. "Matters have moved at such speed... Fitzy... Best of all possible news." The Entail, ended. A Settlement at last. Some financial gain for herself, Mary, and for the other sisters. Especially for Jane. Or for Jane's doctors.

She held the letter loosely in her hand. The seal was heavy; it pulled the pages down. Mary looked more closely: yes, Lizzy had pressed the Longbourn seal onto the page not once, but twice.

She ran the pages through her hands. One, two... three. The third was a post-script. Hesitantly, Mary put the pages in the best position for reading this additional page. It was in a tighter, neater hand than the previous pages.

For your eyes only, Mary. The difficulty I had with Fitzy – which I told you of – please put it out of your mind. He and I are now as we used to be in the first flush of married bliss. These wonders he has wrought, with lawyers and Mr Collins: they have settled it all. He is so clever, so kind. He makes all things good. Oh, Mary, I hope you can experience this fiery glow of bliss with your own dear Robert! He too is a kind and a good man. I pray for you, that you may give and receive married pleasure with him.

Feeling thus energised, I sense a degree of shame about <u>Thwaite</u>. (And of course her little sister.) We should not have acted as we did, Fitzy and I. I told him so at the time, most clearly, at a moment (which I need not describe) when he could not argue with me. I find myself considering some kind of recompense for the poor souls whom we wronged. Though I cannot for the moment think how. At present, Fitzy will agree to any proposal I might make.

Please do not hint at any of this at home. It must be only between ourselves.

Mary folded the letter back into its original shape and pressed its heavy seals as if they could be re-heated and made private again.

How could Lizzy imagine her 'hinting' anything to, or in the presence of, Mr Darcy?

She held the little parcel of confusions in her hand for a moment before slipping it into her drawer under her clean stays, until she delivered them to their intended destination.

୧୨

From Annie: Dear Esther - I have run out of fabric for a third gown. But I have found the enclosed grey shawl, which I shall never wear again, and which you may possibly find useful. I remember with sadness the occasion on which I first wore it. My first-born infant was most frail, and we were by no means certain that she would live; we must go through the necessary ceremonies in haste, in case our fears were realised. Which, after weeks of watching by day and by night, was so. My dear mother-in-law gave this shawl to me, whispering that it had been given to her by Luke's father. Its original purpose, she said, was as a veil for a woman on the ceremony of her 'churching', its grey colour being modest, and suitable for wearing at a later date in chilly weather.

The cloth is of the finest lawn. It is so soft it feels like silk, but silk is cool, and this is warm. I would wear it over and over after we lost our first little girl, imagining her close to me once more; and then later after our first little boy. Though I refused to be churched after having him, it being a horrible thing, making out that childbirth is impure, and so on. Neither would I be churched after my two who survived, and are blessedly alive now. (I can hear them as I write, living noisily.)

But, your master being clergy – and most likely your mistress too, at his behest – may insist upon this ceremony. It is in this spirit that I send you my shawl, my veil, my warmth on a chilly morning, however you may choose to wear it.

I wish this letter to be for your eyes only, so have asked Miss Lizzy for the use of the family seal. I wish to commit to paper two facts that will not leave my mind. The first is something you must already know: about how my Luke came into this world, and what his rights should be, and how no one seems to have awoken to that fact but me.

The other is similar, and equal: that since I now have a mind as to how your son came into this world, and of whose inheritance he should by rights obtain a part, I would like you to be sure that I know it.

I know too that the issue lies in the man concerned being Mr Darcy's closest friend. But, more than that, I know that you must fear to tell anyone the truth of this matter on account of poor, beautiful, beloved Miss Jane.

I will say no more.

   Your affectionate friend – Annie.

∽

Mary stood at the landing window and watched the little group moving along the path that led from the Rectory across to the church of St Michael and All Angels. She had woken at the sound of stirring, unusually early for a day on which there were no set church services. She arose, put on her spectacles, slippers and dressing-robe, and came out of her room to discover what might be afoot.

Down below the landing window, three figures walked slowly in line. From above, as Mary saw them, they appeared as three long, dark, extended shapes moving along the pathway. The man in swathes of black was ahead of the other two, leading and expecting to be followed; after a gap (which Mary interpreted as extreme reluctance) came the first woman, head veiled and bowed; and last came the other woman, also in black, but hatted and shawled and muffed and booted. She was a woman in charge, in authority, exercising that authority even if only from the rear.

Mary watched with breath suspended. *She has done this without consulting me.* Those words held themselves in the air that she was not breathing in. Mrs Beattie had conspired with the man – Mary's husband, the Rector – to bring about this ceremony, this naming of Esther as unclean, and her child as a b...

Then her breath came out in a rush and cut short the arrival of the word *bastard* in her mind. For someone was standing beside her by the window. This person had appeared apparently without taking the necessary steps to get there.

Mary did not turn to look at Milly, but continued to stare at the scene below.

The first of the three figures reached the small Rectory gate that gave onto the next path, which in its turn led, through an avenue of yews, to the church's vestry door. Would the clergyman open the gate and wave first one woman through, then the other? No. He continued to lead, confident that both women would follow him. He had the power. His was the power to declare a woman unclean. The second of the women acknowledged that power, and the first woman was contained between them.

Mary and Milly stood together at the window and breathed together for a while. *How very small she is*, thought Mary. *And she is powerful, too. There is power in every breath she breathes.*

Mary whispered: "Is the child asleep upstairs?"

A quick nod from her side.

"Did she go willingly? Esther?"

There was silence from the other, but when Mary looked down she saw that the two hands had moved out in front and were splayed, as if to say: *Who can say? What does 'willingly' mean?*

Mary, all of a sudden, wrenched herself away from the magnet which was Milly. This grim ritual was unacceptable! She must intervene! Without even putting out a hand for any further garments, she flung herself towards the newel post and the stairs. She would go down there! Her dressing-robe flew out behind her like wings. She could not ignore this ceremony. Though she was a mere wife, she was Mrs Rectory.

Leaving every door open behind her as she descended, she imagined Gladys and Patty in the kitchen hearing her movements and frowning at each other, amazed.

By the time she reached fresh air, Esther had reached

the line of yews and disappeared into it. Mrs Beattie, muffed and hatted, still had several steps to go.

Mary, having paused at the back door, started to run towards the muffed and hatted figure. The figure heard her, turned, and stared in outrage.

Mary's feet responded to that stare, and halted dead in their tracks before her mind caught up with them. She was paralysed, unable to take a single further step. For, in Mrs Beattie's outrage, she saw what Mrs Beattie saw: a wild woman. A wild undressed woman, with wild unkempt hair streaming out behind her, with her wild robe – not wings now – undone and blowing freely behind her in the breeze of early morning. A child-woman, with a cry frozen on her lips – *Me! Wait for me! Don't go without me!* A woman mad with needing. A hysterical woman. A woman out of her own, or anyone else's, control.

"Miss-ess Needle Man!" The Ulster syllables called brutally over few yards between them. "What in the name of the good Lord...?"

"My prayers!"

Mary managed to bring out those two words. *Prayers* meant sanity. *Prayer*, that heavenly medium, brought her back to earth. She said it again: "My most fervent prayer!" She put her hands up to her wild hair to press it down, then ran her hands down to her robe to demonstrate control. "Will you take them? Please? My prayers, for the woman who is to be churched, and for the man who leads her? My husband? And for yourself, Mrs Beattie! Such a holy woman as you are!"

And Mrs Beattie's outrage weakened. She snapped her mouth shut and turned sharply back towards the yew trees.

Mary ran into the house, and up stair after stair after stair, to the place where she and Milly – Milly, whom she loved – had been standing, and might be standing still.

⁖

Milly had gone.

Mary, catching her breath and holding her hands up against the pounding of her heart, looked around to see where she might have gone.

Of course: she was up in the attic, with the baby.

She would go after her.

But first she must quieten herself. She was abashed. She had betrayed herself, in Mrs Beattie's eyes, as a weak, hysterical woman. In her husband's eyes too. Her husband and Mrs Beattie had been united in some mysterious friendship long before she came to Humbole, which would last long after Mary might leave the scene. Women did leave the scene, all the time. Like Lady Manton's Gwentholen. Like their own dear Jane.

Jane! Jane, perhaps, could come to her as she did before, and tell her what to do?

Jane, she murmured inwardly. *Please tell me. Am I a mad woman? Lost to decent society? Can I dress myself properly, and reappear?*

And Jane's voice spelt out a reply: *It is only a ceremony. When the next ceremony comes, all will come clear. The passion that you showed came from the Holy Spirit. It came from love.* The words were silent, but they spoke to Mary.

Now she heard a physical sound. A living sound.

A rustle. It came from the attic stairs. Milly.

Mary turned away from Jane and said, into the space that Jane had left, "I love you, Milly." The words were out before she could stop them.

Then she heard the echo of what she had said, and straightaway closed her eyes and checked in her mind as to who might have overheard her.

Did she? Love Milly, the waif, the crippled maid? Was this the mad woman, the wild woman, the child woman, taking charge of her again?

No. No one was looking at her now, except Milly. Gladys and Patty were the only ones in the house. Hurry was drugged in his bed in the stables; the baby was asleep in the attic; and the three other occupants of the house were now inside the church, doing what they must do. The Rector would have opened the clergy door with its big iron key and led first the veiled woman, then the hatted and muffed woman, into the church through the back way. They were trying to wash *shame* away. The shame of childbirth, the uncleanliness of it. Of any childbirth, not only the illegitimate kind. The shame of being a woman, doing what women do.

Did Esther herself feel shame? Mary, remembering Henry emerging wetly, bloodily, towards the surrounding angels, could feel no shame on her behalf. Her wild venture, which had so outraged Mrs Beattie, was her attempt to subvert the ceremony of shame.

Opening her eyes and turning towards the rustle, she said again, "I love you, Milly."

Then: "Do you love me, Milly?"

Milly was standing a yard or two away from her at the foot of the attic stairs. Her upward gaze was impenetrable.

"Just a little? Please! You came to me. You touched—"

"Sssshhhh!" The sound was harsh and sudden.

"I cannot sssshhhhh!" Mary was breathless and could scarcely speak. "Can you?" She could not bear to say the word *love* again. "A little?"

"Aye owny luth ess."

Mary had learned how to understand Milly. You did it by not speaking back, and not by thinking too hard, but by letting the words stay in the air and receiving them back a second time, this time with open ears rather than the ears of expectation. Then you could hear, and understand, the words.

Aye owny luth ess. Ess. Esther. *I own-y... I only...* "You only love Esther."

"Ess." That could mean *yes*, or *Ess. Esther.* Either way, the meaning was the same.

"But you came to me, you—"

"You wann-ed."

"I did want, yes. But you too—"

"For us. For Ess. For Babba."

"What do you mean? I cannot understand! For me, it meant—"

But she could not continue. Milly's gaze was too strong.

Milly said, and Mary heard it: "Every thing I do is for Ess." Or perhaps it was *for us*.

Staring at Milly, Mary wondered if she could ever

replicate the power that stared back at her. She heard, beyond those words, another phrase: *And not for you.*

Her knees buckled. She knelt now at Milly's level. Their eyes met, and locked.

Mary was begging.

But Milly's gaze did not drop; it was now directed above her, over her head, to things that Mary could not see, could not imagine.

Mary heard the words: *Milly requires nothing for herself. She simply thinks of others. Mostly, she thinks of me.* Who was 'me'? Esther. Those were Thwaite's – Esther's – words, in the Pemberley carriage as they neared Longbourn after her first visit to Derbyshire.

A small noise sounded somewhere, which she could not identify.

Then more of Esther's words came to Mary. *We lost...* Lost? Who? Her *brother.* What was his name? Joel. Her *family.* They had lost their family. Except for each other.

But she too – Mary – had suffered *loss!* Her family did not love her. She needed a family of her own! She needed love! She needed a baby to love! And be loved by in return!

That sound again. Upstairs, in the attic.

It was Baby Henry. He had been asleep, and now he was awake.

She exclaimed to Milly: "He has woken!" But, in the space where Milly had been, there was no one. Milly had already vanished.

Mary struggled to her feet, straightened her spectacles, gathered the skirts of her nightgown and robe, and climbed after Milly up the attic stairs.

Those stairs, so blessed through her carrying of endless jugs of hot water and towels for the miraculous birth, seemed narrow and oppressive now. Near the foot, she managed to take two stairs at a time, but close to the top she had to let go the skirts of her nightgown and pause for breath.

At the top she paused again, then rushed into the room where the baby was.

Milly's back was turned against her. Milly's tiny frame, clutching the baby close, stood in her way. She tried to move round her so as to place herself on the same side as the baby. "*Please!*"

She held out her arms. She was begging again. She had wanted Milly, but could not have her. So she must have the baby. She was Mary of the Annunciation, Mary of the Virgin Birth. The angels were with her, all the angels, the archangel Gabriel, the archangel Michael even. They knew she needed a baby. This baby. In her arms, now.

"Please!" The word had become an order. "Please! Now!"

Milly, her arms full of clutched baby, stared upwards defiantly at Mary.

The baby was bawling. Milly held him ever tighter. "Coo..." she murmured, her head bent down to his. "Coo...coo..."

"Give him to me! I have not held him yet! Let him come to me!" She thrust out her arms and aimed for the baby's clothing.

Milly, while still coo-ing, took a step backwards and held him ever tighter as his cries came ever louder. Mary thrust herself forward in an attempt to grab the child. But there was no space for her hands to get a hold. Henry was disappearing into Milly, disappearing from her sight.

Now came a whirlwind. A hurricane, pushing past her: a hurricane of grey cloth and desperate shrieks.

"Mill! Babba! Come to me, my Babba!"

Esther closed in on Milly to enfold baby Henry between the two of them, and they became three, a trinity, in an inextricable cocoon.

Mary's hands fell loosely at her sides. Then she turned and groped her way back through the low door frame, and away.

22

Towards Baptism

MARY RETURNED to her room, climbed onto her bed and remained there for an uncountable time. A volume of sermons lay on her table, and after a while she set it on her knee as if to read. But she could not read. The weight on her knee was a book, not a baby. She could never hold the baby, if the baby did not want to be held. She could never hold Milly, if Milly did not want to be held.

Sounds from downstairs indicated that her husband had finished his breakfast and gone to his study. She put the book back on her side table and got out of bed. Slowly, she dressed. The lacing of her stays irritated her, and the stays themselves felt scratchy until she came through her bedroom door and paused at the stairs; there she breathed to steady herself, relaxed within her corset, came down and stepped out onto the patterned tiles of the hall. She must prepare herself now to meet Mrs Beattie: as a dressed woman; as a responsible woman; as Mrs Rectory.

She expected Mrs Beattie to be awaiting her at the dining room door. Would she say, as usual, "Good morning, ma'am"? And would Mary say, "Thank you, Mrs Beattie, I shall now break my fast"? Her plan was to follow this up with: "It being a reasonably fine day, I shall take a walk to appreciate the glories of spring." Not so fast. She must ask Mrs Beattie whether there had been any alteration in Hurry's condition. That would re-establish her as a concerned Rector's wife. Then – oh – that would be the moment, too, to enquire whether Mrs Reynolds of Pemberley had found a vacant alms-house in which Hurry might see out his last days, should he be well enough to be moved.

But there was no Mrs Beattie.

Might she have remained in the church, in prayer? Or still be tending to Hurry? But her care for Hurry had never previously interfered with her duties in the house.

Into the dining room. No sign. No sign of her husband either.

Would he be in his study?

Mary sat, and waited.

Through her inner vision, a grey shawl fluttered; then Esther, reaching desperately for her baby through that swirl of grey lawn. Had she, had Mary, seized him from Esther's arms? She had not. She had been prevented.

Patty came in with a tray, transferred a bowl and a plate to Mary's place, and stomped out of the room again. Mary knew not to ask her any questions, as there would never be a reply. Gladys might offer a syllable or two; Patty nothing.

Mary made herself eat what was put in front of her, in case the household thought something was amiss. As she ate, and as she wondered about Mrs Beattie, some words of her husband's returned to her: "Such a surprising woman, Mrs Beattie. She has all the scholarship of St John's College Cambridge at her fingertips! From her father, an Ulster man, and another clergyman, I forget his name, who now resides in Yorkshire. They are most strict, these Ulster men, you know. Especially on such matters as the *sacraments*."

Sacraments. Such as baptism.

She could not *have* Baby Henry. But still he must be baptised! Else he could not be admitted to the Kingdom of Heaven.

Her task was to ensure it was done. She was the one who could make it happen.

However, first she must fill the morning. She would take that walk.

Using the front door, thus avoiding the stables and questions about Hurry, she took the path towards the village. The sun was well up and the lower branches of the horse-chestnut trees were starting to burst into wide fingers. As the lane left Humbole behind, young oak trees displayed their fat buds, and behind them, on the higher ground, larches were sprouting needles in small tufts. Mary felt somewhat congratulatory about what she had learned of God's world since coming to live here last summer. She recalled Mr Needleman's kindness in directing her towards books in his library; most of all, towards Gilbert White's *Natural History of Selborne*. Robert had even prevailed upon Hurry (when he was well enough) not to let the village mole-catcher string up those poor little wizened black bodies on the Rectory gate, because it upset Mary so. Whether the man had then strung them up on other, more distant gates, she had no idea; but today she would fix her mind on the beauty of the Derbyshire landscape and her good fortune in having made it her home.

But (she asked herself as she turned back) how long would that fortune last, if Mrs Beattie reported to her husband that his wife was suffering an attack of the hysterics and could no longer be relied upon? And how, if that were the case, would Mary persuade her husband to give baby Henry the key to eternal life?

She heard the church clock strike the quarter. She must re-enter the Rectory and meet her husband in the dining room. She would set aside her fears and, as they ate their cold meats and cheese together, she would venture her proposition.

She came back the side way, which passed the stables where Hurry was bedded down. Might she do her duty and go and see how the poor man was? She could prove herself a kindly employer – she should have picked flowers for him from the verges, fetched a small vase from the kitchen and taken it to cheer him – she was remiss. Nevertheless, she could offer him the simple act of visitation.

Beside the horses' stalls there another door, split into two as if it also were a stable. The upper half was open, the lower half closed. Not hesitating in case her courage failed, she pushed open the lower half and almost banged her head on the upper as she walked forward. There was straw on the flagged floor under her feet, but she found herself standing in someone's home, someone's living space; there was a pallet bed and, under a loose blanket, an emaciated form.

Beside it, on what must be a milking stool, sat the solid form of Mrs Beattie. The housekeeper had a rough clay mug in her hand, and a spoon with which she was attempting to feed the figure on the pallet bed. The spoon hovered, the form moved a fraction and then fell back; the spoon returned to the clay mug.

Mary could not find breath. The emaciation of the man, and the tender care of the woman, had taken it away.

Mrs Beattie did not turn. She must have heard Mary's entry, but took no heed.

༄

Esther is stroking Henry's belly. It is soft, and full of milk. She senses the milk from her breasts taking its place in him, the one for whom it is intended. Beneath her breasts, small convulsions are happening in her own belly and groin, in memory of their partition. In the soft hillock of Henry's belly lies a small lump; she knows that in due course it will become a cavity (though still, oddly, referred to as a 'button'). Just now, she loves that lump more than anything else in the whole wide world. For it says *We were joined, we two, and will forever remain so.*

Milly, beside her on the bed, breathes in this unity. They both breathe in, then out; in, and out. Everything is standing still. Esther begs it to stay still, in suspension, forever. May it never move forward into becoming; into whatever might come to pass.

Esther says: "Tell me again how it rocks. The crib."

Milly (screwing her face into Mrs Needleman's pious look): "Bought it special, I did, from Mr Thing, the parish j-j-joiner. Cost a mountin o' money, did this crib. I'll rock it, so I will, till it's got the babba in't. Cos that's how yer get a babba, yer ken? By rockin' the cradle!" They roar with laughter before clapping their hands over their mouths in case they are heard.

Esther glances over at Henry's bed-linen and the one soft blanket offered by Mrs N in acknowledgement that, for the moment, Henry needs to be up here, not down there.

Esther: "And it has *soft* sheets? An' *wool* blankets?"

Milly: "It do. Soff. An' woolly. Nowt but best, 'ey are."

Esther's hand on Henry's belly stops moving. He gurgles in protest, and her hand starts moving again.

Milly: "'E'll be a blondie, won' 'e."

Esther: "That black only lasted a week."

Milly: "Blondie." They gaze at the head with its covering of translucent down. "The'll be lookin' to see as who 'e teks after."

Esther: "Sssshhhh."

Milly: "Bu' the' will, Ess."

Esther says, sudden and sharp: "Yer plottin', Mill."

Milly says back: "Course ah'm plottin'! 'S mah job ter plot!"

Esther stops stroking, picks Henry up and clutches him to her body, at which he yelps in surprise and then snuggles in.

Milly, yet again: "Truss me, Ess. Truss me?"

Esther: "'Ave no option, 'ave I?"

She clutches Henry too close, he yelps again and she releases him. Fretting now, his mouth wobbles, and he dribbles down her front.

Milly: "Tell it agen, Ess. In 'church. Prees' sez, woman sez – all that."

So Esther repeats what she heard in the cold church that morning: "Oh Lord, save this woman thy servant." And Milly replies in her turn, *Oh Lord, save this 'ooman.* "Which putteth her trust in Thee." *Whi' pu-th 'er truss.* "Be Thou to Her a strong Tower." *Bi... thou t'er...a stro...* "From the face of her enemy."

"Oh Lord, hear our prayer."

Both: *And let our cry come unto Thee!*

Esther whispers, as if it is a blasphemy: "*You* is my strong Tower, Mill! An' it's them as is my enemy. Them downstairs. Where's we goin' to go, Mill?"

❧

Robert was sitting at his place, hands on knees, quiet as a Quaker. Mary sat down and unfolded her napkin.

"Now that—" she began.

He spoke at the same time. "We need to converse, my dear."

She persisted, and he gave way.

"I have been... I saw...Mrs Beattie seems to care most kindly for Hurry."

"Ah, Hurry! I have known him all my life. His father served my father. The family, historically, used to live in Pemberley."

"*In* Pemberley?"

"The village. It was displaced, generations back, when the Darcys began to build."

Pemberley a village? Not a deer-park? Mary felt shrunk at how little she knew.

But...*sacraments*. These she understood. She must broach the matter which preceded it, the early morning ceremony, and discover whether Mrs Beattie had mentioned her wild intervention.

"Now that the initial ceremony has been accomplished..." She paused, fractionally, in case Robert should ask a question. Nothing came. She could continue. "...the next event would be the baptism of the child."

Robert picked up a knife and fork, then laid them down again. "There you have it. There lies the question." The question was about the sacrament. Not that his wife was a mad woman. "There is a barrier to such an event. That is, the question of bastardy."

Mary shuddered again at the word *bastardy*, but sat up straight. "I have studied the text in your library, and found that such circumstances do not prohibit baptism!"

"You are perfectly correct, my dear. But here, in this parish, it is my duty to maintain standards of morality. As is Mr Darcy, in his original judgement of the case. Mrs Beattie has brought—"

Mary froze. What had Mrs Beattie said?

"...gleaned, at St John's, Cambridge, detailed

knowledge of these matters. And—"

"So have I! Gleaned!"

"But it is I who must make the judgement, Mary. I alone." The use of her Christian name seemed significant. "The fact of the matter is: here, now, there is a moral barrier to the baptism of a bastard child in my church. The child might find some other parochial authority where it is possible. But here, in Humbole, the authority is mine. And that" – picking up his knife and fork and holding them above the cheeses and meats – "*that* must be the final word on this subject." He helped himself to a slice of tongue and began to eat.

Nausea filled Mary's mouth. She burst out: "But where could they *go*? To find such a solution? And he cannot be baptised? Oh, husband, if he, this innocent child, is denied this sacrament, he is banned from life with Christ! For eternity!"

Her husband swallowed a mouthful and leaned towards her. "My dear, we are all born in sin. We must take these matters to the Lord's feet and let them rest there, regardless of our own questioning." She recognised this leaning. He knew how his theological explanations could assuage her longing for spiritual truth. "I beg you, Mary: look to the future. Those unfortunate sisters were taken in, by you, without my consent, at a time when I was too unwell to form a proper opinion. Your task now is to find a place where they, with their infant, may reside; a place which lies, hopefully, at a reasonable distance from ourselves. Be it workhouse, or some other arrangement that has been set up for circumstances of this sort, that is where they must go. I do not *ask* you to do this. I give it to you as a specific *instruction*. It must be *done*."

Mary stared down at the tablecloth, hoping to see some other authority lying there to countermand her husband's order. None came. She had no authority. "Wives, submit to your husbands." There was no argument against her husband.

She wanted to scream. But she could not, without making it worse. Without becoming a mad woman.

"Please… Dear husband…"

He over-rode her. "Do not bring the subject to my attention again. Not unless, or until, you have found an answer to the problem which you, and you alone, have brought upon this house."

⁂

I come back indoors, go to my room, Gladys and Patty come to me with warm water and a sponge. I wash the smell of the stables and the sickness and the balm off of me; I tell myself not to use that phrase "off of" in the hearing of these English folk in case they put me down as a Papist, and I settle myself in my upstairs room, with my own being and my own thoughts.

My mind does its regular check around the house. It is a mosaic of many pieces.

My master sits in his study; having done his duty by the miscreants in the attic, he is no more happy with their future prospects than I am. After our unfortunate but necessary ceremony, he thanked me with a fervent shake of the hand; this restored me somewhat, but was so far from our previous intimacy that I came near to weeping.

My mistress is infected by the witchcraft that emanates from the attic. She wishes for a child. There are others who have also wished for a child, or children, and have been forced to submit to God's Will that there will be no such child forthcoming. Myself included. I had my two sons, my David and Jonathan, my spiritual offspring, but they are no more. *We all have our griefs*, I want to say to her. *Do not suppose that your griefs are heavier than those of others.*

I guess she is in the drawing room, embroidering her latest sampler. Her text is from Psalm 127: "LO, CHILDREN ARE AS ARROWS IN THE HAND OF THE MIGHTY MAN; HAPPY IS THE MAN WHO HATH HIS QUIVER FULL OF THEM".

Gladys and Patty go about their business faithfully, but with much anxiety. One or other of them creeps back to me every hour or two, opens their mouth and shuts it again. They depend upon me. I was their rescuer, as surely as I was the mother of RN and of SH; but that is over now, and they know it. If there were the smallest invitation to move north, they would lose me altogether.

Meanwhile, my patient in the stables is not long for this world. His name is ever more ironic. He knows that his sickness is of the spirit as well as of the body. He has not fulfilled himself in this life; he is on the way to the Elysian Fields, where the Good Lord will lead him into pastures new. He did not wish to go, but is reconciled to it.

And, above me, the miscreants work their wizardry in the attic.

I look back with sorrow at my decision to make my home here in Humbole. The offer seemed like very heaven. The father of SH, a shy and scholarly man, colleague of my father and Mr Prunty at St John's College, spoke to my own father on his death-bed and tried to relieve his mind of anxiety as he prepared to meet his Maker. He had heard of a vacancy for a housekeeper in this Derbyshire parish, which might offer his orphaned daughter security. He said that his son (SH) was of the flighty sort, not suited to the clerical life, but with a brain which toyed with dogmas and philosophies in a way that put argumentative opponents into a spin. My father agreed to this plan and said his last prayers; whereupon I made the needful arrangements. Then I put my hand into the hand of God. And here a miracle was accomplished: having lost my birth family, I became mother to these two men. But the delinquency of the flighty one became his downfall, and the outcome was grief, both for RN and for my good self.

Now comes another piece of the mosaic: Mrs Darcy's newly joyful married state. It shifts the picture. Mrs Reynolds writes (briefly, and after several unanswered enquiries from myself) that Mrs Darcy is in fine spirits. Her soon-to-be-ennobled husband has wrought some Jesuitical settlement of her family's legal difficulties, and she looks forward to reporting all these matters to her dear sister at the Rectory. She will be giving off marital joy, like a perfume that the rest of us are compelled to sniff.

What was it about that place, Longbourn, to produce such disparate and chaotic sisters? All blessed five of them?

As for Mrs Reynolds, I can read between her lines. She disapproves most sternly as regards the events surrounding the miscreants in our attic. She knows that my opinion concurs with hers in every particular; but she looked upon my motherhood of the boys as an aberration. She only tolerated it out of...what? I believe it was out of *unhealthy curiosity*. There are such women, who live vicariously, who thrive on the moral convolutions of others, passing them around their circles of gossip. Some might accuse me of such a position in relation to RN and SH. Yet, for me, it was not vicarious living. It was motherhood of the warmest and most affectionate sort.

The land lies thus. Mrs Reynolds is no longer on my side; RN is grieving in his study; the lead-miner's daughters are setting their plots; and the minx is descending into hysteria. I am beleaguered.

I turn to Mr Brontë's most recent letter. It is marked with his tears. Dear man! He is my last connection with my father, and with my home across the water. Is this the hand of the Lord, giving me a role in the life of his tragic family? He hints that a neighbouring cleric is in need of a housekeeper.

But I cannot leave. Not until Hurry no longer needs my care.

There are two small comforts. First: there cannot, surely, be a bastard's baptism in this parish. I shall receive my reward for that fact, no doubt, on the other side, when I reach my heavenly abode.

Second: Mrs Darcy has survived the issue of her maid's pregnancy without any embarrassing enquiry

into the gentleman responsible. Yes, the *gentleman*.
Rumours among the staff abound that the culprit
is an individual alarmingly close to the Family. Mr
Needleman needs to move swiftly towards a solution
for the two witches upstairs, to give these rumours the
chance to fade.

☙

Esther was not accustomed to receiving sealed epistles.
With eager hand, she cracked open the seal on the
second of Annie's letters, and read:

> *Dear Esther - I can scarcely write this, for I find
> myself too upset by the goings-on at Miss Kitty and
> her husband's behest. They make it clear that Miss
> Lizzy's departure cannot come too soon. I dread
> the time when I and my family are alone here, with
> no protection from the acquisitiveness of that pair.*
>
> *I will, however, find words for a strange little
> incident that occurred the other day. Mrs Darcy
> caught me on the landing and whispered a
> question. Taken by surprise, I begged her to repeat
> it, which she did, with some over-the-shoulder
> glances. It was about offspring, and how I only had
> two (she forgetting my lost ones); how could that be
> achieved, since she wished most fervently to avoid
> the childbirth miseries that were the origin of dear
> Jane's afflictions? Had I some miracle potion, or
> what?*
>
> *I knew not how to reply, and muttered that I
> would think on.*

I wondered afterwards that Mr Darcy had not learned such things from his London visits. For, if he does not visit Ladies of the Night, many of his companions surely do. Even Luke has heard of the rubber mechanisms that some gentlemen try; he says they would be better used for horses than for men. But if they be the only mechanisms to hand, they are better than nothing.

That evening, not wanting to be too long burdened with this, I knocked softly at her door.

On seeing me, she sent her current Thwaite on some errand. (She is quite satisfied with this new young woman, apparently, though in my opinion she is not a patch on your good self.) As quickly and clearly as possible, I found words for what there really are no words for. How, for the woman, the month is different by the week; that Luke and I restrict ourselves to the week before my Monthly Visitor and the week after it; and if we should be taken by surprise during the intervening weeks, then he is especially careful... I could not find words for this to the mistress of Pemberley, only making a small gesture, which gave rise to a hoot of laughter from her.

"So," she said at last. "It is about my calendar? But why did no one take it upon themselves to explain this to me in the weeks before my marriage?"

Then she giggled like a girl and, in the words of the Good Book, 'went on her way rejoicing'.

I called after her – "It is not always effective... reliable..." But she was gone.

Later that day she caught me again, this time

452

on the stairs. Having thanked me most profusely for my earlier advice, she then divulged to me how deeply she regrets her behaviour (though it was under instruction from Mr Darcy) towards yourself and Milly before you were taken in by Miss Mary. She hopes there might be some way to assuage her discomfort in this regard, and wonders if I can offer any wisdom?

I confess, I had no wisdom to offer. I do not know how this repentance might unfold in action towards yourselves and your child. I can only pray that my mother-in-law's shawl may warm you on days when the Derbyshire wind blows chilly, and protect you as often as it has protected me.

I will send this, like the other, as a sealed message - if I can get past Miss Kitty and her husband into the library to use the seal.

From your faithful, but fearful, friend – Annie.

Esther read this over again and again, then the letter that preceded it.

The first seal was neat, the second hasty.

Henry lay in his drawer at her feet; Milly was working in some corner of the Rectory; here, under the eaves, it was quiet. The grey shawl lay across her knees.

How had the letters been packed in Mrs Darcy's luggage at Pemberley? She must have summoned the message-boy and given him orders regarding secrecy. It could only be Mrs Darcy who could have done so; a new, repentant Mrs Darcy.

Annie, in each letter, was telling her something

important, and each was private. The seal ensured that she, and only she, would read the contents. In the first lay the information about the fact that *the issue lies in the man concerned being Mr Darcy's closest friend.* In the second lay the information that Mrs Darcy *deeply regrets her and Mr Darcy's behaviour towards yourself and Milly before you were taken in by Miss Mary.*

Annie would know that she would share these messages with Milly, and Milly alone. But what difference it made to any of them, Esther had no idea.

⟡

Yet again, Mary awaited a visit from Lizzy. As she sat in the drawing room, feeling her husband's distance across the hall in his study, a phrase floated across her mind: *Lo, she comes like clouds descending.* A Methodist hymn, written by those rebels from the Anglican communion, the Wesley brothers.

As the church clock struck eleven there came a rat-a-tat-tat on the front door. Mary did not move, for Mrs Beattie always answered the door when Mrs Darcy was expected; she would appear soon, and announce: "Mrs Darcy, ma'am."

But no. The drawing room door was flung open, and Lizzy herself appeared. She was indeed like a cloud descending, or sunshine from a clear blue sky.

"Mary! Oh Mary, it seems an age since we were last together! So much has taken place! So many questions resolved!"

Mary was embraced. And embarrassed. She released herself and looked towards Mrs Beattie, who was standing, framed, in the doorway.

"Will that be comestibles, ma'am? For two?"

"For three! For four! Mr Darcy is having a word about the horses."

Mary was amazed. "Mr Darcy? He is here? Himself?"

"Why should he not be here? How tiresome that your man has not been well. Have you a replacement?"

"The boy from the village is quite competent. Is that not so, Mrs Beattie?"

"Pemberley's horses will be in good hands, Mrs Darcy ma'am, Mrs Needleman. Comestibles for four, then. I will alert Mr Needleman. He will be honoured…"

"No!" Mary broke in. "I will fetch him myself."

Mrs Beattie made her exit.

"So!" said Lizzy. "The four of us may converse! We will tell our stories, and you may tell yours." She seated herself with aplomb on her usual chair.

Mary left her and walked across the hall. She opened the study door without knocking. Her husband was at his desk, pen in hand. He looked up, surprised.

"Robert, Mr Darcy is here."

He looked shocked, and stood. "Mr Darcy? Is it true, then? That he is to be awarded the accolade?"

Mary did not understand.

"His knighthood? Is it confirmed? How will we acknowledge it? How should we address him?"

She gathered her wits. "Mr Needleman, I would be grateful if you could greet Mr Darcy in a suitable way. I can only recall my father's death and the circumstances arising from that melancholy event."

"Of course, of course. I will finish this sentence,

and then come." He sat down again, still flustered. "There is no need to wait for me, my dear. I will be no more than a moment."

"I am happy to wait." Mary gave a hard edge to her voice, and was not displeased with it. "I would prefer us to go into the drawing room together."

Her husband blinked, and went back to his work; his pen hovered above the page and descended for a scribble. Then he laid down the pen and stood again. He was wearing his usual clerical cravat, and looked at her as if in a mirror while adjusting the cravat very slightly.

"Splendid, my dear," said Mary. "Let us go."

In that moment, she had decided what recompense she might ask Lizzy to make to Thwaite – Esther – and her sister and the baby. There could be a baptism after all. It need not be at the parish church. For did not Lizzy's home, Pemberley, possess the facilities to meet all possible needs, from corporeal to spiritual? Was there not a Family Chapel?

She and Robert approached the drawing room door. It was wide open, and through it she could see Mr Darcy standing against the fireplace, next to his wife's chair. Lizzy was looking up at him, and he was looking down at her. Mary perceived, in a single glance, that everything else – the horses, the servants, herself and Mr Needleman, Mr Bennet's death, the legal negotiations, Bingley, even Jane – had vanished away. They were utterly absorbed in each other.

This image of them together, to the exclusion of all else, recalled the early days of their engagement. Mary remembered how she had felt during that time, because of the warmth, the heat even, of their mutual adoration. On those occasions, embarrassment had so engulfed her that she must retreat to her room and dab her upper body, and occasionally even her lower body, with the water left over in the morning jug of water.

Now, remembering those dabbings, she also recalled a conviction that *they knew something that she did not know*; that she could not, and would never, know. But she knew now. Not as they knew, but in her own, equally precious way.

She took her husband's arm, stopped him in his tracks, and murmured low: "I have a small request to put to them, my dear, in which I hope to have your support." She paused. "Thank you." Robert made no response, and they proceeded towards the open door, making what she hoped was an image of one happy couple meeting another.

Afterwards, Mary could not piece together their four-fold conversation in the order in which it had taken place. Much of the time she had been preoccupied with imagining the conversation as it might be overheard by Mrs Beattie with her ear to the far side of the door.

However, she was proud to have spoken her request with quiet confidence. "You mentioned, Lizzy dear, that you felt some regret towards Thwaite and her sister Milly." There was just a hint of mumble as she said the word *Milly*, but it only lasted a second. "That perhaps you might not have acted kindly enough on the question of the, er, the expectancy." She had launched into the next part, about recompense, and

457

baptism, how it might be conducted in the private chapel at Pemberley. Recalling this, she was paralysed by delayed fear. Mr Darcy's face suddenly appeared, huge, before her: confused, flushed, outwitted. Yet at the same time elated, as if he were still in that bubble of adoration with his Elizabeth.

She had stumbled then, and looked to her husband for reassurance. She recognised in his face, too, something aghast. 'The wind taken out of their sails': that phrase was neither biblical nor literary, but it fitted her purpose. She had taken the wind, and they could not sail on. She, a ship still in full motion, had continued with the question of recompense, and how difficult it was to perform the sacrament of baptism on a "base-born infant" (yes, she had used that uncomfortable phrase) in one's own parish church; but, given that there was this other option, of a private chapel, and that Lizzy was her dear sister, it would be a comfort to the mother of the child, Thwaite (now Esther) – "and also to myself", she added, "who is so close to the situation in hand, and who could readily act as god-parent, as is necessitated in the Book of Common Prayer."

Thus had she continued until the end of her speech was near. "They would receive the blessing of Mother Church, without which, of course, neither mother nor child can enter Heaven on Judgement Day. The contemplation of which" (or had she said *consummation* of which?) "would bring grief to us all, I am sure."

Mary had looked from her husband to Mr Darcy, and Mrs Darcy had looked from her husband to Mr

Needleman. At this point, she became absolutely convinced that Mrs Beattie was indeed eavesdropping at the door.

But she did not care if it were so. Because Lizzy said, immediately and miraculously, "Well, Fitzy, I could not have put it more clearly myself. It is true, I have been feeling twinges of guilt about how ready we were to throw those poor sisters out into the storm. Mary kindly took them under her roof, and now we have the chance to repay her with a kindness of our own. Mr Needleman, would you be prepared to undertake the necessary offices? If, that is, my dear Darcy invites you to do so?"

Mr Darcy, standing imposingly beside his eager wife in her chair, issued a kind of bark, as if to give himself entirely to his wife's desires. He turned to Mr Needleman and said, "I cannot see any difficulty with that, can you, sir? Charity, as they say, begins at home?"

Lizzy followed that with: "Shall we fix a date for the event?"

It was Mary herself who suggested Midsummer Day, the twenty-first of June, and watched with a mixture of panic and satisfaction the nods of agreement from the Darcys and, as if in a dream, her husband himself, too.

❧

Mrs and Mr Needleman stood at the top of the Rectory steps and waved their visitors goodbye. Mary's heart was beating strongly in her chest. For, even as the Pemberley carriage reached the gateway, she realised that having won the battle with the Darcys, she had yet to win the war with her husband; and the notion of 'war' sat oddly in her mind. An unsuitable metaphor, she felt, for a future situation in which the two of them must work together to establish their reconstituted household.

It was with this beating heart and a shiver of wifely apprehension that she turned to her husband, and he turned to her.

His face was flushed, his voice was grave.

"My dear," said Mr Needleman. "Regarding this turn of events. While acknowledging, as I do, that Mr and Mrs Darcy have agreed with your proposed course of action, the future of those visitors in the attic still remains to be decided."

Mary began: "I am aware of that…" But her voice ended in a croak.

"Have you found a solution?"

Words came tumbling out of Mary. "Robert – please – I will stand as god-parent! Or even…*guardian*! They must stay…surely…! Milly is an excellent… They cannot… They must not…go to some terrible…"

Her husband grasped her arm most uncomfortably. "Mary! I beg you to recall our previous conversation!"

She did recall it. That conversation had contained the word *workhouse*. Those places, unspeakable to those from Families like her own, where unthinkable terrors unfolded… Images rushed into her mind, tales overheard in corridors, whispers of servants over the years: *Families torn asunder! Children torn from mothers! Wives sold by husbands! Stone-breakers this way, cripples that! Infants put out for sale! Disease, rife! Deaths, uncounted!*

As these images rushed through her head, she heard unusual sounds from not far away, to her left. They must have come from the stables, where Mrs Beattie would be tending to Hurry. In fact, as they stood in this position of discomfort, Mary glimpsed the hired stable-hand from the village run out of the stables and away towards the water pump. During her next few exchanges with her husband, she heard the splash of water on cobbles.

"My dear." Robert weakened his hold, but only a little. "It is imperative. There must be a plan. There is talk. Mrs Beattie keeps me informed." Was this the moment that he would call her *hysterical*?

"This child must have been fathered. It seems to me that Mr and Mrs Darcy, in their wish not to inject unpleasantness into the situation, have quite naturally hidden the question of paternity."

Mary blinked. This was not about *her*? Robert was not demeaning *her*?

"Mrs Beattie tells me…" Robert let go of her arm, for now he had her total attention. "The talk, as related via Mrs Reynolds, is that this might not be the case. That paternity might, in fact, be nearer to the Pemberley family than is comfortable. If it were so, that would explain why Mr Darcy accepted that the child should be sacramentally baptised."

A memory now fell at Mary's feet. It was a brief exchange with Lizzy at the drawing room door as they had concluded their discussions. *Bingley is returning home*, she had murmured. *Jane is feeling a little better. The dear man needs to be at her side. You will miss him. We will all miss him. But there we are.*

This came together with *nearer to the family than is comfortable.*

Her husband was still speaking. "We need not, must not, name him. The girl would have led him on, as women do. The tragedy of his poor wife must have undermined his resolve. So, the swifter the action the better, so far as we are concerned. To close this matter once and for all. The family in the attic must leave. Must be sent to other premises."

Mary felt faint. She could not take in what her husband was saying. She could not bear it. "The paternity issue is of no account to me. I wish to return to the matter of those individuals of whom we tend not to speak. I am already, in spiritual terms, their guardian. It is my calling to care for the poor, the needy..." She was turning to go in through the door; he must detain her no longer. "I cannot abandon them! Will not!"

As she ran from her husband, he called after her: "But you must!"

❧

Esther, from where she sat on the bed, heard the rapid footsteps reach the top of the attic stairs. "Mill!" she called in a panic through the door, which was ajar. But Milly was elsewhere, scrubbing something. Henry was breathing the sleep of the satisfied.

Mrs Needleman knocked, *rat-tat*. Esther could not let the words *Go away!* out of her lips, so she pressed them together instead. *Rat! tat!* Esther coughed. Mrs Needleman could take that as *Come in*, or leave it.

Mrs Needleman came in. She held some garment over her left arm. "Esther. My dear. I have news. Good news. You will have been anxious. As I have been. Baptism. Of the child. Ah, there he lies. I have brought this." She held the garment in the direction of the sleeping child. But Esther's hand floated above him, protecting him, and the garment fell between them.

Mrs Needleman retrieved it from the floor. "His baptismal gown. I had it made specially. I was not confident of my own skills, I wanted it to be right for him, for his sacramental day, when he became received into God's Kingdom."

Esther looked down at Henry's sleeping form. She could not abide Mrs Needleman's pleading. *Let it stop, please.*

It did not stop. "It is a gift for him, Esther. From me. As his god-mother."

And here was Milly, behind Mrs Needleman, in the doorway.

Mrs N whisked round and saw Milly. Esther rose from the bed, and their mistress was caught between them.

The pleading went on, and on. "May I be? God-mother? Please? After all I have done for you! Surely I have only done right?"

"Whatever you wish, ma'am." Esther spoke to Mrs N whilst looking at Milly. "We are grateful for your kindness. Whatever is…right for, er, him." She could not say Henry's name to Mrs N, for hear that it would somehow give her power over him.

Mrs N's voice droned on. She was clutching the

baptismal gown fiercely to her breast. "The Lord has been leading me in this direction, towards this place in his life, so that I may guide him…"

"He is my babba."

"Of course. But your position is precarious! While I, in my position, have influence! I can be on his side! With Mr Needleman! Even with Mrs Darcy! And this is what I came to inform you of!"

Esther sat back down on the bed, and Milly shuffled forward and sat close to her. Esther waved a hand towards the little chair by the table in the dormer. Mrs Needleman trod carefully along the narrow space and perched there, uncomfortably, with the baptismal gown on her knee.

"I have secured for him a proper baptism. At Pemberley, in the chapel there. Mr and Mrs Darcy graciously acceded to my request. Mr Needleman, at the Darcys' behest, will officiate. A quiet ceremony, of course, though we will no doubt have some sweetmeats. Not at Pemberley. Here. As circumstances permit."

Milly coughed. Esther knew that sign: it was her prompt to Esther to say something that Milly could not say herself.

"Thank you, ma'am. But there are difficulties. Two things."

"Two?"

"The first is, as you will remember, it was at Pemberley, from Pemberley, that we were thrown out under the stars. If you had not saved us, Mrs Needleman, the Lord only knows what would have become of us."

Milly coughed again. Esther clutched her hand for strength.

"But I did save you, did I not? And the second difficulty?"

Esther turned to face Milly entirely and not look at Mrs Needleman at all. "Will there be another, er, god-thing? A god *father*?"

"Oh, I understand you now. Yes, there are normally two or three godparents appointed, who give their promises at the font. But, given the present circumstances…"

"I meant, we wondered… Mr Darcy's friend… We feared…"

She should not have said that. She should not have said the word *friend*, and nor should she have said *feared*. But both words were out there now.

Mrs Needleman put her hand up to her face and adjusted her spectacles. When her hand fell down to her lap, Esther saw that the blood had drained entirely from her cheeks.

"You mean Mr Bing…? No, no, no no no no no. He is not to be present. He is on his way home, to be at the side of his…to be with Jane. Dear Jane. No, no, not at all. I am to be the sole god-parent. The only one. The one who vows to bring the child up in the fear of the Lord. To be unto him a trusty shield in time of…"

Then Esther had to draw in her feet quickly and pull Henry's drawer towards her, for Mrs Needleman stood up in haste, and her feet almost fell over each other as they hastened away out of the room.

23

Baptism, Before and During

MARY WAS AT PRAYER. "Almighty and most Merciful God... We have left undone those things which we ought to have done, and done those things which we ought not to have done; and there is no Health in us. We acknowledge and bewail our manifold Sins and Wickedness..."

She followed the Confession with the Absolution, which she enunciated for herself, to herself: "Almighty God, Father of our Lord Jesus Christ, who desireth not the death of a Sinner but rather that he turn from his Wickedness, and live..."

What should happen to Esther and Milly and the child? Was there a solution, which was the fulfilment of God's will? Or her own, unruly will?

She would pray, and pray, and pray, until she knew.

If it be Thy Will. "Tell me, what is the difference between my own will, and Thine!"

The reply was a profound silence.

There came heavy footsteps and a knock at the door.

"Come in?"

Gladys appeared. "Visitor."

"Yes, and who is it, Gladys?"

"Lade Manton."

"Lady... !"

Lady Manton was the last individual in the world whom she wished to see. But her husband owed his living to her. More even than Lizzy, she was the one who could not be turned away.

She said: "I will be down in just one moment. Show her into the drawing room. Thank you."

She looked into her mirror. She could only think of Lady Manton and herself in terms of horses. The Mary who gazed at her from the mirror was a trifling pony compared with the stately shire-horse that was Lady Manton.

This was the force of nature that had set her on the road to this marriage. Why was she visiting now? To enquire after its progress? To demand why Mary was not yet with child? To berate her for inviting a bastard into the Rectory? Or to admonish her as a wild woman whose needs and views should be suppressed?

She walked unsteadily down the stairs, bracing herself for the verbal cascade that would surely fall from Lady Manton's lips.

"My dear girl!" She was embraced by a body that seemed to have acquired several stones in weight since their last encounter. "I have neglected you shamefully! I have failed in my duty to support you in the parish! My late lamented husband should not have left me with the responsibility of *three* parishes. Not with my temperament! Not with my sufferings! Not with the melancholia that sweeps over me with the close of every year! No one can fathom my wretchedness. My Gwentholen, now *she* was a daughter to me! Not by blood, but by spirit! She loved me as a daughter should! Not as my faithless ones! Faithless, all four of them! So was I granted a different gift, my Gwentholen. But she died, in the same hour as she gave birth."

Patty entered without knocking. She rattled the contents of a tray onto the table and departed.

Mary stood back and reclaimed herself. "Lady Manton. Please do not apologise. My husband and I… Neither of us appreciated just how…"

"Appreciate? But why should you appreciate, dear girl? The people of the parish, they expect one to lead a plain, straightforward life. A family tree, a model to them in their poverty. But this narrow path is not our allotted destiny! Is it, dear girl? Allotted not to me, nor you! Am I not correct in my perceptions? I am so *sensitive*! I *see* things! That is why I cleave so to the *conventions*! Because I find it so hard to cleave to them *myself*! And look at Mrs Darcy now! She tries to play the convention game! And tries too hard!"

They were both sitting down by this time, but Mary did not touch the refreshment tray. It crossed her mind that it was Patty's duty to do the pouring. It was Mrs Beattie's duty to remind her. But Mrs Beattie must still be in the stables. Might Robert be there, too, to say a final farewell to Hurry? She had no idea how he felt about Hurry. She had no idea where he was. She had no idea about anything.

But Lady Manton was talking about Mrs Darcy. Was she trying to convey some information to her about Lizzy?

"Mrs Darcy is…?"

"Dear Mary." Lady Manton sighed, reached over to the table, and poured liquid into cups. "Sugar? We all enjoy our sugar, do we not? My husband would lecture me on how people used to live without it. Imagine! Honey sufficed in the old days, he said. In the smallest quantities. We, he would say, would use honey, grapes, figs, to sweeten our dishes. But then came Africa! The Caribbean! And we were lost to Sugar! …Where was I? Dear me! My beloved Gwentholen!"

Mary was silent. She could scarcely remember who Gwentholen was. She remembered her husband's words about Africa being the dark continent, and thought of what she and Milly had done in the darkness.

Lady Manton's bosom heaved. "And dear Elizabeth. She fears it so, the fate that took away my Gwentholen. Do we not all, we women? With each of my four, I expected every breath to be my last! I bade farewell to my dear husband every time! The terror of it! Men – they have no notion! Elizabeth, she loves her husband, yet she must, on occasions, push him away. She confides in me, did you not know? I am like the mother she never had. You, too, you know now far more than you knew before, do you not? I meant to be a mother to you, but then came my melancholia, and… Oh! My poor Gwentholen. And now, dear Elizabeth."

Mary, catching some kind of thread at last, murmured, "I had not understood."

"You should have leaned on me, dear girl! You needed a broad shoulder to pour out your troubles onto! I *see* your sufferings. I suffer *with* you. So I came by, today…" She leaned forward, breathing crumbs of sponge over the floor between them. "To tell you that I *understand*! Like Elizabeth, you have been given a life you were not born to! And, in addition, you have a great need to be good. As do I, dear Mary, long to be *good*! Ask the servants, I said to her! The servants will have the answer! The answer which I never had! But no, she threw the poor lead-miner's offspring out, and now you are left with the results. And the paternity? Which we all understand? Which, in itself, came from the agony of childbirth in one's wife! Your poor dear… Poor, demented… Do we not understand this? All of us? That a man must take his pleasure where he can? A gentleman, that is, with a maid!"

She took another large bite of cake, and paused to swallow. "My dear. I will have words with your husband. He is lost without his friend, is he not? He does not take enough account of you! He must give you a little more kindness, more support! Let us see what will become of that, shall we? I was right to summon you here from Hertfordshire, I think? Even though he was so wrapped up in his…? I sincerely hope it was the right path? My dear girl, I do hope so?"

Lady Manton was licking the crumbs from around her mouth, but at the same time her eyes were piercing.

She required an answer.

Mary said, "Indeed, Lady Manton. I thank you for inviting me to Humbole. I am content here. I think Mr Needleman finds me satisfactory. It is a situation where, as you say, I can do good. But Mr Needleman needs... He so valued the friendship of..."

"Mr Hepplecraft."

Lady Manton dropped the name between them. There followed a moment of silence. Mary heard the faraway sound of footsteps, and the cry of a baby.

"I will speak to him." Lady Manton's voice was soft. "He will be in the stables, I think? Could you ask your maid to fetch him? You look quite pale, my dear. You need more walks in the sunshine. Leave your husband to me. I will do what I can. You have done well, taking in these lost souls. I shall tell him so."

〰

Extract from the Register of Deaths, Parish of Humbole, Derbyshire, 1821:

Oldfield, Harold, Foundling. Birth datte unknown, found in Old Field Lane Hombole 1791; stable-keeper of The Rectorie. Known to his intimates, and for his staid demeanour, as Hurry. Died Midsummers Day of excess of Laudanum, first took many yeres before, for the purposses of toothacke; mourned by his employere the Rector and house-hold.

"Well donne, thou Goode and Faithfulle Servant."

From Mrs Beattie:

Dear Mr Needleman – When you return from Pemberley and its chapel, you will not find me. Forgive me, sir, for failing to offer this farewell face to face. I am, in the usual order of things, a person of plain and direct speech. You have known this in me, and found it to your profit and to mine. This time, sir, I cannot.

I warn you, sir, that those sinners from up the mines have cast their spell upon your wife. The crippled one even more than the one who committed the obvious sin. If you needed proof of witchcraft, sir, you have seen it this day in Pemberley. They demanded a baptism, they were given a baptism. Mr Darcy acceded to all their requests; and so in your turn did you. How could this ever have been achieved without the intervention of Satan himself?

More sorcery will come, I have no doubt of it. I cannot sit by and watch it happen.

It pains me to write this. I believed myself to be a mother to you and Mr Hepplecraft. You, and he, and I, have fulfilled the spirit of the law here in Humbole for many contented years. You will say, "But it was Sin!" And that is the case, for that is in the nature of being Human, and having Bodies. But we have acknowledged our sins, Sunday by Sunday, have we not? And pleaded for our sin be taken from us? But The Lord chose for that sin to remain with us, and thus offered us forgiveness once again.

The contrasting sin, committed by these two from the lead-mines, has presented no confession and begged no forgiveness. It has now borne fruit, and lives on, brazenly, under your roof. I cannot tolerate its presence. I cannot serve under such a presence. I must up and away.

You know of my acquaintance with the Reverend Mr Brontë: his days in Cambridge with my father, his poorly paid curacies, his travails as regards family and bereavement, his concern for my welfare. I have not had the chance in recent weeks (on account of caring for poor Hurry) to mention Mr Brontë's recommendation of me to the clerk of the parish of Ingrow, by Haworth, in Yorkshire. That distance, for a body so well-travelled as myself, is not too far. He had previously written to me of this housekeeper vacancy, and he would recommend me if I wished; he added that housekeepers of quality such as mine are hard to find; but while Hurry lived, and needed my skills in nursing, I could not leave. That duty being done, I am away.

There is no diminution of my loyalty to you, dear RN. You have been like a son to me. But that is over now, and the witchcraft in the attic, and the persistence of your lady wife alongside, have undone me.

So I gave my answer to Yorkshire in the affirmative, and am on my way.

I spoke to Gladys and Patty. They may be silent, but they have good hearts and an understanding between them. Patty wept a little, Gladys merely set her mouth into a scowl. They have a place here; they are loyal. I trust you will give them a small increase in their emolument this coming Quarter Day.

My dear sir, I shall pray for you, as I hope you will pray for me.

I sign myself as 'Your mother (retired)'.

Eleanora Jane Beattie (honorary Mrs).

❧

Entry in the Directory of Almshouses:

Darcys' Almshouses: Georgian; built by the family Darcy of Pemberley Hall; begun 1795 by Mr Fitzwilliam D'Arcy, completed 1798; refurbished by his son Fitzwilliam Darcy (later to become <u>Sir</u> F D) 1819. A plaque in the centre of the gable has the D'Arcy coat of arms, and reads: 'These Alms-Houses were endorsed by the family Fitzwilliam-Darcy for the lifetime of 18 poor men and women of Humbole, Manton Green and whatever might remain of Pemberley village, in consideration of those who suffered in the late wars in Europe. First inhabited Sept 1798.

❧

Esther and Milly lie on each bed, gazing at each other. Baby Henry lies between them in his drawer; Esther's hand dangles down to him, her middle finger playing with his small pudgy hand; he tries to put the finger in his mouth, and she lets it drift between his toothless gums, then slips it out and away. He chortles, knowing that the finger will come back to him again.

Esther and Milly's eyes are conversing with one another.

Esther: He's gone from Pemberley?

Milly: Aye, he's gone.

Esther: And we've to go to church again today?

Milly: We do.

Esther: For him to get to Heaven. So she says.

Milly: And for us to keep him for ourselves. And be safe.

Esther: But how?

Milly: All it teks is for you to trus' me, Ess.

Esther: I do, Mill. You know I do. But—

Milly: But nowt! *Trus'* me!

Pause.

Esther: They all ken, do they not?

Milly: Sure they do.

Esther: That's what Annie's saying in her private letters.

Milly: Upstairs, downstairs, there and here. They all ken. Excep' for Ma'am.

Esther: But none will say. That's how they work. Nowt is true till it's spoken.

Silence.

Esther: Yer thinking, Mill. Planning.

Milly: I am. He daredn't be there. He went away cos daredn't. He's frit. You mebbe frit, but he's more frit by far.

Esther: What's yer plan, our Mill?

Pause.

Milly: Will see what will see, Ess. (She waves her bent hand over Henry, and he lifts his pudgy hand towards it.) 'Ere's the day he gets 'is place in Heaven.

Esther: Heaven be damned. I want his place on Earth.

Milly: See, Ess. Juss wait n see.

ᘒᕟ

Mary sat beside her husband in the Pemberley carriage.

Opposite them sat the two maids, Esther (formerly Thwaite) and Milly. Mary had provided capes from her wardrobe for each of them, and gloves too. Milly's hands, both the good hand and the bent one, showed how much too big the gloves were: the fingers flapped stupidly whenever she moved them.

Esther was holding the child, rocking him gently with the sway of the carriage. Mary felt satisfied with the baby's appearance: he looked well-fed, and was wearing the exquisite gown that was her gift to him rather than the plain one made by Annie and sent via Mrs Darcy. Mary had feared how she might feel if the child wore Annie's gift instead of hers; that she might show an anger inappropriate to this very special day; but no, Esther had behaved properly, she had set aside her own wishes and done what her mistress would want. Milly might have had a hand in this decision. But Mary could no longer imagine what Milly might do, or think, or feel.

Back at the Rectory, Mary had looked for Mrs

Beattie to hunt for smaller gloves among the servants' wear, but Mrs Beattie was not to be found. She was most likely in the kitchen, preparing the comestibles for later.

Mr Needleman's black clerical outfit was lightened by a covering of white surplice. His face was sombre. Mary could not expect a nod from him to her. This morning he was priest, not husband.

The carriage rocked on its splendid springs. Henry chortled. It was a glorious midsummer day.

Mary watched how Esther held baby Henry. Her manner was quiet and relaxed, but she was moving very slightly, to and fro, all the time. This must be how a baby felt soothed; how he was prevented from crying. She could never do that.

She moved her arms a little, wondering how it might feel to have a baby's weight constantly in one's arms. Henry would never lie in her arms. She had wanted a baby to love, and to love her back. Henry would never love her back. He was Esther's.

∽

Esther saw the dreaded back doors as they approached Pemberley: the servants' doors, from which she and Milly had been ejected only a few months ago. They had been shuffled out at dawn with a handful of clothes between them. The staff they'd worked with would not be given an explanation; they needed none. That miner's kid had ideas above her station; her job would go to someone who deserved it better. As for the crippled one, well, I wouldn't've said it to 'er face, but dont she mek yer flesh creep? The' should put 'em down at birth, like the' do kittens.

Mrs Needleman had explained that the Darcys would meet them at the chapel door; that the ceremony would be brief; and that this carriage would await their return and be followed back to Humbole by the carriage in which Mr and Mrs Darcy would ride.

Esther stepped down awkwardly with Babba in her arms, and heard Milly's intake of breath as she shuffled down after her. Pemberley's man stood back at their appearance and waited to hand Mrs Needleman down onto the step and the gravel. A single maid-of-all-work was to lead them to the appointed place. Milly held close to Esther; they both stared fixedly at the heels of Mrs Needleman's Sunday shoes. Those black shoes, and Babba's sweet head, were all that Esther saw on the walk from the carriage, round the wing, into Pemberley, and to the chapel door, where stood Mrs Darcy and her husband. Mrs Needleman indicated with a flip of her hand that they should continue to follow her as she followed the Darcys through the chapel doors.

A brief glimpse showed the breadth of Mr Darcy's shoulders and the immensity of his masculine hands. Mrs Darcy stood prettily beside him, her hat at a jaunty angle. Esther glanced towards her, hoping for recognition, but there was only an anxious nod from her former mistress.

Her heart began to beat – loud enough, surely, to make the whole of Pemberley hear? Babba gave a whimper. Would the feed she'd given him before they left Humbole keep him going till their return? He'd guzzled, and she'd burped him. Was that enough burping, or would he bring another one up at the crucial baptismal moment? She held him tighter, and he quietened.

This private Family Chapel looked to Esther unlike any of the parish churches she had ever been inside. It had rows of dark, empty pews criss-crossed by shafts of colour from high windows. The whole building echoed to the sound of their feet in procession.

She and Milly leaned in close to each other.

Beside the stone font, which (as Mrs N had patiently explained) held the Holy Water to give Babba the sign of the Cross, Mrs Needleman stepped across to Milly, drew her to one side and shuffled her in front of a pillar. Away from Esther! Bereft of Milly, Esther was cold – naked. Milly, though, stood with chin up, jaw determinedly skew, eyes mainly on Esther but taking in everyone else too.

"Admonished as we are," intoned Mr Needleman, "to baptise only on a Sunday, permission is given, if necessity so require, to baptise on other days of the week. And so it is here, today."

Babba whimpered. Esther gave him her knuckle. He sucked, noisily.

"Almighty and Everlasting God, who by Thy great mercy saved Noah and his family from perishing by water..." She felt Babba's gums loose themselves from her knuckle, and pushed it back in. "They brought young children to Christ, so He might touch them." On, and on, and on.

At last: "Who bringeth this child to be baptised?"

That would be her, Esther. She must say *Yes*,

or something holy that meant *Yes*. She took a step forward.

But Mrs Needleman stepped forward alongside her. "We do!" Her words, high, precise and reedy, rose up between the pillars.

Esther's eyes scanned the pillars to find Milly. Where was she? Had they taken her away? Could they take Milly away from her, and from Babba?

"I am the godmother. She is the mother."

Mr Needleman, waving his hand towards Esther, said, "Let the child be given to the godmother."

Esther could do no other than to obey. As she placed Babba in Mrs Needleman's arms, he did a big burp and a bubble of milk emerged. Mrs Needleman tried to hold him close, but at the sight of the bubble of milk she recoiled. Babba, in Mrs Needleman's arms, looked unbalanced, and Esther moved nearer so as to catch him if need be.

Mr Needleman put up a hand. "Step back!"

Esther, having moved so far, would not retreat. Neither could she move any farther forward. Mrs Needleman, at the *No!*, managed to nudge Babba into a firmer hold, and Esther moved one small step back.

Mr Needleman asked: "Dost thou, in the name of this child, renounce the Devil and all his Works, the vain Pomp and Glory of the World, and the Covetous Desires of the Flesh, that thou wilt not be led by them?"

Mrs Needleman gazed at her husband and declared confidently: "I renounce them all." From somewhere out of sight, Esther heard Milly gasp.

Mr Needleman asked his wife: "Wilt thou keep

God's Holy Commandments, and walk in them all the days of thy Life?"

"I will."

Babba was so quiet now that he might almost be listening.

The Rector put his hand into the font and brought it up. The Holy Water splashed loudly back into the font. "I baptise thee in the name of the Father, and of the Son, and of the Holy Ghost, Amen." The dripping hand moved over Babba's face.

Esther felt a movement at her side. She was there. Milly was there, beside her.

Would Mrs Darcy come and push her back behind that pillar? She did not.

There was stillness behind Esther and Milly, stillness from Mr and Mrs Darcy, stillness while Mr Needleman raised his voice to pronounce the sacred words.

And Babba gave a howl. It was a howl fit to fill the whole chapel, right up to the stone arches of its roof.

Mr Needleman's voice tried to rise over Babba's, but Esther could scarcely hear him. Mrs Needleman clutched him ever more nervously.

"We receive this child into the Congregation of Christ's flock, and do sign him—" moving a still-dripping hand in some invisible pattern, "to be His faithful Soldier and Servant..." The howl echoed up into the vacant air of Pemberley's chapel, out through its many-coloured windows and away into its deer park and its lake and the whole of Derbyshire beyond... "Until his life's end."

Then, in the space left by Babba's curtailed howling, the voice of Mrs Needleman could be heard to say, lightly but clearly: "Now may this Child live the rest of his Life according to this Beginning."

⁓

As she said *according to this Beginning*, Mary recalled the words pronounced over her own head, and her husband's, a year ago: "I now pronounce you Man and Wife." She looked up at her husband the priest, and wondered whether he recalled those words too. But he was not looking at her; he was gazing over her shoulder at Mr and Mrs Darcy beyond. Was he asking himself how Mr Darcy could tolerate a *woman* taking the words out of the priest's mouth, at this time and in this place, his own *Family Chapel*?

The baby ceased his bawling for a moment, then started up again, and more milky dribbles spattered out of his mouth and down onto the smocking of his embroidered gown. Mary called out to her husband over the child's noise: "My dear, might we omit the subsequent prayers and proceed to 'inheritor of God's everlasting kingdom'?"

Robert's eyes flashed, but he followed her suggestion. During the passage of this prayer, Mary took the few steps over to Esther and transferred the child back into her arms. In that moment of relinquishing the baby, Mary's mind returned to the next – and still wholly indeterminate – question. Now that she had secured Henry's baptism, she must somehow ensure that the baby and Esther and Milly had a home. And she had no idea how she might accomplish that.

Suddenly, she remembered another illegitimate

child: Luke. He stood beside her, clear in her vision as if the two of them were standing in the stables at Longbourn and talking about saddles.

And Hill! Mrs Flora Hill! She was here, too!

Those two were son and mother, as Henry and Esther were son and mother.

And who was Luke's father? Her father. Mr Bennet.

And who was Henry's father?

Mr Darcy's friend. Mr Bingley.

Of course. That was why Lizzy had said what she did about Charles's return home to dear Jane. Otherwise he might have been invited to be the child's godfather... But he could not. Not for Esther's sake... Not for Jane's sake...

Ah! It was true! Bingley was like her father. Like Mr Bennet.

These things were clear now. She knew. Everyone knew. Everyone had known except her. Now, finally, she knew too.

She must forget this. Must continue as before, as if she did not know. Must say nothing, as they all did. She must live as if it were not true. As if it were not known.

How could she *do* that? But how could she *not*?

Her husband's final prayer came to its *Amen*. Then, head bowed, he walked round the font and processed forward. They must follow his black and white robes back down the aisle and out of the chapel: Mary, then Mr ('soon to be ennobled') and Mrs Darcy; behind them, Esther with the baby, and Milly taking up the rear.

When they reached the outside doors of Pemberley

and stood looking across to the two carriages, Mary heard Lizzy say to Darcy in cheerful tone: "May I propose a different arrangement for the journey back to Humbole? We sisters to ride in the first carriage together, with the men taking up the rear? Then you may speak together as men do, in ways that we women cannot possibly understand!" She slid easily alongside Mary. "Shall we, Mary dear?"

☉☉

So here she was, Esther, with Babba fussing under her cape and trying to get beyond her chemise, and Milly at her side, and her old mistress and her new mistress sitting opposite. Mrs Darcy had even helped Milly up the step and into her own Pemberley carriage! Which implied something almost unimaginable: Mrs Darcy had *touched* Milly. Mrs Darcy of Pemberley had touched *Milly*, *her* Milly, the Milly that no one at Pemberley, Family or Servantry, had laid a finger on – either in fear or in sympathy – ever.

At the Rectory, it was different. For reasons known only to herself, Milly had gone in to her – into Mrs Needleman's – bedchamber, into her bed. That would be for touching of some sort, would it not? Esther did not understand why Milly had to do that. But there it was. Milly knew and understood things that no one else could know and understand.

As these thoughts fell through Esther's mind, her hands were busy at Babba's cheek and nose and gums to stop him whimpering for the breast. She could not feed him in front of Mrs Darcy. She simply could not.

Not when Mrs Darcy had not fed her own darlings but had put them out to wet-nurses, leaving her own breasts slim and firm and free from interference, ready for her husband.

A few moments after the horses had set off smoothly on their way, Mrs Darcy said briskly: "Thwaite dear – Esther – do please let the child under your chemise, will you? And give us a moment's peace?"

Esther did as she was told, and eventually relaxed into feeding Babba quite peacefully.

After a pause, Mrs Darcy said to her sister, "Was that to your satisfaction, Mary?"

"Quite, quite."

"So sad about your man. Harry, did they call him?"

"Hurry. Because he never did hurry. Indeed, very sad."

"How will Mr Needleman manage for a stable-hand?"

"He has made some temporary arrangement in the village."

"Oh." Mrs Darcy paused again. "I hear Lady Manton called to see you?"

"She did. I appreciated her condescension."

"She is kind, Lady Manton. She understands one in a remarkable way."

"Oh?"

"You must see that? Since she arranged your marriage to dear Robert?"

"Of course. She did. Indeed."

Esther stroked the baby's cheek as she listened. The three of them – she, Milly and the baby – had now become invisible to Mrs Darcy as she chatted on with Mrs Needleman. This was the blessing of being a servant – the blessing, and sometimes the curse – that they were invisible to their masters and their mistresses.

"She confides in me, as I confide in her," said Mrs Darcy. "She tells me if she is ill at ease with herself. Asks herself whether she did quite the right thing."

Mrs Needleman seemed scarcely to be listening. She was looking out of the carriage window. "Swallows! Or are they house-martins? Skimming over the field there?"

"I beg your pardon?"

"I am learning the names of birds. I have been reading Gilbert White."

"Gilbert who?"

"Of Selborne. Clergyman. Nature-lover. From the Rectory library."

"Mary, we have not long together to speak about what has happened and what may yet come to pass. I have so many questions. Lady Manton wondered, and I wonder: is your life with Robert *fulfilled*?"

Mrs Needleman still gazed out of the window. "Of course it is."

"And, what was his name, the friend? He was ever there, but is now gone?"

Mrs Needleman's voice was directed toward the birds and the fields, but she spoke very precisely. "Does Mr Darcy not have *friends*? Such as Mr Bingley?"

Esther kept her gaze firmly on Babba's downy head, while the sound of the word *Bingley* changed something about her breathing. Would her trepidation travel through her breath and upset Babba's feeding, and would he bawl again and upset those who sat

486

opposite, talking, on the other side of the carriage? No. Henry sucked on.

Mrs Darcy said nothing; she was probably frowning. Esther imagined her biting her pretty bottom lip before speaking again.

"Lady Manton is concerned about your future, Mary. As are we all. Whether you, in your high-mindedness, are being foolish."

"Are we not all, Lizzy? Foolish?" Esther dared not look up, but the strength of Mrs Needleman's voice showed that she had turned her face towards her sister. "Do any of us know what is wisdom and what is folly? I understand Robert. Not, perhaps, as you understand Fitzy, but well enough, in my own way. My concern today is not for myself at all. My concern is to help these..."

Now Esther cannot resist looking up, and she sees Mrs Needleman's hand waving in her and Milly's direction. Babba's mouth is off the breast just now, and he burps a little more milk onto the baptismal gown.

"...To help us extricate ourselves from this complex and sensitive situation."

Mrs Darcy's eyes betray confusion. Those beautiful eyes are looking across at Esther, but they do not see her, because her confusion is too great. Babba latches on again; Esther bows her head as Mrs Darcy continues her confusion.

"And how will you, Mary? Extricate yourself, and the Rectory, and everyone? The present situation cannot continue indefin—"

Mrs Needleman breaks in sharply. "Yet the situation

as regards Mr Darcy's friend, our brother-in-law, seems to continue indefinitely? Does it not?"

There is a frozen silence, during which Esther can see in front of her, against the carriage floor, a whisky tumbler half-full, and a wistful man's eyes. The eyes harden as they go from wistful to lustful. She steps into his arms. Or does he step into hers? Surely it is her fault? She was only being motherly, but... She must go! She must fetch the balm from the cupboard behind him! But he is strong, and he bears her along with him, and under him, until he has done what he may or may not have been meaning to do since the very beginning when the whisky glass was still full.

Milly's voice – "Ess!" – brings her to herself. Mrs Darcy may or may not have spoken during her time with the whisky and the balm cupboard; she has no idea. Milly's arm is around her back, and Babba is staring at her through a wet blur. Esther realises that they have driven through the Rectory gates, and the horses are slowing.

Mrs Darcy says, "Thwaite, dear. I should say, Esther. You are weeping!"

Mrs Needleman echoes her: "Esther dear. Milly dear." Then her tone changes. It changes back to the tone of *seems to continue indefinitely*. "Let us see what can be done, shall we?"

Mrs Darcy leaps to open the door, presumably so she can go out and help Esther with Babba through it. But she has moved too quickly, there has been no time for the footman to climb down and take round the step for their descent from the carriage door. Esther, from the carriage doorway, sees Mrs Darcy half-fall, then land on the gravel, then wobble, then regain her balance. She turns, shakes herself, and puts both arms out for Esther and Babba to drop down beside her.

Then, shaken, she touches Esther's arm and, as they walk away together, Esther feels Mrs Darcy's touch like a flame. It is, Esther realises, the flame of envy.

24

Baptism, After

MARY IS SUDDENLY ALONE in the carriage with Milly, who is standing immediately behind her. She is overcome with the desire to whirl around and embrace her.

She can do the first – whirl around – but cannot do the second – embrace her – because Milly has caught hold of her sleeve. Mary's cape has slipped to her elbow, and this is her summer muslin frock; the sleeve is a three-quarter-length summer sleeve. Milly has used her crippled hand to grasp this sleeve, and is holding her mistress fast.

Mary cannot move.

"Msss Needa!"

"Milly dear. Set me free, please."

"I need to speak." Mary hears these words as if they

were spoken clearly, though she realises that they have come out in Milly's impenetrable speech.

"Very well, dear. Quickly. Then we must go."

"I need to ask. Are you taking him? For your own? Our Babba?"

"What? I? Take him? Henry? No! Why should I? He is Esther's!"

Her reply is dishonest, she knows that; but it is only a small dishonesty. She had wanted to take Henry for her own. But only for a little while. That is over and gone.

Milly breathes deeply, her twisted little chest rising and falling. "Good, good."

"Now, dear, let us go. They are waiting, the Darcys will be—"

Milly bursts out, "Goddam the Darcys! I need to speak!"

"You are speaking, dear. And I am listening. But we must—"

"Speak in *there*! I need to speak in *there*!"

"There is no need for you to worry about that. I will speak. I will say what must be said, do what must be done."

"It must be *me*! For Ess, for *us*! I will speak, and you will say what I have said!" Every few words, she tugs for emphasis at Mary's sleeve.

Mary's cape is slipping further from her elbow. She takes a single breath, then adopts a heavy tone. "Milly, I cannot do that. I will speak for myself, and say what must be done."

"Msss Needa, you must remember *you an' me*. What we *did*. What you an' me *did do*. You *must* let me say what we *must have*. Else I will say what *we did*. What *you* did. Wi' *me*."

The words, together with the tugging of the sleeve, hit Mary like a series of hammer blows. She thinks that she will faint. The cape now falls on the carriage floor. She manages to blurt out: "But they will not understand what you are saying!"

"They will. 'Cause you will say it after me. *Come night, she and I did lie in twain...*"

"Very well! You may speak! And I will support you in what you ask. And repeat it to them. As you request." Again she feels faint, and sways. "But not *that*!"

"So long as you let me *speak*."

"I will let you speak. Milly, we must go. To welcome Mr and Mrs Darcy to the house. I do not know where Mrs Beattie is... Where the step is... What to do with this…" Her foot moves the cape, which lies between her and the carriage door.

Milly lets go of the sleeve, and Mary whirls back around and peers out into the dazzling sunshine. The step is below her; the cape falls onto it; she steps onto the cape and step, then onto the gravel; retrieves the cape, and surfaces into the world.

Surely this turning world has stopped on its axis since she yearned to fling her arms around Milly out of sheer and complete love for her and was rewarded only with threats? Mary is clear; there has been no love. Not if there is now a threat.

Surely there was desire? If she, Mary, felt desire, there must have been desire in the one who gave her to feel it?

Who knew? There may, from start to end, have been only bargaining.

Out here in the sunshine, the Pemberley footman patiently picks up the step and returns it to its place. Mary prepares to move forward over the gravel, but then realises that the footman has denied Milly the help she needs in order to descend. Mary calls to the footman – "My man!" – and offers him her cape. Startled, he takes it. Mary turns herself round, places her hands firmly under Milly's arms, and lifts her out of the carriage doorway and down. Milly completes her descent without a glance at anything but her two feet.

They walk side by side, as if the best of companions, across the gravel, up the steps, and in through the Rectory's open doors.

⁊

I sit, rocking and buffeting, in the north-bound stagecoach, and let the tears flow down my cheeks. It does not concern me that the other passengers stare and mutely point out my tears to each other from the far bench.

I realise with some surprise that I am not weeping for Mr Needleman, or for Mr Hepplecraft, or for the family ties that bound us together and that are now severed. I am certainly not weeping for the minx. I am weeping for the future of the small, motherless Brontë daughters whom I shall shortly encounter for the first time.

But I am weeping, too, for Gladys and Patty. I

rescued them from their father, and they became as kin to me. Their rescue was much to my cost, but eventually to my benefit, and theirs. That is another story, and one which I may tell at another time.

Yet, again to my surprise, I also weep for the little witch in the attic and her sinful sister, for no doubt they too have their story.

And for SH, because his father will weep for the way he has become obsessed and degraded. He has made his choice, and must live with the consequences.

So, I weep for Gladys and Patty, and I imagine that they are weeping for me. But I have left on the kitchen table, on the Rectory's prettiest paper doyley, resting on the finest of the china plates, a set of my best fruit breads. Taken out of the top oven at six o'clock this morning. Cooled on trays, and buttered. Mrs Darcy enjoys my fruit breads. Mine are superior to Mrs Reynolds'; she told me so. Whatever emerges from the day's events, that plateful of my fruit breads will smooth the path.

☙

Robert sat at the diagonal across the carriage from Darcy. He never knew what to say to the man. His teeth shone. His frown was like a crater.

Robert could not stop himself, in these circumstances, pondering the name *Fitzwilliam*. Of course, in Norman parlance, 'Fitz' meant *fils de*, son of. But it also, if said in a certain tone, raised an eyebrow. On the Darcy crest there was no *bend sinister* to give the sign of *Fitz*, the open acknowledgement (when speaking of the king's line, say) of the 'wrong side of the blanket'.

No, no: it meant *distinguished on the battlefield*! The concept of 'battlefield' had now moved into the commercial or even the industrial sphere, where the Darcys had certainly distinguished themselves. Their estates on both sides of the Atlantic were famed; their investment supported swathes of employment among the masses; their endowments graced many a charitable venture. If the Darcys, way back in their line, were of royal or ducal blood, that blood should surely command respect. And, before long, if tittle-tattle were to be believed, Sir Fitzwilliam would arise from his knee before the young king and return to Pemberley with his Lady on his arm. Then all speculation would be at an end.

Speculation, that is, about Darcy.

Speculation about his friend Bingley, on the other hand, was another matter.

Darcy spoke. "My wife, you know, is very fond of her sister Mary."

"That affection is reciprocated most warmly," replied Robert.

"None of us are saints, of course. But she may be the nearest."

"Indeed. Her parish work is…" He could not quite think what it was.

"My wife did have words with Mrs Reynolds."

"Oh?"

"Via your housekeeper, about your man. From the stable. His indisposition."

Robert was startled. These lowly matters did not

normally impinge on the consciousness of a Fitz. He murmured, "The man has since, sadly, died."

Mr Darcy said, "I heard so. Mrs Reynolds' query had been about an alms-house. For the man, in his distress. But that will no longer be necessary."

"No, indeed. How kind of you to think of it."

Robert waited for Darcy's next remark, which would be that it was no trouble, no trouble at all. It did not come, and the two men spoke no more to each other until the carriage drew to a halt at the Rectory.

ఌ

Esther said to Milly, in a voice clear enough to be heard by those around them in the Rectory hall: "I must deal with the baby's gown. It needs changing."

Milly nodded, but stood her ground. Milly knew what she was doing. She was not coming upstairs. She was staying near the Family.

Esther took the stairs slowly. She would give Babba a bit of time, the two of them alone, after all that messing about with water and devils and such. Henry was gurgling now, fed and happy. This would be their few moments together in their own space. She would take off his fancy gown and blow raspberries on his tummy. Why did they call it 'blowing raspberries'? She neither knew nor cared.

Oh, the bliss of it.

What was happening down there? They would be in the drawing room by now. Milly said Mrs Needleman was after having Babba for herself, but Esther could not believe it of Mrs Needleman. Yet, in a way, she could at the same time believe it of her. She was all *our Lord* this, *our Lord* that; she could persuade herself of anything if *our Lord* gave the word.

But no one could take Babba off her, off Esther, off the mother.

Oh, but Mr Bingley could! If he chose! If he confessed, and wanted his son by this lady's maid to be his own proper son!

But Mr Bingley had set off for home. For home, and Miss Jane, the beautiful, the sad; the mother who could not cope with her own children, never mind another child, a child that her husband had fathered on another woman, and a servant at that.

But gentlemen did behave in this way. They possessed things. They possessed people.

Esther looked for, and found, the gown made by Annie and sent from Longbourn with a letter for her – Esther – signed and sealed. The gown was not so fine as the one that Mrs Needleman had bought for Babba; it was simple, with only small flashes of embroidery around the arms. But it was right.

She took a damp cloth and dabbed Babba all over his face, under his pudgy chin, down his milky front. He gurgled, and she blew raspberries on his belly, and he chuckled. Yes, he was going from gurgles to chuckles. He was growing, he was thriving. He would live. He was hers.

She slid Annie's gown over his head, and when his face appeared above it, she gave a shriek of delight, and he chuckled with her.

She grew solemn, and he stared solemnly back at her.

She must go downstairs and face those people. As Milly would be facing them at the moment. How could she do that? She could do it; Esther trusted Milly to do whatever was necessary.

She settled Babba comfortably against her front, and carefully they made their way down the flights of stairs.

ᦰ

"Patty!" Mary called after the maid as she dashed out through the drawing room door. "Why such haste? Where is Mrs Beattie?" Patty's face flashed round, red and swollen. "Whatever can be the matter? Where is Gladys?" But Patty tumbled away, down towards the kitchen.

As Mary headed back to the drawing room she realised that Milly was no longer beside her. When she went through the door, she scanned round the room to locate her.

Milly stood to the right of the fireplace, between the fire-screen and Mr Needleman in his chair, and fading into the background of both. Lizzy and her husband sat on the left side of the screen.

The three of them were not talking. All of them looked up as Mary came in, as if expecting her to begin a conversation of some sort. Then a flash of creamy white appeared in Mr Needleman's hand: he was waving a letter.

He called across the room to her. "My dear, it is from Mrs Beattie! She cannot be with us! Excuse me" – turning to Mr and Mrs Darcy – "for interposing these domestic matters. We need speak of it no more just now. She – that is Mrs Beattie – has baked us these splendid fruit breads."

Mary was confused. "Milly dear, where is Esther? Oh, she will be up in the attic, dealing with the child. She will be here soon. No matter, I will pass the plate." She put up a hand to indicate that Milly should stay in the shadows.

But Milly did not. She hastened over to the table in the centre and deftly rested the plate of fruit breads on her crippled hand while holding it steady in the other. Then she went from each to another, inviting the guests to partake.

Mary, muttering "No matter, no matter," passed round a small plate for each piece of fruit bread to sit on. Then she poured cordial into the glasses. "Elderberry; our own – Mrs Beattie's own. Lizzy? Mr Darcy?" And over to her husband. "My dear?" Mr Needleman's look was of horror. What was he horrified of? Was it Milly's presence? Mrs Beattie's absence? It must be the fact that she, his wife, was waiting on them.

With a peremptory nod, Mr Needleman took a glass and spoke loudly to Mr and Mrs Darcy. "A wonderful cook and manager in every way. But Patty and Gladys – good women both – they do splendidly too."

Mr and Mrs Darcy left their fruit breads on their plates, sipped their cordial, and said nothing. Finally Mary sat down without either cake or cordial for herself.

She saw Milly position herself in front of the fire-screen and open her mouth to speak.

"Msss Needymun?"

"Yes, Milly dear?"

"Mun I?"

"You may speak."

Milly's eyes flashed towards the door. There came a cough from Esther, then a small cry from the child. Esther and Henry were declaring their presence, but they did not proceed any further than the doorway.

Milly said, "Will you come and help me speak?"

Mary heard the words clearly, but the baffled expression on the faces of Mr Darcy, Lizzy and Mr Needleman showed that they did not understand a word that Milly was saying.

"Of course." Mary stood, and walked across to the fireplace on her husband's side. She placed herself by the screen, a few paces away from Milly.

Milly looked straight ahead, at no one in particular, and spoke. "Mr Darcy, Mrs Darcy, I need to tell you about my sister."

Mary repeated it: *Mr Darcy, Mrs Darcy...* There was a murmur from the baby in the doorway, but otherwise all was silent. *About my sister.*

Milly: "How Esther, and how the baby became."

"How the baby became." Mary could not help it: she was sliding behind the fire-screen, she was disappearing, so that the words remained Milly's but she herself was hidden. She raised her own voice a little, to ensure that she was heard.

"Mr Bingley." Milly spoke the word. "Yes, him, did take advantage of her, and she had no part in making it happen."

Mary: "Mr Bingley, him, he did take... My sister had no part in making it happen."

"So there is no blame for Ess, and much trouble, though the Babba is a darling and we will look after him always."

"No blame. We will look after him always." Mary swallowed, and missed a few words.

Milly repeated those words again. So Mary must repeat them too.

"So, as Babba must be looked after, there must be a home for us. And we must have the *means*. The *means* to live, and to look after him, and help him to grow. Because the fault is Mr Bingley's."

Mary was completely behind the fire-screen now. Even as she spoke the word *Bingley's*, she could hear Esther begin to weep in the doorway.

Mrs Darcy, Lizzy, rose from her chair and ran over to Esther. "Thwaite! My dear! I am sorry! So sorry!"

Milly ignored Esther and Lizzy and went on speaking, somewhat louder. Mary raised her voice and faithfully repeated everything she said. "Babba has been done in the church, and will go to Heaven like he should, as child of a gentleman. But what happens to us now is our question. Where shall we be? We cannot stay here with Mrs Needleman, whatever she may say."

Mary said it all, right up to *cannot stay here with...* Then she baulked at the dismissiveness of Milly's last words. "Stay here in the Rectory."

"It is for you to give us a *home*, and *means*. That is the right way, considering what did happen."

"Considering..." Mary's voice cracked, then recovered. "Considering the behaviour of the man, which may or may not have just cause on account of his sorrows, but was wrong in how it became for the young woman who…"

"We have understood!" Mr Darcy stood sharply. "What is being alleged!" His face was grim, his mouth so tight that he had to spit the words out of it. "Thank you, dear sister-in-law, for the interpretation you have offered. Please come from behind the screen." Mary stepped to the side, and emerged. "I have no doubt it was an accurate rendering of what…of what Mrs Needleman has thought it necessary to suggest. It may be that my friend, unfortunate as he is…"

Now Mary stepped forward. She realised that since the first enunciation of Mr Bingley's name by Milly and herself, no one else had spoken that name, and now Mr Darcy was unable to speak it either.

She said, carefully, as if Darcy himself needed interpretation: "Unfortunate as Mr Bingley is…"

Darcy coughed into his hand, and continued. "Therefore, in recognition of the needs of the child, his mother and his aunt, I will make the necessary arrangements. One of our alms-houses is available. And there will be an annuity, sufficient for due maintenance."

His eyes rose to stare at his wife and Esther. "There seems to be a good deal of knocking at the Rectory's front door, and no member of staff to answer it?"

Mary saw Esther and Lizzy move apart from each other, and realised that there was indeed some heavy knocking coming from the far side of the hall. But none of them had heard it. She strode across, past Lizzy, past Esther and the baby, into the hall. Lizzy came swiftly alongside Mary, and, in the absence of any servants, the two of them together pulled open the heavy front doors.

Outside in the sunshine stood the family from Longbourn: Annie, Luke, their two children, and a few small scatterings of luggage.

Epilogue

1821-22

Annie took up the pen, dipped it in ink from the well, and wrote:

> *The Rectory, Humbole, Derbyshire.*
> *Michaelmas, year of our Lord 1821.*
>
> *Dear Longbourn,*
>
> *Never did I expect to write a letter of farewell to you. But here it is.*
>
> *It is clear now that our separation is not some brief aberration, but a permanent condition. So is the fact that I and my family will be making this little Derbyshire village our home.*
>
> *Do not fret for us, Longbourn. Miss Mary, bless her, is a home-maker. A year past June she set about making a home for herself here, and she sympathises*

with the adrift-ness we have felt since our arrival. She has welcomed us as if we were her own blood. (Which, of course, we are. But that is the one aspect of this upside-down world that we do not mention.)

"Head for Humbole," I said to Luke when Longbourn, under Miss Kitty and her husband, evicted us from employment and the roof over our heads. "Humbole, and Miss Mary." It was the only option. I saw I was right when the Rectory doors opened. Miss Mary herself opened them – with Mrs Darcy, astonishingly, at her side – and behind them stood Esther with her baby in her arms! And the baby, when I looked later, wore the gown that I made for his baptism!

Not that Luke wished not to come; just, he was nervous of it. He knew Miss Mary well, but dreaded the condescension of her husband and the suspicion of Mr Darcy. But we need not have feared. Mr Darcy seemed almost relieved to see us. Maybe he thought that if we had not made a claim on the Bennet estate on Luke's behalf by now, we most likely would not make one in the future. He shook our hands vigorously, ruffled the children's hair, then stood very close to his wife. His wife took no notice of him at all, but ran up to us and embraced us. Then, with warm words and hopes for our future, the two of them hastened away in the Pemberley coach. Mr Needleman was nowhere to be seen, but when encountered later, was alarmingly pale but perfectly polite.

So began our settling in. The only place we could be accommodated, at first, was in the stables, where we all four must share the pitiful mattress of the man who preceded us there, with a truckle-

bed beside. We none of us gained a great deal of sleep, and there was some bad temper among us. So Miss Mary called a little 'Meeting' as she sweetly called it, in the kitchen. She invited Gladys and Patty too, and asked those two original maids to consider making their home in the stables, after the alterations which Luke would undertake, with speed. (She had not consulted Luke on this task, but he nodded.) This notion gave poor Patty palpitations, for she has a great fear of 'them four-leggedy beasties'. But Luke described the wood and even the metals which he would put in between her and the beasties, and her fears abated. Within just under three weeks a proper home was made for the two of them. It is still not clear to me whether they are in fact sisters, but they do not invite queries as to their history or status. All Miss Mary will divulge is that they owe their life to the former housekeeper, Mrs Beattie.

And that is how we came into the House. To the attic rooms for sleeping, and the said Mrs Beattie's room as our Day Room and Play Room. Imagine! The luxury!

And did Mr Needleman condescend to us? Dear Longbourn, he has not the energy to assert his status. He is a sad man. He leans on Miss Mary most heavily. The two of them spend their mornings in the study, hard at work on his sermons. Miss Mary has read most of the volumes in his library, and points him to the ones relevant to the date in the Church Year which is upon us at the time. He offers these compilations from the pulpit to the parishioners, who mostly snooze through them, or use the time to catch up on whispered gossip. The afternoons take Mrs Needleman out into the village and down the lanes with her charity baskets and her smile.

The parishioners, I can see, live in <u>awe</u> of Miss Mary. It is my suspicion that they realise it is <u>she</u> who chooses the hymns, <u>she</u> whose words come to them from the pulpit, <u>she</u> who even sets the agenda for the Parochial Church Council. Mr Needleman is the gentle ghost whose weak and bony hand they touch briefly as they leave the church after Matins and Evensong, while Mrs Needleman – with the full support, it seems, of her sponsor Lady Manton – runs the parish.

Yes, she has the support of her sponsor, but she does not have the support of her <u>stays</u>. She has removed them to the bottom drawer, where they languish, rejected. And she will not use my assistance to dress in the mornings, either. Which is a great blessing, as I can in remain in my night-clothes a while longer, and play more games with the children, before I run downstairs to share the chores with Gladys and Patty.

As I continue my role as maid to a member of the Bennet family, I remember my dear mother-in-law. I often feel, in fact, that I am turning <u>into</u> her. I say to Miss Mary: "Shall we have a moment of remembrance for Mrs Hill?" And we stop in our tracks, close our eyes, and give thanks for all she did for us.

I frequently take the two-mile walk to the alms-houses, which lie in a little by-way at an angle to both Pemberley and Humbole. I call at Number 14, and Esther welcomes me; Milly too, from her place in the background of everything. In the foreground of everything is Henry; he is so adored that I worry he might become as Mr George has become at Pemberley, careless of anyone's feelings but his own. But Henry's home is not a mansion, it is an alms-house. That will tell him his proper place in due time.

Esther has taken to making delicate little figures out of pastry, which Milly puts in the oven – "for just eight minutes" – with the weekly bake. Their brother apparently used to do the same with scraps of lead, and this activity renews her bond with him. These little baked people are mostly given to Henry, who mulls them between his toothless gums and swallows the soggy bits with whoops of delight.

I understand that Mrs Darcy too calls at number 14, but less frequently now that her latest pregnancy weighs her down. She also comes less frequently to visit Miss Mary, and stays less than half an hour. Not long ago she caught me at the top of the kitchen stairs and said hurriedly, "Annie dear, might we have words? Some time? There are matters which I need to ponder, and you have been such a strength and stay. Yet Fitzy says we must take what we are given and be thankful. And he promises to summon the finest of doctors." Then she turned away, not wishing to show me her tears. I could weep for her in my turn; for it is clear to me that all the 'Lady Darcys' in the world, all the ten thousands a year, cannot save her from the fear of child-bed.

Dear Longbourn. You seem so far away. If it were possible to visit you, who would be there to receive us? Luke could pay his respects to his dear mother's grave in the churchyard, and give the stone

of his father a kick. But, when I picture it, I feel the
small hands of Edie and John-James slipping into
mine and pulling me away. When they grow up
(as, God willing, they will) and need to give an
account of themselves, they will say, "I come from
Humbole, in Derbyshire". I will have to jog their
minds even to recall the name of Longbourn.

I will sign off, and go to the kitchen, and see
if my fingers can create little people in pastry like
Esther's. Gladys is preparing the bread dough.
Might fragments of bread dough shape up into
little people? They would rise, and be plump! I shall
try it and see.

Your affectionate Annie.

∽

It was past Candlemas and coming towards Holy
Week, and spring. The trees were still bare of leaves,
but some buds in the garden were fattening. Mary
and Robert sat in the study and gazed out at the view
which Mary had first seen – *properly* seen, with her
soon-to-be-husband's discarded spectacles – so long,
it seemed, ago.

Mary noted a little more colour in her husband's
cheeks. He had been thrice to Buxton now, to take
the waters. Those waters smelt strange, he reported;
yet the smell and the penetrating warmth had given
him hope of improvement. There was an excellent
library in Buxton, he said. There, sensible men went
to sit between their sessions in the Spa, reading and
occasionally making conversation. (Ah! Hence his
recent acquisition of a monocle.) He had so missed

conversation. Mary knew what that meant: he missed *SH*.

But, clearly, Buxton was doing Robert good.

Mary herself was reading Daniel Defoe. Not his *Journal of the Plague Year* – that was altogether too gloomy – but his *Tour through the Whole Island of Great Britain*. She had turned yet again to Mr Defoe's description of the lead-mines, their horizontal 'adits' leading to deep shafts, with the miner emerging, 'heaving himself out...uncouth...lean as a skeleton, his face lank...an inhabitant of the dark regions...' Could this have been Milly's and Esther's father? How did that square with the pretty little home in which they were now ensconced, with posies of flowers from their garden even this early in the year: snowdrops, and the first primroses? How was such a transition possible within a generation? And could they, in their alms-house – and she and Robert in the Rectory, too – ever live in comfort and safety, without the need for those skeletal men to toil their lives away in waterlogged mines in order to put lead on everyone's roofs and keep the rain out?

Irked by these questions, she closed the book and opened it again at her favourite page: when Mr Defoe visited the 'wonder' which was Chatsworth, and the fact that 'the lady was the mover of the first design...', how she had 'finished the whole in a magnificent manner'. *She* had done that – the *Duchess*! Not the *Duke*!

And so could she, Mary, in this parish, work her own wonders.

But first she must care for dear Robert.

"I am so glad," she said. "About Buxton. I might accompany you, perhaps, as the spring strengthens, and the journey becomes less arduous?"

"Do not tax yourself with such a thought." Robert's response came languidly, but she knew its tone: she must not interfere. This was a man's world, the world of libraries after one's bath. She would be in the way.

But he added, unexpectedly: "I hope, my dear, that you will find a friend for yourself around here. I should not like you to be lonely."

"I, lonely? I have the Lord, and my parishioners, and my piano. And our sermons, and occasional visits to Esther's little family. Besides, Annie is here, and Luke is busy about the place. The children are such a delight. I hope they do not disturb you – little Edie and John-James?"

"Oh, they do. But it is a small price to pay. The loss of Mrs Beattie! I still can scarcely speak of it. The sound of children's laughter is something I had not thought to relish. It fills the space."

What had he meant, she might find a *friend*?

Perhaps he had made a *friend* in Buxton.

As she had had in Milly? Friend...or whatever?

She could manage without a friend. She was, in fact, managing very well without. Milly had shown her *herself*. In the depths of the night, she was rediscovering that self. It was enough.

Out there, through the study windows, in the garden, were molehills.

"Look, Robert! They are returning! The moles!"

"My dear, I have told you, you must get Luke to deal with that."

"Oh dear. Is there not some other way than killing?"

Robert sighed. "We have these conversations too often, Mary dear. Shed no tears. Just ask Luke."

Mary gave a parallel sigh. He was right. She had wept too often for the moles.

This thought gave rise to the other conversation that had a habit of returning again and again. Luke. How to correct the anomaly of his brotherhood without upsetting the whole apple-cart of familial and communal relations.

Robert spoke again. "My dear, please will you ask Luke about the moles, and only about the moles. Let the other matter rest. You have raised it; he has said he is satisfied; there is no need for further action on your part."

Once again, he was right. Moreover, it was unnerving that he could so easily read her intentions. She had indeed been planning to raise the matter once again with Luke. Even though it was pointless. And unseemly. And, probably, in their attic room, pointless and unseemly for Annie too. She really must accept her husband's advice on this particular question. It rankled, that necessity to give way. But, in this case, she must obey.

Then she remembered something rather startling. She had noticed, immediately Annie and Luke and the children had exchanged rooms with Gladys and Patty, that Annie and Luke had pushed the two narrow beds in their room together. They had rearranged the two beds as one, with the sheets and blankets lying cross-wise and the counterpane diagonal, all neatly tucked in.

Such lengths to go to! Just to be closer together! Marriage, it was a mystery. Annie and Luke's marriage was as much of a mystery as Lizzy's with Fitzy.

Sir Fitzy! *Lady* Elizabeth! Did that make a difference when they were in bed together?

And sisters: they were a mystery too. The latest news from Jane held a little morsel of hope. Lizzy had said, last time she came, that Jane had written her a little note. A brief one, but such an event! In her own hand! Might she suggest that Lizzy take her new baby, when it was born and baptised and seen to be thriving, to visit her? Might that be possible? If so, it would be a miracle.

Lord be praised, there were miracles. She knew it, and Esther knew it, and most of all Milly knew it. Those miracles might vanish almost as soon as they had come, but they had come. There was no denying it. And they might come again.

Acknowledgements

The Unexpected Marriage of Mary Bennet has been over sixty years in the making. In the 1950s I studied *Pride and Prejudice* for my O-Level exam, which at the time was the major external test for teenagers. For the next stage, A-Level, I studied Virginia Woolf's *Orlando*, which offered a more exotic take on sexual identity and relationships, though equally among the super-rich.

Something happened between my reading of these two novels which had a profound effect on my thinking. I came from a conservative middle-class home. Capital was sacred, and if you wanted something doing, you paid someone to do it. My parents didn't clean their own house; they hired a 'treasure' to do their cleaning. Anne, our treasure, became almost part of the family; as well as cleaning several mornings a week, she would bake apple pies or see us to bed if our parents were going out for the evening. One day, my sister and I were finishing a late breakfast and Anne was cleaning around us. Anne asked, conversationally, looking at a book on the windowsill: "Who's reading *Emma*?" I said, "Me – why?" Anne said, "Oh, everyone said I should call my daughter Emma because I read it over and over when I was expecting her." My head sort of burst open. I realised that Anne was paid a pittance to clean up after me, but she read the same books as I read.

The back-burner of my mind held that knowledge for decades, and informed almost everything I read and wrote, up to and including this novel. So my first thanks must be to the late Anne Morton.

From my thirties onwards, I wrote fiction with publication in mind. Sometimes, in the dark hours of the night, my mind would wander into unpublishable fantasies. An image would arise of Elizabeth Bennet and Fitzwilliam Darcy's married life, and it was not a romantic scene. After the wince-making discoveries on their wedding night, Lizzy would find their sexual relationship full of delight. But, as childbirth succeeded childbirth, each with its threat to her intimate health, her needs would start to run counter to those of her patriarchal, heir-seeking husband. None of their wealth and power – 'ten thousand a year', with its gracious home and spacious estate, its London house, its personalised carriages – could compensate for the loss of bodily health and beauty to pregnancy and childbirth. And there were the additional responsibilities: to community, to status, to staff, to 'moral tone'. All these would conflict sharply with the pain emanating from Lizzy's womb. The fears from her bleedings (or the lack of them) would lurk in her wounded places and lead to a revulsion from the act of sex itself. For they were a threat to her very life.

In the daytime I ignored these prides and prejudices with their accompanying sexual anguish and got on with chasing publishers, theatre directors, the BBC and other outlets for my imaginative work.

Meanwhile, in the world of popular culture, Andrew Davies's dramatisation of *Pride & Prejudice* encompassed a pond-dipping scene in which Colin Firth's Darcy flipped Jennifer Ehle's Elizabeth emotionally upside down. Before long, a medley of talents such as Helen Fielding, Colin Firth (again), Renée Zellweger and Hugh Grant brought forth Bridget Jones I, Bridget Jones II, and so on. 'Mr Darcy' became established in the British female psyche as the most desirable of all possible mates. Here was Darcy – glum, proud, stiff, but desperately fancying Elizabeth – as Romantic Idol. Did he deserve it?

One of the subsidiary lessons I had learned from my study of *Pride and Prejudice* was the existence of the strange moral code underlying early British capitalism: for the upper and rising-middle classes, it was essential *not* to work, rather than to *work*. Thus Landed Money was superior to Money from Trade; Leisure was superior to Labour; and Service – the effort that went into keeping all this upper-class Leisure going – was inferior to all. And, of course, ladies never worked. Truth lay in the comic quip: 'Horses sweat, men perspire, ladies only *glow*.'

I began to let go of the values of my conservative upbringing and explore other political paths. I was especially interested to read the French economist Thomas Piketty's commentary on the Bennet family of P&P. In his 2013 book *Capital in the Twenty-first Century* he demonstrated with facts and figures how wise the Bennet sisters were to wait around for Messrs Darcy and Bingley to come along with their leisured wealth rather than to earn their living by their own toil; for any attempt at the latter would leave them with vastly lower status, and most likely poverty-stricken in the end.

So: thanks go to my English teachers (Miss Bell and Miss Gault), to Andrew Davies and Helen Fielding and company, and to Thomas Piketty.

Next, thanks go to the late, great, Margaret Forster. My interest in the relationship between Family and Servantry was fired by Margaret Forster's novel *Lady's Maid*. Forster had been outraged, when writing the biography of Elizabeth Barrett Browning, at how appalling was the celebrated poetess's treatment of her devoted maid Wilson, demanding every moment of her time and refusing to let her find love in her own life. *Lady's Maid* was the result of giving fictional embodiment to that outrage.

Outraged, too, in the world of television drama, were Jean Marsh and Eileen Atkins. These two first-rate actors watched John Galsworthy's Forsytes accomplishing all their deeds in TV form without even mentioning the staff who made possible the whole shebang. So they created the revolutionary series *Upstairs, Downstairs*. I had devoured the original text of *The Forsyte Saga* and its successors in the summer following my O-Levels, and adored this re-interpretation from Below Stairs. So my thanks go to those two luminaries, Marsh and Atkins.

Then there's the issue of Darcy's and Bingley's involvement in slave ownership, and slave labour on Caribbean sugar / slave estates. I have drawn, with gratitude, on many opinions, such as Joanna Trollope's in 2015 and David Olusoga's entire opus. The major research comes from University College London's Centre for the Study of the Legacies of British Slave-ownership.

At last, when I was well over seventy, and had declared myself retired as a writer, the Bennet sisters began to knock on my inner door and let out their hopes, their frustrations and their sexual longings.

Mary Bennet took her time to rise to the top and demand central status. But when she got through, she appealed to me more than any of the others. Mary was the sister it was permissible to mock, along with her shameful, nerve-ridden, daughter-heavy mother. Yet Mary read improving books, she practised the piano, she was (as her father cruelly teased) 'a young lady of deep reflection'. She, surely, yearned; but she channelled her yearnings into religion rather than into romance.

A Reverend gentleman slid alongside Mary: Robert Needleman, with interests and needs which Jane Austen could not possibly have understood. (Or could she?) Other characters began to take shape around these two: Mr Needleman's lover with his exotically laced cuffs, Mrs Beattie the abrasive cook-housekeeper from Ulster, Hurry the languid stableman.

And Esther, Lizzy's lady's maid. And her little sister Milly.

Esther – known to Mrs Darcy as Thwaite, named after her previous lady's maid – is in a situation all too familiar, from *The Marriage of Figaro* onwards. She is a hugely valuable asset: sensitive, hardworking, entirely focused on her mistress, alert to her every need. All too soon, though, she 'falls' pregnant. Few people enquire into the manner of that fall. The disgrace is all hers. As Thomas Hardy put it in *Tess of the D'Urbervilles*, 'The woman pays.'

Milly's situation is far rarer: she is a half-crippled maid-of-all-work who merits a crucial place in my story. At the turn of the 18th and 19th centuries, a child with cerebral palsy would hardly ever survive. In the last decade of the 20th century I helped a small group of people with cerebral palsy to write their life stories, and I discovered how raw is the struggle for physical and psychic survival, even today, for those living with this condition. So what hope for a Milly, back then?

But most plots need an element of luck to propel them on their way. The ingredients of Milly's luck were the devotion of her parents, the brain inside her head, and the intimate connection with her sister Esther. Further thanks go to members of the group *Disabled Not Daft* for allowing their stories to inspire mine.

Philip Pullman says that every writer is a magpie, so my fervent thanks go to all those writers who left shiny ideas lying around for others to pick up. I have asked permission where possible, and for advice where not.

(Thank you, dear Society of Authors.) Special thanks to Jo Baker for her revelatory novel *Longbourn*. Mrs Hill is the only servant actually named by Jane Austen in P&P, and I have continued Jo Baker's surmise that she gave birth to a child by Mr Bennet, a child who returned to Longbourn and married a Longbourn maid.

Thanks too to the Jane-ites, the Austen bloggers: all those who fill the internet with their research into the difference between a phaeton and a gig: you saved my day more often than you could imagine.

My thanks fly through other worlds to my first reader, Diana Sidaway. Diana didn't manage to see it through to the end, but she asked the questions to which my writing became the answer. She is the novel's dedicatee.

Thanks beyond measure to Sheila Rowbotham, Adèle Geras and Paul Jeffery for their generous reviews. Thanks too to my friend, neighbour and fellow-writer Deborah Delano, with whom I have sat, walked and run as we shared experiences and possibilities around our novels. Then to Jeff Phelps, poet and novelist and fellow Quaker, whose enthusiasm for the work buoyed me up in hard times. To my other early readers – Elin Robson, Heather Jeffery, Patsy Wilson, Nick Wilde, Anna Carlisle, Rosemary Daley, Sonya Remmen – I can only say that you are those without whom this novel would never have seen the light of day.

Scott Pack has been an invaluable mentor (without whom, etc); thanks, too, to Nell Wood and Clio Mitchell for their professionalism.

And the biggest 'without whom' is for Frank.

Printed in Great Britain
by Amazon

29847422R00300